WILLIE
WILDEN

ᘓᒻᒻᒻᒻᘌ

This is a work of fiction. Every character and incident in this book is imaginary, with the exception of real persons who are referred to by their actual names. All other names, characters, places, and incidents either are the product of the author's imagination or are used fictitiously. Any resemblance to actual persons, either living or dead, business establishments, events, or locales is entirely coincidental.

WILLIE WILDEN

〰

A NOVEL BY

JOSEPH DOBRIAN

REX IMPERATOR, NEW YORK, N.Y.

To my dear friends Bill and Erlinda,
who exemplify why "old-fashioned"
is my favorite compound adjective.

WILLIE WILDEN

Tuesday, May 18, 1999

Roger Ballou liked to imagine, when he was out on the streets of Manhattan, that people were noticing him, and he carried himself so as to be noticed. He was 42, but looked younger. He was six feet tall, and heavy, but in reasonable shape: meaty rather than fat. He stood almost too erectly, his wide shoulders thrown back and his chest outthrust, head high, and he walked quickly and with long strides, despite a limp caused by an improperly corrected clubfoot.

Already, at 9:30 in the morning, the weather was warm and humid, foretelling a brutal summer. Ballou hated summer. He guessed that this might be the last day, until fall, that he could wear his favorite suit, a charcoal-grey double-breasted pin-stripe, so perfectly tailored that it appeared to have been painted on him. His shirt was white, his tie the darkest possible red. A white linen handkerchief peeped out of his breast pocket. His dark hair was slicked back, Jack Nicholson-style. In all, his dress and grooming habits had stabilized in the men's fashion renaissance of the mid-1980s, and had hardly changed at all since then.

Ballou's face was large, pale, and smooth. His nose was aquiline but slightly askew, his mouth narrow and lipless. His eyes were tiny and Asiatic — almost piggy — and they gave Ballou a menacing, violent aspect, even when he didn't want them to. He would often try to make eye contact with people as he passed them in the street, just to see how they'd react. Women particularly. He usually tempered his threatening affect with an ironic little dimpling – not quite a smile – and a tiny twinkling of the eye, as though reminding the other person of a naughty secret.

By the time he'd reached his destination – the Alliance Capital Building on Sixth Avenue at 55th Street, two miles from his apartment – his appearance had deteriorated considerably. His face and hair were dripping; his shirt collar was soaked. He would have paused in the enormous lobby for a few minutes, to let the perspiration process slow and stop, and to let the sweat evaporate somewhat, but he no longer had that time to spare. He went directly to the elevators and rode to the 28th floor, to the American Association of Executive Management, giving his face a fast toweling with his for-blow handkerchief on the way up, and re-combing his hair.

Ballou could have done business with the AAEM – his biggest client – entirely via e-mail, but he felt that regular face-time was key to client retention, so he made a point of monthly visits to the company's editor-in-chief of periodicals, to get his assignments. He was on a $2,000-a-month retainer – had been, for the past five years – to write articles for AAEM's several newsletters.

Linda Bierschaum was a peppery, elfin old lady with a braying voice, who wore too much jewelry and a spicy perfume that revolted Ballou. Her office was a tiny cubicle, no more than five feet by five. Ballou sat in the visitor's chair, going knee-to-knee with Ms. Bierschaum when she turned her chair from her desk to face him. Ordinarily it amused Ballou to observe that the AAEM – a think tank that claimed expertise in modern, high-powered management – kept its employees in the same uncomfortable, undignified conditions that it criticized in its books and seminars. This morning, he wasn't in the mood to smile about it. He was still pumping sweat and trying to control it with his handkerchief – and trying to breathe lightly.

"Blanca, get this poor guy some water," Ms. Bierschaum hollered to her assistant, who sat in the next cubicle. "Roger, why not take a taxi?"

"It's my Calvinist ancestry, no doubt," Ballou replied. "Life is supposed to be uncomfortable. Besides, walking everywhere keeps me in control. If I'm on foot, I'm on time, see? Being late for an appointment is like missing a deadline. I don't allow it to happen."

"You're such an A type! You'll give yourself a stroke."

Ballou shrugged. "It's a good day to die."

Ms. Bierschaum shook her head.

"Roger, you are *so* weird."

Blanca squeezed into the cubicle and handed Ballou a small bottle of Poland Spring, which he drained in a few seconds.

"You need a vacation, Roger," said Ms. Bierschaum.

"Can't afford one. If I take a few days off, there's nobody running the store. When I'm not working on an assignment, I'm selling myself, looking for new clients."

"Well, you might want to take one now. I'm afraid I've got some bad news for you. We've got a new editorial director, and this guy — well, he's one of those guys who either he's a genius or he's insane, but whichever it is, he's overhauling the department, and he's decided that from now on, AAEM's publications are going to be entirely Web-based. No more newsletters or magazines. So that means my job is now redundant, and I don't mind, because I'm 70 next month and I've been getting ready to retire anyway — but I guess it doesn't do you any good."

"Wait, though," said Ballou. "Won't he still need content?"

"That's what I asked him," said Ms. Bierschaum, "and he just pooh-poohed me, or actually he didn't even answer me. That's why I wonder just how stable he is. But bottom line is that I've been told not to assign anything further to my freelancers. I'm sorry. Really. It's been wonderful to work with you, and if I could have persuaded him to keep using you, you know I would have."

Ballou stared.

"So... that's the end of my retainer? Just like that?"

"I'm sorry."

"But that's almost half my income. That's two grand a month that I don't have anymore."

"I know, it's terrible. But at least you're not losing your whole job. You only have to make up a couple of thousand a month, not all of it."

Ballou was about to snap back something angry and sarcastic, but before he could, he heard Ms. Bierschaum saying, "I'm going to look around for you. Believe me, I feel awful about this, and I really will see what I can do for you."

"Well, thanks." Ballou forced himself to keep an even tone.

"It can't be easy, spending half your time looking for clients. Haven't you ever thought of going back to a real job?"

"I've been out of that market for too long," said Ballou. "I've been freelancing for 15 years; I'm probably unemployable. Even if someone hired me, I couldn't command a salary similar to what I make freelancing. As an associate editor, or some such thing? Forget it. I can barely pay my rent as it is."

"How about getting out of the city?" Ms. Bierschaum asked. "You could freelance from anywhere. Why not move somewhere cheaper, and spend more time writing poetry or fiction or whatever it is that you really want to write?"

"Move to some Hooterville or other where I just sit around all day missing Manhattan?" Ballou replied. "If you're not in the city, you're camping out. That's why I came here after college – and I could never have made any kind of career for myself anywhere else. Besides, any ideas I ever had of being a poet or a novelist evaporated years ago. I don't have the talent. Writers who can write, write creatively. Those who can't, write commercially."

Ms. Bierschaum looked rather severe.

"That gives me an idea," she said. "Have you ever thought of teaching?"

"Never, and who'd have me? I've got no credentials. Don't you need some sort of certificate, at least? Not to mention a graduate degree of some kind?"

"Not at a lot of places," said Ms. Bierschaum. "Private schools. Some of the smaller colleges. My son-in-law is chair of the English department at Van Devander College. Upstate, in Wildenkill. I could ask him."

"I'm not moving up to Wildenkill; come on!"

"I'm not talking about that. But maybe he knows of some schools here in the city that need someone to teach writing. Would that interest you?"

Ballou sighed. "I suppose it might."

"Roger, I should have put poison in that water you just drank," said Ms. Bierschaum. "You are so negative. Just what do you want out of life, anyway? I mean, if you'd wanted to be a great writer badly enough, you'd have worked at it. Instead of cranking out crap for clients like us, just so you can afford to stay in Manhattan. And you're not even enjoying it. I think it's the idea of living in Manhattan you're married to, more than the reality. And that's another thing. Why don't you get married? Find a nice girl to support you." Finally Ms. Bierschaum smiled a little, and Ballou chuckled grudgingly – and bitterly.

"Yeah, sure, there are plenty of women who'd marry me. Years and years ago, I used to have actual dates: just imagine. It's not that easy anymore."

"You should go for someone younger, Roger. I'm sure you could get plenty of young girls. You'd impress them."

"You'd think, right? Given my stunning good looks and all. But, no. Ordinarily, the only way a young woman will go for an older guy is if he's in a position of power. I'm supposed to have a date tonight with a woman who says she's 25. A blind date. Met her through a personal ad on the Web. We're supposed to meet for a drink and I have this awful premonition

that I'm going to be stood up. We talked on the phone a couple
nights ago, and when I told her I was 42 she just said, 'Oh,'
as though she couldn't quite bring herself to back out of the
date right then and there. If she shows up tonight, I'll be stag-
gered. See, it hasn't even happened, and already I'm feeling
homicidal."

"Could be your own attitude that's getting in your way, then,"
said Ms. Bierschaum, severe again. "Women can read attitudes,
even over the phone. Listen to this, Roger. A woman only ever
has one criterion when she's choosing a boyfriend. It doesn't matter whether she's looking to get married; the question is always
going to be, 'Would I breed from this guy?' Even if you're not
planning to have children – even if you're as old as I am – that
is going to be the question, every time: 'Would I breed from
this guy?' So evidently you're doing something wrong, or going
after the wrong women. And if it's important enough to you to
figure out what you're doing wrong, you'll figure it out, and you'll
change it."

Ballou shrugged. He felt he was being scolded – and scolded
for being unattractive to women, at that: a fault he believed he
couldn't help.

"Maybe it's the way you present yourself," said Ms. Bierschaum.
"You know, you're so formal-looking – and you do look like you
could kill someone. I'm used to it now, but I used to be a little
afraid of you. It's your eyes. You look so scary."

Ballou shrugged again, this time in a "What can I do?" gesture. He was getting angrier and angrier.

"Anyway," said Ms. Bierschaum, "it's just something to
think about. Don't take my word for it. I'll call my son-in-law
today, and I'll let you know what he says. And again, I'm sorry.
I wish I could give you a final set of assignments, anyway, so
you'd have time to look for some new clients, but they just
dropped this news on me the other day. Let me walk you to
the elevator."

Ballou said not a word as Ms. Bierschaum led him through the long row of cubicles, toward the elevator bank. When the elevator arrived, she stood a-tiptoe and kissed Ballou on the cheek. She'd never done that before.

"Good luck," she said. "Don't kill anyone on your way home."

Home, for Ballou, was 450 square feet — two tiny rooms, a kitchen, and a bathroom — in a dark, dilapidated walkup near the corner of Second Avenue and 26th Street. The apartment was barely big enough to contain his books, his clothes, and what passed for his office. He sat at his desk — in a cheap plastic-upholstered swivel chair from Office Depot — and stared into space.

He could have made cold calls to prospective clients. He could have called a few established clients, to try to drum up more work. But he could not get himself to move.

Ballou spent an hour rolling cigarettes: enough to get him through the next week or so, he guessed, as he was not a heavy smoker. He thought about doing a little housework, but told himself that even if this blind date went well, it would certainly not end at his apartment, so why bother?

He heard a scratching outside his apartment, and looked up to see an envelope being slipped under his door. He got up and opened it, and found a letter that began, "Dear Valued Tenant," which in his experience meant, "Drop your pants and assume the position."

Dear Valued Tenant:

As you probably know, your lease is due to expire in 90 days. Tenant retention is important to us, and we always try to keep our rents as low as possible. A small increase at the beginning of a new lease term is usually unavoidable ...

The proposed increase for the upcoming year was 25%. Forty percent if he would agree to sign a two-year lease. Ballou read the letter over a second time, and a third, as though reading it again would cause it to say something different. He suddenly jumped out of his chair and ran into the hallway, looking for the super, who'd probably been the one who'd delivered the letter – but he ran up and down the stairs, looking on every floor, and saw no one.

In effect, Ballou was to be evicted from the city. Sure, he could get another apartment in Manhattan, of about the same size and quality as the one for which he was now paying – but he'd probably pay about 50% more, rather than the 25% his current landlord was proposing. And he had just had his annual income reduced by $24,000.

For the past 20 years, he'd been comforting himself with the thought that whether or not he'd made a success of himself – and he hadn't, by any measurement that he used – at least he was making a living, and in Manhattan at that. Now, all of a sudden, both the living and the location were beyond his grasp.

And in a couple hours he'd have to buy drinks and dinner for a woman he'd never met before. So far, she hadn't called him to cancel the date.

Ballou got out of his sweaty clothes, showered, shaved, put on clean underwear and a clean shirt, and at that point he wanted to go out for another stroll, just to kill time before his date – but he wanted to give the young woman every opportunity to get in touch with him and cancel, and he was not certain: Had he or hadn't he given her his cell phone number? So he sat, waiting in vain for the phone on his desk to ring or for a new e-mail to pop up.

At 7:45 he walked over to La Vièrge, a bar/restaurant on Park Avenue South and 21st Street that was his local, and where the date was supposed to begin. It being a Tuesday night, the bar was nearly empty, and only a couple of tables in the dining room were occupied. Ballou sat down at the bar at 7:58. The bartender was a handsome, muscular young man in a black T-shirt. Ballou didn't recognize him.

"Brian's on vacation?" Ballou asked.

"Brian's gone," the bartender said. "Quit or got fired, I don't know. I'm Tom."

A good bartender can be an invaluable ally on a first date, and Ballou had been counting on Brian to help him through this one. He ordered a seltzer, and nursed it for 30 minutes as he watched the door.

A Black Demon appeared, hovering in the air above Ballou's head. That's what Ballou called them, in his mind. He'd never told anyone else about them. The Black Demons were imaginary creatures that had plagued him since he was a toddler, although he'd not named them the Black Demons until well into adulthood. (When he'd been very small, they'd just been "Them.")

"Them" amounted to eight or nine demons in all. Naked bony hairless creatures, each about half Ballou's own size, with ink-black skin, hominoid bodies, gargoyle faces, gaping mouths, and enormous pterodactylous wings. Often, if Ballou were alone with his thoughts after having said or done something that struck him as maladroit, one or two or sometimes all of the Black Demons would appear, flapping their wings, berating him, offering sarcastic commentary, calling him unoriginal names, or just curling their lips and shaking their heads.

One of them would sometimes play Ballou's defender, but in a reluctant, patronizing way, as though egging his fellows on to greater insult. Another one, Ballou's particular nemesis, would appear only in extreme cases. He would never speak, but when the verbal abuse from the others was reaching a crescendo, this one would clamber onto Ballou's shoulder, gibbering like a monkey, and cling with furious tenacity with both legs and one clawlike hand, slapping Ballou hard on the head with the free hand, again and again and again.

A second Black Demon appeared, hovering, then a third.

"Well, really, Rog," said one of them, "you should have known this would happen."

"He *did* know it would happen, obviously," said another. "And he went ahead and made the date anyway."

"Yeah," said the third Demon. "You know what I think? He gave up looking for a girlfriend long ago. Now, he's just actively seeking abuse. Inviting abuse, every time he asks someone for a date. Funny, isn't it?"

"Funny – and pathetic," said the one who'd spoken first. "How did he get this way? It can't be just his looks. And it can't just be because he's not successful. He can scare a woman off when she doesn't know a thing about him! That's talent."

The Demons faded from his view. For the first time that day, Ballou felt moved to compose. He took from his pocket a pen and a small leather-bound notebook.

> Dear Hosebag: You have behaved properly, on the principle that if a man is deemed insufficiently interesting, the rules of polite society may be waived when dealing with him. Let me apologize for forcing you to stand me up – not that you thought twice about it, nor should you have...

Years before, Ballou might have sent such a letter. He'd done so more than once. He was, despite his sarcastic tone, not kidding. He did not blame this woman he'd never met, for standing him up, so much as he blamed himself for being the kind of man a woman would stand up in such a manner. Linda Bierschaum had been quite right, he reasoned: A cool guy, a guy who struck a woman as acceptable breeding material, would not be treated so.

Eight-thirty-five. Ballou decided to concede defeat and order a real drink.

Eight-thirty-six. The street door opened, and a woman entered the bar. Ballou's date had described herself on the phone as 25, short, "and I've got long black hair like Pocahontas." This new woman was nearer 40 than 25, though, and rather tall, with reddish hair and a statuesque figure. She seated herself halfway down the bar from Ballou, just as Ballou called Tom over and ordered.

"A double rye old-fashioned, please," said Ballou. "And do *not* muddle the fruit, okay?" He always ordered a martini from Brian, having taught him exactly how Roger Ballou's martini was to be made, but he didn't feel like giving this new guy a lesson in martini-making right now, not in his current state of mind.

"Want to start a tab?" Tom asked.

"Please. I'll probably order something to eat, in a bit."

Ballou glanced down the bar. The lady wasn't beautiful, but certainly attractive. He looked her up and down, not being too obvious about it, trying to notice something about her that he could remark upon and thus start a conversation.

Tom served Ballou the old-fashioned, and poured a glass of merlot for the lady. Ballou took a sip of his drink, and found it acceptable. He selected one of his home-rolled cigarettes from a silver case, fitted it into a short ivory holder, and lit up.

Non-smokers can never imagine the pleasure of smoking just a few cigarettes a day, and heavy smokers have long forgotten it. This was the ceremony that Ballou looked forward to every day, as a mystic might look forward to prayers. He seldom smoked except when he was having a drink – sometimes he'd puff on a pipe during the day, but even that was rare – so that first smoke of the day, with his evening cocktail, was like falling into bed with a beautiful concubine who desired him as much as he desired her. The delight of it never palled; it would never have occurred to Ballou that it could.

He inhaled, felt the rush of smoke into his lungs and the lovely blonde aroma in his nostrils, and suddenly it mattered just a little less that he'd been stood up, that one more woman had informed him that he wasn't good enough to deserve ordinary courtesy. He watched himself in the mirror behind the bar: watched himself blowing out the smoke, watched himself watching it rise to the ceiling; watched the merlot-drinking lady watching him. He took another sip of his drink.

"Excuse me," the woman called over to him. "Could you please not smoke that in here?"

Ballou stared at her.

"Ma'am, this is a bar. And smoking is still legal in bars, for all that some people are trying to outlaw it."

"No, not if someone objects," said the woman, waving her finger at Ballou. "If one person objects, you have to put it out. That's the law. I know; I'm a lawyer!"

"And I'm Oprah Winfrey," Ballou replied. "You should be ashamed of yourself, lying like that." He took another sip and another drag, hoping he could at least force himself to keep a calm tone of voice, but doubting it. "But you anti-smoking fanatics are all alike, aren't you? No sense of shame. What, do you just pick out a different bar every night, and go in there to hassle smokers?"

"Bartender!" cried the woman. "I'm going to call the Health Commission in a minute."

"Sir, maybe you'd better put it out," said Tom.

"Like hell I will. And you're not doing your employer any favors, backing her up. If it comes to that, get Peter over here, if you please. He knows me."

"Peter won't be in till about ten," said Tom. "I'm sorry, I'm new here, and I don't know what the policy is about smoking, but just to be on the safe side I'm gonna ask you to put it out. Please."

Ballou goggled at the bartender, his jaw working.

"You... you..." he stammered. Ballou's eyes blazed; the bartender actually took a step backwards, his face registering not quite fear, but wariness. Ballou's voice dropped to a murderous whisper. "You have got to be *kidding*, you little snot-nosed *fuck*!"

"Sir. Sir. Listen, I'm tearing up your tab, here, you don't have to pay for that drink, but I need you to leave now."

"Are you out of your mind? I've been in here three-four nights a week for five years!"

"Sir, please. I need you to leave."

"You know what? I've got a good mind to sit here and let you call the cops on me, and see how your boss would like that." Ballou stood up. "You've lost yourself a regular customer, your first night on the job. You're doing your boss real good, pal. And you're in for a terrific evening as long as this... this *thing* is sitting here!"

Ballou took a five-dollar bill out of his pocket, and slapped it onto the bar.

"Here's for the glass," he snarled, and limped out, taking glass and cigarette with him.

"Sir! Sir!" the bartender called. "You can't have an open container on the street!"

Sunday, August 29, 1999

"We should invite Dora to the next bridge party," Frances Quagga told her husband. They were sitting in the dining room of their home in Wildenkill, N.Y., after supper on a Sunday night, drinking coffee, picking at a plate of cookies, and listening to the crickets outside. Their younger daughter, Emmeline, had left the table after having hardly eaten anything – that was her custom – and their elder, Miffany, had not shown up for the meal at all, having gone on an all-day picnic with some friends.

Mrs. Quagga still wore the light blue tailored dress she'd worn to church that morning, and her husband had removed his jacket but had not loosened his tie. Mrs. Quagga was a tall blonde woman in her 40s, with a heart-shaped face that looked haughty in repose but sweetened up considerably when she smiled. Donald Quagga was a few inches shorter than his wife, and remarkably resembled Thomas Dewey: a trim little man with a clipped moustache and dark, perfectly barbered hair parted almost but not exactly in the center. He had a sharp and no-nonsense affect; his smile, which he didn't use much, was usually too sardonic to be friendly.

"She seems lonely, poor thing," Mrs. Quagga continued. "Although she's sure to make plenty of friends soon enough, with her catering."

"Didn't know she played bridge." Mr. Quagga had the deep, rich voice of a trained singer.

"But she's obviously very intelligent," Mrs. Quagga protested. "And I taught the Planktons easily enough. And they'll be here, and Runs will come, and Hugh and Effie, and Frank and Lois. I just thought Dora would be an interesting new face."

"Good Lord. You're not thinking of hooking her up with Runs, surely," said Mr. Quagga. "You're incorrigible, you are."

Mrs. Quagga giggled. "Don't be so silly," she replied. "No, probably the perfect match for Dora would be that scary friend of yours. Can you imagine that?" She shuddered a little.

"You mean Roger Ballou? He's hardly my friend. I rented him a house."

"Well, I've seen him on the street a few times, and he looks like he might have Girl Scouts in his freezer. You'd better keep an eye on him."

"Wonder how he'd behave at the bridge table," Mr. Quagga mused.

"Please! You're giving me the creepy-crawlies! Who is he, anyway? What does he do? You said he's teaching at Van Devander, but where did he come from?"

"Up from the city, temporarily," said Mr. Quagga. "Apparently Jack Hogenfuss, in the English department, hired him to teach a couple of classes because Jack's mother-in-law more or less blackmailed him into it. I don't know the whole story. But he's harmless. Although certainly a little odd."

"Maybe we should get him together with Charlotte Fanshaw," said Mrs. Quagga, giggling again. "That would give her some new material for her next book, anyway. If she survived to write about it."

"Oh, no doubt the classic outcome would ensue." Mr. Quagga began packing a pipe: a large, well-used billiard. "Boy meets girl, boy and girl take instant dislike to each other, boy and girl exasperate each other to the point of infatuation. And it concludes with some delightful rice-throwing in front of a little white church on a lovely spring afternoon."

"Charlotte would want to get married nude, under a waterfall," said Mrs. Quagga.

"True enough," Mr. Quagga conceded. "But yes, why not invite Dora? At least we know she'll bring us something nice to eat." He nodded at the plate of cookies. "As for Roger Ballou," he continued, "you've given me an idea. It'd be a slap in the face if the *Advertiser* didn't run a review of Charlotte's latest, but I'm surely not going to write it. Maybe I'll call Ballou in the morning and see if he'd like to."

In addition to being real estate brokers, Mr. and Mrs. Quagga published the local weekly newspaper, *The Wildenkill Advertiser* — mainly to promote their own operation.

They heard the front door opening, and in a few seconds Miffany entered the dining room with her boyfriend, Greg Dandridge, both dressed in jeans and t-shirts, dirty and reeking of horses. Miffany was 17, tall and blonde and demure like her mother. Greg — as far as one could tell through the lank hair falling into his face — was half-glowering, half-sneering at nothing in particular, and he bestowed a nod and a grunt on the Quaggas.

"*Sex and the City* is on," Miffany announced, as they passed through the dining room and into the kitchen on the way to the TV room. "Aren't you two just *dying* to see it? Didn't think so!"

"Perish forbid," Mr. Quagga called after her. "Once was enough for me, with that show."

"Besides," he added to his wife in an undertone, "I have it on Roger Ballou's authority that there is no sex in the city. He was complaining to me about it, for much of the time we were looking at houses. His complete lack of a romantic life, I mean."

Greg — in the kitchen, presumably thinking he was out of earshot — asked Miffany, "Does old Ward wear his tie to bed, too?"

Mr. Quagga raised an eyebrow.

"It's remarkable how that character has survived," he mused. "Ward Cleaver. He's become an archetype. Or a meme, rather. That boy knows who he is, if only at second hand. I suppose I should feel honored."

"You're not Ward Cleaver, my sweet," Mrs. Quagga replied, standing behind him, her hands on his shoulders. "You're much more interesting." She picked up the cookie plate and made to follow the two teenagers, then paused, taking a deep breath. "That's such a nice combination, isn't it? Your pipe-smoke, and... horse poopie."

Mr. Quagga fell back in his chair, guffawing. He hugged his wife around the waist and held onto her, his shoulders shaking, until he'd calmed down and wiped the tears from his eyes. "Oh, God. Oh, God, Frances. There should be a law against you."

He sighed, and remembered where he'd been.

"Ward Cleaver was much taller than I, though, and he didn't have a moustache. And he and June did not sleep in the same bed." He swatted Mrs. Quagga on the butt backhand as she walked out of the room, and she yipped.

Monday, August 30, 1999

Wildenkill, N.Y., a town of about 4,000 people (and that's only if you count the 1,800 students of Van Devander College, its primary industry), sits on hilly terrain near the west bank of the Hudson River, 105 miles north of Midtown Manhattan. Its most famous inhabitant at that time (or nearby resident, to put it more accurately) was the aged and legendarily reclusive poet, Llandor, who lived on a small horse-farm a few miles to the west of the town. Nobody in the area (newcomers were told) could claim to have seen Llandor in many years. People who drove by his place reported that a car was usually parked in the driveway of the farmhouse. A red-haired woman who looked to be in her 30s sometimes drove that car into town to do the grocery shopping, but she hardly spoke a word to anyone and pretended not to hear if anyone asked her about Llandor. Two or three hired men could be seen working with the horses, most days. If Llandor himself ever emerged from his house, he evidently did so in a manner not observable from the highway.

Two concentric fences topped with razor-wire surrounded Llandor's farm, and so far nobody had bothered to verify the rumor that booby-traps had been laid besides — nor the rumor that

Llandor had shotgunned and killed an uninvited visitor once (or two or three times, or perhaps he'd blown away a couple of dozen over the years, depending on who was telling the story) but had escaped prosecution because of his eminence.

Still, the occasional teenager or college student would make a pilgrimage to the high wire gate to leave there a bouquet, or a thank-you note in verse. Sometimes a slightly older person would leave a photograph of a baby who'd been christened Llandor, or Nicolette, after the eponymous heroine of Llandor's most famous poem.

Roger Ballou had heard of Llandor, all right. Who hadn't? But he was only vaguely aware of Charlotte Fanshaw.

It was because of Llandor that Wildenkill was all abuzz about Charlotte Fanshaw's new novel, *Gains and Losses*. Ballou, recently arrived, knew that Ms. Fanshaw lived in a big old falling-apart house on the outskirts of town, with several children, and wrote a column that appeared weekly in the Family section of *The Wildenkill Advertiser*. In the two weeks he'd lived in Wildenkill, he'd never given that paper more than a glance – a glance that did not include Ms. Fanshaw's column – and he'd not known that she had a small reputation nationally, as an author of books about travel and householding.

Ballou had learned, however, that she had long ago been the subject of local gossip. Some 25 years earlier, at age 18, Charlotte Fanshaw had had a brief romantic relationship with Llandor, a man more than 40 years older than she. Donald Quagga had told Ballou that story – what he knew of it – earlier that summer, while taking him on a house-hunting excursion. One of the properties that Ballou had looked at stood half a block away from Ms. Fanshaw's old grey house, which was ramshackle but had a bizarre charm to it, with its attached dog-kennel and several bicycles parked in the front yard, where various flowers grew – not in a garden, nor in arranged spots, but apparently at random.

"Quite a story about the woman who lives there," Quagga had commented, and recounted it.

"And then not long after that affair, she married a local good-for-nothing," he'd concluded the story. "A folk singer, the kind that every college town has. And they traveled all over the country while they were married, living here and there. That's how she got her reputation: writing books and articles about all the different places they lived, and about bringing up a family in... in that sort of nomadic *milieu*, you might say. Then when the marriage broke up, by George if she didn't bring all her children back here and settle into that old house – where she'd grown up. Her parents are gone now. There was a crazy couple, if you like: her parents.

"Her children all seem nice enough – in fact my daughters are friendly with her daughters – but... well, Charlotte is very fond of attention. Some people find her interesting – and some don't."

As it turned out, Ballou had gotten a lease with option to buy on a different house, one that Quagga himself owned, nearer Wildenkill's tiny business district: only four small rooms, but it had a shady little yard and a swing on the front porch, and was only a five-minute walk from Van Devander College.

"Not that I plan to stay long," Ballou had told Quagga. "I came up here because I had to. Needed the job, needed a place to live. I guess this'll be my Wilderness Period, until I can rebuild my client list; then maybe I can afford to get back to the city."

It was early on the morning of August 30 – early for Ballou, that is, five minutes after nine, just as he was finishing his coffee – that Quagga phoned him to commission a review of *Gains and Losses*.

"I'd rather have someone do it who doesn't know Charlotte," the realtor/publisher explained. "If you do a good job, we can talk about giving you a regular column. The pay won't be more than token, but it'll be an opportunity for exposure, and who knows? People have gone on to national syndication from humbler beginnings than the *Advertiser*."

Ballou dropped by the offices of Quagga Realty that afternoon – it was a glorious cloudless day, not too warm – to pick up a review copy of *Gains and Losses*.

"Give me about 750 words," Quagga instructed. "You'll have to work fast; I'll need it Thursday night, for Saturday publication. If you like it, fine; if you don't, don't be shy about saying so."

"It's nice to have a newcomer who knows how to dress," Quagga added. The two men were wearing light summer suits, white shirts, and conservative ties.

"In the city, now, you see people going to work in polo shirts," Ballou replied, "so I assumed it'd be even less formal here – but, no. It's like I stepped into a time machine and went back a couple of generations."

"Yes, Wildenkill is still Old New York in a lot of ways," said Quagga. "You still see some of the older ladies wearing hats, and children riding bicycles without helmets and padding, if you can believe that."

"How Rockwellian," said Ballou – reminding himself to smile so Quagga would take it as banter rather than put-down.

Ballou had his first encounter with Charlotte Fanshaw herself a few minutes later, on Wildenkill's Main Street. He'd walked from Quagga Realty to Giant Foods, and now was walking back up-hill with two paper bags full of groceries, taking long strides as was his custom. At the intersection of Main and Elm, he would turn right and walk two more blocks to his house.

Main Street was lined with wooden frame buildings. These housed retailers that were geared to weekend visitors – antique shops, art galleries, ethnic clothing boutiques, restaurants, "artisan" food shops – and several real estate offices, two law firms, a barber shop, and a funeral home, along the stretch that led up to the Town Square at the crest of the hill. Two churches (Episcopal and Reformed Dutch) stood across the square from each other. Wildenkill was a little too self-consciously quaint, Ballou felt.

From one of the law offices emerged a thin woman of about Ballou's age, of middle height, wearing a tight, short red dress and a wide-brimmed straw hat, a manila folder full of papers in her hand. She walked smack into Ballou. Ballou stopped short and swayed a little to prevent the groceries from spilling, then righted himself.

"Sorry."

"It's okay," said the woman, apparently somewhat distracted. "Only, there's so much legal stuff I have to worry about in connection with my book, I'm just running around like a *nut!*" She laughed breathily. She had strawberry-blonde hair that hung well past her waist, with bangs in front, and freckles. She looked a little like Mia Farrow but even skinnier. Her legs were long and shapely, and she was showing a lot of them. She looked expectantly at Ballou, as if inviting a response.

As happens with most men when they encounter a strange woman, the "Would I, or wouldn't I?" question appeared in Ballou's mind instantly, and in this case he decided he wouldn't. This woman was quite pretty – but the nervousness, and the too-loud laugh, raised a warning flag in his mind.

"Well, good luck," he said, and walked on, only realizing some seconds later that this was probably Charlotte Fanshaw he'd just bumped into.

*

Gains and Losses was a fast read. Ballou started it that afternoon, and by Tuesday night, he'd finished it. The book contained enough exposition of human failings to keep Ballou deeply interested –

and to make him angry. As he read, his resentment grew more intense.

From as long ago as he could remember, Roger Ballou had wanted fame, and it was a source of much self-directed bitterness that he'd never achieved it. Not that he'd ever tried all that hard for it, partly because he was a lazy man, and partly because he knew that if he did become famous, it would disrupt his quiet, solitary life. Thus, he had always satisfied himself with daydreams: performing a song he liked, when he heard it on the radio; conducting an orchestra, when he attended a concert; being elected President of the United States, when following a political campaign.

A quick and easy way to get famous is to effectively attack a celebrity. Fame is relative, and it sometimes doesn't travel well, so one can achieve notoriety in a small town by exposing the faults of a local hero, yet never have it remarked upon outside of a radius of a few miles. On the other hand, if the target's big enough, and the shot's small enough, the fame may be spread thin, widely noted but largely ignored. It appeared to Ballou that Charlotte Fanshaw's book would make her notorious – probably worldwide – and would pay off many of her old scores, particularly the one against Llandor.

"You're just envious because if *you* wrote a book like that, nobody in the world would give a shit – least of all a major publisher," one of the Black Demons commented, over Ballou's shoulder. "Too bad you're not enough of a writer to make it happen."

Gains and Losses was a stark, gloomy novel about a serial seducer and the women he exploited. Stylistically, Ballou thought, it resembled Jacqueline Susann's work, only rather more gothic.

The story mainly took place in a small, remote college town in upstate New York: one that could be compared to Wildenkill. It concerned the parallel stories of several female students, each of whom, in the course of her studies at the fictitious college, was seduced by a professor who was also a world-famous poet: a man who might well be compared to Llandor. In each case, after an affair that might last a few weeks or a few months, this character would unceremoniously dump the young lady.

"I've taught you all I can teach you," he said to one of them. "It's time for you to try the world on your own." This was typical of his technique. Invariably, shortly thereafter, another young woman would move in with him – to be mentored with similar vigor.

The professor – to the author's evident regret – never got any comeuppance. He eventually retired to his farm, to grow old in seclusion. Meanwhile, the pain and psychological damage that this poet/professor had inflicted on his defenseless students would stay with them forever. (And male professors all over the world, it was implied, were pretty nearly as bad, and something should be done.)

The final quarter of the book took the reader through the 25 subsequent years of the life of one of those students: her efforts to gain a reputation as a poet; her successes as a writer of non-fiction; her marriage (which ended in divorce but produced two girls and two boys); and coping with the nomadic, chaotic lifestyle her ne'er-do-well husband had imposed on her. *Gains and Losses* ended with this woman's final encounter with the poet.

> I had been on the move for a great deal of my life [the protagonist related], since I left Gossage. Buying an old Volkswagen and driving across the United States and Canada for a year, just driving by day and writing by night, to escape from the ruins of my parents' marriage and the memory of Gossage. Marrying John and moving with him 14 times in the 15 years of our marriage as he tried to make a go of a job here, a business venture there. As my marriage fell apart and my career blossomed, giving readings at colleges and bookstores all over the English-speaking world.

All that, only to settle again in my parents' old house, my mother a suicide years ago – accidental death, the official report said, but how could it not be said that she had spent most of her life trying to end it, and finally succeeded? – and my father, crippled, blinded, and deafened by strokes, confined to a nursing home, unable to recognize me or his grandchildren.

The idea of reclaiming the old homestead was not what brought me back. I had run away from the town where Gossage lived – because it was where he lived. Now, I was ready to live near him again – in defiance of him. And to do that, I knew, I must face him once more, once and for all.

[The narrative went on to describe her resolution to visit Gossage's farm once more, and to speak with him again, however little he might want to see her. But she, too, had heard the rumors of booby traps and shotguns, and she had seen the razor-wire.]

I bring along a favorite snapshot of each of my children. Beth in her sophomore Spring Dance gown. Lula at 13, posing beside a painting she'd just completed of our Irish Setter, Valerie. John Jr. bouncing a soccer ball on his knee. Barnaby asleep on our living-room sofa in the midst of a Christmas party that ran late. I tape them to my bra, each picture precisely equally near to my heart. I know I might not be coming back alive.

John Jr. says to me later, "Mom, you should have had a plan to get in there. Why didn't you just wait for one of the hired men to leave, and run through while the gates were open?" Of course he's right, but I don't think of that at the time.

I have two pairs of heavy work gloves, in case I have to climb over the razor wire. I have a thick shearling coat that might resist the wire, and might protect me if someone comes at me with a knife. And I have the car: My father's Cadillac, bought new when I was a little girl and now ready for the junk heap – but I have one last mission for it. I wonder how the Vikings felt, when they set out to burn the ship of a departed relative. I imagine I'm feeling much the same, now.

It gets dark early in the Catskills in December. The last autumn leaves have fallen. Gossage's farm, its trees, its stables, stand skeletal in the afternoon gloaming. I turn off the road onto the short driveway that leads to his front gates: two wire fences, one inside the other.

I stop my father's car. Its front end is almost touching the gate, on which there's a squawk-box with a buzzer I could press to ask to be let in. But I have wasted enough time in getting to this point. I back up slowly, to give the car a running start. I back clear across the road, so that my car sits on the opposite shoulder, now, perpendicular to oncoming traffic on both sides.

"Visualize it," I can hear Gossage saying to me, as he used to say when I was stuck on a line of poetry. "Visualize it." So I do. I visualize my car ripping through first one gate, then the other, at top speed, and continuing up the driveway, right to the front porch of the farmhouse.

I floor the accelerator.

My car tears across the highway and slams into the gate. It bursts through. I expect some kind of electrical explosion, but there are no sparks, just the sound of metal crashing through metal. I keep my foot on the gas as I hit the second gate, about ten feet inside the first. But apparently I have lost momentum; anyway, the car crashes against the second gate and stops, the hood crumpled, the gate unyielding.

Almost without thinking, I turn off the ignition, open the door, and roll out onto the ground. In case anyone tries to shoot me. I make myself as small as I can, crawl quickly to the fence, and begin to climb. As I climb, I weep, sob. My gloves resist the razor-wire, so does my coat. My jeans don't.

I have one leg over the top of the fence when the other leg of my jeans snags on the wire. My grip slips. I know I have to fall in one direction or the other, so I hurl my body forward and fall 12 feet or so, face-first onto the ground. I feel the wire ripping into my calf as I fall, but I remember from my high-school judo classes to slap the ground hard with my palms as I hit, to absorb the shock.

The right leg of my jeans is sliced from the knee down, and although it's too dark for me to see how badly I'm cut, I can feel blood on my leg. I start to GI-crawl, still sobbing, but realize that it's at least 200 yards to the farmhouse and it will take too long. I'm sure I've been seen, and have to assume that someone will start shooting at me.

I get up and run, not directly toward the farmhouse, but approaching it zig-zag, veering first left, then right, diving to the ground and rolling for a few feet, then getting up to run again. By the time I get to the front porch, I realize that I'm no longer crying. I'm laughing. Exhilarated. Straightening my coat, putting my gloves in my coat pockets, patting my hair into place, I walk up the steps and ring the doorbell. I know I have a big grin on my face, and I do not want to wipe it off. I could not, if I wanted to.

Lights are on, and I can hear movement. I know someone's home. I ring again. If Gossage doesn't open up, I'm
prepared to sit on his doorstep for as long as I have to, dar-
ing him to call the police. I'm also prepared to be shot to
death. I'm not prepared for how I feel, though. Peaceful.

The door opens. Now, only a screen door stands between me and him. I can sense, still, an energy about him,
but he is very, very old. Frail. His face is even more bitter,
angry, than I had remembered it. He coughs, and spits
into a handkerchief.

He has a shotgun cradled in his arm. It's pointed at
the floor, and he doesn't raise it. Instead, he lays it on a
hall table.

"I've been wondering when you would show up," he
says. His voice is a harsh, rasping croak: a sick man's voice.
"Every year or two, one or another of you girls shows up
here, thinking she's going to tell me off once and for all.
Excuse the gun, but when someone plows a car through
my front gate, I have to take precautions."

We stand silent for a few seconds, facing each other.

"Do I need to call the cops to get your goddam car towed
away?" he asks. "Or are you going to go down that hill and
drive it the fuck off my property?"

It only takes that moment. My fear of Gossage, my love
of him, my hatred, my despair, my rage, all that I have ever
felt for him, is gone. He's not my old teacher, my old lover;
he's almost not Gossage. Just an angry old man, with not
much left but his anger. He's a stranger – but I feel an urge,
now, to comfort him.

I don't, though. I smile at him.

"I think it'll run," I tell him. "I'll say goodbye now. I just wanted to show you I'm still here – and I'm happy – whether you like it or not."

I turn, and walk down the steps, down the hill toward his front gate. I do not look back. But I hear him – the last words he will ever speak to me, this man who once called me "My Soul's Beloved":

"Why should it bother me that you're happy?" he shouts after me. "Fucking crazy broad!"

As I reach the inner gate, it slowly swings open. Evidently Gossage has thrown a switch inside the house. I walk out of his prison, into the world. Miraculously, the pictures of my children are all still secure, next to my heart.

It did not occur to Ballou to let his thoughts settle overnight – and in any case, well indoctrinated in the principles of successful freelancing, he wanted to be sure to make the deadline. He still had a couple of hours before he needed to go to bed, so he sat down at his computer and typed almost without stopping.

Payback Time
By Roger Sullivan Ballou

Every so often, a book is published that one expects will be too tasteless to read – but one reads it anyway, for fear of missing something naughty. *Gains and Losses,* by Charlotte Fanshaw, is one such.

Gains and Losses is compelling. You'll want to finish it in one sitting – just as you wouldn't be able to tear yourself away from any story in which the teller is unwittingly performing a psychological strip-tease.

Many an author has written a book (whether journalism, memoir, or disguised fiction) about a failed romance, with a view to exposing the faults of the ex-lover. The numerous affairs of a reclusive poet are the principal subject matter of *Gains and Losses.* One major objective of the book is to invite the reader to despise that poet.

The other, apparently, is to show the reader that romantic relationships between student and teacher – even when both are legally adults – are invariably destructive, injurious to the student, and morally wrong by definition.

Ms. Fanshaw does manage to mildly amuse the reader by making her antagonist – the reclusive poet – into a cartoon villain, through voluptuous descriptions of his odd habits, his various neuroses and obsessions, his arguably evil friends, and his general son-of-a-bitchery. But who knows? Perhaps she really has met a poet who behaves this way.

• Did you know, for example, that this poet habitually hangs upside-down from an inversion apparatus to induce a trance-like state, whence his literary inspirations?

• Did you know that he has a particular favorite chair in which he likes to sit and think or write, and that he once barked at a lady friend (when she had disturbed his creative ecstasy), "When I am in this chair, you are not to speak to me; you are not to touch me; you are not even to enter my field of vision or make any noise that I might hear. The only possible exception might be if the house were on fire"?

• Did you know that every time he makes a remark that might be interpreted as optimistic or positive, he feels compelled to tap his own head twice in the "touch wood" gesture?

• Did you know that three times a day, he ate a bowl of Baskin-Robbins' banana-nut ice cream with maple syrup on it, threw a furniture-smashing tantrum when the manufacturer discontinued that flavor, and contemplated a lawsuit to compel them to supply it, before deciding to bite the bullet and settle for cherry-vanilla with chocolate sauce?

• Did you know that his few friends (in the mid-1970s, in which this book mainly takes place) were political conservatives? ("I spend much of that evening listening to Gossage telling Joan and Bob Danziger that Ronald Reagan might be the country's best hope," a narrator writes, describing a dinner party during her stay with the poet. "I am horrified. We have never discussed politics before, and when I hear him praise a Republican it's like – I imagine – what Bluebeard's wife must have felt when she opened the door to the secret room and discovered the unimaginable evil that was her husband's secret.")

I would like to ask the author this, about *Gains and Losses:* "If we apply a calculus to what a certain ex-lover did to you, and to what you've written in this novel, would you say that you're even with that man now? And if so, on a scale of one to ten, how good does it feel?"

In literary terms, the book is about as tasteful as its subject matter. You might get the impression that the author meant the book to be an epic, but she's left so many sub-plots dangling that you'll probably conclude that she was in a hurry to get paid – or that her editor warned her that the book wouldn't be publishable unless she cut it down to a beach-read.

Quite aside from questioning the taste of *Gains and Losses*, I question its apparent message: that physical relationships between teacher and student are invariably predatory and exploitative, and should be forbidden, with severe sanctions against any professor who indulges his swinish passions.

I don't downgrade books – or any other artistic effort – just for the sake of doing so. I might have praised *Gains and Losses* if it had been essentially the same story, better written. I might have done the same if the story and the message had been worth reading, even if clumsily presented. But I find this book preachy, tendentious, and – above all – anti-æsthetic. And I'm a hypocrite for finding it so amusing, despite all that. Having to admit my own hypocrisy is what *really* annoys me.

Monday, September 6, 1999

"Congratulations," Quagga told Ballou over the phone. Ballou was at his desk in the second bedroom of his house, which he'd set up as his study. "I thought my wife was going to die laughing when she read your review. And I've been getting a ton of calls and e-mails, ever since it came out. Mostly from women, and they all agree that you must be some kind of unspeakable ogre, to attack a courageous woman like Charlotte Fanshaw. And I got a long rebuttal of your review – from a man – and I'll publish it this coming weekend. Hang on and I'll e-mail it to you."

A few seconds later, the note popped up on Ballou's computer.

> To the Editor:
>
> Roger Ballou's review of Charlotte Fanshaw's *Gains and Losses* was obviously intended to be witty in the way of that critic in the old movie *Laura,* who claimed that he wrote "with a pen dipped in venom." But instead of being a legitimate review, much less a witty review, it's blasphemy for its own sake. Sour, angry, creepy garbage, reminiscent of bad stand-up comics who have to rely on insulting the audience because they have nothing of their own to say.

The review says more about Roger Ballou himself than the subject he seeks to skewer. His *ad hominem* attack on Charlotte Fanshaw makes him look the coward. All the great critics have the guts to attack the work they are critiquing. Roger prefers to dehumanize an obviously kind, compassionate and sensitive woman by implying that she's neurotic and vindictive. In doing so, he displays his own deep want of something worthwhile to do with his life. This kind of meanness is always, in my experience, self-loathing turned outward.

I – for one *male* reader – consider *Gains and Losses* a masterpiece. It's honest. It made me laugh, and cry. It made me feel that I know Charlotte Fanshaw. (I haven't met her yet, but I hope to!) It made me blush for my own gender. Bottom line: *Gains and Losses* truly moved me.

Roger, your review reeks. Of failure and frustration. It's a midlife crisis in print. You are so transparent. And so pathetic. Why don't you just do a Hemingway and get it over with? You do master the trick of being both hateful and beneath contempt in the same moment, which is some kind of Zen achievement. May we never see your by-line again, in this or any other lifetime.

– Parzival

"That's from someone connected with the college," said Quagga. "parzival@vandevander.edu. Other than that, I've no idea who it is."

"Obviously one of my fellow faculty," said Ballou. "That's not a young man's voice. He's trying to show off to all the single women in the area – especially to Charlotte Fanshaw herself."

"Why, Roger, you seem to know everything," said Quagga. "But if you're right, you'll probably have a chance to see it unfold next Saturday afternoon. Charlotte's going to kick off her signing tour, over at Mountain Lights Books. You might want to show up there and ask her a question or two. Oh, and speaking of Saturday – do you play bridge?"

Wednesday, September 8, 1999

As he stood before his Poetry Workshop class, in room 208 of Van Devander's Liberal Arts building on Wednesday morning, Ballou remarked that some of the girls were still girls, and all but one of the boys were still boys. College students had not been that young, to him, the last time he'd been in a roomful of them. Twelve of them sat around a large oblong table. They'd left the end of the table nearest the door for Ballou, presumably, and he set down his briefcase there and said "Good morning" to it. None of the students responded, and he immediately scolded himself for not having looked right at them. He did so, then, circling the room with his glance and making the briefest eye contact with each student.

"I can fake anything," he repeated to himself. "I can fake anything."

He ran down the roll, remembering to employ a device he'd learned from one of his own college professors for retaining a large number of names.

"Michael Brooke?"

The one black student – or light brown, actually – raised his hand. Ballou noted, Brooke, black, same as Edward Brooke the black U.S. Senator.

"Kelly Curley?"

Miss Kelly Curley had very curly hair. Easy. And, yes, Ballou decided: he would.

Lee Grossbaum was far and away the prettiest girl in the class – slender, with a rosy-porcelain complexion, small black eyes, and long curly black hair – and thus Ballou memorized her name automatically. (He definitely would.)

Curtis Wandervogel was tall, with dark wavy hair, and thin, with a stiff, nervous manner. Vogel, bird, and the young man was certainly birdlike.

The last name on the list, Sherrie Zizmor, belonged to a girl with an unfortunate complexion. Zizmor, more zits. (He wouldn't.)

"Okay." Ballou consciously straightened up. "I'm going to stay on my feet, because I talk better that way. You're here to learn to write poetry, or to write better poetry, if you already write it. Mainly, you'll improve your poetry in two ways: first, by reading poetry, good and bad, but more importantly, by writing poetry.

"You are all going to write quite a lot of poetry for this class. We meet three times a week, and in each session we're going to critique at least two poems. That means that on the average, each of you will be up for a critique every other week. However, I will require you to write considerably more than one poem every two weeks. The minimum required to pass this class will be 20 lines of poetry every week, and if you want a better grade, you'll have to either produce more, or really knock my socks off with those 20 lines, or both.

"It's all very well to talk about how you have to be inspired to write great poetry, and that may be true, but you won't write great poetry until you've written a lot of poetry that's not so great. So, if you don't feel like producing a certain amount of poetry every week, you're just going to have to force yourselves.

"Don't worry about having your poems critiqued in class. I will sometimes point out to you where you might be doing better with your words, but I didn't agree to teach this class just for the pleasure of destroying baby poets' egos."

(This got a few smiles, which encouraged Ballou.)

"I'm going to be hard on you – because I want you to succeed. If you ever feel that I'm treating you too roughly, bear in mind that I'm doing it because I'm on your side. I'll expect all of you to participate in the discussion of each poem, and I expect you to be polite but honest. I don't want you to praise something that stinks, just to be nice. If it stinks, explain why it stinks. Don't be a know-it-all, don't be snide – but be critical.

"If you're being critiqued, I've got one rule for you: shut up. If someone says he doesn't like this or that about your poem, or doesn't understand this or that, or says, 'I think it would be better if you said thus-and-so,' you are to sit there and take it. No matter how much it hurts you to hear people tearing your work apart, you are not here to argue. The only time you're allowed to respond is if someone asks you a direct question, like if he asks you the meaning of a word he doesn't know. Come to think of it, if you don't understand a word or phrase, ask me, not the author. If I know, I'll answer. If I don't, I'll ask the author. That's how you'll find out how little I know."

Someone shrieked, falsetto, as though she'd been stabbed. Ballou looked around and determined that the sound came from a pale, thin, long-faced young woman in a loose dress – and that the sound was evidently a laugh. She blushed almost purple – the blush was as abrupt and extreme as her laugh – put her hands over her face, and looked down at her lap. Ballou ignored the outburst. (Tonia Kampling was her name, and he wouldn't.)

"Now, each one of you is in a very fortunate position, with regard to your future as a poet. Anybody want to tell me why?"

Silence.

"Okay, I'll tell you. You're all between the ages of 17 and 22, I'd estimate. As a matter of fact, there's quite a lot of people your age around these days, and there'll be more. You're just the crest of the wave. See, we had a lot of babies born in the early and mid-1980s, and now the first of those kids are just entering college.

"There's one fact. Let me give you another. Let me name you some names. Samuel Taylor Coleridge. Walter Scott. Lord Byron. John Keats. Percy Shelley. William Cullen Bryant. Do those names mean anything to you? Anybody?"

Sherrie More Zits raised her hand.

"Are we going to be concentrating on dead white males?"

"That's a fair question, and the answer is no. For the most part, you'll be free to read whatever poets you like. At the end of the semester you'll submit a term paper of about 3,000 words – that's about 10 typewritten pages – in which you compare and contrast your own poetry with the work of other poets of your choosing. But the people I just mentioned do happen to be dead white males. They're dead because they were all born more than 200 years ago. And that's part of my point.

"All those guys were born within about 20 years of each other. They all became world-famous poets in the first 25 years or so of the 19th century. Now, I don't know why or how it happened, but many people consider the 19th century, and in particular the early 19th century, the high point of poetry in the English language.

"You're going to find, if you read history, that in just about any field, whether it's literature, or sports, or industry, or architecture, or what-have-you, there will be periods of a few years where everything seems to come together and a huge wave of talent comes onto the scene, and you have what you might call a golden age of poetry, or sculpture, or baseball. That portion of the 19th century – when all of those guys I mentioned were young men, mostly in their teens and 20s – was one of those times.

"And now, we're about to start a new century. We have a population that's rather heavy with teenagers, as most of these guys were when their century turned. So my point is that we have a chance to create another golden age of poetry. If a bunch of you work hard and get good, a professor 200 years from now might be asking his class what they know about Sherrie Zizmor, Lee Grossbaum, Michael Brooke, etc.

"Many famous poets – including most of the dead white males I just mentioned – became famous when they were still in their teens. And that's no accident." Ballou paused again, and looked around the room. "You may not believe it now, but you all are really lucky to be 18, 19, 20, and writing poetry. Can anybody tell me why?"

"Because life sucks when you're our age," said Michael Brooke. "You gotta suffer to write great poetry, right?

(Another shriek – although a slightly less violent one – from Tonia Kampling.)

"Right you are, Mr. Brooke," said Ballou. "Contentment might be delightful, but you don't get inspiration out of contentment, do you? Has any one of you written a poem, when you were feeling happy, that you liked a long time after you'd written it? Or did you pick it up a year later, when maybe you weren't feeling so positive, and did you go 'EEEEW!'? Wasn't it, in retrospect, the worst piece of crap you'd ever written? Didn't you go and burn it immediately?"

"That is a bullshit," said a round, bulky, balding young man with a sullen face and an Italian accent. "I write a lot of appy poems."

Vecchia means "old." Giulio Dellavecchia was probably not much past 20, but his balditude gave him 10 extra years.

"*Bene*, Signore Dellavecchia," Ballou replied. "Bring them in."

"*Parla l'italiano?*" Mr. Dellavecchia looked surprised, for Ballou had pronounced his name without stumbling.

"*Un po', si. L'ho etudiato durante due anni, all'università. Ma... ma non ho alcun'opportunità per praticare, dunque il mio italiano è... è... non è molto forte. Mi dispiace.*"

Dellavecchia inclined his head, apparently half-impressed, half-dismissive.

"Okay," Ballou continued, "so, it's my opinion that the teen years, and the early 20s, are a great time to write poetry because it's a difficult, frustrating age when emotional turmoil is more interesting than it is in adulthood. When you're feeling lousy, you want to tell people, right? And you want to do it artistically, and memorably, so that everyone else will feel your pain and discern the beauty of your soul."

All the students were smiling and paying attention, even Giulio Dellavecchia. Ballou took heart, and proceeded.

"So, you all are in a position to write better poetry than a lot of older folks can write, on account of your age, and what-all is going on in your heads at the moment. In this class, you're going to use your ideas to create poetry; meanwhile, it'll be my job to teach you the mechanics.

"Can anyone tell me what a metrical pattern is? Miss... Motski?"

"That's, like, the rhythm of it?" Wanda Motski was pretty in a buxom way, a dumpling, or a matzo ball, matzo, Motski. "Like, the beat, almost? Like, ta-TUM, ta-TUM, ta-TUM, or something like that?"

Ballou quickly undressed Miss Motski in his mind.

"That's about right," he said. "If a poem 'scans,' so to speak, then it follows a proper metrical pattern. For example:

I knew an old man from Spokane,
Whose limericks no one could scan.
When his friends told him so,
He said, "Yes, I know,
And that's because I always stick as many gosh-darn syllables
into the very last line as ever I possibly can!"

"So, when you scan a poem you identify a regular rhythm. And you'll observe, in the limerick that I just recited, that the rhythm was okay, and identifiable, through the first four lines, but on the fifth and final line, it kind of fell apart, didn't it? His limericks, no one could scan – because I always stick as many gosh-darn syllables into the very last line as ever I possibly can. See?

"We're going to work on scansion, this semester, and we'll discuss rhyme, and poetic forms, we'll discuss the differences among blank verse, free verse and free form. Some of this will be kind of dry, no doubt, but it's necessary that you know these mechanics if you expect to become good poets. You can't be a poet unless you know it. Yes, Mr. ... Taylor."

Scott Taylor looked like the stereotypical Campus Radical, with unkempt hair and clothes and a languidly cocky manner.

"Yeah, why do we need to learn that stuff anyway? Why can't we just make a poem rhyme if we want it to rhyme, or not? Hardly any poetry rhymes or has regular verses or any of that stuff anymore, does it?"

"Thank you, Mr. Taylor: That was the question I was waiting for. You're right, that you seldom see poetry nowadays that rhymes, much less poetry that has a specific form. But could you tell me why poetry used to rhyme, and have form, long ago? Or if you're not sure, can you guess?"

"I don't know for sure," Scott Taylor replied, "but I'd imagine it was because people in general were more formal. Y'know, they wore fancier clothes, and their way of talking was, y'know, fancier, too, and they all called each other 'Mister' all the time."

Ballou joined in the laughter, although a bit resentful that he hadn't been the first to cause it.

"That's what a lot of people assume, Mr. Taylor. But that's not quite right. The reason that poetry rhymed in the old days – or if it didn't rhyme, it used some other kind of repeating sounds – was for almost the opposite reason. It was because so many people, hundreds and thousands of years ago, were too poor to go to school. Even elementary school cost money in those days, and in any case the children had to stay home and work, or their family wouldn't eat. They were not fancy or formal people at all. They were poor folks who wore rags and never had enough of anything, and they led short, dangerous, and very boring lives – *and they couldn't read!* Most of them couldn't even write their names!

"Now, how would these people have amused themselves, in the few minutes they had each day to relax and have fun? Well, they'd have sung songs and told stories, wouldn't they? So, if they couldn't read, if you wanted to tell these folks a story in a way that they'd remember it, you had to make it easy to remember. Now, what's easy to remember? Miss Zizmor! Who's your very favorite modern poet? A poet who's still alive or who died just recently?"

Sherrie Zizmor glared at him.

"Excuse me, but what is this 'Miss'?" she demanded. "Do you also call African-Americans 'colored people'?"

Ballou stopped himself just short of going into a long tangent about racial nomenclature, and paused an extra second to make sure he didn't do it.

"Do you really want to be called 'Mizz Zizmor'?" he asked. "Doesn't 'Miss Zizmor' fall much more pleasantly on the ear? I daresay, if your name were Sissmor, I'd call you 'Mizz Sissmor,' for the same reason. See, this is a perfect example of what you'll have to keep in mind when you're writing poetry. Poetry is meant to be spoken aloud, so you have to be mindful of how it sounds. You have to choose words that sound well together.

"I certainly can call you 'Mizz Zizmor' if you have a strong pref-erence. I believe in calling people what they want to be called, but I do think 'Miss Zizmor' sounds nicer. Or I can call you 'Sherrie' if you insist on it, but my own strong preference is for surnames. I believe the best poetry is formal in the sense of 'having form.' And I believe the best relationships between student and teacher are formal in the sense of 'proper and reserved.' I'm sure you're aware of the kind of abuses that can take place when that relationship becomes too familiar. Maybe one day I can call you 'Professor Zizmor.'"

Miss Zizmor rolled her eyes and fluttered her hand in the "whatever" gesture.

"Anyway, your favorite living poet. Do you have one?"

"Maya Angelou, I guess. Or Jorie Graham."

"Okay," said Ballou. "And probably a lot of people would agree with you. They are possibly the most respected living American poets – except possibly for Llandor. What do you think of Llandor, by the way?"

"As a poet, or as a person?"

"Yes, you're right, his personality has received a lot of publicity lately, hasn't it? I'm just curious: Do you like his poetry?"

Miss Zizmor wrinkled her nose a little. "I did. It's been a while since I read him. I concentrate on women and third-world poets."

"Okay. That's fine. We all have our favorites. So, two of yours are Jorie Graham and Maya Angelou. Now, please understand that I respect your opinion, but here's mine. I believe that those two women might be good *writers*, but I have a serious doubt in my mind as to whether they write *poetry*. Jorie Graham's work, in my opinion, is prose with odd line-breaks, and Maya Angelou is more of a speech-writer than a poet. Can any of you *recite* a poem by either of them?"

No takers.

"Okay, and neither can I. But that was the important thing about poetry, back in the old days. Because not many people could read, poetry had to be *memorable*. It had to be memorable enough that if you heard it, you could recite it later. Poetry evolved as a method by which people could remember old stories that were never written down. If it had a strong rhythm, if it rhymed, it would be far easier to remember.

"Therefore, in my opinion, the final point of distinction between what is poetry and what is prose is whether the work employs mnemonic devices."

Ballou moved to the blackboard and wrote the word "mnemonic" thereon.

"A mnemonic device is anything that makes the poem easy to remember. Does it rhyme? If it doesn't rhyme, does it at least have a metrical pattern? Does it use alliteration?

"Alliteration" (Ballou wrote this on the board too) "is a word we'll come back to frequently in this class, by the way. It means using words that begin with the same sound, so as to make the phrase memorable. Like 'dumber than dirt.' Okay, and if a poem doesn't use rhyme or alliteration, does it at the very least have a rhythm to it that will help you to memorize it?

"Of course, you're all free to disagree with me. And you're welcome to bring free-form poetry into class, and any of you is welcome to praise it. But I hope that by the end of this semester, most of you will have come to prefer formal poetry. And perhaps, by teaching this class, I'll come to appreciate free-form poetry.

"The trouble is, most teachers of poetry don't communicate the importance of form – that is, distinct patterns of rhyme, rhythm, and verse – and most poets lack the discipline to impose form on themselves. They just won't make themselves do it. I wrote almost no formal poetry until I was well into my 30s, but I'm convinced that if I had forced myself, as a teenager, to write sonnets, villanelles, and pantoums, I'd be a much better poet today. Mr. Tisquantum?"

Little Chuck Tisquantum, Jr. (that was the name on the official class list, although he was of middle size) was obviously an Indian. The roach-style crest of black hair atop his otherwise shaved head emphasized that fact.

"Yeah, why'd people stop writing formal poetry?" he asked.

"Several reasons, Mr. Tisquantum. For one, as time went on, more and more people could read. More and more people could afford to buy books and pamphlets of poetry. If you have a poem in print, in your house, it becomes less important for you to memorize it. If you want to entertain your friends, you can just take the book off the shelf and read aloud. That's probably the biggest reason. Poetry no longer *needed* form, at least not as much as it did back when most people couldn't read and didn't own books.

"Another reason was that many poets felt that poetic forms were too restrictive, and prevented them from experimenting. So they tried new forms, and some of these forms were not recognizable as forms to anyone but themselves. And so, inevitably, formal poetry went out of style. Eventually, poets who used form, and rhyme, and so on, ran the risk of being considered very old-fashioned and kind of corny. And if there's anything a poet is really paranoid about, it's that he might sound corny.

"I'm sure you all know that as well as I do. A lot of people think poets are corny by definition. How many of you, when you were kids, used to write poetry in secret, because you were afraid you'd be made fun of?"

Ballou raised his own hand, and more than half the students raised theirs.

"It's an unfortunate myth, but let's face it, a lot of poets believe it themselves. According to the stereotype, poetry is for sickly, sentimental girls or weak, wimpy men. Except for Rudyard Kipling. If you add in the idea that formal poetry is old-fashioned and contrived and affected, it's no wonder nobody writes it anymore.

"Just by the way, though, I would point out that George Washington and Abraham Lincoln, who were two of the toughest dead white males in history, both wrote poetry. As a matter of fact, one of Washington's poems is used as an example in *The Complete Rhyming Dictionary*" (Ballou held up his copy of that book for the class to see), "which I strongly recommend that all of you buy."

The beautiful or beauteous Lee Grossbaum (Ballou couldn't decide which she was; the latter word implies a mystical element) put up her hand.

"Isn't that cheating?"

"Would you say that using an ordinary dictionary is cheating?"

"No."

"Why not?"

"Um…"

"Well, okay, never mind why not. If it's not cheating, then why is it cheating to use a rhyming dictionary?"

 Silence.

"Right," said Ballou. "Maybe it would be cheating, if we poets all got together and made a rule that you couldn't use a rhyming dictionary – but that'd be about the same as a bunch of carpenters getting together and agreeing that they couldn't use hammers. A rhyming dictionary is a tool. Sure, you could build a house without using a hammer – it used to be done all the time – but guess what? Once hammers were invented, you didn't have to, so why should you? I'll repeat: Buy a rhyming dictionary. It's cheap, and if you use it, you'll write better poetry and have a lot more time left over to party."

"Professor Ballou." Curtis Wandervogel had a kind of sing-song voice which Ballou thought made him sound rather self-important. "If you have to resort to a dictionary to find a word that rhymes, don't you destroy the integrity of the po-em? Wouldn't it be a better po-em if you used the word that came from your heart, instead of the word that rhymed?" The young man raised his eyebrows, pursed his lips, and gave his head a triumphant little tilt at the end of each question.

"You might use the word that comes from your heart *first*," Ballou replied. "You'll probably find your heart less eloquent than your head, however. If you stretch your vocabulary by looking for the rhyme, and keeping to the form, you will usually discover precisely the right word."

Ballou looked at his watch, and saw that he had ten minutes left. He reached into his briefcase and brought out a dozen copies of a poem, which he handed out to the class.

"Probably the best way to end this first session is to let you read what is maybe the worst poem I've ever seen. And I can say that confidently, because I wrote it myself. I was 15 years old at the time – a sophomore in high school – and I had a terrible crush on a girl in my school who was a senior. I was obsessed. I could hardly eat or sleep or study for thinking about this girl. And of course she, being a senior, was not interested in being my girlfriend. As dumb and socially retarded as I was, I didn't understand that senior girls simply did not date sophomore boys. I thought she was just being unreasonable!"

That got the laugh he'd been waiting for – but not from Tonia Kampling. As the rest of the class giggled, she gasped audibly, and stared at Ballou open-mouthed, horrified. She moaned, and her eyes actually welled up in compassion for his clueless teenaged self. Her reaction almost embarrassed Ballou in its excess – but it touched him nonetheless.

"And as I got older I got worse," he said, directly to Miss Kampling. "Anyway, the poem:

Sometimes
I think about you so much
And
I just want to tell you
How much I miss you and want to be with you
I am
Nothing without your love

Most of the students were looking at each other out of the corners of their eyes.

"Okay, it's pathetic, and not just because I gave you the context. Just look at it. You've got arbitrary line-breaks, which occur because the author has noticed that modern poetry has a lot of arbitrary line-breaks. Because the poem has no form, it just rattles along, and tells us nothing.

"'I think about you so much.' Well, *how* much? The poem doesn't tell us how much. And then, 'I just want to tell you/How much I miss you and want to be with you.' He wants to tell her how much he misses her, see, but he *doesn't*! And why doesn't he?

"*Not* because he's not writing from the heart! No! It's precisely because he *is* writing from the heart, and not from the head! It's because the poet didn't appreciate how much more effective the poem would have been, if he'd given it form. If he'd chosen his words carefully. If he'd made it *memorable*."

Ballou paused – to make "memorable" memorable.

"One factor that distinguishes good poetry from bad is *control*. Reading good poetry, you're aware that the poet paid close attention to every word. Reading bad poetry, you're aware that the poet did not express his thoughts as precisely as he could have done. That's true whether you're reading formal or free-form poetry.

"Formal poems are not, by definition, better than free-form poems, but unlike free-form poems, they do teach you control. With the strict limits of the form imposed on you, you're forced to think hard about each word, and thus you're more likely to be precise. A formal poem – especially one that employs one of the stricter forms, like a *ballade* – is jeweler's work.

"Some people who don't know any better will argue that rhyme, and other formal expedients, restrict you unnecessarily. I say just the opposite. When you use form, you expand your knowledge of the language, and this gives you more possibilities.

"For that reason if for no other, I find formal poetry more fun to write. You can whip out a free-form poem in minutes, because it's just prose, only easier. It doesn't even have to be written as a complete sentence. A formal poem can take a very long time, and you forget everything else during the composition. The sheer pleasure of composing it is indescribable. Yes, Mr. Taylor."

"If you'd made that poem memorable, would she have dated you?" Mr. Taylor asked. Again the class tittered.

"Poetry may be powerful, Mr. Taylor, but it's not all-powerful," Ballou replied. "I don't care if I'd written a poem that won a Pulitzer Prize. Nerdy tenth-grade boy does not get twelfth-grade girl who looks like Reese Witherspoon."

Ballou paused again, to indicate that he was about to close.

"To end with, I'm going to recite the first poem I ever learned by heart. It's by Robert Frost — who, by the way, once said that 'Writing poetry without form is like playing tennis without a net.' This poem is called 'The Pasture'."

I'm going out to clean the pasture spring;
I'll only stop to rake the leaves away
(And wait to watch the water clear, I may)
I sha'n't be gone long. You come, too.

I'm going out to fetch the little calf
That's standing by the mother. It's so young,
It totters when she licks it with her tongue.
I sha'n't be gone long. You come, too.

Ballou paused. Lee Grossbaum was looking at him as though he'd written the poem himself. Ballou almost forgot to start speaking again.

"I was not quite five years old, and we were living in Madison, Wisconsin, and one day my mother told me that Robert Frost was in town, and we were going to go and hear him read his poetry. We had some phonograph records, you know, those old vinyl things, of Frost reading his poetry, and that was how I'd learned to recite 'The Pasture.' By listening to them. So naturally I was pretty excited. The reading took place in the afternoon, and we went to a restaurant for lunch beforehand, and as we were eating, we noticed this old white-haired couple at the table next to us, must have been in their 80s, and my mother leaned over to me and said, 'Now, don't turn around, but over there is Mr. Frost!' And you know, five-year-old boys don't whisper, so I yelled, 'You mean *Robert* Frost?' And the old lady, over at the next table, she says, 'Why, Robert, that little boy knows who you are!'

"And then my father introduced me to Frost, and he saw that I had a little pad of paper, where I'd been drawing a picture of a clown while we waited for the food to arrive, and he asked me what was the clown's name, and I said, 'Joe Smith,' and he signed the picture, 'Joe Smith and Robert Frost, September 16, 1961.'

"Think about that for a moment. I probably made Robert Frost's day, and the reason that I knew who he was, at age four or five, was that he remembered the primary function of poetry, which is to speak to the reader vividly enough that the reader remembers the poem."

Ballou paused again.

"Now! Your first 20 lines are due next Monday, the 13th. I want at least two of you to volunteer to read to the class on Friday, this week, and I'll need at least two volunteers for every day of class thereafter. Anybody? Mr. Wandervogel? Good. Miss Motski?

"That's two, and I doubt we'll have time for a third, but Mr. Taylor, you be prepared just in case, and if you're not called on Friday you'll be first up on Monday. The three of you, I want you each to bring enough copies of your poem for all of us. There's 13 of us in all, and possibly one or two new people will show up on Friday, so bring maybe 15 copies, okay? Mr. Tisquantum and Miss Schlegel, you'll please have something ready for Monday too.

"And despite what I said about formal poetry, bring free-form poetry if that's what you write, and that's fine with me. See you all on Friday."

*

At the end of Ballou's afternoon class, Expository Writing, as he was putting his papers into his briefcase and preparing to leave the classroom, a student accosted him.

Andrew Florence was his name on the roll: a spindly young man of 19 or 20 with liquid dark eyes, feminine lips, and straight dark hair that he wore in a bowl-cut, like a small child. He'd drawn Ballou's attention almost immediately because he was extremely fidgety. He hadn't spoken in that first session, but he tended to snicker frequently. Not in the way that Tonia Kampling had done that morning, which had made Ballou doubt her sanity. This young man's laughter seemed more malicious: as though he were mocking every other person in the room. But it hadn't been disruptive enough for Ballou to say anything about it.

"A... about my name," the young man said. "I nee... d a favor. My name on the register is Andrew Fl... Florence, but call me Firenze... Q... Tanquiz. F... Fi for short." He stopped, but Ballou could tell that he wasn't done talking, because his mouth was working desperately and foam was collecting at the corners.

"Firenze Q. Tanquiz," the young man repeated, pronouncing it "fye-*ren*-zee." "Dynamite Jock, on WVDV cam... campus radio. Ni... ni... ni... ninety-nine-point-eight on your FM dial!" This was followed by a huge gasp for breath.

"Write it out for me," said Ballou, passing the class list to the student. Firenze Q. Tanquiz did.

"Where... where you h... h... eaded now, Professor?" Tanquiz asked, falling into step with Ballou as they walked down the hall. Ballou was already feeling a bit bemused, about the name the student had given himself, and this question struck him odd, as well: too personal, almost. Firenze Q. Tanquiz, Ballou suspected, liked to push himself on people.

"Over to the athletic building," said Ballou (almost adding, "If it's any of your business").

"Tha... t's where I'm going," said Tanquiz. "What? You got..." Again he got stuck; his mouth twisted horribly as they continued to walk together, now outside the building. "You got a gym class too?"

"No, of course not." Ballou tried not to sound stiff, for he felt that the student didn't mean any harm, and in any case he didn't want to be accused of unfriendliness to a stammerer. "I'm just going to buy some football tickets. I figured I'd better hurry up before the good seats are gone – if they're not already."

"You... shouldn't have a problem," said Tanquiz. "I bet they never sell tuh... tuh... too many tickets. Athletically, we suck. You like fuh... you li... ke football? You're gonna hate it here."

"I'm actually not much of a football fan," Ballou admitted. "But I don't know anybody here. If I buy two tickets, I'll have to invite someone to use the other, so I force myself to make some friends – see?"

Ballou felt immediately embarrassed that he was telling a student about his lack of a social life.

The foyer of the athletic building, which housed the ticket office, was almost empty: just the odd student passing in or out. Ballou glanced up at the purple-and-orange fresco that covered the wall opposite the ticket window. It displayed the team's logo and mascot: a cute, pot-bellied, stumpy-legged little Indian with a scalp-lock and loincloth, holding a football under his left arm and an upraised ball-head club in his right hand, his eyes squeezed tight shut and his mouth wide open, presumably giving voice to an adorably blood-curdling war-cry.

"Has he got a name?" Ballou asked.

"That's Willie Wilden," said Fi Tanquiz, pronouncing the name with obvious scorn. "He's one reason why we... suck. Look at him. He's all cuddly. He... looks like a kid's... toy. How you gonna win football games with that? Give us a tough-looking guy, maybe put a bloody scalp in his hand, and call him Big Chief Slap-Yo-Momma. Maybe..." (Tanquiz gasped and gagged briefly, then recovered.) "Maybe then we'd win three or four in a season."

Tanquiz talked in bursts. He'd be all right for a few words at a time, but then he'd choke and lock up.

"I bet you're wondering how I got to be a radio DJ with this impe… impe…"

"Impediment?"

"Let me say it, God damn it! Don't ever prompt a stammerer! That's really bad manners."

"Sorry."

"Forget it. It's part of my act. The st… the st… stammer… is real… but, but, but, I make it part of the act. You got it, use it!"

"When's your show?" Ballou asked. "I'll catch it if I can."

"Wednesday and Thursday nights, eight to eleven. Like tonight," said Tanquiz. "Tonight and tomorrow. I gotta get, get, to class, then… gotta… gotta get home and get, get, get my beauty sleep before the show." He pointed. "Ticket office is that way."

Saturday, September 11, 1999

Mountain Lights Books, a store of a size suitable to a little town, had only a small area indoors for lectures, signings, and such events. On this bright sunny afternoon the owner had set up a podium outdoors on the Town Square, with as many metal folding chairs as he could organize: not nearly enough. Ballou arrived early and got one, front and center, and as he sat waiting, a crowd collected of perhaps 300 people: three or four times as many women as men, most of them in the 20 to 50 age range, including quite a few mothers with their college-age daughters.

A few minutes before three, Police Chief Jorgensen and Officer Perdue pulled up in a patrol car, got out, and went over to the owner of Mountain Lights, who was standing near the podium.

"No, I haven't got a permit," he admitted to the Chief. It was a picture: this rather scrawny, thirtyish man with bushy hair, wearing jeans and a Che Guevara t-shirt, standing next to Chief Jorgensen, who was about the same age and looked like Dick Decent: blond and big-jawed, with an immaculately pressed uniform, whitewall haircut, and straightforward manner. "I didn't think it would get this big. Yogi, you're not going to shut us down, are you? I'm sure it'll be orderly. And it'll only run maybe an hour, 90 minutes tops."

"Oh, heck, I guess not," replied Chief Jorgensen. "What do you think, Boo-Boo?" he asked his subordinate. "Much chance of a riot here?"

Perdue was small, dark, and wiry, a little rumpled-looking. He called out to the crowd, "Just everybody keep quiet and nobody'll get hurt," and got a general laugh.

Ballou stood up to look around. Donald Quagga had emerged from his office across the street and joined the standees, a few feet away. Ballou recognized no one else.

A few minutes after three, the owner of Mountain Lights stepped up to the microphone, Charlotte Fanshaw standing a few feet behind him.

"Some of you are new to this town," he began, "and you may not have met Charlotte Fanshaw, who was born and raised here, and after a life of travel and adventure, who recently returned here to raise her family in the house where she grew up in." (Ballou grimaced at the syntax.) "But we all know why she's here, and we all know why we're here: We're here to celebrate the publication of her latest book, *Gains and Losses*. Which I'm sure we all hope... uh... brings her the fame she deserves. And so without further ado, I give you Charlotte Fanshaw."

The author wore a bright yellow dress, which suited her complexion no better than the red one had, but showed off her legs equally well.

"This is my fifth book," she began, in the strong, clear voice of one accustomed to public speaking, "and my first novel, and for each book, I've come back to Mountain Lights, but I've never seen a crowd like this — just as my previous books never got a tenth as many reviews in the press as this one has — so I'd like to start by acknowledging each and every one of you for coming here today. It's great to be back, and I'm especially happy to be speaking to so many women of my own age who are here with their daughters.

"In many of the reviews *Gains and Losses* has received, the words that come up over and over again are 'abuse' and 'exploitation.' And strangely enough, they're usually used to describe what I did, in writing this book, rather than what someone else might have done.

"I wrote this book for every woman who has ever been exploited and abused by an older and more powerful man – or by the patriarchy in general – and for every woman who has ever sublimated her true being in order to please a man she was involved with. I also wrote this book for every mother who might have a daughter in danger of being placed in this position. My own eldest daughter is entering her last year of high school this fall, and will turn 18 this winter…"

Following her set-up, Charlotte read a few of the juiciest bits of her novel. Ballou thought her a fine dramatic reader. She concluded with the final confrontation between poet and ex-student, which drew loud applause, then declared that she was about to open the floor to questions.

"But before I do, I want to address a question that appeared in a review… well, the review that ran in *The Wildenkill Advertiser.* The reviewer asked whether I got even with anyone by writing this book, and how good did it make me feel. My answer to that is that first of all, I'd like to know if a man would ever be asked a question like that!"

Applause from the crowd. A man a few yards away from Ballou shouted "Right on!"

Ballou glanced over. The man looked about 50 years old; he was tallish and quite fat – close to 300 pounds, Ballou estimated, as best he could tell since the man wore baggy jeans and a loose sweatshirt – with wavy, greying dark hair and a full but close-clipped beard that merged with the body hair that grew above the neckline of his shirt. He had with him a boy of about four, who sat on his shoulder. Ballou caught Quagga's eye, cocked his head toward the fat man, and winked. Quagga looked perplexed for a moment, then lifted his chin in comprehension.

"Second, I had a story to tell. I told it because I thought it was an important story for people to hear – especially for women to hear – and if it helps even one of them, or keeps one of them from having to go through something like that themselves, then I'll feel very good about that."

"And now I'll take questions." Ballou had been looking right at Charlotte, and she saw his hand first. "You."

Ballou stood, slowly. He kept his expression, and his voice, bland and polite.

"I have a question, and then a brief follow-up, if I might."

"Just a minute." Charlotte indicated that Ballou should look behind him, and he did, to see a TV camera trained on him, and a young man carrying a boom mike moving toward him. Ballou waited until the mike was just over his head, then proceeded, speaking extra clearly so that the mike would pick up his voice properly.

"First of all, from your account, I fail to see how this fictitious poet actually exploited or abused anyone, other than being a little crotchety. Could you please elaborate on why this fictitious situation needed to be aired as a warning to other young women – as opposed to airing it in order to pay back a man who scorned you?"

Charlotte looked displeased, but she didn't pause for more than a couple of seconds.

"The abuse and the exploitation lay in the imbalance of power, between an older, wealthy, and famous literary figure, and an 18-year-old girl. If you ask me, this came pretty close to pedophilia. And I wrote it partly because I *don't* believe the story's unique. It goes on all the time. Look at Bill Clinton and Monica Lewinsky. There are predatory men out there, and women and girls need to know that. Any time you have an imbalance like that, I'd call it an exploitation."

"Okay, then, here's my follow-up," said Ballou. "It so happens that my own parents met when he was a 55-year-old professor at the University of Wisconsin, and she was a 19-year-old under-graduate. They got married on her graduation, and I was born a few years later. I have to say that in my observation it was a very happy marriage, save that my father died after only 20 years of it. My mother still speaks highly of him. And he was a pretty good father, in my opinion. Should I explain to my mother – or should you explain to her – that she was in an exploitative situation?"

A few gasps and murmurs from the crowd, and several dirty looks directed at Ballou.

"The difference is obvious," Charlotte replied, in the tone of someone being deliberately respectful to a retarded person. "Your parents had a committed relationship that lasted 20 years. And I only have your word for how happy their marriage was. It's too bad your mother isn't here. But thank you for your question." She pointed to a woman a few feet behind Ballou. "Yes?"

Ballou sat down, rolling his eyes.

"I just want to say that you changed my life," said the next questioner: an intense-looking, heavyset, frizzy-haired woman in a seersucker shift. "I recently ended a relationship with a very demanding, controlling man, and for all this time I've been asking myself, you know, 'What's wrong with me? What's wrong with me?' and your book made me realize for the first time that maybe I was okay, maybe there wasn't anything wrong with me, and…"

The "question" continued for a full minute, by Ballou's watch, and when it concluded, there was no question after all, but Char-lotte responded anyway, graciously acknowledging the woman's praise and adding, "There are a lot of us out there, all right, and we have to convince each other that we *are* okay, and that we don't have to fulfill someone else's impossible demands in order to *be* okay!"

She recognized another woman, of about the same age and build, who gave a similar speech. This one lasted 95 seconds before Charlotte tactfully cut her off. The author then pointed to the back of the crowd. Ballou turned in his seat but couldn't see the questioner.

"I'm Fi… renze Q. Tanquiz, Dynamite… Jock, with WVDV cam… campus radio, tape for broadcast," came the amplified voice.

"About L-l-l…" Firenze Q. Tanquiz choked briefly, and recovered. "I'm sorry, I have a sta… a sta… "

"That's okay," said Charlotte. "Take your time."

"About Llandor… is he a h-… is he a h-helmet, or an anteater?

"I'm sorry, what was that?"

"Is Llandor a helmet, or an anteater?"

"A helmet or an anteater?"

"Y-y-you know, circumcised or un-un-un-uncircumcised?"

Charlotte's eyes widened just a bit, and she paused for a second, but otherwise kept her countenance. "I think I'll let that one alone," she replied, and indicated a woman some distance away from the young man.

But Tanquiz persisted. "Charlotte! Charlotte! When you were with him, did you let him use all three inputs?"

Chief Jorgensen, some 50 yards away, started toward the young reporter, who saw him and began backing through the crowd. Jorgensen let him go, and resumed his post. Ballou missed this, as he was holding his hands over his face, trying to stop laughing long enough to get his breath.

"First of all," said the next questioner, a woman of about 60, "let me apologize on behalf of that young man."

"*I dare you to apologize for me, you old bag!*" Tanquiz bellowed, from a safe distance.

"Oh, don't worry," said Charlotte, with a loud laugh. "I expect to get a lot tougher questions than his!"

"Okay, well, speaking of what you expect," said the older woman, "did you expect to see Llandor here today?"

This, at last, seemed to surprise the author, as though she'd never thought about it, and realized that she maybe should have.

"No, I didn't," she said. "At least, I assume he's not here. I don't see him. I don't think he'd come; I doubt he'd want anyone to know he was paying any attention to me. But he'll read the book. I'll bet you anything on that. He'll probably have some way of getting hold of it secretly, so that only one or two other people in the world will know that he has it. Then of course he'd have to kill them."

Off to the side, the man Ballou assumed was Parzival kept trying to gain recognition, waving his hand whenever it looked like a new question was about to be invited. His little boy, meanwhile, alternately insisted on being set down on the ground, and hoisted back onto the man's shoulder. Each time, the man obliged cheerfully – until this moment. The boy jumped up and down, trying to climb onto Parzival's shoulder yet again, but now Parzival was ignoring him, waving insistently at Charlotte. At last she gave him the floor.

"Charlotte, I'm really glad to meet you at last," he began. He had a grand, self-important voice, with more rising and falling in the intonation than is usual. "I know you've taken a lot of abuse for this book, including even in our local paper which you write for, and I wish the guy that wrote that review was here, so I could punch him right in the nose." (Titters and scattered handclaps from the crowd.)

"What I'd like to know is, you've talked a lot about what you want women to get out of your book, and we've heard from so many women here today about what they did get out of it – and they got a lot out of it obviously. But what message do you want men to take away from this book? How can men in general learn from your experiences?"

Charlotte beamed. "That's such a good question! Thank you so much for asking it! I think men can take quite a lot from this book. First of all, they can understand that women have stories to tell too, that a story doesn't have to be about war, or money, or politics, or sports, to be interesting. A story about a woman's journey can be just as interesting and just as important.

"Second, they perhaps can learn from my story, how *not* to treat the women in their lives. To nurture their relationships with women. I hate to use such a clichéd expression, but maybe this book will teach men to examine their feminine sides." (More scattered applause.) "Finally, very simply, this book can teach men what is an appropriate relationship, and what is not." (Louder applause.)

After a few more questions, Charlotte thanked her audience, got a big hand, and moved to a table a few feet away from the lectern, where she sat preparing to sign copies of her book. Parzival, being near the table to begin with, was among the first to get his signed, and Ballou observed him chatting briefly with the author and shaking her hand a little longer than perhaps he needed to. The little boy jumped up and down, crying "Da! Da! Da!" until Parzival introduced him to Charlotte – whereupon he shrank from her outstretched hand and hid behind his father. The two adults exchanged that conspiratorial/indulgent smile that means, "Kids!"

The boy began running through the rows of folding chairs, tagging bystanders as he darted past them, and the fat man looked after him with a wistful gaze, then glanced back at Ms. Fanshaw as though inviting her to share the sweetness of the moment.

Ballou supposed some of those in attendance knew he'd written the unfavorable piece in the *Advertiser*, and that Parzival – and Charlotte Fanshaw – would learn that fact soon enough. Not that he thought for a moment that Parzival had been serious about wanting to punch him in the nose. Still, he didn't want to leave any possibility that he'd been offered a challenge in public and had shrunk from it. So as Parzival turned away from the author's table, Ballou walked up to him, a slight smile on his face.

"Sir," he said. "I beg your pardon. I'm Roger Ballou. I wrote the review in the *Advertiser* that you referred to. So, if you want to punch somebody in the nose, I guess I'm the guy you're looking for. At your convenience."

Parzival was taller and heavier than Ballou, but older, and Ballou knew perfectly well that he was not going to launch a physical attack — and in any case Ballou was mostly kidding. Parzival straightened, sucking in his gut.

"Roger." (He replied in the same grand voice he'd used before, with an almost audible period following the vocative.) "This act of yours is tired and nonsensical. You're just another pathetic hack writer who can't think straight, and who can't stand to see anyone else make something of themselves. Especially if it's a woman. Now, you might have some talent; I don't know. Why don't you use it to try and do something constructive?"

Ballou felt himself tingling; then he felt almost outside of himself. An amazing sensation, one that he'd felt from time to time before in his life, in moments of greatest anger: the urge to kill a man with his bare hands. Even in the moment, he remarked on it: the horrible thrill of it, and its near-irresistibility. Just a few seconds before, he'd been only mildly irritated, and had only approached Parzival as a way of insuring his dignity while having a little fun. But the name-calling and Parzival's loaded, sanctimonious question almost blinded him with rage. His hands tensed into claws, his jaw set, his breath came harder — and he forced himself to pause, and recover.

"Talk is cheap, fat boy," Ballou said softly. "If you're feeling froggish, jump."

"I'll tell you what we'll do," Parzival said, in a voice loud enough to carry to a generous radius. Several people looked in their direction. "My hunch is, you fight worse than you write. So I'll reserve the boxing ring at the Phys Ed building, for next weekend. We'll spar. Three rounds. Then I'll buy you a drink, whatever happens. If you've got the guts. I'm betting you won't show."

A clever move, Ballou admitted to himself.

"No, pal, I'm not gonna spar with you." Ballou's voice hardened, but stayed conversational in volume. "I'm not gonna put on headgear and 16-ounce gloves and have a goddam pillow-fight and be buddies afterwards. If you want to fight me on principle, then let's have a real goddam fight. Come at me in the street, any time you feel like it. Or have a few of your friends hold me down – if you have any friends – and you can beat the shit out of me with your purse."

"Oh, ouch," Parzival sneered.

"Well, come on," Ballou urged. "If you want to fuck me up, try it. Any time. My address is a matter of public record." Ballou was focusing on Parzival, but peripherally he noticed that they'd attracted a few spectators – although the crowd was already dispersing and most appeared not to notice them at all.

"Oh, lighten up, Psycho," said Parzival. "I'm talking about a little sparring. I don't want to hurt you."

"Well, I wouldn't mind hurting you, fat boy. In fact I hope you'll attack me with deadly force, so I can legally kill you."

Chief Jorgensen stepped between them. "What seems to be the trouble here?" the policeman inquired.

"A little disagreement, sir," Ballou explained. "We're discussing terms."

"Yeah, right, if threatening to kill me is 'discussing terms,'" said Parzival.

"Oh, and I called you 'fat boy,'" Ballou reminded him. "Aren't you going to tell him that, too?"

"Okay, gentlemen, cool it," said Jorgensen. To Ballou, he said, "Now, sir, do me a favor, would you? I need you to walk in one direction, and," (to Parzival) "maybe, sir, you could walk in another direction. Okay?"

"Okay with me," Ballou replied, keeping his expression even. He turned, and threaded his way through the folding chairs on the lawn, going toward the sidewalk. Once there, he paused, and noticed that his hands were trembling. He stood, staring into the distance but registering no sights, as he tried to collect himself.

He must have stood there longer than he was aware of, for by the time he looked around again, almost the whole crowd was gone. Even the cops had left. There was no sign of Parzival, and only a few stragglers hung about Charlotte Fanshaw's table, where she continued to sign books.

Ballou thought about going back and introducing himself, in the hopes that he could come up with a little dig disguised as a compliment; then he realized that that would come under the heading of Trying Too Hard, and in any case he was in no condition to talk to anyone.

That Evening

The Quaggas lived only three blocks away from Ballou, so it was no problem for him to walk over with a large laden platter in his arms. He'd thought about bringing fried chicken, but no: finger food, crumby and greasy, inconvenient at a card-party. And fried chicken for up to a dozen people? A lot of chicken and a lot of frying. Filet of beef he'd considered and dismissed as too expensive and probably requiring some sort of hard-to-make sauce to accompany it. So, he'd decided on coulibiac, the Russian salmon pie: not hard to make, economical as long as he used canned salmon, and can be made of any size since it doesn't bake in a pan.

The Quaggas lived in a white Colonial Revival with dark green shutters, on a big lot at the crest of a steepish hill. Three mature oak trees stood in the front yard. Frances Quagga, in a dark red dress, answered the door and let Ballou into the front hall. As he introduced himself, Ballou heard the stereo playing and male voices from the living room, on his left – and female voices from the kitchen, somewhere beyond the dining room on the right.

"I'm so glad you could come," said Frances. "Let me take that into the kitchen."

"No, ma'am, it's pretty heavy," Ballou replied. "I'd better carry it. If that's okay."

"You might run right out of here if you see the kitchen. It's a fright! But don't say I didn't warn you. This way." Frances led Ballou through the dining room and into the kitchen, which ran horizontally along the rear of the house. The counters were loaded with salads, casseroles, cookies, and a large cake. Two other women stood with their backs to Ballou, arranging the food and assembling plates and silverware. The larger, older one wore a flowered dress; the smaller, younger one a tailored dark blue skirt and dark blue middy blouse. All three women wore high heels. They smelled angelic.

"Set it there," Frances instructed, indicating a bare spot on the counter. "What kind of pie is it?"

Ballou resisted the urge to say, "Fish and finger," and explained the dish.

"That sounds lovely," Frances exclaimed, gazing at him as though he were the cleverest, most thoughtful man in the world. Ballou gazed back – she was really pretty – and he felt envy of Donald Quagga welling up within him, as well as bitterness directed at himself, even as he smiled at her. "Now let me introduce you. Effie, this is Roger Ballou, who's just moved here. Roger, I'd like you to know Effie Hoo."

Ballou looked quizzically at Effie Hoo, trying to reconcile the surname with this large, blonde, pink-cheeked woman. "Effie... ?"

"Hoo. It's a Chinese name. My husband's Chinese. Makes me sound a bit like a knock-knock joke, doesn't it?" Mrs. Hoo spoke briskly, with a Scottish accent. "I was born a MacIntyre. But 'Effie MacIntyre' won't quite do for a punch line!"

"I'll try to come up with one for you," Ballou replied, "before the evening's over." Mrs. Hoo was good-looking, but heavy-set and past 50, and Ballou's heart still belonged to Frances Quagga.

"Dora, this is Roger Ballou," said Frances. "Roger, this is Dora Fox. She's brand-new in town, just as you are."

"Hello, Roger," said Dora Fox in a tiny, childish voice, smiling brilliantly up at Ballou and extending her hand.

She looked, Ballou thought, like an other-worldly princess drawn by a DC Comics artist. That idea amazed Ballou as it occurred to him, and he held it in his mind: Dora Fox actually looked more like a toon than like a real human being.

She might have been Ballou's own age, or even a bit older, but exceptionally well preserved. Just a shade over five feet tall, and very slender – a girl's figure, almost – with prominent cheekbones and a ski-jump nose. It's been said that while good health and regular features make a woman pretty, the flaws make her beautiful, and in this case it was her nose – too long, upturned, and chiseled at the end – that captured Ballou. Her mouth – rather wide, full-lipped, a little pouty when she wasn't smiling – was made to be kissed. She had almond-shaped eyes, set rather close together, and long lashes. Her eyes were light purple, which Ballou had heard of before but never seen. She wore her abundant tawny hair in an immaculate French twist.

In an instant, in Ballou's mind, Frances Quagga had become merely a charming and gracious lady. Ballou had never seen, never imagined, never hoped to imagine a woman as lovely as Dora Fox.

"Love at first sight" does happen. Many people censoriously (and perhaps a bit enviously) insist that it's "not really love," but nobody has yet come up with a better word for it. It causes actual physical sensations. The first, and most immediate, is that it's like walking into an invisible pillow. You're not hurled backwards, as you would be if you'd hit a wall, but you're *stopped*: You lose, for a moment, your ability to move forward. Thus it took a fraction of a second for Ballou to persuade his right arm to move, and his hand to take Dora's, which was very small but with long, thin fingers.

"Ha-how... di-da-dyado?" Ballou half-croaked. His mind groped, and grabbed the lifeline Frances Quagga had tossed him. "You just moved to Wildenkill, too?"

"Well, not *just*-just," Dora Fox replied. "It's been almost three months now. I feel completely acclimated, and as oriented as I ever am!" She gave Ballou a half-smile, half-simper, looking right into his eyes as though she'd invented the witticism expressly to please him.

His first good look at her, and that pretty "Hello, Roger," had been the one-two punch that sent him staggering into the ropes. That look of hers back at him was the left hook that finished him. An *ache*, Ballou felt then, an actual ache in the pit of his stomach, the physical manifestation of the sudden yearning he had to take her in his arms, to stroke her hair, kiss her eyes and her lips, hold her tight, protect her against anything that might possibly threaten her perfect happiness. His arms actually started toward her, just maybe a quarter of an inch, not enough for anyone to notice, before he got control of himself.

"Dora has opened a delightful little bakery just down the road in Verstanken, haven't you, Dora?" said Frances. "That's her cake, and her cookies, on the counter."

"Oh, now you've let the cat out of the bag, Frances!" Dora exclaimed. "I was going to deny authorship if nobody liked them, but now I can't! Roger knows the secret!" She looked at him again, in mock-appeal.

"Madame, if nobody likes them, I'll claim them as my own work," Ballou replied, fingertips to heart. "You may have credit for my coulibiac."

Dora gasped, glancing at the pie and then back at Ballou, eyes shining. "That's *coulibiac*? Did you know I was coming? I *love* coulibiac."

Ballou almost replied, "And I love you." Instead, he said, "I'm impressed that you've heard of it."

"My mother makes it. She's Russian. I mean, her forebears were Russian. It was my favorite dish when I was a little girl. She'd make it for my birthday."

Suddenly Ballou saw Dora Fox at four or five, in mary janes, white socks, and a little party dress, her curls still a baby's white-blond, soft beyond imagination, as delicate as spun glass, with the sun shining on them...

"I'm glad," was all he could think of to say aloud. "It's just a happy coincidence, I guess. I hope it's as good as your mother's."

"Oh, it will be, I'm sure," Dora said. "I expect you're a very good cook."

At this point, with Ballou almost literally on his knees, Donald Quagga entered the kitchen from the living room, bringing in empty glasses. "Roger, there you are. Go on in there and meet a few more people. Frank Leahy will introduce you."

Frank Leahy occupied the law office next door to Quagga Realty, downtown. Quagga had marched Ballou over there, on the day they'd signed the lease on Ballou's house, and presented him to Mr. Leahy, with the clear implication that the lawyer was one of the town's bigger shots. Ballou had not seen him since.

"We'll talk later," Dora reassured Ballou. "Maybe we'll be partners!" She went back to whatever she'd been doing before, leaving Ballou with no excuse to defy Quagga's directions.

Ballou stopped at the swinging door that connected the kitchen to the living room, and listened for a moment, trying to identify the music, which sounded like something from the 1930s: a woman singing in American-accented French, so probably Josephine Baker. He then entered the living room to find two card tables set up. At one of them, in wooden folding chairs, sat Frank Leahy and an old lady in a long robin's-egg-blue dress – a striking old lady with light-brown skin, and white hair piled high atop her head. She sat bolt-upright in her chair, her posture that of a woman in her 30s.

Immediately to Ballou's right, behind a small wet-bar, stood the most enormous man Ballou had ever seen, and possibly the ugliest: an Indian, if not seven feet tall then close to it, with an immense barrel chest, a broad flat face decorated with several big knot-like moles, tiny black eyes, thick twisted lips, and a sharp nose. His greying hair was braided into two long queues down his back. He wore a dark green jumpsuit, like an auto mechanic.

"Roger!" Frank Leahy jumped to his feet. He was a thin, spry man, past 70, with one of those long, ruddy, toothy Irish faces, and hair that was still mostly brown. He held his right elbow tight against his body and stuck out his hand stiffly. "I extend the short arm of friendship!"

"Dear," he said to the white-haired woman, "let me introduce Roger Ballou, new man in town. Roger, this is my wife, Lois."

"I am so pleased to meet you," said Lois Leahy with very precise diction, smiling and shaking Ballou's hand. Her accent sounded foreign, but Ballou couldn't place it. She wore a lot of bright silver jewelry, including a silver-and-pearl ornament in her hair.

"And over here," Mr. Leahy continued, "is the man to know. Roger Ballou, meet Runs-Away-Screaming."

The Indian stepped forward, hand outstretched, his face expressionless. He reeked of Aqua Velva. Ballou could discern undertones of tobacco and marijuana as well.

"Yep, that's my name. Believe it or not. Call me Runs." Runs' accent was flat, Southwestern. "Get you a drink? I'm temporary bartender. Anything you want, they got here."

"Well, how are you on Manhattans?" Ballou replied. "In honor of the fair city I left behind me." Runs grunted, and returned to his place behind the bar.

"You need to talk to Runs," Leahy told Ballou. "If you haven't bought a car yet, Runs will sell you one. Maybe you've seen his lot, over on the West edge of town. Big sign that says, 'Runs.'"

"Yep, see, the name's an advannage," Runs remarked, working on Ballou's drink. "My name's my slogan. Kinda my guarantee." (He pronounced it "*gah*-ran-tee.") "Anything you buy from Runs, it runs. Runs stakes his name on it."

"You should see the crap he sells there," said Leahy. "Some of those cars, I swear they still haven't cleared the dead people out of. Some of the rustedest, twistedest old junkers you ever did see."

"Francis X. Leahy!" Lois remonstrated, slapping his hand. "That is not very nice!"

"It's the truth, dear, and I'm sure Runs won't deny it!"

"But they run," said Runs. "They all run. You want a car for a few hunnerdollars, call Runs."

Ballou, seeing that ashtrays were laid out, brought out his makings, sat down at the card table with the Leahys, and began rolling a cigarette. Runs delivered the Manhattan – a large one – and sat down next to him, making the chair creak. "Make me one of those too, wouldja?" he asked Ballou.

"Runs, tell Roger about your name," Leahy urged. "Roger, this guy has stories you could listen to all day."

Runs shrugged. "Well, Injuns have lots of names," he told Ballou. "There's the names your parents give you, first of all. They usually give you two names at least. The name they call you by, and then your true name, and your true name's a secret. Then as you grow up, other people give you other names. Nicknames, whatever. And lots of Injuns have names they use among themselves and then they have a white man's name. Like my white man's name is Jimmy Dan Powell. It's what they called me in the Army, and on all the official shit.

"This name I use, well, when I was a kid, being big, I could knock the shit out of anyone. Only I never had to, because nobody was fool enough to try me. Once when a bunch of us were playing together – I must have been ten years old or so – I got mad at this kid for something and took after him, and he ran... man, he ran fast. Ran home, screaming at the top of his lungs, like he was afraid I was gonna physically kill him if I caught him.

"We most always spoke English, even at home, but one of the kids liked to talk Cheyenne, and he give me the name, in English it means 'His Enemies Run From Him Screaming.' And one of the other kids started calling me 'Runs-Away-Screaming.' Which I didn't like much, at first, but the other kids thought it was kinda funny, and it didn't do me no harm. So that's what I been, ever since."

"This is what's so endearing about Runs," Leahy told Ballou. "You never can tell if he's putting you on or not."

Ballou glanced at Runs to see if the Indian were offended, but he couldn't tell a thing from Runs' face, which didn't smile, didn't frown, barely even moved when he spoke.

"Look at that mug," Leahy continued. "Imagine playing poker against that. I've known this sonofagun for 15 years, never seen him smile. Not once, I don't think."

"Injuns can't smile," Runs growled. "It's a genetic thing. Our face muscles don't work that way. See?" He showed Ballou a slight stretching of his lips back from his teeth (which were too white, too even, and thus false, Ballou concluded). "That's the best I can do for a smile. You never see a bald-headed Injun, you never see one with hair on his chest, and you never see one smile."

"Aw, bullshit," crowed Leahy, and again Ballou glanced surreptitiously to see if Runs' eyes were twinkling at least – but they weren't.

Ballou handed Runs a cigarette, and lit it and his own. "You're a Cheyenne?"

"Half," said Runs. "My father was Cheyenne. I grew up in southern Kansas, mostly. My mother's people came from right around here. The Wigwags. Small tribe. You want to be politically correct, you can call them the Ui'q'aq'i." Runs pronounced this word with an odd, clicking glottal stop. "Some of the tribe is trying to get people to change the spelling, and the pronunciation. I figure what the hell difference does it make?"

"Funny how you never see any reference to the Wigwags in any of the historical documents of this area," Leahy mused.

"Like I said, small tribe," said Runs.

Donald Quagga and Effie Hoo entered, each of them bearing a large plate of *hors d'œuvres*. Frances Quagga and Dora Fox followed.

"Runs, how *are* you?" Dora exclaimed, as though thrilled beyond description to see the Indian. Ballou felt like he'd been kicked in the belly. "You know, my jaunty jalopy is running just like a dream! It's the nicest car I've ever had!" Dora turned to Ballou. "Runs sold me the most wonderful old car, a 1971 Plymouth Cricket. I got him to paint it bright yellow for me. It's so much fun to drive! If you need a car, you have to see Runs."

"So I've been told," Ballou replied grumpily, even as he clenched his teeth at the sight of Runs-Away-Screaming gazing back at Dora.

"It looks like there'll be eight of us," Frances announced. "The Planktons went down to the city for the weekend, and Hugh's working on that patent case, isn't he, Effie?"

"I'm afraid so," Effie replied. "He's off to London tomorrow to present it, so I expect he'll be up the night, the silly man."

"Effie's husband's a partner in my firm," Leahy told Ballou. "He's the chink in our armor, you might say. Just joined us a couple of years ago. He'd been practicing in England, and he brought a bunch of his English corporate clients with him as they went global – so now we can call ourselves an international firm, small as we are. It's too bad he's not here, Roger. You'd love to meet him. He's an Old Etonian. He'd probably be worth an article."

Frances Quagga picked up a deck of cards, fanned them out, presented them to Ballou, who took one; so did each of the other guests. "High cards at this table," she decreed, "and low ones here. The two lowest are partners, and the two highest are partners. Roger, and Dora, the stakes are a penny for every 20 points." Ballou had a deuce.

"Move aside, Frank Leahy," Dora mock-snarled, hipping Leahy out of the seat opposite Ballou. She showed Ballou her card – also a deuce – and gave him another of those right-in-the-eye smiles. "Howdy, Partner."

*

As Dora dealt the first hand – she and Ballou were playing against Frank Leahy and Donald Quagga – she warned Ballou, "You're going to have to be very patient with me, because I just barely remember how to play." She put on a pair of wire-rimmed reading glasses, which made her look schoolmarmish but even more beautiful, Ballou thought. They accentuated the shape of her eyes.

Despite her warning, Dora demonstrated at once that she knew what she was doing. She worked that hand into a five-club contract: often the sign of a beginner or a fool. But she played it perfectly. Ballou, as dummy, stood behind her as she played, to observe (and to smell her: she had a sharp but pleasant personal musk that complemented her perfume). On the next hand, after Ballou had opened one spade and Leahy had passed, she said mournfully, "Oh, Partner, I don't know! Raise, or shift? I'm *torn*!"

Leahy laughed sharply, and managed to look amused and annoyed at the same time. "In my day, that kind of table-talk would have got you thrown out the window," he warned. But it had done the job. When Dora said, "Two hearts," Ballou knew she had spade support, and they ended up bidding and making six spades.

"You're so clever," Dora cheered as Ballou claimed the last tricks. "I would never have been brave enough to go to slam!"

Ballou remarked to himself that he should have deliberately misplayed, to prolong the rubber and their partnership. As it was, they would have to switch almost immediately. "I'm going to get something to eat," Dora announced. "I can't wait to try your coulibiac!"

All four of them went to the kitchen to fill their plates – with coulibiac, pickled meat ("That's probably muskrat, or possum,"

Leahy warned, "courtesy of Runs," but Ballou tried it anyway and it wasn't bad), several types of salad, and homemade bread — and by the time they'd returned, the other table had wrapped up its first rubber and the partnerships were rearranged. Ballou drew Leahy this time, against Effie and Frances. He willed himself to ignore Dora, now at the other table.

"Roger, this is *delicious*," she called over to him. "It's every bit as good as my mother's!"

"Yes, it's very good," Frances agreed. "You're definitely getting invited back."

Ballou and Leahy won the first game, lost the second. Effie dealt the next hand, and opened one club.

"Double," Leahy snapped.

At the next table, Runs-Away-Screaming growled something that Ballou couldn't catch, but it elicited a quick trill of laughter from Dora. "Oh, Runs, you're so *funny*!" she gasped, swatting his arm. Since Runs had his back to him, Ballou couldn't see the reaction, but he tingled with hopelessness.

"Roger, dear?" Frances prompted him.

"I'm sorry. Gosh, I'm sorry. I wasn't concentrating. Did you bid?"

"Yes. One club, double, and three hearts, to you."

"He needs another drink, Frances Q," Leahy suggested.

"Maybe he's got something on his mind, Francis X," Frances replied. "Roger, your classes have barely started. You couldn't have fallen in love with one of your students yet, could you?"

"He's blushing," Effie observed. Ballou held his cards closer to his face.

"Four spades, bedads, or we die in the attempt!" Ballou declared.

"Mother of Finn McCool!" Leahy wheezed. "Roger, you're a wild man! If we go down, I'm taking it out of your hide!"

"Five hearts," Effie bid.

"Double," said Leahy, shaking his head the least little bit at Ballou. Frances passed.

"Sorry, Frank," said Ballou. "Five spades."

Leahy groaned. "Roger, we're vunnerable!"

"I know," said Ballou. "Trust me."

"I never trust anyone who says, 'Trust me.'"

Leahy did not look pleased, and Ballou figured he'd be black-balled from future parties if this didn't work out. But when Effie led a low heart, and the dummy came down, he saw that the contract was unbeatable. He played out the first few tricks, and claimed 12.

"We had the slam, Roger, if you hadn't been so eager!" Leahy remarked. "If you'd bid three rather than four, I'd have supported you, and we might have worked it to six."

"Yes, and what if the diamonds hadn't split?" Ballou asked. "We'd have been up Shit Crik!" It was out of his mouth before he could stop it, for Leahy's certainty made him a little defensive, even though he believed he had the stronger argument.

"I'm sorry, ladies," Ballou added. He looked down at his lap, clenching his teeth.

"D'ye think we've never heard that expression in this room?" Effie demanded. "It's almost a technical term. Ye'll probably find it somewhere in Goren."

"And you should hear how Francis X talks, when he has to partner Lois," Frances added, touching Ballou's arm.

"That's different, Frances Q. She's my wife! In any event, a slam might have been difficult to bid. You done good, Roger!"

Ballou absconded to the kitchen, where he cut himself a large piece of Dora's chocolate cake, which turned out to be exquisite: very dark and not too sweet, with a creamy white frosting accented by crystallized flower petals.

In the next rubber, Ballou discovered that Lois Leahy was indeed a challenging partner: inclined to make highly speculative bids in one hand, then meekly underbid the next. She wasn't the best at guessing where the opposing cards lay, or remembering what had been played. But she played with such funny exclamations and quick, excited gestures that Ballou couldn't get too angry; he was so busy enjoying her enjoyment of the game – and he nearly forgot about Dora. Runs and Donald Quagga were all business, and the Leahy-Ballou partnership went down to ruinous defeat.

"By the way, Roger, I made a few inquiries about your fat friend," Quagga remarked as he added up the score. "Parzival. His real name is Martin Wandervogel. He lives over in Kingston. Apparently he's pretty well off. He has a big house, anyway. And I understand he's got a name in the film industry. He's a Van Devander alumnus, class of 1970, and he was involved with some of the noisier student radical groups, and he's directed several films since then: documentaries about various social issues. I haven't seen any of them. But I guess they've made him some money. That's about all I can tell you."

"I've got a Wandervogel in one of my classes," said Ballou. "Could be his son, I guess. That's not a common name."

"Who's this?" asked Runs.

"Oh, a fellow who had a letter in the *Advertiser*, in response to something Roger wrote. Apparently Roger offended his sensibilities."

Runs grunted. "I never look at the *Advertiser* except to make sure my ad's in the right place," he said. "I like comic books and *Motor Trend*. The news just depresses me. Roger, you got another of those butts?"

"Say, may I try one too?" Quagga asked. "I haven't rolled a cigarette since college."

"Oh, me too," said Lois, waving her hands eagerly. They passed the papers and the tobacco pouch around, and soon Frances Q and Francis X came over to partake of the novelty. Only Effie and Dora abstained – and Ballou's heart sank yet again as he wondered whether Dora was just a non-smoker, or a rabid anti.

Ballou drew Runs as partner for the next rubber, against Effie and Dora – and Dora smiled hugely as she sat down between the two men, her eyes shining brighter than ever. She appeared to be drinking Cinzano and soda. Ballou had switched to bourbon and water; Effie was on Scotch; Runs, as he'd been doing all evening, sipped coffee from a mug that looked the size of a teacup in his enormous fist.

"Ye're fortunate that Runs and I aren't partners," Effie remarked. "He and I bring each other luck. 'Twouldn't be fair to the newcomers."

"True dat," said Runs-Away-Screaming. "The cards just fall right into place when we're on the same side. It's 'cause we're both Injuns."

Dora looked wide-eyed at Effie. "No! You're an *Indian?*"

"A-well, I'm a Highlander, and we're very much like your Indians. Our clan system is nearly the same as a tribe of Indians, and for hundreds of years we were a different breed of people from other Scots. So, Runs has decided that I'm one of his ilk."

"And you wrap yourselves in blankets like we used to," Runs added.

Mrs. Hoo sniffed, dealing the cards. "We know how to fold 'em properly; we don't just drape ourselves like a tattie-bogle. And I'd say we're more civilized than the Lowland Scots, who call us the savages. We speak better English, for one thing, when we're not speakin' the Gaelic, which they can't speak at all. One club."

"And you can't handle the firewater any better than we can," said Runs. "Pass."

"Is that really true, about Indians and alcohol?" Dora inquired. "One no trump."

"You bet it's true," said Runs. "Injuns have a different way of processing alcohol. Something to do with metabolism. You never seen drunk till you seen a drunk Injun. It's why I stick to coffee. I've tried alcohol maybe three-four times in my life, back in the army. And I'm a slow learner, but the time I woke up hogtied in a jail cell, gagged with a broomstick, with my head feeling like it was gonna come off, and couldn't even remember what I done to get there… that learned me. Never tempted me after that."

"I'll pass," said Ballou. "Effie, do Highlanders have 'inside names' and 'outside names,' the way Indians do? Runs was telling me all about his various names."

Effie nodded to show that she'd heard the question, then glowered at her cards. "Damn it. Pass."

Runs passed, and Ballou led a low heart.

"Many of us have Gaelic names and English names, if that's what ye mean," said Effie, as she laid down the dummy. "But it's not a matter of two different names. For example, my name's Euphemia MacIntyre. In the Gaelic, that's Oighrig Nic-an-Tsaoir. Same name, different language. Just as... well, just as Giuseppe Verdi would be Joe Green."

"And d'ye know what's a funny coincidence, speaking of Indians and Highlanders?" Effie continued. "Van Devander's College's football team is called the Wildens, which is what the old Dutch colonists called the Indians, because the college was originally – " Mrs. Hoo called over her shoulder to the next table. "Frank, Van Devander was founded as a school for Indians, long ago, wasn't it?"

"That's right," Mr. Leahy replied. "Founded in 1773. New York's answer to Dartmouth, I guess. Although it has hardly any Indian students nowadays. And of course the name of this town – Wildenkill – is Dutch for 'Indians' Creek.'"

"Anyway," said Mrs. Hoo, "at halftime, at their football matches, they've got a regular Highland pipe-and-drum corps, with the kilts and all, instead of the brass band that most schools have."

"That must be wonderful!" Dora exclaimed. "I love going to football games. I'm no expert, but I love the atmosphere. When I was a girl, my father was an instructor at West Point, and I used to go to the games with him. It was so *thrilling*, all those cadets in the stands, in their long grey coats."

Ballou saw his shot – and funked it. He knew Van Devander played its first football game of the season in two weeks, and if he could make a connection in Dora's mind between himself and her father, it'd put him at a huge advantage – but he didn't have the nerve, not with Runs and Effie right there.

A Black Demon appeared, hovering in the air above Ballou's head. "You dick," it hissed at Ballou. "You stupid, spineless dick."

As Runs dealt the next hand, Ballou scrabbled in his mind for a new subject. "Runs," he announced, "I'm going to come see you during the week. I thought I could get along with just my feet, when I moved here, but that's madness. If you've got something cheap and junky like Frank says, maybe we can do business."

"Runs does *not* sell cheap and junky cars," Dora protested. "At least, he didn't show me any!"

"Well, he wouldn't, would he?" Ballou countered. "Not to you. I'm sure you saw nothing but his best. But I demand the worst; I insist on it!"

"We'll find you something," said Runs. "Pass."

Dora passed, too, but Ballou, with a very strong hand, drove the bidding up to four spades – and made it. He whistled out loud a few notes of the tune that had been running through his head for much of the evening.

"Darn it, Dora," he said, "ever since you mentioned your Plymouth Cricket, I've had the advertising jingle running through my head. I haven't thought about it since I was a teenager, and now here it is, and I can't get rid of it."

"Keep whistling it, and it'll go away," Dora suggested. "I don't think I've ever heard it."

Ballou did, softly, and Runs' eyes lit up in recollection, and he joined in, whistling along – on key, note for note, even rest for rest – and tapping out the beat on the table. Ballou conducted, and he and Runs cued each other with upraised forefingers. By the time they'd reached the third bar, Dora and Effie were looking at each other slack-jawed in horrified amusement.

"Brand new Cricket (Tweet-tweet!), comin' throooooo!" Runs and Ballou chorused. Runs, solemn as ever, leant across the table to punch fists with Ballou. From the next table, Frank and Lois Leahy applauded.

Unnoticed by everyone except Ballou, the Black Demon snickered contemptuously.

"You two!" Dora exclaimed. "You must have eidetic memories! Oh, but that's not right, is it? Phonographic memories? I guess that would be the word, but it doesn't sound like it should be."

"It's funny how memory works," Leahy remarked. "Lois, here, can sing any song she's ever heard. Even if she doesn't know the language, she can repeat the sounds. But damn if she can remember whether she's pulled all the trumps!"

"That is because the songs are more important," Lois replied complacently.

"Not when we're playing for a whole twentieth of a cent per point, dear!"

"Dora, and Roger," said Frances, "you've never heard Lois sing any of her songs from the old country! That's such a special treat. Lois, you're going to have to give them a song at the end of the rubber."

"Oh-*kay!*" cried Frank Leahy. "Let's wrap up."

And in a couple of hands, they did. As Mr. Quagga took charge of all the scoresheets to determine who had won what, Lois stood up and began to sing.

She had a pretty voice, with only a little of the old lady's quaver to it, and she sang in a language that had somewhat the cadence of Spanish but was not Spanish. On the whole it sounded like an Asian language, and the tune sounded more Asian than European. From the way Lois performed it, it seemed to Ballou like a sort of debating song, meant to be sung back and forth by two people.

Ballou glanced sidelong at Dora, and caught her eye, and they smiled at each other. "It's so lovely," Dora whispered to him.

Ballou could smell her again, and he admired the wispy red hairs on the back of her neck, and wanted to draw her to him and kiss her right on that spot...

"Brava!" cried Frances, as Lois came to the end of the song.

"That was beautiful, dear," Leahy seconded, and everyone clapped, while Lois curtsied.

"What language is that?" Dora asked.

"That is Ilocano," Lois replied. "The song is called a *dal-lot*. It is a traditional wedding song from Ilocos Norte, in the Philippines, which is my homeland. Ilocos Norte is the most beautiful part of the Philippines. And most of our presidents have come from Ilocos."

"I wouldn't brag about that if I were you, dear!" said Leahy.

"Could we have another?" Frances asked.

"Why, I think you should sing," Lois demurred. "Or Donald. Donald, I have not heard you sing in such a long time."

"I agree," cried Leahy. "Give us one of your show tunes, Don." He turned to the newcomers. "Don should have been on Broadway," he explained, "but he makes too much money in real estate, I guess."

Quagga looked a little abashed, but Frances stood and tugged at his hand. "I'll play if you'll sing," she offered. An upright piano stood in one corner of the room, and she stepped over to it, sat down, and played a few introductory measures. Quagga said, "Oh, Frances, no, I haven't thought of that one in years!"

"It'll come back to you," she teased. "I'll start you out. Just try it for me, my sweet." She repeated the passage on the piano, then she began to sing, in a soft alto: Nellie Forbush's part of the "Twin Soliloquies" from *South Pacific*.

Quagga straightened up and came in with a full bass voice on Emile deBecque's part. His singing was nearly professional-level. His wife's voice couldn't stand up to his, but she kept him going through the song, then she played the introductory notes to "Some

Enchanted Evening," and Quagga, now getting warmed up, sang it through.

Ballou looked over at Dora again, but could not catch her eye this time. Quagga was singing at his wife, varying his volume dramatically, and Frances gazed back at him as she played.

Ballou forced himself to pay attention to the song, which he knew was technically difficult, and he was interested in finding out whether Quagga could handle the tricky breath control at the end, and the last prolonged and very high note.

Quagga gasped ever so little, but he hit that last note, and held it, and the room fell dead silent for a second before everyone clapped and hollered. Frances just about glowed with pride – and Dora, too, looked awed, Ballou observed.

"That was how we met," Frances explained. "I was a junior at Holyoke, and Don was a senior at Amherst. I was Nellie and he was Emile. And we were engaged by the time the show was in performance. Our parents insisted that we wait for almost two years, until I'd graduated – but we got married the very day after my graduation!"

"That's so sweet, we're all gonna need insulin," Runs muttered to Ballou.

"Oh, Runs, that's mean," said Dora. "You should sing us an Indian love song now."

"Not sure I know any," Runs replied. "I'm an old bachelor. I forgot what it's like to court a girl." He thought for a moment. "Wait, though. I do know one. Not exactly traditional to my tribe."

Runs got to his feet. "Roger, you're gonna have to give me the beat." He demonstrated by drumming on the card table, the stereotypical Indian beat: *boom*-boom-boom-boom, *boom*-boom-boom-boom.

Ballou picked it up, and Runs puffed out his chest and threw his head back. Ballou expected to hear a voice that broke from the bowels of the earth, but to his surprise Runs' singing voice was majestically high-pitched, like that of a medicine man invoking Manitou in an old movie.

Runs sang "Kaw-Liga": the Hank Williams song about the cigar-store Indian who fell in love with the Indian maiden in the antique store across the street – admiring her from afar, unable to speak or give her a sign, until the Indian maiden was sold, leaving "Kaw-Liga, that poor old wooden head" to pine for the love that could never be.

Realistically, Ballou told himself, Runs-Away-Screaming would be no more a rival for Dora's affections than the Pope. But if Ballou sat quiet, after that performance, he'd look like a wet noodle. As long as Dora could see him trying his best, Ballou's poor singing might not lower her opinion of him. No effort at all, however, would doom him. So, before anyone else could volunteer, Ballou got to his feet, still racking his memory for something to sing. Dora – West Point – military family – he had it.

"Back when I was in high school, my best friend was an Army brat," he told the audience, "and he taught me this one." He straightened up and sang, reminding himself to hold the tune and not go too fast:

Now, Old King Cole was a merry old soul, and a merry old
    soul was he
He called for his pipe, and he called for his bowl,
    and he called for his privates three
"Beer! Beer! Beer!" said the privates; merry men are we
For there's none so fair as can compare
With the field artillery!

He could see that Dora recognized the tune. So, apparently, did Runs and Leahy, who came in on *"Beer! Beer! Beer!"* Up the chain of command he went, verse by verse, and soon everyone was coming in on *"Beer! Beer! Beer!"*

Now, Old King Cole was a merry old soul, and a merry old
    soul was he
He called for his pipe, and he called for his bowl, and he
    called for his Colonels three
"Duh... What's my next command?" said the Colonels
"Oh, what a lovely war!" said the Majors
"Oh, what a bloody mess!" said the Captains
"We do all the work!" said the shave-tails
"Right by squads, squad right!" said the Sergeants
"Dress that goddam line!" said the Corporals
"Beer! Beer! Beer!" said the privates; merry men are we
For there's none so fair as can compare
With the field artillery!

"That deserves a refill," said Quagga, taking Ballou's empty
glass. Ballou was shaking, internally, and hoped it didn't show too
much, but he felt he'd done the job. Dora had applauded as loudly
as anyone.

"Who else?" asked Frances. "Francis X, you must have something."

"Nothing you'd care to hear, Frances Q. I don't know any nice
songs."

Frances cocked her head at Leahy – coquettishly, Ballou
thought. "Then sing a not-nice one."

"Well, I can sing you one I knew back in college."

There was an old farmer who lived by a rock
He sat in the meadow a-shaking his

Fist at some boys who were down by the crik
Their feet in the water their hands on their

Marbles and playthings and in days of yore
There came a young lady, she looked like a

And on it went, in that vein, for a good many verses. Ballou was laughing so hard his sides hurt, his eyes were streaming, and he knew it was a terrible reflection on him that he was finding it funny. He didn't dare to check Dora's reaction, but he heard laughter and applause from the others, and reflected that old age held small but obvious advantages.

Effie Hoo, still laughing, moved to the piano. She took a deep swallow of Scotch.

"I'll give ye some Robert Burns," she announced, as she sat down. "Or as we say in the old country, Rabbie Burrrrrrns."

"Oh, he wrote such pretty songs!" Dora exclaimed. "'Annie Laurie,' that's one I really love."

"Well, this is a love song of sorts," Effie replied. She played the introductory passage, a somewhat pastoral-sounding tune in three-quarter time, and commenced to sing in a thin but pretty soprano, and with a heavier accent than she normally used:

Come rede me, dame, come tell me, dame,
My dame, come tell me truly,
What length o' graith, when weel ca'd hame,
Will sair a woman duly?

The carlin clew her wanton tail,
Her wanton tail sae ready -
I learn'd a sang in Annandale,
Nine inch will please a lady.

Ballou, knowing Burns' poetry well, recognized this one with horror. Effie sang all six verses. The Leahys and the Quaggas were chuckling as they clapped, as though they were aware that they'd heard something naughty even if they weren't sure they'd got it all. Dora, looking quite serious, exclaimed, "Oh, Effie! That's such a pretty tune! But I'm afraid I didn't understand a word of it. Is that Gaelic?"

Ballou didn't know whether to believe her or not.

"Certainly not," Effie replied. "It's Scots. What the Lowlanders speak. A heedious bastard dialect. And I believe ye've not given us a song yet, Dora."

Dora quailed. "Oh, I can't sing. I really can't. I have the littlest voice, you see, and when I try to sing with it, it just sounds awful. Believe me, you don't want to hear it. But I could play you something."

Effie motioned her to the piano.

"I'm *very* out of practice," Dora warned the company. "I'll choose something easy." She sat at the piano, staring at a point high up on the wall; her eyebrows jumped once, and then she began moving her lips and her gaze shifted up and to one side as it does when a person's trying to recall something. Watching her, Ballou noticed that his mouth was wide open, and he shut it fast.

She played "The Golliwog's Cakewalk," and Ballou was too busy watching her hands (and the back of her neck, which was beginning to obsess him) to tell whether she played it well. He liked the piece, anyway, so he clapped enthusiastically and restrained himself from doing anything any more effusive.

Mr. Quagga then announced that Roger Ballou was the night's surprise winner – one dollar and thirty-four cents – beating Runs-Away-Screaming, who came in a poor second with 62¢. Lois took last place with a loss of $1.29.

"Bravo, Roger!" cried Dora.

"Dear, you'd better hope I outlive you," said Leahy to his wife. "I'm keeping score, and in my will I'm going to take the equivalent of all the money you've lost on bridge, and use it to endow a bridge professorship at Van Devander!" He reached into his pocket and counted out $1.07. "That's minus the 22 cents I won," he said, placing it in front of Quagga. "I'm just lucky I got to partner Roger for one rubber."

The guests all took the announcement of the score as a signal to leave. Ballou tried desperately to think of a discreet way to get Dora's contact information, or at least the location of her bakery. But instead he offered to help clean up – and much to his relief Frances informed him that traditionally, the hosts cleaned up, in exchange for being allowed to keep the leftovers.

"Anybody need a ride home?" Runs asked.

"I would, but it'll be so nice to walk home in this weather," Dora remarked, looking out the window. "Or actually, no, I wouldn't, because if I'd driven, I would have brought my Cricket, wouldn't I?"

"You didn't drive?" Ballou asked. "Don't you live in Verstanken?"

"Oh, no. My business is in Verstanken. I live right here, over on Valley Road."

Ballou didn't let this one go by.

"But that's right near me. Would you dah-do me the honor of letting you – letting me see you home?" In fact, Ballou's own house lay three blocks in the other direction, but only the Quaggas and Mr. Leahy knew this, and they certainly wouldn't mention it.

"Why, of course, sir," Dora replied, and Ballou's heart leapt. "Runs, it's such a pretty night, why don't you come with us? Runs, can you walk?"

"Hah!" whispered the Black Demon, in Ballou's ear. "Not that she's interested in that guy – but she wants an escort to protect her from you! You do have that effect on girls, Rog, don't you?"

"I better drive on back to the garage," said Runs. "Three's a crowd, and I believe I'll do a little work yet tonight. Don't guess I'll get to bed till morning. Roger'll see you home okay. He's near as big as me." Ballou felt relieved, and grateful to Runs, but it still smarted that Dora had asked Runs along in the first place.

"Before ye go, Roger," said Effie, "I'd been expecting a punch line for my name. Ye're forgiven, though."

"I'd forgotten," Ballou admitted – and just then, the obvious one popped into his head, and he grimaced. "Come over here," he muttered, motioning her to him and whispering.

Effie shrieked.

"Oh, dear Lord, listen to this, everyone," she commanded.

"No, no," Ballou pleaded, wincing, clenching his teeth, looking for Dora out of the corner of his eye.

"Knock-knock," Effie proceeded, undaunted.

"Who's there?" asked Leahy.

"Effie."

"Effie who?"

"Effyou, too, ye rotten big bastard!"

And of course it would have been folly for Ballou to pretend it hadn't been his work. Leahy winked at him, as though sensing his discomfiture.

Runs gave a little wave to the Quaggas and lumbered out the front door. Ballou turned to Dora.

"Ms. Fox, shall we?"

*

A distant chorus of girls' voices, singing "We Are Family," drifted over from the direction of the Van Devander campus, no doubt from one of the sorority houses a few blocks away. Almost all the neighboring houses were dark by this time, and there was no moon, so Ballou couldn't look at Dora as much as he wanted to. Behind them, Ballou fancied he could hear the flapping of wings: three or four of the Black Demons now following, watching, but saying nothing.

"I love being in a college town at this time of year," Ballou said. "Even when I was in college myself, it used to give me kind of a thrill. Seeing the students arrive, seeing the rush parties with all the freshman girls all dressed up, all that."

Although he was pretty sure he hadn't utterly disgraced himself yet, Ballou was choosing his topics carefully, to avoid revealing flaws that might be unknown even to himself. "I went to the University of Wisconsin, which has a beautiful campus. It's a huge school. Much bigger than Van Devander, obviously. Anyway, I always used to love those first few days – which is funny, because when I was in K through 12, I hated going back to school."

"I always loved school," Dora replied. "I wish I could go to school all my life long, full time. I love learning."

"Did you go to a cooking school, then, to be a baker?"

"Oh, no. I'm a complete auto-didact as a baker. Well, my mother taught me when I was little, of course. But this is my second career. And maybe temporary. I'm a plastic surgeon. I practiced in the city for... well, for a long time. I'm not going to tell you how long, or you'd be able to guess my age."

"Quite the career change."

"It's something I thought about for a while. I went into plastic surgery because I wanted to do some real good for people. By improving their appearance, I could improve their quality of life. I always strive to create beauty, in everything I do. If I had to sum up my life's vocation, I would say I'm a creator of beauty."

"What decided you to get out of surgery?"

"That's a long story. Which I won't go into right now. I'll just say it wasn't fulfilling. Some of my patients, oh, it was so demoralizing to work with them. The ingratitude. And finally I said to myself, 'Dora, wouldn't you rather be doing something you really love to do?' And I'm not good enough to be a concert pianist, as you heard a few minutes ago. But I've always loved to bake, and I'm so good at it, and I decided that perhaps my fellow *homo sapiens* would be more grateful to me if I were feeding them, than if I were cutting them."

"Must be quite a change for you financially." Ballou wondered whether he wasn't being too familiar, hinting at money, but the words had gone out of his mouth.

"No, I could retire now if I wanted to. I've always lived very simply. I have a pretty little house, and that's all I want. And I have a dog. I got a collie puppy as soon as I moved here. She's my best friend in the whole world."

"Must be nice." Ballou almost added that he wished he could think about retiring even 30 years on, but he stopped himself. Crying poor at this point? An almost certain deal-breaker. "Did Don sell you your house?"

"Frances did. They're both licensed. She's just the sweetest woman. They're all such nice people, aren't they? Frank and Lois, and Effie with that funny accent. And Runs is a scream."

"So to speak."

"Oh, goodness, did I say that? Did he tell you how he got that name?"

"He sure did. Interesting fellow." Ballou could feel himself tensing; he could almost hear his body humming like a tuning fork.

"And I was going to recite an Indian poem for him, too!" Dora sounded dismayed. "But I can recite it for you, instead. Would you like to hear it?"

They had just turned onto Valley Road. Dora stopped, and laid her hand on Ballou's arm to indicate that he should turn to face her. What was this?

They stood only about 18 inches apart. Dora looked into Ballou's face, and smiled, but Ballou could see that she was trying to look solemn instead. He noticed the tiniest dimples at each corner of her mouth; noticed her throat set off by the big blue bow on her middy blouse; her little hands up at chest-level, palms out, nearly touching him, as though to position him. He wanted to kiss them all: lips, throat, hands. Again, he felt his arms almost willing themselves to enfold her, but he forced them to keep still.

"Okay," Dora said, dropping her gaze for a moment. Deepening her voice, sounding as masculine and stentorian as she could with her almost babyish timbre, she intoned:

By the shores of Gitchigumi
By the shining big-sea-water...

"Gitchigumi!" she shrieked, prodding Ballou hard in the belly. She danced backwards a few steps and doubled over laughing, clapping her hands in glee. Ballou stood staring open-mouthed, and several seconds elapsed before it occurred to him to ask himself whether Dora wanted him to chase her and kiss her, but by the time that thought crossed his mind she had straightened up, several yards ahead of him, evidently waiting for him to continue the walk.

"I used to do that to my little brother, when he was a baby," she explained.

"Cute," Ballou said, smiling more than he felt like. He was flattered, but he couldn't ignore that she had intended to pull it on Runs, not on him, and there came to his mind the image of Dora naked, straddling the gigantic Indian, ecstatically impaling herself, riding up and down on his mammoth...

"Arrgh," Ballou said aloud, forcing the thought out of his head as they walked.

"Is something wrong?" Dora asked.

"Oh. No. No, but I remembered. You said you loved football. Van Devander plays its first game two weeks from today. Against Cornell. Can you come with me?"

"I should be able to," Dora replied. "It's a good thing you gave me so much notice, though. I want to be sure to clear the decks so I can go."

It was all Ballou could do not to leap into the air.

"Well, here we are," Dora announced, indicating a little stone bungalow at the end of a cul-de-sac, with a white picket fence round it and woods behind and to one side of it. "Time for me to walk my perky puppy."

"May I come along? It's awfully late to be out alone." Ballou knew he was overreaching, but it would have been ungentlemanly not to offer his protection.

"Oh, that's so sweet of you! But this is my time to be alone with my best girlfriend. Wait right here, though, and I'll introduce you before we say goodnight."

Dora passed through the gate and up onto her front porch. She entered her house and switched on the lights in the foyer. A few seconds later, Ballou heard barking and scrabbling, seemingly from the other end of the house, or perhaps behind it. This got louder, and then he heard Dora cooing at the dog, although he couldn't make out the words. In a couple of minutes she emerged, with a half-grown collie straining forward on the leash, bucking up on its hind legs as Dora held on with all her strength.

"I haven't got her completely trained yet," Dora called apologetically from the porch, "but here she is." The two of them bounded down the path, through the gate and onto the sidewalk. "Pegeen, behave yourself, and say hello to Uncle Roger."

Ballou squatted down, and let the dog lick his face.

"Roger, be careful, she's going to get her dirty paws all over your jacket! Pegeen, down!"

"No, it's okay," Ballou protested, trying to keep Pegeen's tongue out of his mouth. She still had a little of that puppy smell. "That's what dogs are for. Hello, sweetheart!" He scratched Pegeen behind the ears and along the ribs and let her lick for a few seconds more before pulling himself upright. The dog kept leaping at him, and he couldn't stop himself from continuing to pet her.

"I just made up a poem about Pegeen," he told Dora.

Pegeen and Margaret, Gretchen and Meg
Went to the hen-house in search of an egg.
They found a nest containing four;
Each took one, and left three o'er!

Dora considered. "So... Pegeen and Margaret, Gretchen and Meg... they're all... ?"

"Forms of the same name, or diminutives."

"So they're all the same person! And you just made it up? Just now? You are so smart! Isn't he smart, Pegeen?"

"About some things, I guess I am. Other things, not so much."

"Oh?" Dora looked serious again. "Like what?

"I expect you'll find out, if you hang with me much more."

"I don't believe you. I'm sure you're very bright about everything."

They were walking uphill, returning the way they'd come, up Valley Road. Ballou knew not what to say that might be particularly witty or charming, and he hoped that Dora didn't feel that he was forcing himself on her by walking along when she wanted to "be alone with my best girlfriend" – but he had to walk back up Valley Road to get on the way to his own house.

"Two things I need to get now," he said. "A car and a dog. I never had a dog in the city; I didn't think it'd be fair, making it live in my little apartment."

"Oh, yes, do get a dog!" Dora pleaded. "Then Pegeen will have a playmate!"

"I'm going that way," Ballou told Dora at the intersection of Valley and Herkimer, hoping she'd choose the other direction.

"Then I'll see you for the football game, anyway. But I'm sure we'll run into each other before then. Goodnight, Roger."

Dora didn't give even the faintest hint of presenting her cheek, so Ballou dared not do any more than shake hands. He could hear the Black Demons laughing.

Ballou walked south for a block, then turned west, getting out of Dora's sight – and removing the temptation to look back at her – as quickly as he could. He had a few cigarettes in reserve in his tobacco-pouch, and he stopped, halfway home, and lit one. His hands trembled so hard he could barely get the match to strike.

He leaned against a tree and smoked, trying to collect his thoughts and put together some kind of general strategy, but he felt too flustered to come up with anything even vaguely coherent. Besides, five-and-a-half hours (more or less) of suppressing certain normal functions had created pressures of another kind. Ballou looked about him, right, left, before and behind. No house light was on in the immediate vicinity. He was quite alone. He let rip a thunderacious fart.

Tuesday, September 14, 1999

"You'll have to write fast, again," Quagga told Ballou over the phone Tuesday morning. "I'm going to e-mail you Charlotte's latest column. I've told her that I'd ask you to write a rebuttal, and she sounded fine with that. But I also promised her that next time, if she wanted to, she could rebut something you wrote. If we can get a rivalry going, here in the *Advertiser*, maybe circulation will go up, and we'll sell some ads.

"Meanwhile I can send out some of your stuff to Charlotte's syndicate, and maybe a few papers will pick you up as a columnist alongside of her – her column is only going to get more popular, now that she's written this book – and eventually we all make money. So, I'll need it Thursday again, but the sooner the better."

"Okay," said Ballou. "Ms. Fanshaw will be livid, I'm sure."

"You never can tell," Quagga replied. "She hates criticism, but she loves attention. And I'd bet the attention trumps the criticism. You're not going to get on her good side, but I doubt you'll be hurting for female admirers around here. Frances and Effie and Lois are planning a free-for-all to see which of them gets to leave her husband for you. Only, Frances has the notion that you'd be just right for Dora Fox. I don't know if that prospect pleases you."

"Ah," said Ballou, trying to show no reaction. "She is a charmer, all right."

*

Few students showed up for the meet-the-faculty garden party that afternoon. It took place on the green in front of the small student union, and the only person Ballou recognized when he arrived was the new president of Van Devander College, Faye Bannister: a large, jovial woman in her 50s with buzz-cut grey hair. She wore a sweatsuit for the occasion. Ballou reminded her of his name and department.

"You're so formal!" Dr. Bannister exclaimed. Ballou was wearing what he'd assumed would be proper attire: blue blazer, pressed chinos, white shirt, rep tie. "Everyone's so formal here!" Dr. Bannister continued. "Ha! I can see I'm going to have to stir things up. Introduce yourself around, Roger."

Some people fear snakes above all else; some fear enclosed spaces. Speaking in public is commonly mentioned as *the* greatest fear: greater than the fear of death, disease, or destitution. Ballou's great fear was of finding himself at a party where he knew nobody. The other night, the Quaggas had been there to guide him, and even at that he'd been uncomfortable enough, but this afternoon he was on his own. He stood on one spot, making no move toward the refreshments, and watched the people circulate around him for about 20 minutes until the chairman of the English department, Jack Hogenfuss, arrived with his wife. Hogenfuss greeted him – clapped him on the shoulder, in fact, and stuck his beard right into Ballou's face, grinning and breathing peppermint.

"Well, Roger, another year! You remember Audrey, don't you?"

"No, Jack, we never met. I'm brand new this fall, remember?"

"Roger's teaching a couple classes this year, just getting his feet wet," Hogenfuss told his wife. "Your mom recommended him to me, and I took him 'cause he's dumb enough to take the shit salary we pay!"

"Vi!" Hogenfuss called to a plump, severe-looking woman standing a few feet away from them. This woman was about 60, with iron-grey hair scraped back in a bun.

"Roger, I'd like you to meet our department's oldest inhabitant," said Hogenfuss. "Been here about 25 years, right, Vi?" The lady professor cocked an eyebrow at Hogenfuss, not smiling. "But still the prettiest Southern belle in all New York!" the chairman added hurriedly. "I'm not going to tell you her name, Roger, I'll let her do it. It's a tradition with her."

"Howdy, Roger," the lady professor drawled, not smiling at Ballou either. "I expect you'll find this institution fairly amusing. I know I do." Her demeanor conveyed world-weariness and a mild general annoyance: certainly no amusement. She reached into her purse and handed Ballou a little printed card.

"We'll talk one of these days, I'm sure," she sighed, as though she were not looking forward to that ordeal. She gave Ballou a little nod and strolled off, greeting other professors here and there. Her card read:

HOW TO SPELL AND PRONOUNCE MY NAME

A damsel named Violet Menzies
Asked, "Mama, do you know what this thenzies?"
Her Mama, with a gasp,
Said, "My dear, it's a wasp
And you're holding the end where the stenzies!"

The Hogenfusses, too, went off to mingle, leaving Ballou to stand alone again — but only for a few seconds, for looking across the green he spied the massive form of Parzival (now known to him as Martin Wandervogel), dressed much as he'd been on Saturday, but without any children this time.

Wandervogel made straight for Dr. Bannister and her crowd. A couple of minutes later, he stepped over to the refreshment table and began filling his plate. Ballou couldn't stop himself. He followed.

"Martin Wandervogel!" he exclaimed, holding out his hand. "You're quite well, I hope? What brings you out here today?"

Parzival/Wandervogel started, and glared disgustedly at Ballou, but Ballou kept his hand right there, and kept the smile on his face, so Wandervogel had to shake, but the glare didn't diminish.

"I didn't know you were on the faculty here."

"Gosh, Martin, I didn't know *you* were! This is just the nicest surprise! You're in the film department, I suppose."

"Yes." Wandervogel appeared to relax a little, although the suspicious expression remained. "I'm here on a visiting professorship. Just for the year. And I'm working on a film. Faye thought I could help her drag this school into modern times."

"Really? What is that going to entail?"

"Oh, a lot. I think you'll be pleasantly surprised. I'm sure the school and the town, both, will benefit from this coming year. Have you been teaching here a long time?"

"No, this is my first year, too."

"Then maybe you haven't found out what I mean, yet." Wandervogel drew himself up, tilted his head back, and looked down at Ballou. "But this place is rotting, just *rotting*, for want of a change. Faye and I agree on that. She's just starting here too, you know. And she has no intention of treading softly as many first-year presidents do. Things are going to happen, and fast. And I'm grateful to be involved in it. Maybe you will be, too. Faye is a genius, in case you haven't noticed yet. And she's maybe the most socially conscientious person I've ever known."

"Ah." Ballou nodded sagely. "A social conscience is a dangerous servant and a malicious master. I can't wait to see what the two of you have in mind. Say, Martin, have you met Jack Hogenfuss?

Jack, have you got a minute?" Ballou handed Wandervogel off like
a ripped dollar bill, and strolled to the other end of the green. He
forced himself to smile at two or three people in hopes that they
would introduce themselves, but none did. He left as soon as he
decently could.

Ballou walked away from the campus and onto Herkimer
Road, which was Route 212B and led, about five miles along, to
the nearby town of Verstanken – and a little farther than that, to
Llandor's farm. Ballou wasn't going that far, though. The highway
was prettily wooded on both sides, and thus quite dark and cool
even in full daylight, but after he'd walked two miles, the woods
ended, and past a sign that said "Leaving Wildenkill Town Limits! Don't Stay Away Too Long!" 212B intersected with a four-lane
highway, 9W.

This larger road was sparsely lined with gas stations, ware-
houses, a supermarket, a Dairy Queen – and, on the other side of
the road, a crummy-looking service station and used-car lot. Atop
the lot's chain-link fence stood a big yellow sign, on which "RUNS"
was painted in plain red block letters. Above it flew two flags: an
American flag – and to its left, a purple Van Devander banner, with
its orange lettering and the little Indian, Willie Wilden, brandishing his war-club and bellowing his challenge. Route 9W had little
traffic at that time of day, and Ballou limped across.

The cars on display in the lot were as various a collection as
Ballou had ever seen: anything from late-model cars and SUVs in
fairly good shape, to panel trucks and pickups from the 1950s, and
junkers that seemed to be made entirely of rust, held together only
by force of habit. Ballou passed through the open gate and toward
the main building, a cinderblock triple garage with an office on one
side and a car-wash in the back.

A newish black Subaru, a blue Volvo, and an old purple Chrysler sat atop hydraulic hoists inside the garage. Two gaunt old-young

white men, both wearing ponytails beneath baseball caps, their arms sporting crude tattoos, worked on the Subaru and the Volvo. Runs-Away-Screaming stood underneath the Chrysler, tinkering. A brown-and-white pit bull, wearing a spiked collar, slept in a far corner of the garage.

One of the white men was smoking the scrag-end of a doobie, and he passed it to Runs. Ballou's jaw dropped. A spark falling in the wrong place in that oil- and gasoline-impregnated garage… but the men obviously didn't consider that. The marijuana stench nearly blotted out the various automotive odors.

"Ugh," Runs greeted Ballou. He took a hit on the doobie. "Been expecting you." Holding it carefully at the very end with his grease-blackened fingernails, Runs handed the soggy butt to Ballou – who without hesitation took a hit also, just to show Runs that he wasn't too good to accept it.

"Yeah, I come about a car," Ballou replied in a strangled whisper, holding the smoke in his lungs. There wasn't enough left of the doobie for another hit, but he didn't think it polite to discard it himself. It belonged to Runs, so it was his call. Ballou handed the tiny scrap back, and Runs examined it critically to determine whether it was at all smokable before flicking it into a can of sand.

"Coffee?" asked Runs, motioning Ballou to accompany him into the office.

"Just a sec," said Ballou. He indicated the pit bull. "May I?"

"It's Pruno's dog," Runs grunted, indicating one of the white men. "Sure," said Pruno, smirking. He and the other white man glanced at each other.

Ballou walked over to the pit bull and put his hand out. The dog sniffed it, gave it the barest lick, and went back to sleep. Ballou shrugged, and the two white men laughed, apparently from surprise.

"You're good, bro," Pruno drawled.

"Okay," said Runs, sitting down at his desk, lighting a Marlboro with a stinky Ronson lighter, and taking pencil and paper. "Let's go down your wish-list. How much can you spend, what are you looking for, how are you gonna use it, all that good trash."

"Well, I'm not sure," Ballou replied, a little embarrassed. "I guess I just got the idea that I need a car. Something dependable, as cheap as you can go. Old is good, big is good, I'm not particular how it looks as long as it's going to hold up. Doesn't have to be a car; could be a van or truck, I guess."

"You gonna do any hauling?"

"Not that I know of. I'll take whatever you got that's cheap and that'll take me around. I probably won't use it much. Driving around on weekends mostly."

"You said old. You want something vintage? Something classic? That can run into money unless you want something that's got some wear and tear on it. I can sell you a salvage title and fix it up for you. I got lots of those. That Cricket that I sold Dora was a salvage, but you'd never know it. She show it to you?"

Ballou got that awful watery feeling in his belly at the mention of Dora's name, especially from Runs. He hoped he wasn't showing a reaction, not by a movement, a change in breathing rate, a dilation of the eyes, anything.

"'I got others near as good. Like that Chrysler I got up on the hoist. Nineteen-sixty-two, but solid as she comes, mechanically. Body's all fucked up, and the interior would make a rattlesnake vomit, but she'll run... shit, she'll take your coffin to the cemetery. Course the gas mileage'd put you in an early grave, for sure."

Ballou sipped his coffee and thought. He looked away from Runs for a moment, and noticed on the office wall a miniature version of the Van Devander pennant. Ballou told Runs about the conversation he'd had the previous week.

"That kid was right," Runs replied. "You're a bettin' man, never bet on a team with a cute mascot. Not in football, anyway. I kinda

like that little bastard, though. Willie Wilden. You know, I'm a
Cheyenne, and we tell stories about a guy named Wihio.

"White men have stories about Superman types. Your
Paul Bunyan, your Pecos Bill. But Wihio was kind of the anti-
Superman. Little puny guy. They say Wihio's wife could stretch
out her arm at the shoulder, and he could stand under it. And poor
Wihio, he wasn't just little, he was also not that bright – but he
was always tryin' to outsmart folks. Maybe once in a blue moon
he'd do it, too, but mostly he'd just end up gettin' outsmarted
hisself. Like Homer Simpson. Or that Honeymooners guy, Jackie
Gleason, or Rodney Dangerous, you know, 'I don't get no respect.'
That's Wihio. There's all kinds of stories about Wihio. And I figure
Willie Wilden, he's probably just another Wihio. Little man who
can't do nothin' but talk big."

"I understand that that's how the Wildens play football, anyway," said Ballou.

"Hell, yeah. I love to gamble; I'm an Injun, right? I'll give you
free advice: Never bet the Wildens to cover the spread. Not that
there's ever much action on them. The secret to gambling is to
let the stupid folks pay for your time. Bet the Hurricanes, bet the
Yankees, bet Duke in college basketball. In the long run you'll
do okay. Anyway, I got that Chrysler. I got a GMC pickup that's
older'n you are and sounds like a lawnmower with tuberculosis. I
got a couple old army Jeeps. Lemme walk you round the lot."

Again, Ballou marveled at the assortment. "Whoa!" he cried,
pointing to a teal-blue 1968 Ford Mustang. "That's magnificent!"

"Yep," Runs agreed. "Outside your price range, though. That
there's a true classic, in top condition. Original paint job. Museum-
quality, just about."

Ballou sang: "Only Mustang makes it happen! Only Mustang
makes life great!" Runs joined in: "Mustang moves you! Mustang
moves you! Mustang, Mustang, sixty-eight!"

"There's one you might go for," said Runs. He pointed to a huge old Cadillac Fleetwood, the front end of which had obviously been smashed up and hammered back into place – sort of.

"Nineteen sixty-five. Salvage title. I was thinkin' of keepin' her myself; it's why I fixed the front end already. Mechanically, she's not a hunnerd percent, but close. A little heart murmur, a little arthritis, but pretty much okay. I bet I could make her run as long as you wanted to keep her. Like you can see, she's got some rust. Imagine. Dumb sonofabitch who bought her new didn't go for a couple extra bucks to get her Ziebarted. This was one of the most expensive cars on the market back then, too."

"It's us – or rust!" Ballou reflected. "But wait a sec. I remember those ads from, like, the mid 1970s. Are you sure Ziebart was around in 1965? I'd never heard of it before the 70s. Maybe it wasn't available."

"You know, I'll have to look into that," said Runs. "Believe it was around way earlier, like late 50s, early 60s, but I'm gonna google it and see. Shit, now I'll be wondering about that till I find out. If I don't find it on the Web I'll have to call the Ziebart people and ask them. You're complicating my life, Roger. Not a good idea. I'm a simple man. Don't complicate my life.

"Anyway, this car's got your name on it. I can make her look some better. You want to spend the money, I'll treat the rust with a latex solution that'll arrest the corrosion. She'll look okay, not great. But check the interior."

The car might originally have been any color from green to tan, but the paint job – insofar as it had survived the rust – had faded to the color of snot. The interior, though, remained in fine shape. The well-cushioned beige leatherette seats bore stains here and there, but weren't worn or ripped. The dash and control panel had the no-nonsense lines that were fashionable in the 1960s.

"Just about makes your dick hard, don't it?" said Runs.

Ballou knew his own eyes must have been shining. He forced his mouth to maintain a straight line.

"May I take it for a spin?"

Runs walked back to the office, and returned with the keys. "Bring her back," he warned as he handed them over.

Wednesday, September 15

"It's tiiiime – for the Firenze Q. Tanquiz show!" proclaimed a Don Pardo-like voice on the radio.

"Hi, I'm Fi… Fi… Firenze Q. Tanquiz," came Tanquiz' voice, somewhat higher and squeakier than the voice he used in regular conversation, "and… and… I wanna be a duh… a duh…" (various gasping and fizzing noises) "I wanna be a disc jockey!"

"You're *hired*!" boomed the first voice, followed by the sound of a massive explosion. Then a chorus of female voices, singing, "Fiiiii Tanquiz! Dynamite – joooooock!"

Ballou didn't much like the show. Tanquiz evidently aspired to be another Howard Stern, but he had no sidekick to play off, and the music was mainly rap. Ballou listened to it, nonetheless, through his evening martini and through dinner (soup and a pastrami sandwich from the quaint little deli near the Town Square), so that he could tell Tanquiz he'd done so.

Dinner over, Ballou switched off the radio, opened a beer, and decided to call his mother and have that chore out of the way for a while. He'd not spoken to her since he'd moved from New York City to Wildenkill. Nor had he seen her in almost five years. She still lived in Madison, Wisconsin, rarely venturing out of her house since Ballou's father had died. Ballou only kept in touch for the sake of his conscience, and her will.

His mother began the conversation as usual with a sigh. "I'm glad you could call."

"Are you well?"

"Oh, well enough. The usual aches and pains that come with being 68."

"Well, Mom, just think." Ballou imitated Butt-Head. "Next year you'll be – huh-huh – *sixty-nine!*"

His mother sighed again. "I wish you wouldn't make remarks like that," she said. "I don't know what the joke about 69 is, but I know it's something I wouldn't like. That's probably why you have trouble attracting anyone, Roger, because you're always making some kind of off-color reference."

"Yeah, yeah."

"And don't 'yeah, yeah' me, either. You should listen to your old Maw."

"Yeah – I mean, undoubtedly I should. For example I'd never have left Wisconsin if I'd listened to you. I'd still be living with you. Anyway, let's not start. Anything new over there? You're not getting married yet?"

Mrs. Ballou gave just the barest ghost of a laugh.

"Who'd marry me?" she asked. "I'm broken machinery. And anyway, I've never really thought about anybody since… since my old boyfriend went away." (Her voice caught.) "I miss him every day." (She blew her nose.) "I just miss the conversations, more than anything. Your father was such a wonderful talker. That's where you get it from, I guess, except that your father never made any of those… suggestive remarks. You're not talking that way to your students in class, are you?"

Ballou swung his fist in exasperation. "No, worse," he replied. "I try to work as many 'fucks' as possible into any sentence I speak in class, okay?"

"Oh, Roger, stop. Have you met any nice girls up there?"

Ballou told his mother about the bridge party, and Dora, and the tentative date.

"Be on your good behavior when you're with her. I know how you get nervous when you're around girls, but watch what you say to her. And wear nice clean clothes."

"Mom, I'm nervous enough, already. I'm practically crapping my pants. I'm trying not to get my hopes up, okay?"

"You're not smoking around her, are you?" his mother asked. Ballou clenched his teeth. "I just read an article where several women said that's the biggest turn-off, worse than overweight, or bad grooming, or even drugs."

Silence.

"Are you there, Roger?"

"I'm counting ten. Very slowly. I have never known a day to go by when you haven't 'just read an article.' If I had a dime for everything I wasn't allowed to do as a kid, things that every normal kid was allowed to do – but not me, oh, no! because you'd 'just read an article'..."

"Oh, that's not true. You just say that. And you know I'm right about this one. *Please* don't smoke around her. Or anywhere."

"Mom, I'm asking you as nicely as I know how..."

"But I worry. It breaks my heart every time I hear you lighting a cigarette, and I have a feeling that you drink a little too much sometimes, and I bet you haven't lost any weight since the last time I saw you..."

"Mom, knock it off or I swear I'll hang up right now."

"Roger, you know I just say these things because I care about you. And you know if you'd listened to me, you would *not* have still been living with me. You'd have had your doctorate long ago and you'd have a tenured position somewhere instead of always wondering where your next cheque is coming from..."

"*God damn it Mom, I fucking warned you!*" Ballou screamed, and rang off.

Ten minutes later his mother called back and Ballou only picked up because he preferred hearing her weeping into the phone to having to listen to it on voice-mail later.

"If you had let me finish," she sobbed, "I was only going to remind you that there's still some money in your trust, and you could very easily use it to go back to school. It would only take you a few years." She snuffled, and appeared to have calmed down a bit. "And then you'd have a regular, steady job and you wouldn't have to be scrambling for new clients every month, or wondering what you'll have to retire on."

Ballou let his breath out slowly – and imagined steam escaping from his ears. "I blew the trust fund on a brand-new Cadillac," he said.

"You *whaaat?*"

"Relax. I only spent a very little money, on a very old Cadillac."

"Oh, Roger, a *Cadillac?* That's so… I don't know, so… *ostentatious.* Really, what are people going to think? And I just read an article about how people really hurt the environment when they keep those big old cars on the road…"

By the end of that conversation, Ballou had been so wound up and exasperated that he'd neglected, for several minutes, to entertain any thoughts of Dora Fox. He knew this because he noticed it when she popped back into his head – that is, he noticed that he had been too busy being steamed at his mother to think of her.

Dora hadn't been at the front of his mind for every waking second, but she'd been there oftener than not: sometimes like white noise or background music that can be almost ignored but never entirely switched off, and sometimes with a longing that Ballou couldn't remember ever having felt for anyone else. He was able to go about his business with only a barely noticeable loss of efficiency, but on some level Dora was never away from him: her face, her figure, her laugh, her hair, her smell.

Ballou figured that any contact with Dora was out of the question for at least several days, unless he wanted to destroy any faint chance he might have. He felt thankful that she lived on a dead-end street, since if she'd lived on an ordinary street he'd not have been able to stop himself from just happening to stroll by at an hour when she might chance to see him. As it was, he could not come near her house without her knowing that it was on purpose to see her – so he didn't.

He had a car. Runs had lent him a Toyota Camry for the few days until the Fleetwood would be ready. Ballou could have called the Quaggas to find out the location of Dora's bakery, but he could just imagine the chuckles and the raised eyebrows. Instead, he browsed the Web, googling "verstanken chamber of commerce bakeries catering." But he couldn't find anything. No doubt the business was too new to be listed. The Verstanken Chamber of Commerce Website did provide a map of that little town – population 860 – and it listed several local restaurants, including one called the Brookside Tea Garden.

> The ideal place for a quaint but unpretentious lunch, dinner, or weekend brunch: Family-style four-course table d'hôte dinner $24.95, children $17.95; limited-menu lunch and brunch in a spacious, airy, family-run white-tablecloth dining room. Traditional American cuisine: specialties pot roast, Southern fried chicken, homemade soups; vast array of old-fashioned side dishes and tempting pâtisserie. No alcohol. All majors. T-F 11:30-2:30 and 5:30-9:00, Sat 10:00-10:00, Sun 10:00-4:00. Closed Mondays.

Him for brunch at the Brookside Tea Garden and a leisurely drive around Verstanken on Sunday, Ballou decided. Dora's bakery was likely to be closed, so she'd never know he'd been doing his research. Then maybe on Monday or Tuesday he'd drop by ever-so-casually, buy a little something, chat her up for five minutes, and see where that might take him.

Meanwhile the wait was torture. What if she met someone else before then? What if she already had met someone, who'd been patiently working on her for months, waiting for just the right moment to make his move and have her eating out of his hand, and what if that moment had arrived, before Ballou could do anything about it?

Ballou reflected that a really enterprising fellow might kid-nap Dora, keep her confined, and wait for her to develop Stock-holm Syndrome. But that would be problematic. She'd certainly be missed, sooner rather than later, and even if she were never traced to him, it wouldn't be practicable to keep her locked away indefi-nitely – and once she was out and about in society again, no matter how hard she'd fallen for him by that time, she'd have a hard time answering well-meant but prying chit-chat such as, "Where have you been keeping yourself for the past few months? We were all worried sick about you! The FBI was looking for you and every-thing! I'm afraid your house is in pretty bad shape, what with the police turning it inside-out looking for DNA, and they had to take your dog to the pound, and..."

No, that was just not going to work. Dora would surely resent it in the long run, especially the part about the dog.

Ballou supposed that this obsession was not unique. No doubt, he told himself, other men had similar ridiculous fantasies in response to their infatuations, and he couldn't imagine that no man had ever felt the same for Dora as he did. And since nobody needed to know about his fantasies besides himself, he indulged them. Most of them, after all, were pretty tame. Imagining, embel-lishing, perfecting what he imagined would be his and Dora's first kiss occupied him at least four or five times a day. The thought of the two of them living together, married, in a bigger house with two dogs, appeared and reappeared.

But far more so than the obviously absurd one about kidnapping, the fantasy about marriage disturbed Ballou. Aside from that first kiss, and sometimes subsequent kisses, the marriage fantasy was pretty well confined to the comradeship they would enjoy, the beauty and grace with which no doubt Dora would fill his life, and his own appreciation of it. He was utterly unable to use Dora as inspiration during his private moments. Granted: memories, not futurities, best feed the muse of masturbation. Still, Ballou would have expected that Dora would have been worth something to him in that regard. Instead, his mind would (apparently involuntarily) snap to thoughts of one or another of the few women he'd actually lain with. He wanted to bring his mind to bear on Dora then; he tried to – but he could not.

Friday, September 17

"Miss Zizmor, your day of glory has arrived," Ballou announced. "Pass the copies of your poem around, and when everybody's got one, would you like to read it to the class, or shall I?"

"I will," Sherrie Zizmor replied, looking down at the table as she passed the papers in either direction. When everyone was ready, she read, slowly and clearly:

To My "Best Friend"

You've done me favors, which I have returned
And so my memories of them are vague.
They take a lot of work to recollect:
So pointless, wiping off the coat of dust
That covers all the debts we pay and file.

Your biggest gift, I do remember, though,
And if I live forever, always will
For it's the one I never can repay
I wish I could: It cost you nothing; yet,
It was quite boundless in its wealth and depth

Glib artistry you showed, an adept's touch
You styled it, added to it down the years;
You'd whistle bits and pieces, now and then,
Embellishing, perfecting, even if
You hadn't hoped to craft so great a work

So brilliant its conception! Well I knew,
When it was done, you'd made a masterpiece
With words and glances, by slow increments
You wrote for me a symphony of scorn
And still it plays within me, note by note.

Tonia Kampling, seated across the table from Miss Zizmor, gasped aloud, her red-rimmed eyes widening dramatically. She stared at the author, appalled.

"Miss Zizmor, this is impressive," Ballou said. "And I'm pleasantly surprised. What you've written here is quite traditional and old-fashioned in its composition. Which is good as far as I'm concerned, but I'd expected something more modern from you, and less formal.

"Has anyone in this room taken a course on Shakespeare?" Only Sherrie Zizmor's and Wanda Motski's hands went up. "I want to point out to you that Miss Zizmor has written this poem in iambic pentameter, which is what Shakespeare used in his plays. Not only does she use iambic pentameter, but you'll notice that she doesn't cheat, at all, anywhere in this poem. Even Shakespeare cheated a little, here and there – but look at this poem! She maintains the integrity of the meter all the way through. Miss Motski, could you please tell us what iambic pentameter is?"

Miss Motski could and did.

"Thank you, Miss Motski. Now, you're going to find that in ordinary English conversation, you will use iambic meter quite a lot, even without being conscious of it. Thus you will use a lot of iambic meter in your poems, simply because the English language falls naturally into iambs.

"I want you all to be aware of this, as you write and experiment. I don't mean you should set out to write a poem in iambic meter, or trochaic meter, or whatever, unless you decide that you're going to work on a certain meter as an exercise, which might not be a bad idea. What I do mean, though, is that I want you to be aware of how each word or phrase will affect the meter of your poem. If you have several lines of iambic meter, and you suddenly throw in an anapest, you're going to dramatically change the composition of the poem – maybe for the better or maybe for the worse, but just that variation, caused by a single syllable, could make your poem much better or much worse. You'll learn to beware of this as you go along, and indeed it is *vital* that you beware of this.

"Note also that the author of this poem kept strictly to form. Five lines to each verse, five feet per line, and each verse contains a unified idea. Moreover, as I interpret the poem, it touches on a universal subject. It's a poem we can all relate to because we've all been there. Miss Zizmor, I call this fine work."

Miss Zizmor smiled just a little.

"But it's not perfect," Ballou continued, stabbing his finger at Miss Zizmor in mock anger. Again Tonia Kampling gasped, and visibly flinched, as though Ballou had brandished a weapon. "So now we'll rip it up and tell you what-all's wrong with it. Who'll start?"

"Of its kind, it's not bad," Scott Taylor began, as if to suggest that even so, "its kind" ought to be taken out and buried. "I'd start with the title. Why the scare quotes? Did you put them there like a big sign to say, *'Warning: Sarcasm Coming Up'*?"

"Is it sarcasm, or irony?" asked Annette Schlegel. "I thought it was more ironic that her supposedly best friend was doing whatever she was doing to her."

"It could be both," Ballou decided. "But Mr. Taylor makes a fair criticism. Sometimes you have to trust the reader to see your point, without your hanging lights on it. But sometimes you do have to belabor the obvious. Only the individual poet can make that call, but you have to keep that in mind – particularly in the late stages of composing a poem, when you're down to polishing and perfecting. Miss Curley?"

Kelly Curley had that fresh, wholesome, bubbly look that suggested "cheerleader." She smiled a little apologetically at Sherrie Zizmor before she spoke.

"I think this poem is really good?" she said. "I think it could be better? But, Sherrie, it really is good? Here's what I think, though? It's, like, I just didn't like the second line? I can't really say why, but… it just didn't sound as… artistic?… as the rest of the poem? Does that make any sense?"

"Okay, let's ask ourselves why you didn't like that line," Ballou said. "I agree with you that it's a weak line as it stands now. I can point to two things I'd question in that line. First, you have 'And so.' I would call that a too-ordinary phrase for a poem like this. It looks like it's there just to provide an extra metric foot. And that's commendable, that the author strove to maintain the meter, but if she'd spent a little more time on that line, she might have found a stronger way to do it.

"But what I really don't like about that line is the use of the verb 'to be.' In my opinion, we should use that verb sparingly in poetry. I don't say that it's a bad or useless verb, but I will say that excessive use of 'to be' can lead to sloppy writing. You tend to take the easy way out, and use 'it is this,' or 'there is that,' when you might write a more effective line, and say what you mean more exactly, if you say 'it becomes this,' or 'it seems that,' or 'I see suchandsuch.'" If you take care not to overuse 'to be,' you force yourself to look for other verbs, more dynamic verbs.

"So, Miss Zizmor, you might consider revising that line, finding a substitute for 'And so,' and getting rid of 'are.' Anybody else? Mr. Brooke?"

"Yeah," said Michael Brooke. "In the first line. I hate 'favors.' Favors means something you do for somebody because they asked you to, and maybe that's what you mean but even if it is, I don't know, it doesn't sound right." Michael Brooke grinned and ducked his head. "I keep thinking, like, 'sexual favors,' you know?"

"Is there another word you'd prefer?" Ballou asked Brooke. "Or maybe she did mean 'sexual favors.' I didn't get that, from the rest of the poem, but maybe I'm missing something."

"No, I don't think she meant that. Like... uh... 'kindnesses,' maybe?"

"Okay. Another reason why 'kindnesses' might work better relates to the tone of the poem as a whole. Miss Zizmor has written a poem of what I might call 'quiet wrath.' She's not jumping on her friend with both feet and beating the crap out of her. No, she's stealthily strangling her with a silken rope. Aren't you, Miss Zizmor?"

Miss Zizmor smiled again.

"Therefore," Ballou continued, "you have to consider the sound of the words. 'Favors' sounds so harsh and rough, all those f's and v's fizzing and popping around in there. Sounds like Alka-Seltzer. But try 'kindnesses.' So soft, so smooth, so enticing, almost like you're luring this friend of yours to come closer to you so you can get that rope round her neck. See what I mean?"

"But that messes up the meter." This was from Tim Dance. He was a hulking, tough-looking blond kid with a mullet, a Fu Manchu moustache, and a chain-link tattoo around his biceps. He was also enrolled in Ballou's Expository Writing class, but this was the first time Ballou had heard him speak.

"Yes, it does," Ballou admitted. "So let's see how we can fix it. In this case it's easy. Just say, 'You've done me kindnesses, which

I've returned.' You've got the same meter, and the contraction 'I've' sounds less stilted than 'I have.'"

"'Kindnesses' is a dactyl, isn't it?" Scott Taylor pointed out.

"Mr. Taylor, it's people like you who cause unrest," said Ballou. "Yes, you're right, it's a dactyl. So, the author will have to decide whether to use that dactyl, or find some other word. A poet will have to ask questions like that all the time: Can I compromise a little bit, here or there? And will that compromise enhance the poem, or detract? See, this is what makes poetry so maddening and yet so much fun. Good catch."

On they went, for the first half of the period, until Ballou concluded, "Thank you, Miss Zizmor. Now, Mr. Dellavecchia, you're on. Have you got copies for all of us?"

"You read," said Giulio Dellavecchia, with a sly smile, as he passed the papers around. "I am a shy."

The poem was in Italian. There was no translation.

"Mr. Dellavecchia, if you want to write in Italian, that's fine, but from now on I need you to provide an English translation of each poem, because my Italian just isn't that good, and probably most of the class can't speak it at all. Okay? So I'll read this one, and I'll try to translate it, but you'll have to help me. And then we'll discuss it."

Ballou read the poem (mercifully a short one) silently, twice, to get the gist of it, then read it aloud, surprising himself that he could do it smoothly.

"You speak Italian like a Frenchman," Giulio Dellavecchia commented.

Ballou exhaled sharply through his nose, but he forced himself to smile back.

"Yes, Mr. Dellavecchia, I probably do. I studied French in high school, so that was my second language, and I still speak French a lot better than Italian. I only had two years of Italian in college, so you'll have to forgive me.

"Now, let's work on the translation. Actually, class, this is a good little exercise. Many of you will find, as you go through your careers as poets, that you'll be called on to translate poetry from other languages – or you might even have to translate your own work. You are all studying at least one foreign language, aren't you? Hands?"

Four hands went up.

"Did any of the rest of you take a foreign language in high school?"

Two more.

"Ladies and gentlemen, by your favor, this is unsatisfactory. In fact it just about makes me want to throw things. All those of you who are not taking a foreign language class this term, I strongly advise you to add one if you can, or at least resolve to take one starting next semester. Any foreign language at all, any one that interests you or that might prove useful to you in some other endeavor. If you're going to write well in English, you must understand the language, and part of that understanding will come from learning how English relates to other languages.

"Now, is there anyone else in this class, besides me and the author of this poem, who could translate this into English for us?"

Lee Grossbaum put her hand up, shyly. "I can't speak Italian," she said, "but it sounded so pretty. And I've heard songs in other languages that I liked even if I didn't understand them. Do we really need to translate it? Or can we just appreciate it for what it says to us?"

"No, Miss Grossbaum, we don't *need* to translate it. We could do just as you suggest, but in that case I would not be doing my job, and they'd kick me out of here so fast that I'd actually travel backwards in time."

Tonia Kampling gasped yet again, and looked at Ballou open-mouthed, apparently shocked at his sarcastic tone – although Miss Grossbaum hadn't seemed to mind.

"The first two lines," said Ballou, "are: *Contro gli uomini/Contro gli uomini e le donne.* That means, 'Against men/Against men and women.' It could mean 'Against mankind and womankind.' Or it could mean 'Against the men and women' – in other words, against a certain group of men and women. At this point it's ambiguous. But let's translate the whole thing as literally as we can, and then we can refine it and give it definition – in other words give it a literary as well as a literal translation into English."

The literal translation took 10 minutes, which left very little time in which to work on a literary translation. Still, Ballou felt satisfied. Several of the students murmured "You, too," when he wished them a good weekend, and both Lee Grossbaum and Kelly Curley smiled at him as they left. Giulio Dellavecchia looked peeved, as though he felt his poem hadn't been sufficiently critiqued. It hadn't been, either, and Ballou congratulated himself for not having called Dellavecchia an arrogant, neurotic, self-sabotaging peckerhead in front of the whole class.

*

The Wildenkill Advertiser September 18–24, 1999

Living Life
Charlotte Fanshaw's Column

May I Plead "Truth"?

Call me naïve, but I believe in truth. Fiction has its place – and I know, because I write fiction, and I love it. Fantasy has its place, too. If it didn't, there would be a lot fewer art museums, and hardly any movies that anybody would want to see. But I believe that truth has its place in art, too: in graphic art, performing art and literature. When my novel, *Gains and Losses*, came out a few weeks ago, I felt a true sense of accomplishment for many reasons, and one reason was that for the first time in my career, I had completed a work of art – something that I considered art, anyway – that was fiction, and yet told the truth.

A lot of people – and I won't say "readers," because I get the impression that it's mainly people who heard about my book, heard what it was about, and made up their minds about it without reading it because "I don't have to read that garbage; I know what's in it" – disapprove of my decision to write a book in which I told the truth. At least, *this* truth.

I've been asked a lot of questions, via letters and e-mails, by phone, and in person, especially now that I'm about to go out on tour, promoting my book. Almost all of them start with "Don't you think… ?"

"Don't you think there's such a thing as being too truthful?"

"Don't you think the people you wrote about might be hurt or offended?"

"Don't you think you're being unkind to all the people who have admired [a certain poet] for all these years?"

"Don't you think you should have left an old man alone?"

And then there are the statements. The statements almost all begin with, "You ought to," but "because" hardly ever gets explained.

"You ought to be ashamed of yourself."

"You ought to be horsewhipped."

"You ought to never be published again."

"You ought to pray for forgiveness."

Where does all this anger come from? What is it, about the truth I've written, that so offends people? Have I smashed a holy idol? Would the world be better off if I had not created a fictional character whom many people took as a reference to a man so many people admired? Are these people really just saying that if you can't say anything nice, you shouldn't say anything – especially if you're a Lady? Are they saying that certain people should be immune from comment – especially from comment by someone whose literary reputation isn't as great?

My intent in writing *Gains and Losses* was not to destroy anyone's reputation. I don't write about "good people" or "bad people" in this book. I just write about characters. Readers may form their own opinions.

For one thing, no, I don't think I'm being unkind to the people who know and love a certain person's art. A person might be a great artist. His art can still be loved even if he is not a perfect man.

For another, no, I don't think I should have respected the privacy of anyone to whom these people might refer. Do I worry that I've offended anyone? No, because I've only told the truth, if only in fictional form. If anyone finds the truth uncomfortable, so be it.

Women are expected to keep people happy, to say kind and comforting things, and not to air dirty laundry, and for years that was what I did – glossed over my problems – but I've crossed a bridge. I can't and won't feel obligated to live, and write, in that way.

And finally, no, I don't think there's such a thing as being too truthful. Not in this context, anyway. This particular book had to speak the truth, or it would not have been the book I wanted to write. Had to write.

Also, it would not have been as good artistically. Readers might not agree that *Gains and Losses* is good literature, but I can tell you this: If I had been less than truthful, it certainly would not have been.

Art is what it comes down to.

Have you ever looked at a famous painting of an old person? There are many, and not all of them are flattering. The subject of the painting might look sorrowful, or tired, or bitter. Their jowls might sag. Their wrinkles might show. Maybe they were hurt and offended when they saw the painting. And yet, if the person had not been painted truthfully, it would not have been a great painting.

That's the line of distinction: between portraying a wrinkled old man in a great painting, or in a plastic surgeon's advertisement. You can use truth to create art, or abuse it for the sake of commerce. When an artist expresses truth, he or she should ask, "Am I doing this for my art?"

And I hope people can understand that I must be truthful if I'm going to be true to my art. If they can't, too bad.

*

Does Art Justify Truth, Or Vice Versa?
By Roger Sullivan Ballou

Ordinarily, when we speak of "artistic license," we mean the right of an artist to embellish or distort the literal truth (in writing), or divert from photographic realism (in painting or sculpting), to produce a more interesting or pleasing piece of art. Occasionally, however, the opposite act – to hew uncomfortably close to the truth – is also considered an artistic license, and artists sometimes debate the morality of indulging in such behavior.

The following question has come up, lately, in specific regard to Charlotte Fanshaw's novel, *Gains and Losses*: Is the artist morally justified in setting aside the human considerations of how the work might affect its subjects, in the interests of creating the best and strongest piece of art?

In response to this question, Ms. Fanshaw has suggested that yes, the artist does have such authority, adding "You can use truth to create art, or abuse it for the sake of commerce." She declares that there is (or should be) a sharp distinction drawn "between portraying a wrinkled old man in a great painting, or in a plastic surgeon's advertisement."

This response invites a number of questions:

1. Who determines what is art, and how does one do it?

2. Why is it okay to (say) paint an unflattering portrait of a person and excuse it on the grounds of artistic license, but not okay to publish that same painting as an ad for plastic surgery?

3. Why, deontologically, is it important that "art" be the driving force behind any strong and candid expression?

4. Who can honestly say that art and commerce are mutually exclusive?

5. Cannot a good artist create a worthy piece of art in which he takes care not to distress or insult any living person, if such be his objective? And if yes, is it

morally okay to produce a work of art without consideration of who might get hurt by it?

As to question one, I say art is whatever the artist says is art. The question of whether that work of art is any good is, of course, left to the individual observer.

I can address questions two, three and four all at once, by expressing my disagreement with the underlying premise. Art and commerce, after all, overlap almost entirely. I, and Charlotte Fanshaw, both make our living by writing, and neither of us is ashamed of that. Neither she nor I, at this stage of our careers, would invest a solid year or two in writing a book unless we knew we'd be paid for it.

Artists of all types sometimes create art for which they know they will never be paid, but in the majority of those cases, they do so hoping that one day their art will pay. To my mind, it is outrageous snobbery to imply that art (whatever that is) is somehow on a higher moral plane than mere commerce, and that those who produce art for its own sake are not bound by ethical considerations to the same degree as are those lower persons who pursue mere mammon.

I'd say the answer to question five is "probably." And Ms. Fanshaw's answer to the second part of that question is apparently "yes."

And I would agree. An artist does indeed have the right – the same as anyone else – to hurt another person's feelings, to expose another person's faults, to subject another person to censure or ridicule. However, I must reject the provision that this must be done only in the name of art. Perhaps Ms. Fanshaw would agree with me that it might also be fairly done in the name of protecting society from a villain (by exposing him as such), or to publicly humiliate the person in hopes of changing his behavior – or to take revenge.

If, for instance, I were to write an article characterizing a person as dishonest, brutal, sociopathic, and foul-smelling, I would expect him and his friends to be very angry at me, and possibly to retaliate, even if I had written the truth. It would not matter whether I'd attacked him in an artistic way or in a crude way. Nor would it matter whether I'd done it for the love of my Muse or for filthy lucre.

Useless, to plead that in writing that article I was merely an artist doing justice to my art. If it had mattered to me that I not offend him or his, I'd have taken care not to.

Thus, at last, my own answer to the question at the beginning of this essay: As in all of life, you have license to do whatever you please. With license, however, comes the implicit acceptance of reactions to your actions. That holds good, whether you're painting a man's picture or punching him in the nose.

Sunday, September 19

Ballou got up early enough to arrive at the Brookside Tea Garden at 10:00, to avoid any possible crowd. He left off the jacket and tie, instead putting on a lightweight plaid shirt, the better to look unremarkable. (For this semi-undercover operation, he did not want to attract any notice.) He thought about taking his briefcase with him so that he could work through brunch, but decided that that would make him conspicuous, so he bought *The New York Times* at a gas station along the way – just like all the other yuppies up from the city.

Aside from where it intersects with 9W, the road to Verstanken is prettily wooded all the way along, a drive so charming and green and bucolic as to be almost saccharine. Verstanken's main commercial street is just a 200-yard stretch of Route 212B that looks even quainter than Wildenkill, and more rustic.

Ballou found the Brookside Tea Garden a block off the main drag, in a residential area: a simple but sprawling white frame building on a huge lot, with a lavishly windowed annex that apparently formed at least part of the dining area. Much of the front yard had been dug up and paved for parking spaces. It must at one time have been a community building of some kind, Ballou supposed, rather than a private home, and it must have been in business for some time, since he doubted its owners would have been able to get the zoning variance needed to open a restaurant there anytime recently.

A thirtysomething group of two men and two women emerged from an SUV parked there; also in the lot was a bright yellow Plymouth Cricket.

That would be the killer. If Dora Fox were there, brunching at 10 o'clock on a Sunday morning, with a date, Ballou would have to write the whole thing off. He wondered whether he should just turn around right away, find breakfast at a truck-stop, and head home. It would beat sitting there watching Dora out of the corner of his eye as she played the morning-after love-games at a nearby table with some guy who'd been wearing her out all the previous night. Worse, she might invite Ballou to sit with them.

Best to know now, Ballou decided. He parked the Toyota next to her car – into which he took a glance as he emerged. He saw no detritus or decoration, save that the back seat appeared to have been replaced, or covered, by a wide plank shelf.

Ballou headed toward the front door of the house, through which the four people from the SUV had entered, and just as he mounted the stoop the door opened and Dora Fox emerged, looking as though she'd just arrived from the previous century. She wore an ankle-length, high-necked, puff-sleeved white seersucker dress that made her hair (which was tied in a simple ponytail that morning) look brighter and redder than Ballou had remembered it. She almost walked into Ballou, recognized him at once, and grasped him by both elbows, almost shaking him as she laughed up into his face.

"Roger Ballou, you are my *hero*!" she exclaimed. "You really are! That column in the *Advertiser* yesterday! You absolutely made my whole day! You made Charlotte Fanshaw look like a complete fool – which she is!" Dora let go of Ballou; her face grew grim, almost angry. "How *dare* she disparage plastic surgery like that? How *dare* she? But you showed her up, and you did it just right! You didn't use a single unkind word, but you exposed her for an ignorant, hypocritical... oh, I can't call her names, I really can't, because I don't know her at all and I've never read any of her books, and maybe she's a perfectly nice person. But that crack about plastic surgery really antagonized me."

"Well, don't bottle it up, Dora. Tell us how you *really* feel," Ballou replied, but he was a little shocked to hear Dora expressing anything remotely resembling anger, about anything. He'd somehow had the idea that nothing could ever upset her enough to make her anything less than cheerful.

"Anyway," Ballou added, "I'm sure she didn't mean anything against plastic surgery, really. I think her point was to put down commerce, generally, and plastic surgery just seemed to be the handiest example."

"Yes, probably it was synecdoche," Dora conceded. "But it irked me. Luckily you saved the day. But she made it sound like plastic surgeons go around trying to make people feel bad about themselves, so they can perform operations promiscuously. And goodness knows I never did."

"What? You didn't? You mean, you don't think I need a little work? Look at me! My eyes are too small, and my nose is way crooked."

Dora looked at him critically.

"Why, you have very pretty eyes," she declared. "And you have a beautiful facial structure. You really do. And your nose is just deviated a tiny bit, certainly not enough to need surgery. I absolutely do not recommend surgery lightly. You'd be surprised how many people I've talked out of it. If I felt differently, I would have had my own nose fixed long ago! Not to mention that if I approved of breast implants, obviously I could have used them." She laid a hand delicately across her modest bosom.

Ballou wanted to tell her that her nose was perfect and that his favorite letter of the alphabet was A, but instead he asked her, "Have you eaten yet? Come and join me."

"Oh, I would love to, but I just came by to drop off today's desserts. They get their pies and cakes from me. And I'm hoping that they'll want me to supply some of their bread too, eventually. But, no, I've got to get home. I've got a lot of work to do. I've got medical journals to read that have been just piling up lately."

Ballou had expected her to decline, so he moved on: "Well, since I've got you here, let's make plans for that game on Saturday, shall we? Kickoff is 1:30, so I'll come calling for you between 12:30 and one, okay?"

Ballou did not think it would be okay. Even before Dora's face could contract in apparent disappointment (as it did), he was pretty sure of what he would hear.

"Oh, Roger, I'm not sure I can! You know, we're supposed to play bridge again that night. It's at the Leahys' this time. And if I go to the game with you, I don't know how I'll have enough time to get everything done that day!"

Ballou fought back the panic and rage; fought back the urge to snarl something to the effect of, "Yes, I was pretty sure you'd think better of it, once you realized you'd agreed to a date with *me*. How can I blame you?"

Instead, he said, "Aw, Dora, it'll be fun. First game of the season, and I'll buy you a Van Devander pennant, and we'll get to hear the bagpipes. Besides, this'll be a chance to give you a ride in my new... well, not new, my old Cadillac. I'm getting it on Monday. I bought it from your boyfriend, Runs!"

"Oh, yes, Runs *is* my boyfriend," replied Dora, wide-eyed. "How did you know? We were trying to keep it a secret! He's just the handsomest man in the world; he's my ideal! We have the most wonderful sleep-overs at his house, and he takes me camping and hunting with him, and he's just the most marvelous man I've ever known in my life!"

Ballou figured she was putting him on, but he was dumb-struck. He goggled at her, and babbled, "Ah, ah-huh," and tried to turn the sounds into a chuckle, without much success.

"That's a hell of a note," he said at last. "I had a pretty bad crush on him myself, but I know I can't compete with you. Anyway, listen, Dora, do come. I got seats at midfield! You can't say no to that!"

"Okay, I know what you can do," said Dora after thinking for a moment – and no doubt noticing the disappointment in Ballou's face. "Come over at, like, noon that day. I've been restoring this wonderful antique dressing-table, and it should be done by then, and I need to get it from the garage to my bedroom. You can help me with that, and then we can go to the game."

That was far, far more than Ballou could have dreamed of.

"Done!"

"Okay, then," said Dora, moving off the stoop. "I need to get going."

A family of two adults and two half-grown children had pulled into the parking lot as he and Dora had been talking, and now Ballou – almost floating – entered the building right behind them. They stood in a dark, homey foyer that was decorated with an oriental rug and a couple of rocking chairs, as well as a cashier's stand and the obligatory side table on which sat a rack of fliers that advertised local shops, attractions, and events. Ballou supposed the staircase must lead to living quarters upstairs. On the right-hand side, a door led into a large dining room with walls and floors of blonde-finished pine. Looking in, Ballou noticed that about half of it was part of the original building, and the rest of it extended into the annex. The tables, with plain white cotton tablecloths, were mostly large ones, set up for six or eight people. Al Hirt's "Java" played softly.

Ballou, his mind elsewhere, almost followed the family, when the hostess led them to a table, but he remembered himself at the last instant and stayed behind, hoping that none of them had noticed him. The hostess, a round, motherly-looking woman in her mid-50s, came back and conducted him to one of the smaller tables, against a wall, where he could observe the whole room. In another few seconds, a boy of about 15 or 16 came over to his table: a thin, delicate-looking boy in black slacks and a white shirt. He moved like a dancer, Ballou thought.

"Good morning," the boy said, in a very soft voice. "My name is Bartholomew; I'll be your waiter today. May I offer you some fresh orange juice, and tea or coffee?"

The menu, as suggested in the advertisement, was short but appealing. Ballou ordered the soup du jour (cream of turkey) and a Western omelette. The soup was an exquisite red-brown – a surprise; it turned out to have a tomato base, and a good deal of paprika – and puréed to an almost unbelievable smoothness. It came with a little basket of corn sticks, spice muffins, and white bread, all hot from the oven, with butter and homemade black-berry and cherry preserves. Bartholomew also brought dishes of piccalilli, corn relish, pickled watermelon rind, and dilled string beans.

The omelette turned out exactly as a Western omelette should but almost never does: the eggs fluffy, cooked barely to the point of solidity; the ham, onions, and peppers minced fine, rather than diced. Potato croquettes accompanied it.

The dining room filled up quickly. By the time Ballou was halfway through his omelette only one of the large tables remained open – and toward it the hostess led Martin Wandervogel, with his little boy perched on his shoulder and Charlotte Fanshaw at his side. Behind them, a bit noisily, trailed four freckled adolescents – two girls of 16 or 17, and two boys a little younger – and Ballou's pupil, Curtis Wandervogel, bringing up the rear.

Ballou bit the insides of his cheeks, to hold back the laugh. He kept eating, pretending to read his paper, but in fact trying to overhear the newcomers' conversation: impossible since two tables stood between him and them, all four of Charlotte Fanshaw's children (as Ballou supposed) were talking at once, and the two adults sat side-by-side and didn't need to raise their voices. Ballou felt so disappointed that for a few seconds he forgot how much he was enjoying the food.

However, that didn't last long. He finished up, and Bartholomew reported, "For dessert today we have cherry cake, dark chocolate cake, blueberry-peach pie, lemon meringue pie, and chocolate, vanilla, or strawberry ice cream."

"Hmmm. The pies and the cakes are all courtesy of Dora Fox, I suppose?"

"Yes, they are," said Bartholomew, smiling shyly. "Do you know her?"

"She's a friend of mine," said Ballou, aware that he was boasting. "We play bridge together sometimes."

"Awww." Bartholomew sounded so envious that Ballou almost felt sorry. "You're so lucky to have her as a friend. She's such a beautiful person! I'm so in love with her!"

"When are you gonna let her know about it, tough guy?"

Bartholomew looked down at his shoes. "Oh, I don't mean *that* way," he whispered. "*You* know what I mean."

"I do. She's got it together, no question."

"She's such a *sweet* person," Bartholomew added. "And I love the way she dresses. She always looks so perfect, and so *festive!*"

"Chic but conservative. Anyway, I had better try the cherry cake. And more coffee, if you please."

The cherry cake went down beautifully. Ballou left Bartholomew a large tip and saw that he had a choice of two escape routes: he could walk across the room and right past the Fanshaw/ Wandervogel table, or he could take a peripheral route, keeping to the wall, walking past the kitchen door and the waiters' station – which he figured would put him in the way of the staff.

"Hey, there, Curtis Wandervogel," said Ballou. "Brought the whole family with you, I see. And then some. Martin, how are you? Ms. Fanshaw, we've met, but we've never been introduced, which is a shame since we're developing into quite a team in the *Advertiser.* I'm Roger Ballou."

Charlotte Fanshaw smiled a little sourly. Her daughters glanced at Ballou and then looked, at each other, obviously suppressing giggles. "Yes, of course," Charlotte said, and shook hands briskly. "I'll look forward to letting you go first, next time."

"Is your book moving nicely?" Ballou asked her.

"I honestly don't know. I don't pay attention to that sort of thing."

"Ah. That's commendable. Money is so sordid, isn't it? Martin, your son, here, has been making some very intelligent comments in my poetry class. And the students love vilifying his work." Curtis gave a small forced laugh.

Ballou decided to walk around Verstanken before driving home, to help him digest and to find Dora's bakery. Then he decided, no, he'd better drive around, rather than walk, so that if her bakery were open he'd be less likely to be spotted near it. After all, if she saw him coming around after they'd already had one conversation that morning, she might think he was a little too pushy at best and a stalker at worst.

The question of whether he should have walked or driven became academic in about one minute, when he turned the Toyota onto 212B and immediately passed a little grey up-and-down duplex that stood between two similar buildings (an antique shop and a cabinetmaker) with a sign above the front door that said, "Dora's Bakery & Catering," and another sign, on the door, that said "CLOSED." He'd obviously gone right by it on his way to the Brookside Tea Garden, without noticing it. He reckoned that Dora must have got up very early that morning to bake the cherry cake, chocolate cake, blueberry-peach pie, and lemon meringue pie, lock up the store, and make the delivery.

Which meant that if she'd done the same thing the weekend before, after having played bridge and walked her dog until all hours of the night, then she was not much of a sleeper. This worried Ballou a bit, for he loved nothing better than lying around and doing nothing – and sleeping late on weekends.

Only then did it occur to Ballou that if Dora wanted him to help her move a dressing-table, before the football game, she didn't have anyone else to do it for her.

Thursday, September 23

The Fleetwood stood on display at the front of Runs' lot, with a "SOLD" sign on the windshield. Ballou kept himself from actually jumping up and down, as he and Runs walked over to it, but otherwise the sensation was not much different from opening presents when he'd been very little. Only a sharp eye could spot where the rust had been covered, and while the front end didn't look like new, it would pass.

"She'll run good," Runs remarked. "You want to accelerate slow, and give her plenty of time to warm up when it gets cold – and otherwise just treat her good, and she should last a lot of years yet. You got a cheque for me?"

Ballou used the hood of the car as a desk – almost afraid that he might scratch it with a button from his jacket as he was writing.

"C'mon in the office," Runs suggested. "You still got the insurance binder to sign, and all. Have some coffee. Car'll still be here. Scout's honor."

"Tell me something," Runs sat down at his desk and dumped about a quarter-cup of sugar into his coffee. "You know a fat guy, calls himself Wonderful? Morton Wonderful, or something like that? Is that the guy you and Quagga were talking about the other night? Says he's a film teacher or some such shit?"

"Yeah." Ballou gave Runs the short version.

"He was by here this morning," said Runs. "In a Mitsubishi Montero, had a few kids with him looked like students, and they had a bunch of film equipment. And before I can say Word One to him, he tells me he's making a movie about Van Devander, a documentary movie, and he wants to know can he take some footage of me talking about what it's like for me, being an Injun – only he calls it Native American, right? – what it's like being a Native American in... shit, lemme see if I can quote him right..."

Runs drew himself up in his chair and recited, in a near-perfect parody of Martin Wandervogel's sing-song:

"I want to hear about how the Native American population around here has been *marrrr*-gin-al-iiiiiized" (Runs drew this word out for about five seconds, with a long downward inflection) "both by the town and by Van Devander College. I want to learn from *you*" (Runs gestured toward Ballou with a slow, open-handed motion, gracefully emphasizing the "you," as a lecturer or a salesman might) "how Van Devander College should be helping *your*" (again the gesture) "*pee*-puuuulll. I want you" (gesture) "to describe the *holistic* experience of the Native American in this environment."

Runs shook his head. "It was that kind of shit. And I didn't know what to say to that. What do I know about it? Then he showed me this waiver thing – I guess he called it a release form – that he wanted me to sign, so he could use me in this movie. Only I didn't.

"What I did was, I laid some lingo on him. I told him, 'Me think. Paleface pay plenty wampum? You no pay, me no touch pen.' Only I couldn't tell if Cap'n Wonderful was dumb enough to take me serious. You know, he laughed kind of, and then when I didn't say nothin' more he got all earnest again like maybe he thought I wasn't funning him after all. Don't guess he knew what to make of me."

"Don't underestimate him," Ballou warned. "He just might be that dumb. I'll tell you I'm not one of his admirers, but it's your call."

"Yeah, he gave me the fantods. Can't explain it, but I felt like I needed to go and *warsh* after he left. So they all took off, but they didn't go far. They went off across the road, and set up their shit there, and it looked like he and the kids were filming – you know, the cars going by, and my place from a distance. Beauty shots, maybe. He hung around for an hour or so anyway."

Runs shoved the bill of sale, insurance papers, and other documents across his desk. He had signed each of them "Jimmy Dan Powell," in a tiny, neat hand.

"Touch pen, Paleface," said Runs. "Sign there and there. And, listen, this is just a 30-day binder, so shop around for a better policy. I can give you some leads. Meanwhile if Cap'n Wonderful comes back I'll let you know. I better start wearing feathers."

Ballou drove slowly back to Wildenkill from Runs' place, marveling at the hugeness of the car, at the way it still ran almost as quietly as it must have done when new, at the smooth handling, as smooth as he'd ever experienced. It was a warm day, warm enough for air conditioning, and the unit in the car worked just fine, and be-damned to the strain on the gas mileage.

The time was past four, and Ballou had some minutes to kill. He'd received an e-mail from President Bannister that morning, asking him to stop by her office at five. He'd no idea what that would be about. He'd felt a little apprehensive at first, wondering whether a student had complained that he was doing a bum job, but then he'd decided that if that were the case, he'd be called on the carpet by his department head, Jack Hogenfuss, not the president. Probably, Ballou thought, she was scheduling private meetings with each member of the faculty in turn – the new ones, anyway.

Ballou pulled into the parking lot of the Wildenkill post office, got out, and walked almost sideways – looking back repeatedly to admire his car – until he'd entered the building.

Ballou knew, from common talk, that Llandor's wife – or housekeeper, girlfriend, or whatever she was – picked up the mail there every day at around five. Llandor's post office box number had not been hard to discover, as other members of the Van Devander faculty had tried writing to him before, with no response. Ballou was virtually certain his letter would be ignored. But he saw no point in not sending it. It read:

Dear Mr. Llandor:

I'm a beginning instructor at Van Devander College, teaching a poetry workshop. I'd like to invite you on an outing. Would you care to visit my class, any day at your convenience, to give your views on the art? Don't worry, this won't be one of those sessions where the students will be asking you "Like, where do you get your ideas?" I intend to keep this as focused as possible. I suggest that you come prepared to discuss your mechanics, not your inspiration – but that would be up to you of course.

My class meets from 10.30 a.m. to 11.20 a.m., Monday, Wednesday, and Friday. On the day you designate, I can be at your door at 10.00 – in a Cadillac – and run you home immediately thereafter if you wish. Or I can buy you lunch, the only honorarium I can offer. I suggest this Friday morning. You may contact me via letter, phone or e-mail

[contact information followed].

Yours faithfully,
Roger Sullivan Ballou

Having handed the letter to the clerk at the window – she arched her brows and smiled, but didn't comment – Ballou got back into his car and drove to campus. He had to park a couple of blocks away from the administration building, since he didn't yet have an on-campus parking permit. Not that he minded leaving his car where any passerby could admire it.

Punctually at five, Ballou presented himself in the anteroom of Dr. Bannister's office. As he gave his name to the assistant, he looked past her through the open doorway that evidently led to the office proper, and saw several people milling about in the small space, including – as near as he could tell since the man had his very broad back to him – Martin Wandervogel. The assistant pressed a button on her phone, said, "Roger Ballou is here," and told Ballou to go on in.

It was Martin Wandervogel after all, and three of his students – including one of Ballou's poetry students: pale, red-eyed Tonia Kampling. They were adjusting lights and cameras around Faye Bannister's desk, at which the president sat – again, clad in a sweat-suit – watching the proceedings with an indulgent smile. Already in one of the visitors' chairs sat Jack Hogenfuss, who nodded at Ballou without smiling. Ballou judged that a bad sign. Hogenfuss was perspiring. The room was very hot on account of the lights.

"Hi, Roger," Dr. Bannister greeted him. "Take a seat. I hope you don't mind. Martin is doing a film about Van Devander; isn't that exciting?"

"Yeah, Roger, I need you to sign this release form," said Wandervogel, handing Ballou a printed paper, "so we can go ahead and use this footage if it makes the cut. This is just a standard form that says you know you're being filmed and you give us your consent to use your words and image."

"Naturally you're under no obligation to sign," said Dr. Bannister, "but of course it'd be a big help to all of us. And I'm sure you've got nothing to hide." (This with a huge, gingival smile.) "Martin's just filming the day-to-day operations of the school. Who knows? You might end up a star!"

Ballou read the release and thought for a moment. Here was Wandervogel, a guy who had no use for him, and he'd be giving this guy the power to film him, possibly over a long period, possibly when he was unaware, and then possibly fiddle with that film, take bits out of context and so on – to make him, Ballou, look like an idiot.

"I'm much more interested in filming Faye than I am in filming you," Wandervogel reassured him. "This sequence is going to be about her, showing her going through the routines of her job."

"Tell you what," Ballou replied. "I'll write, on both copies of this release, that I authorize you to use my words and images that you record between now and six o'clock today, one hour from now. And you'll sign too, while I watch. For any other scenes, you'll have to get me to sign another release."

Ballou didn't see how a session in Dr. Bannister's office could provide much opportunity for unfavorable distortion – and at the same time, he had to admit, he was curious to see just how this guy proposed to mess with him.

"What are you afraid of, Roger?" Wandervogel demanded. "Afraid I'm doing a hatchet job on *you*? I've got a lot bigger fish to fry than trying to make *you* look bad. You do a good enough job of that on your own."

"Good," Ballou replied, "then you'll have no problem with that condition." The papers signed, Ballou sat up straight in his chair, hands on his knees. "So, Dr. Bannister, you wanted to see me?"

"Faye, please," Dr. Bannister replied.

"Just a sec," said Wandervogel. "Okay. Rolling. And... action."

"I need to talk to you, Roger," Dr. Bannister began slowly, "about some complaints that have come to me about your conduct in the classroom."

Ballou froze. Even at his best, he never could take criticism well; it just wasn't in him to do it. Criticism from someone who was paying him was almost unbearable. Invariably, it caused a mixture of terror and anger to well up in him, a paranoid reaction, as though he'd known all along that the critic had been waiting and hoping for him to make some mistake for which he could be dismissed, perhaps with his fee withheld to make up for his incompetence.

"The student in question," Dr. Bannister continued, "didn't want a formal grievance procedure, so… so neither the student nor h-… nor the student's representative, is participating in this discussion. The student just wanted to be sure that the grievance was known, and that I'd brought it to your attention."

"Excuse me a moment," said Ballou. "Are these matters not usually handled through the chair of the department, rather than at the presidential level?"

"Ordinarily yes." Dr. Bannister looked annoyed that Ballou would mention this. "In this case, though, the complaint was made directly to me. I have an open-door policy, you know. Students are always empowered to come and see me. So I decided to deal with this myself, with Jack present. The student had several concerns, actually."

She donned her reading glasses and picked up a list on her desk. Ballou resolved to heed what he'd told his students: shut up, no matter how egregious the criticism.

"First of all," she commenced, with a little exhale, and a stern look, "there was some talk, and the student wasn't clear on this point, but she thought you might have referred to African-Americans as 'colored people.'"

Resolution forgotten.

"Now, wait right there!" Ballou said, more sharply than intended, and Dr. Bannister looked shocked, as though he'd threatened her. Ballou registered this at once. In a softer tone, he went on: "I'm sorry to interrupt, but on that point I have to correct the information. What happened was, a student asked me, 'Do you call

African-Americans "colored people"?'" He repeated the conversation as close to verbatim as he could.

"I see." Dr. Bannister's expression had changed to one of pee-
vish disappointment. "That does put a different light on it, I'll
admit. And the student did sound a little confused about that
point. Frankly I would have been surprised if you had used such
an expression.

"Still, you have to be very careful to not even let a situation
arise where that kind of confusion might happen. I'm not saying
you did – it sounds like you didn't – but it's the kind of thing you
always have to be on your guard against."

Ballou said nothing.

"In any case, in that same incident, in roughly that same conversation, there was some feeling that you made fun of a student's
name."

Ballou blanched. He wondered if he could really have slipped,
and called Sherrie Zizmor "Miss More Zits." He was almost sure
he hadn't, but there lay the problem: he was *almost* sure. But if
he had, Dr. Bannister would have taxed him with making fun of
Sherrie Zizmor's complexion, not her name, so, no, he couldn't have
done.

"You were telling her why you called her 'Miss.' And the student who reported this to me was uncomfortable with the way
you... well, I guess you could say the way you played on the sound
of her name. Again, I wasn't there, and I'm sure you meant it very
innocently, but you have to remember, you're dialoguing with
young men and women who can be very sensitive."

"I know you're just starting out as a teacher, so just keep in
mind that... that this is the kind of thing you have to keep in
mind." Dr. Bannister smiled maternally at Ballou. "We want to
try to create an environment here that's *welcoming... * and *NURRR-
churrrrr-iiing.*" (She drew that last word out in exactly the same

style as Runs-Away-Screaming had used, imitating Martin Wandervogel earlier. Her smile broadened.) "Do you see?"

"I think so," Ballou lied.

"And that's another thing," Dr. Bannister went on. "You might want to reconsider the use of surnames in class. Most modern educators believe that students tend to learn better, because they feel more nurtured, if the environment is as friendly and informal as possible. It could even be seen as patronizing, almost as a form of sarcasm, to take such a formal tone with your students. Do you see?"

This time Ballou kept dead still.

"I don't want to micromanage, so it's your decision what you call your students," (again the smile) "but we do take student evaluations into account when it comes to tenure and salary."

"Did the complaining student tell you why I choose to use surnames in class?"

"If... if the student did, I've forgotten."

Ballou repeated the gist of the explanation he'd given to Sherrie Zizmor.

"I would think you would appreciate that," Ballou added. "The student-teacher relationship is so tricky. Especially when the teacher's a man, wouldn't you agree? The imbalance of power can create an atmosphere where misunderstandings can arise. Sometimes inappropriate feelings, and even inappropriate relationships, can develop. I do appreciate your point, about creating a nurturing atmosphere, and I will surely take that good advice. But perhaps you can understand that as you say, I'm dealing with very sensitive people here, and I want to be very sure of my ground at all times. Which is why I will probably err on the side of formality."

Dr. Bannister inclined her head, serious again.

"There was also a complaint that you looked inappropriately at two women students as you were dismissing class the other day."

"*Whaaat?*"

"I'm sure it was all very innocent behavior on your part. You seem to have a sense of what's appropriate and what isn't, and you'll become more sensitized as the year goes along. But this student was uncomfortable with it. It's something to keep in mind."

"Next," Dr. Bannister said. "The student described your method of teaching the class. Again, I don't want to micromanage, and I realize that you're starting out and you're going to make mistakes and learn as you go along. But keep in mind that I intend to move Van Devander's teaching style away from the traditional 'chalk and talk.' Do you understand what I'm talking about? It's all part of our plan to modernize this school."

Dr. Bannister bridled, then leaned forward, looking right at Ballou, the muscles around her eyes contracting just a bit to communicate an intense earnestness.

"I want Van Devander to become a byword for progressive education," she explained, her voice softening dramatically to a near-whisper.

"A little louder, please, Faye," advised Martin Wandervogel.

"I want to make Van Devander a showcase for the most modern methods," she went on. "A place where the most forward-thinking students and faculty can realize their potential and sing their own songs. And that means that I envision our faculty as facilitators, who instead of teaching their students, help the students to teach themselves. Do you see the difference?"

Ballou was genuinely puzzled. He wanted to answer, "No, I'm afraid I don't understand what you want me to do," but he knew better than to give her more ammunition.

"And now we come to the more serious matters," said Dr. Bannister. "You advised your students to study foreign languages, I understand. And that's not a bad suggestion. But you have to remember that there was a Native American student present. There was a feeling that you showed insensitivity to him, by stressing the importance of foreign languages, when you might have advised him to study some of the other American languages instead. You might create the impression that you consider those languages unimportant, that you were somehow marginalizing him and his culture. Do you see what I mean?"

"Does Van Devander offer any courses in... in languages indigenous to the Americas?" Ballou asked. "I'm pretty sure we don't."

"That's not really the issue," replied Dr. Bannister. "And I'm certainly going to look into adding some to the curriculum. It would be great if we found someone who could teach... well, at least one of the languages that are native to New York State."

Ballou almost challenged her to name one.

"Also," Dr. Bannister continued, "I wonder if it's a good idea to require your students to bring in an English translation when they write a poem in another language. If they want to, fine, but to require it... that sounds a little Anglo-centric to me."

"But this class is in the English department."

"Yes, I know, but still..."

"Besides, what if Little Chuck Tisquantum brings in a poem in his tribal language, with no translation? I wouldn't begin to know what it meant, nor I suppose would anyone else in that class, and how could we discuss it?"

Dr. Bannister looked outraged – almost as though she'd been struck. She drew herself up and stared levelly at Ballou.

"Do you routinely refer to your students as Little This or Little That?"

"No, Dr. – Faye, that's his official name. It's on the register. Little Chuck Tisquantum, Jr. Look it up if you don't believe me."

"Oh."

"And that's another thing. Would you prefer that I address him as 'Little,' or as 'Chuck,' or as 'Little Chuck'? Until he advises me differently, I'll stick to 'Mr. Tisquantum.'"

"You also," Dr. Bannister went on, unfazed, "apparently used the word 'retarded' at some point in your... lecture. I know you haven't had a lot of experience in the world of education, but that is such an outdated term! It's such a loaded, inflammatory, offensive word! The preferred term nowadays is 'special needs.'"

"The term I used was 'socially retarded,'" Ballou explained, "and I was using it to refer to myself, to some behavior I engaged in as a teenager."

"Still, I'd advise you not to use it, in any context at all."

Ballou closed his eyes for a moment, so that he wouldn't roll them heavenwards.

"And I was told that you used the 'general he,' several times," said Dr. Bannister. "As in, 'If a poet wants to do thusandso, then he must do suchandsuch.' You need to work on that. I understand that it will slip out, if you're used to talking that way, but it's best to avoid that kind of phrasing."

Ballou cocked his head to the left, raised his right eyebrow, and drilled Dr. Bannister with that one eye. "As Winston Churchill once pointed out," he said, very slowly, "'Man embraces woman.'"

"Oh, you see, Roger, that's the kind of thinking you've got to be very careful about," Dr. Bannister lifted her chin triumphantly. "Sometimes man embraces man, and woman embraces woman. We welcome all students here: gay, straight, bisexual, transgendered, or questioning.

"Another item. It was reported that you said, 'I'm hoping you will come to appreciate formal poetry.' Now, is that right, to impose your values? Any more than if you'd declared to the class that Picasso was a better painter than Georgia O'Keeffe? And you mentioned George Washington and Abraham Lincoln as great poets? Come *on*, Rog-errrrr!" (Dr. Bannister's eyes twinkled with genial condescension.) "I know they're supposed to be great men, but great *poets*? And Roger," (the serious expression reappeared) "you have to keep in mind that today's students are much more aware of the kind of men they were, than when you were in school."

"Excuse me," said Ballou, "I did *not* say Washington and Lincoln were great poets. I said they wrote poetry."

"But why do you have to bring them up at all? George Washington was a slave-owner, for God's sake, and Lincoln was a white supremacist, and both were responsible for the deaths of maybe *millions* of people. You're going to alienate a lot of your students if you hold them up as role models."

Dr. Bannister shook her head, sighed, and assumed an expression of great patience and wisdom.

"This is what I mean, Roger, about being progressive and forward-thinking. You have to be sensitive to these issues. It's just not a good idea to mention people like that, when you have minority students in the room – or ever, really – unless you put them into context, and point out that these people were maybe not as heroic as we were taught years ago. Glorifying people like that might be seen as very exclusionary, very white-male-centric – even if they weren't responsible for so much bloodshed."

"And finally," said Dr. Bannister with a regal exhalation, "I understand that you want your students to work hard. All teachers do, especially when they're just starting out and trying to assert themselves. But 20 lines per week strikes me as a little excessive. And telling the students that they'll be graded partly according to the quality of the poems, well, that's so subjective. I'm planning to abolish grades entirely at Van Devander, and this class might be a good place to start. Or at any rate you might consider honoring their work, whatever you might think of its quality, and grading them according to their class participation, as long as they do submit a certain amount of poetry. And a 3,000-word term paper: that's *huge*. Some students might call it unreasonable. I know one did."

Ballou was getting short of breath. His face dripped from the heat; he could not understand how Dr. Bannister still looked as comfortable as if the room had been 70 degrees. He took his handkerchief from his right inside jacket pocket and toweled his face and neck vigorously, not giving a shit what Dr. Bannister thought.

"Faye, that's about 10 typewritten pages, double-spaced. I had to write a lot of papers that long, when I was in college – and take mid-terms and finals, which of course are not a part of the work-load in this class. Didn't you have to write that much, when you were a student?"

"Times have changed," Dr. Bannister replied. "Students today are used to thinking in short phrases. TV and video games have done it to them, I know, but those are the conditions we face nowa-days. I've had students complain to me when a teacher asked for a 1,000-word paper. Frankly I think it's the number that intimidates them. They hear the word 'thousand,' and they panic. They come out of high school, where a two-page paper is considered a long project. I understand that you mean well, but you may find that you'll need to lower the bar to accommodate the abilities of all your students."

"We want to create a nurturing environment," Ballou added, in a tone so solemn that he supposed nobody could have missed the satire.

"Now you've got it," said Dr. Bannister. "Roger, I'm sure you're going to work out just fine here. It's not going to be an easy adjust-ment for any of us. Van Devander is way behind the times, and we're all going to have to come to grips with that. I'm glad we've had this little talk, and I'm sure we understand each other a lot better now. Just keep in mind what I've told you, and consider what you need to do about it." She turned to Jack Hogenfuss, not having looked at him since Ballou had sat down. "Jack, is there anything you'd like to add?"

"No," Hogenfuss replied, "I think you've covered it, Faye. Thank you." Hogenfuss got to his feet; Ballou did the same. He felt slightly disoriented as he stood, and almost upset his chair. He came out of himself, remembered for the first time in many minutes that he was being filmed, and that Martin Wandervogel was in the room – and one of his own students! – and a fresh wave of fury engulfed him. He wanted to turn back to Dr. Bannister and demand to know how she dared – but knew it would do him no good whatever. He squared his shoulders and strode out of the office, through the anteroom and into the hall. Jack Hogenfuss was yards ahead of him, walking fast, not looking back, heading for the exit.

From behind him, Ballou heard Martin Wandervogel's voice: "That was great, Faye. Just great."

"Ha!" Dr. Bannister whooped. "Let 'em hate me so long as they fear me!"

*

Who might have denounced him? Scott Taylor? No. He was mischievous, but this wouldn't be his style, and Ballou felt that Taylor didn't wish him ill. Michael Brooke? Little Chuck Tisquantum, Jr.? Unlikely. They both seemed pretty normal. Tim Dance? Never.

Giulio Dellavecchia? A real possibility. A nasty, hostile person, with "weasel" written all over him. It'd be just like him to do something sneaky like that, just for meanness. Curtis Wandervogel? The obvious suspect. On discovering that his son was in Ballou's class, it would have been perfectly natural for Martin Wandervogel to ask Curtis to do him a favor.

Kelly Curley? Annette Schlegel? Wanda Motski? So far none of them seemed like the type. Sherrie Zizmor? A good candidate. But, no. She'd have had a better memory. She'd not have offered a confused story about how he might have said "colored people."

Tonia Kampling, who'd been helping Wandervogel with the filming? Would she have been allowed to witness the interview if she'd made the complaint? Who knew? Maybe Faye Bannister had offered Miss Kampling this option, so that she could see Ballou getting spanked without having to reveal herself as the accuser.

And that sickly-looking and possibly half-mad girl would be just
the type to go around looking for offenses against her tender sensibilities, and lodging earnest complaints at the highest levels.

And as soon as he'd thought this, Ballou realized he'd made all
kinds of assumptions about a girl who'd so far not spoken a word
in his hearing, about whom he could not possibly know anything.
He almost physically slapped himself.

Finally, Lee Grossbaum. Her few comments and questions
so far had bordered on fatuity. She'd have had neither sufficient
motive nor imagination to complain of him. Besides, Ballou reasoned, Lee Grossbaum was beautiful. Beautiful women don't play
such tricks on men without extraordinary provocation.

Ballou was so upset, angry, indignant, just plain violated – and
so absorbed in the mystery – that he walked right past his Cadillac.
He went a full block further on – near the intersection of Herkimer
and Main Street – before he saw that he'd overshot.

He decided to keep walking toward Main. He should buy
a second cassette recorder, he thought, to keep in his office and
take to each class. He also figured he had better talk to a lawyer, and fast. Forgetting the recorder for the moment, he went
past the Town Square, past Quagga Realty, toward Frank Leahy's
law office. It was almost six o'clock, but there was a chance there
might still be someone there. If not, he'd stop by first thing in the
morning.

Leahy was stepping out of the front door of his office, just as
Ballou approached the building. He wore a dark grey suit and a
plain maroon tie, and he was walking very slowly alongside a man
even thinner and older than himself: probably 100 years old, with
thick glasses and wispy white hair under a Red Sox cap. Ballou
hailed them.

"Roger!" cried Leahy, offering that odd stiff short-armed hand-
shake of his. "Roger, I'd like you to meet another Francis X." Leahy
turned to the older man. "Dad, I'd like you to meet a friend of

mine, Roger Ballou. Roger, may I present the founding partner in our firm? Francis X. O'Dell."

Francis X. O'Dell shook Ballou's hand.

"X is the secret middle initial of every Irish-Catholic boy named Francis," Leahy explained. "Probably every French-Catholic boy, too, eh, Roger?"

"I guess," Ballou replied. "My family were Huguenots."

"I don't care if they were forget-me-nots, I'll still invite you to join us," said Leahy. "Frank O'Dell and I are going over there to Smitty's." Leahy pointed in the direction whence Ballou had come. "Frank O'Dell wants a cheeseburger. Don't you, Dad?"

"Cheeseburger *deluxe*, Frank," Mr. O'Dell corrected him in a reedy croak. "Make me one with everything, as the Buddha says."

"Smitty's has the best damn burgers in the Eastern United States," declared Leahy. "Well, actually they don't, but they have the best burgers in Wildenkill, and that's all we can offer. How are you anyway, Roger?"

"I've been better," Ballou confessed. "I've got quite a story I could tell you, if you feel like being really bored."

"If it's something to do with Van Devander, I'm all ears," Leahy replied. "I'm a trustee, you know."

Good news – or so Ballou hoped.

"Then I will come along, thanks. I'm afraid my appetite's been pretty well taken away, so I might not be able to handle a burger right now, but I'll tell you the story."

They proceeded. Ballou, who normally walked at top speed despite his bad foot, could hardly bear to go at Mr. O'Dell's pace.

"Young man, I'm sorry, I didn't get your name," Mr. O'Dell said loudly, as though straining to make his voice audible to himself. "Are you a student?"

"No, sir, I'm on the faculty. Roger Ballou is my name."

Leahy winked at Ballou.

"I've known Frank O'Dell all my life," Leahy explained, speaking loudly and distinctly for the old man's benefit. "Literally. Frank is my godfather, and my former future father-in-law. He and my father grew up together, and his daughter and I were sweethearts when we were growing up. And when my father died, when I was a teenager, it was this guy here who put me through college. I graduated Van Devander in the class of '42, and I had intended to go to law school at Columbia, but the war got in the way. And I had also intended to marry Frank's daughter, but I came home from the Pacific with Lois.

"And this old sonofabitch understood perfectly. He said to me, 'It's one of those things that happen in a war, isn't it, Frank?' And he still financed my law school and took me into the firm when I'd finished. Greater love hath no man."

"It was well worth it," said Frank O'Dell. "You're a fine boy, Frank. You have always been a fine boy."

Smitty's was a traditional-looking diner with a soda fountain, a counter with stools bolted to the floor, and a few upholstered booths and small tables with Formica tops. The place was crowded, almost entirely with students, but they found an open booth.

"If I learned one lesson from that whole episode," Leahy told Ballou, as the waitress handed round menus, "it's that one way or another, most things happen for the best. I know that sounds corny as all hell, but it's true. Biddy O'Dell and I were fond of each other, we still are, but we wanted different things out of life. She wanted to be a lawyer too. And I didn't want to be married to a lawyer. I wanted a wife who'd stay at home and bring up my children. Biddy would have been miserable with that kind of life.

"In any event, Biddy went on to law school, too, and she was one of the best tax attorneys, down on Wall Street, for many years. Just retired recently. And here I am, a simple country lawyer. But I've had 54 glorious years with Lois – although we never could have children – and I wouldn't have traded that for anything." Leahy turned to Frank O'Dell, raising his voice. "I'm after telling Mr. Ballou about Biddy, Dad. About what a great career she's had."

Mr. O'Dell nodded – with slight irritation, Ballou thought – and turned to the waitress.

"I will have... a cheeseburger... deluxe." Mr. O'Dell spoke very slowly and loudly, with long pauses between every few words. "That's with everything. Cheese, bacon, lettuce, tomato, onion, fries, coleslaw, pickles... and whatever else I might have forgotten. And I would like that rare. Very rare. Just scorch the outside a little. And bring me... a large root beer."

"Hearing it described restores my appetite," said Ballou. "Bring me exactly the same thing, please."

"Make it three," said Leahy.

As they waited for their burgers to be delivered, Ballou told Leahy all about his meeting with Dr. Bannister, and the appreciative film crew. Leahy looked somber throughout, not saying a word, nodding slightly every now and then.

"This makes me a little nervous, I have to admit," said Leahy, when Ballou had finished. "She's here on a three-year contract. We're stuck with her, at least for the time being.

"We hired her because we needed an administrator. Most of our previous presidents were good men, but they've been scholars, you know, and not always practical. Bannister has been in administration for almost her whole career. She'd been the provost at Faber College, down in Pennsylvania. But what you're telling me... Look, I don't care if she's got a few cranky ideas; we can probably survive that. What I worry about is the litigation we might find ourselves involved in, if she gives other faculty the treatment she just gave you."

"Lots of lawsuits arising from wrongful terminations, I suppose, which I'll bet I'm being groomed for," said Ballou.

"Yes, that, and God knows what else," said Leahy. "Academic litigation is already plenty big, and it'll only get bigger. You're going to see a ton of lawsuits, on all kinds of issues. Students suing for sexual harassment, or because they didn't get into the fraternity they wanted, or because they got a C on some exam or other. And there'll be all kinds of lawsuits on just the general issue of academic freedom. That puts our law firm in a difficult position, since we represent Van Devander College. We have to make sure that the administration doesn't do anything crazy that it might get sued for, and at the same time be ready to defend against frivolous claims.

"That's one reason why our firm was so happy to get Effie's husband, Hugh. He's still learning the ropes of American courts, but he's a top-notch corporate barrister. I'm planning to retire in two years, when I'm 80, and Hugh is already taking over most of the litigation involving Van Devander. So I would suggest, Roger, that you give Hugh a call. Informally. He can't represent you against the school, obviously, but he could advise you. Off the record."

"I will."

"I'll tell him you'll be calling. If you play golf, he and Effie are fanatics — as a matter of fact, Effie used to play professionally — and they're always looking for partners." Leahy turned to Frank O'Dell and raised his voice again. "Dad, I'm after telling Mr. Ballou about our new litigator." He turned back to Ballou. "Frank O'Dell predicted this situation before I did. Didn't you, Dad?"

Mr. O'Dell looked vacant, munching his burger.

"Academic freedom, Dad," Leahy reminded him.

Mr. O'Dell swallowed, and his look changed to one of concern. "Damn right," he replied. He continued to speak slowly, haltingly, but with great energy. "Academic freedom is in grave danger at this school. I've been saying that for years. Frank, if you're wise you'll pick this young man's brain and find out what's going on. That's what a trustee is supposed to do."

Mr. O'Dell turned to Ballou. "My godson, here, is a trustee at Van Devander College," he explained. "Speaking of trustees, Frank, just recently I read a new book by a young man named Buckley.

He had a lot to say about how the trustees and the alumni at private colleges today are neglecting their duties and letting the wrong people take over. It's a... a sobering book. It's called *God and Man at Yale*. You should read it, Frank. Remind me to lend it to you when you take me home tonight."

"I will, Dad," Leahy replied. "Frank O'Dell has been retired for years," he told Ballou, "and he has neighbors to look in on him and all, but Lois always worries about him, so a couple of times a week I bring him by the office, just to keep him informed, and then we come here for a burger. Meanwhile Lois is making sure his house is in order and he's got plenty of food in the cupboards."

"That's a fine girl, Lois," said Frank O'Dell. "A nice prize of war, wasn't she, Frank? You know, uh... Robert," he turned to Ballou, "I was in the First War. And I met a lot of elegant French ladies, but not the kind you'd marry. Frank was lucky he served in the Pacific. A lot of boys came home with brides from that theater. All we brought back from France, in my day, was a few interesting diseases."

"Speaking of elegant ladies, Roger," said Leahy, "how are you making out with Miss Dora Fox? Has she proposed to you yet?"

"Oh... ha-ha. No, not quite."

"I want to hear the full story before I have to hear it from Lois, because she'll get it all wrong, and I want to know the facts so I can enjoy the fiction all the more."

"I don't know that there's a story," said Ballou, "but I might as well tell you. As you say, you're sure to hear something, especially if there's nothing."

Ballou told Leahy just the facts – his and Dora's walk after the bridge game, his inviting her to the football, and their conversation at the Brookside Tea Garden – in as much detail as he could remember, just as though he were talking to his lawyer. He went on for several minutes. Leahy just nodded and grinned.

"And you haven't seen her at all after that?"

Ballou shifted in his seat. "Well, since I found out where her bakery is, I did stop by there once. Last week. I bought some stuff. Not too much. I figured that was innocent enough. And I didn't stay long, just chatted with her for not even five minutes."

Leahy still looked skeptical. "Only once?"

"Swear to God. I wanted to make it over there every day, but... okay, I'm not as smart as you are, but I knew better than to do it more than once. Anyway, she told me, 'Don't be a stranger.' I've no idea if she was just being nice or what. I asked her for her e-mail so I could tell her how I liked the cookies I bought."

"You're a smooth one!" Leahy crowed.

"Yeah, yeah, but what the hell else could I do? Anyway I waited two whole days before I used it. And she e-mailed me back to say she was glad I liked the cookies... and ever since then I've been forcing myself not to contact her again. Anyway I'm pretty sure I'm wasting my time. Hell, Runs probably has a better shot with her than I have." Ballou threw his wadded napkin onto the table and reached for his wallet. "What's my share of this, by the way?"

"Damn it, Roger, put it away!" Leahy exclaimed. "Your money's no good here."

"Robert, that young lady might be a tease." Ballou started at the sound of Mr. O'Dell's voice. The old man had been looking about the room, smiling at customers and waitresses who passed the booth, apparently uninterested in Ballou's tale, but suddenly he'd turned back to the conversation. "I'll bet every boy on campus is in love with her, but I'll bet half of them will claim they can't stand her."

"I'll bet you're right, Dad," said Leahy. "I can't figure out a girl like her, and I'm not inexperienced. The charm of someone like Dora is the way she makes you feel like you're the most fascinating guy in the world, even if you're a bum. My Lois can do that to some extent, and so can Frances Quagga, but this Dora – she's in a class by herself. And what the hell are you talking about, Roger? You think she likes *Runs*?"

"Nah, not really, no way. Just a thought I like to torture myself with."

"You know, I don't know what goes on with Runs," Leahy replied. "If I had to put money on it, I'd say Runs might not swing that way. I've never seen him with a woman, never even heard him talk about a woman. He plays with Dora, he flirts with her, and probably he's attracted to her the way that type of guy is attracted to pretty girls."

"As though she were the china doll in the antique store."

"That's it," said Leahy, as they all got up to leave. "Mind you, Dora might not suspect that about Runs. She probably assumes he's normal, and she figures she could get him if she wanted to."

"Whatever goes on with his preferences," said Ballou, "Runs has one thing going for him: Nothing seems to faze the guy, nothing at all. That complete coolness that he has, you know? Women love that. And I utterly lack it."

"It sounds like you have a… an *inferiority complex*, Robert," said Mr. O'Dell, loudly enough to make several heads turn. "You need to stop worrying about what the other young men are doing, and just do *your* best."

Ballou cringed, and looked away from the old man for a moment as though to announce to the room that he didn't know whom Mr. O'Dell had been talking to.

Slowly, they moved toward the door, past booths full of kids whose grandparents hadn't even been conceived when Frank O'Dell was their age. Mr. O'Dell smiled and nodded here and there, as he passed them, and one or two of the kids smiled back, then shrugged at their mates.

"You know why girls like Dora so often get to be friendly with guys like Runs?" Leahy asked. "It's because Runs enjoys kidding with her, but deep down he's not interested in taking it any farther. Meanwhile, every normal guy she ever meets turns into mush as soon as he's introduced to her. I saw you. Your tongue was dragging the floor, and everyone in the room could see it. If I could, she could."

Once outside, the three men moved even more slowly than they had done an hour before. Ballou's car was only a few yards away; he pointed it out to his companions.

"It's a corker, Roger," Leahy remarked, as they walked over to investigate. "You know who used to drive a car like this? Chumley Fanshaw. Used to be a professor here. His daughter is that lady writer you're having the feud with in the *Advertiser*. He had a Cadillac Fleetwood that he bought brand-new back... God, it must have been about the same model as this one.

"Then in the last year or two, ever since she moved back here, I'd see Charlotte driving it around sometimes, with all her kids..."

"Holy shit," said Ballou. "This has got to be the same one. Look at the front end. See, Runs told me it had been smashed up, and you can tell. See how the grille is a little off?" He told Leahy about the *dénouement* of *Gains and Losses*, in which Charlotte Fanshaw recounted a character ramming a Cadillac through her ex-lover's front gate.

"I wonder if she really did do that," said Ballou. "Or maybe she just had an accident, and wrote that episode as wish-fulfillment."

"I'll be damned, that would have to be the car," said Leahy. "She must have sold it to Runs, and here you are."

"Oh, God." Ballou leaned against the car, holding his head in pretended despair. "She'll never forgive me now. Maybe she could take my ragging her in the *Advertiser*, but now I got her car?"

"Ask her for a date," said Leahy. "If Dora sees you and Charlotte together, she might get interested."

"That's a thought," Ballou conceded. "You guys need a lift somewhere?"

"No, thanks. We don't have far to go, and I like to keep Frank O'Dell moving, so he doesn't catch rigor mortis. Besides, it'd take most of the night to get him out of that car, once we got him in."

Leahy pinned his right elbow to his side and stuck out his hand. "Godspeed."

Friday, September 24

Ballou sat in his cubicle in the Liberal Arts building, jotting notes on students' papers from Expository Writing, which would come up at 1:30. Poetry Workshop had been quite fun that morning. Michael Brooke had submitted a ballad – in the general style of Robert Service, but full of obscure literary and historical references, which had astonished Ballou – called "The Bard Of Stanky Booty." It had inspired quite a lively debate as to whether a poem could be funny and have serious literary merit, both.

(Pale, red-eyed Tonia Kampling had spoken in class for the first time: "Michael, this is brilliant! *You're* brilliant! You're going to be a *great* poet, no, you already *are* a great poet!" Then she simultaneously giggled and wept.)

Lee Grossbaum's poem, equally to Ballou's astonishment, had turned out to make some sense, once the grammar and usage had been cleaned up. Still, Ballou had had a hard time enjoying himself, what with second-guessing every sentence he uttered, wondering what would be used to nail him this time.

As he finished marking the papers, Ballou decided to go ahead and call Frank Leahy's partner – Effie Hoo's husband – as Leahy had advised him to.

"O'Dell Leahy Hoo," said the receptionist at the other end. "Please hold for a moment." The hold-music was a lush, sprightly string-orchestra version of "The Lonely Goatherd."

"I'm sorry to keep you waiting. How may I direct your call?"

"I'm Roger Ballou, that's B-A-L-L-O-U. I'd like to speak to Mr. Hoo."

"One moment, please." The hold-music returned, for a few seconds, then a man's voice came on the line.

"Hugh Hoo."

"It's Roger Ballou, Mr. Hoo. How do you do?"

"Tickety-boo! And you?"

"Getting through. Anyhoo, I'm a client of your partner, Frank Leahy, and did he mention that I'd be calling?"

"That he did, Mr. Ballou." Hugh Hoo had a high voice with an outdated "teddibly upper-clahss" British accent. "And of course Mrs. Hoo had told me all about you, after the other evening. Do you play golf as well as you play bridge?"

"No, way worse. I play, sort of, but I've lived in the city for the past 20 years, and I got to play maybe two or three times a year, so you can imagine."

"Then we shall undertake to improve your game. Have you got clubs, and can you get away late this afternoon, six-ish? Effie and I try to play a quick nine holes at Mourning Wood, as many evenings as we can. In full summer, if we keep up our speed, we can usually do 18 before it gets too dark to see the ball. You know how to get there? Jolly good. In that case we'll meet you in the clubhouse at six."

So, Ballou had another worry to get him through the afternoon. He hadn't so much as touched a golf club in three months. Even at his best he'd been lucky to break 100, and now he was going to blow an evening making a fool of himself. He'd need to get home by five at the latest to change into golfing attire and load the clubs into his car – and in the meantime he'd have to teach his afternoon class, do all the research he'd been intending to do that day, and complete the class preparation that he'd intended to leave for that evening.

Just before five, he heard a soft knock on the doorframe of the cubicle, and a slender, pale woman with long, fading, straight red hair stepped in. She wore jeans and a lacy antique blouse, large round glasses, and a little simper of apology. She held an envelope in her hand. She moved to Ballou's desk, placed the envelope in front of him, inclined her head slowly, and left, glancing back at him, her eyes converting her smile from one of excuse to one of farewell.

Ballou, having decided in that three-second transaction that she passed the "would I or wouldn't I?" test (and then some) got up to call after her, then he saw that the envelope was addressed to him in a masculine hand. He remembered who the woman must be. He took up the envelope and ripped it open as he walked out of the office, reading it as he limped downstairs and out of the building.

Dear Mr. Ballou,

Thank you for your invitation. I get at least one of these per semester from Van Devander, and of course hundreds if not thousands from other teachers all over the world. They all want to play Dill Harris to my Boo Radley. I never answer those letters but I thought to do you the courtesy of answering yours because I like your pieces in the Advertiser. The answer's no. But it's no to everybody.

Best regards,
Llandor

The letter was hand-written, evidently with a fountain pen. Ballou had got out the door of the building and halfway across College Green when it hit him: a holograph letter from Llandor. Probably worth a nice piece of change now, and priceless once

Llandor was dead. He refolded the letter and replaced it in the
envelope as gently as he could, mentally scourging himself for having been so eager to open it that the envelope was badly torn. Torn,
but certainly not destroyed – and the mucilage, presumably, would
have Llandor's DNA on it. As though he were handling gossamer,
Ballou slid the envelope into his inside jacket pocket.

*

The course at Mourning Wood Golf & Country Club consists of
18 holes laid out on a piece of land that appears to have only had
room for nine. The architect got round that problem by laying
each hole parallel to another, so that each fairway blends in with
another. Only the ninth and 18th have out-of-bounds to one side.
Moreover, only the ninth and 18th holes have greens of ordinary
size. Each other hole features a huge double green that it shares
with its neighbor: Holes one and 17 share a green; so do two and
16, three and 15, and so on, with the two pins distinguished by
different-colored flags.

"Ye can very nearly see the entire course from any point," Effie
Hoo remarked. She and Ballou stood on the first tee, waiting for
Mr. Hoo to emerge from the men's locker room, where he was
changing. "Ye'll not find any rough to speak of, ye see, nor trees,
but ye'll find swales and depressions and mounds and deep bunkers exactly where ye'd hope not to find 'em. Och, I love Mourning
Wood. It's very long, and very hard."

"It's lucky that they let you walk this course," Ballou remarked.
"On most American courses, now, a cart is compulsory. I hate that."

"Och, that's the worst," Effie agreed. "It throws your rhythm
off something hellish, when ye ride. I'm a scratch player, and I find
that a cart can add five strokes to my score, easily."

"Yes, Frank told me you'd played for dough."

"I was on the European Women's Tour for a few years," Effie replied, "when I was much younger, of course. Hugh and I met when we were both teenagers, for he was one of the best amateurs in the U.K., although we didn't start to court, let alone get married, until many years later. And by that time I'd become a teaching professional. That's what I do now. I give lessons and seminars, all over the country – mostly to businesswomen. I teach not only the fundamentals of the game, but the etiquette, and the unwritten rules, which are even more important than playing well. Ye might be the worst golfer God ever blew breath into, but if ye're well-behaved on the course ye'll be tolerated."

Hugh Hoo emerged from the clubhouse in plus-fours, an argyle sweater, and an old-fashioned tweed newsboy's cap. He was tall for an Asian, slender, with a small round head and a pencil-line moustache. Ballou hadn't had time to change clothes, except to put on his golf shoes. He still had on his dress slacks and white button-down shirt, and his tie. Effie wore culottes (which did not flatter her broad beam) and a windbreaker.

"Cool outfit," Ballou remarked. "Almost as impressive as your work clothes." Hoo had arrived at the club wearing grey-and-black striped trousers, black waistcoat and jacket, silver-grey tie, a shirt with an old-fashioned wing collar – and a homburg on his head.

"Cheers," said Hoo. "Who is that chap who always wears the cowboy clothes in court?"

"No," Ballou corrected him, "Hoo is the chap who wears the striped trousers and the wing-collared shirt. It's Gerry Spence who wears the cowboy clothes."

"That's the chap. He goes to show you, a sartorial trademark never hurts. Hence mine own attire. In English courts one wears the robe and the periwig, of course, but here I can take that little advantage. It's been a battle, ever since I came Stateside, to keep myself from adding a tall silk hat to my business uniform. But I had to admit that that might have been a bit much."

"That's like the girl who orders a banana split with all the works, and then leaves off the cherry because she's on a diet," Ballou countered. "Get the hat."

"Ye're not supposed to tell him that," Effie howled in despair. "Now march up to the tee, ye miserable man, and show us the way."

"After you."

"Not a bit of it." Effie now looked grim. "Guest goes first. And ye'd better hit a good one unless ye fancy being outdriven by an old woman."

With that delightful prospect in mind, Ballou unlimbered his driver, swinging it at the ground a couple of times to loosen up. It was an ancient club, one of a set of hickory-shafts that had belonged to his father – a set so old that the iron clubs had names, rather than numbers, stamped on the sole. So as not to look like a wimp in front of the Hoos – and against his better judgment – Ballou pegged his ball up at the back tee.

"If you're going to miss, on this hole, don't," Hoo warned. "There's that burn on the left, as you see, and if you go at all to the right you'll find bunkers you'll be very lucky indeed to dig your ball out of. Straight down the fairway, that's your ticket, and don't worry about length. Sooner let Effie out-drive you, just so you hit a straight shot."

Ballou swung as slowly as he could and came through the ball perfectly, knowing just from the feel that it was as good a drive as he'd ever hit. Sure enough, the ball roared dead straight through the air, smack down the middle of the fairway. Ballou was a little disappointed not to see fire trailing from it. What felt like a full minute later, it finally hit the ground, bounced, and rolled, settling nearly 300 yards along. "Aye," said Effie. Hoo nodded approvingly. "Yes, that's Position A," he said.

Effie, stony-faced, also set up at the tips, scorning the ladies' tee about 50 yards ahead. She, too, hit a perfect – indeed a professional – drive: shorter than Ballou's but just barely, and on nearly the same line. Hoo hit the shortest drive of the three, although perfectly placed.

"Put your arse into it, Aoidh, for fuck's sake," Effie scolded her husband. Ballou supposed she called him by a pet name. It sounded like "euyh." Hoo showed no discomfiture. Ballou supposed he was reconciled to being not quite as good a golfer as Effie.

However, Hoo hit his second shot just as straight as his drive, and it put him on the green within 10 feet of the cup. Effie, although she had a shorter shot and could take less club, ended up outside her husband's ball. She shrugged. "I'm longer, he's steadier," she explained.

Ballou had only a little over 100 yards to the pin, so he took his wedge. He swung at the ground once – and it felt awful. He swung again, but just could not get the feel of it. He squared up to the ball, trying his best to visualize a smooth contact, praying he wouldn't get under it. He swung, and as he came through the ball his whole brain filled with white light – as though he'd been at the center of an explosion. For the barest instant, he was insensible. He came to himself to see the ball skittering pathetically along the ground, bouncing crazily, coming to rest about 10 feet short of the green, in some deep fringe. He'd skulled it.

Ballou sank to one knee, seizing the back of his head with both hands, moaning. He got to his feet, shaking his head. He couldn't look at the Hoos.

"Now you see how I really play," he said.

"Ye're not in bad shape there," Effie reassured him. "Just knock it close."

It looked an easy enough shot. The ball stood up pretty well in the high grass. Just an easy swing of the sand-wedge would get it onto the green and let it roll close to the hole. Again, Ballou took two practice swings, then a third. He felt he had the shot in his mind, and had the feel of it. Focus, he told himself. Focus. He stepped up to the ball, concentrated, and swung, ever so easily.

The club stubbed into the grass a good two inches behind the ball. Momentum carried it forward so that the clubface just barely popped the ball into the air. The ball almost landed in the deep fringe again, but cleared it just by a hair, landing on the apron, leaving Ballou a putt of about 60 feet on a wickedly undulant green.

Again, he kept staring at the ground. God forbid he should see the expressions on the Hoos' faces. He took a deep breath and exhaled very slowly, wishing that a trap door would open beneath him and transport him into eternal emptiness.

"Roger, listen to me a moment," Effie commanded. Ballou raised his head and glared at her, his face set in defiant fury, wishing he could tell her to shut the fuck up and fuck off and just fucking die.

"I know how disconcerting it is to get advice on the golf course," she went on. "But, Roger, if ye *insist* on decelerating your club before ye've even hit the ball, that'll be the result. Now take your putt. Ye still only lie three. And take your time."

Ballou's putter was as old as the rest of the set, a "Calamity Jane" style, slightly lofted. He'd tried several more up-to-date (and supposedly more effective) putters over the years, but for the way his father had taught him to putt – with the wrists, instead of from the shoulders in the modern style – the old-fashioned putter suited, and he kept coming back to it.

Ballou didn't want to inconvenience the Hoos by taking a long time to study the line, when he knew he'd end up taking three or four putts anyway. If you can't be good, he reminded himself, be fast. He aimed about 10 feet to the left of the hole, and took a long, slow backswing.

He'd guessed the line almost exactly – and the speed as well. The ball followed the line, broke right and downhill, straight for the hole, but at the last moment veered just off, ending about six inches to the right.

"Brilliant!" cried Effie. "Now, why can't ye do that with your wedge?"

"I think we can let you have that," said Hoo.

"No way," Ballou replied. "I'm gonna putt out. Under the circumstances." He tapped in the six-incher for a bogey.

"That and better may do," he snarled. "That and worse will never do."

But worse it got. Flustered, Ballou could not come close to finding his rhythm. By the time they'd come up to the ninth tee, his score stood at 48, and it was nearly dark.

"I'm sorry," he told the Hoos. "If you hadn't had to drag me around, you might have got your 18 in after all."

"It's a brutal course, and your first time playing it," Hugh Hoo replied. "You've a fine swing, but you'll never play at all if you only play twice a year. We'll have to get you out here oftener, old thing. And schedule a lesson or two with Effie."

Hoo hit another annoyingly straight drive off the ninth tee. Effie hooked hers slightly, but it was the longest ball she'd hit all evening. Ballou, completely demoralized, hit a horrible high slice – a true "banana ball" – that curved out of bounds, hit a boulder, and ricocheted back: into play, but only about 125 yards from the tee. Ballou was close to tears.

"I should try to perfect a bank-shot myself," Effie remarked. Growling, Ballou picked up his bag and almost ran to the ball.

"Slowly, slowly," Effie called after him. "If it'll make ye feel better, swear at us for a minute, before ye take your shot."

With theatrical deliberation, Ballou dropped his bag on the grass, turned back toward the Hoos, and confronted them, fists on hips. "Dag nag you two frickin' Limey bastards anyhow!" he roared, giggling despite himself.

"Limeys?" echoed Effie indignantly. "You're calling us *Limeys*?"

"You're *Limeys*!" Ballou insisted, stamping his foot and swinging his fist like a hammer. "Limeys, Limeys, *Limeys*!"

The ball lay down in a swale, a good 300 yards from the flag, in thick grass, so Ballou had to take a lofted club. He popped the ball out with his niblick, advancing it another 100 yards or so, then took his kleek and tried to get it to the green – but the shot went well to the right and found another pot-bunker instead.

He lay three, in a bunker so deep that the green was above his eye-level. The ball had plugged in the sand, too. Ballou thought about hitting it out backwards, just getting the ball back onto the fairway and trying to reach the green on his next shot. As it lay, though, one direction offered as little hope as the next.

"Ye've got plenty of green to work with," Effie called from well above him. She was only a few feet away, but Ballou couldn't see her; it was like being called to while underwater. "Just blast it out!"

That was fine, Ballou thought, if only he knew how to do that in the first place, and take advantage of the green in the second. He aimed well to the left of where he thought the pin was, opened his clubface as far as it would go, and swung like hell.

He had no idea what had happened to his shot. His eyes and mouth were full of sand. He shut his eyes tightly and spat, and he heard Hoo exclaim, "Oh, I say!" and Effie cried "Fuckin' hell!"

Tossing his club out ahead of him, Ballou scrabbled on all fours up the side of the bunker and onto the green. The ball was not to be seen.

"Where is it?" he cried, getting to his feet.

"In the bloody hole, ye muggins," replied Effie.

The Hoos both stood well away from the hole; they could not have interfered with his ball if indeed it had been going toward the hole in the first place. Still, Ballou looked suspiciously at both of them. Careful not to step in the lines of their putts, he walked clear across the green and there, sure enough, the ball lay in the hole.

"Simple game, isn't it?" said Ballou with a shrug.

"Aye, that's the shot that'll bring ye back," said Effie. "How the hell did ye do that, Roger? That was not a makeable shot. Not if ye were Tiger Woods himself."

"Well, don't make me do it again. That gives me a 52. I'd better just go home and sit down in the study with a bottle of brandy and a pistol, and do the decent thing."

"Our lips are sealed," Effie told him, "and we've both seen much worse. I believe ye've forgotten to rake the bunker."

The Hoos both shot 37 for the nine holes. "That's about our game," Hoo declared, as they walked back to the clubhouse.

"I wonder if my friend Martin Wandervogel had one of his students hiding in the bushes, getting my game on video," Ballou remarked. "Hugh, Frank Leahy told you about that little episode, didn't he?"

"He did indeed. Disgraceful. But consider yourself lucky that that interview was filmed. Evidence, don't you know. If your president tries to sack you, and you end up in court, you could subpoena that video – and if it's as Frank described it to me, it might hang Dr. Bannister, not you.

"As Frank warned you, I can't give you more than a little off-the-record advice, and that is this: Use your common sense, do your duty, and let the good lady destroy herself in her own way, if she will. But be advised that she'll be gunning for you in particular, unless I miss my guess."

"Why me in particular?"

"Because, my dear chap, as you're new and quite powerless, you might well serve as the chicken who's killed to frighten the monkeys. Do you know that in China, zookeepers will often keep the monkey-house in order in that way? If the monkeys are acting rebellious, their keeper will slaughter a chicken before their eyes. And the monkeys are just intelligent enough to understand the implications. They'll calm down right smart, as you say over here.

"That's why you'd better decide, now, that if she tries any further outrages – such as bushwhacking you in front of one of your
students as she did the other day – you'll stand up to her. As you
saw, anything might be used as an excuse to put you in trouble.
You might be the best-behaved little boy in the whole school, but
she'll find a way to have you flogged before School House, depend
upon it."

"Aoidh, your metaphors so often involve flogging!" Effie
exclaimed, as they arrived at the clubhouse. "And no wonder. He's
more English than the English themselves, Roger, d'ye notice? I
hate him, I do."

"What is that you call him?" Ballou asked. "Is that the Gaelic
for Hugh?"

"Right in one," Effie replied. "Hugh, Aoidh, Hugo, Kay: all the
same name."

"And that leads to the same surname sounding very different in
different languages spoken not too far from each other," Mr. Hoo
added. "In Scotland you have MacKay – son of Aoidh – and in
Wales you have the surname Pew, shortened from Ap-Hugh, which
means the same thing."

They had drinks outside, on the clubhouse terrace. Ballou fit
one of his hand-rolled cigarettes into a holder and lit up.

"You look like Walter Hagen," Hoo remarked. "The tall drink,
the cigarette holder, the tie. I should start wearing a tie with my
golfing attire, shouldn't I, Effie?"

"Roger should tie the end of that tie to his ballocks," Effie
replied. "That'd force him to keep his head steady."

Ballou raised his glass appreciatively to Effie. "Yeah, Hugh,
what are you doing without a tie?" he demanded. "I wouldn't have
thought you'd dream of going without one on the course, any more
than you would do in court! Speaking of which, do you miss wearing the wig, when you're working an American courtroom?"

"Why, yes, to tell you the truth, I do a little," Hoo conceded. "You might laugh, but it's those… those identifiers, you might call them, such as the wig, that I for one find so appealing. It wouldn't be entirely wrong to say that I was drawn to the law partly because of things like the wig, the robe, the formal language, the rituals of the courtroom – for the same reason that many small boys are drawn to the military, I suppose. I did consider, many years ago, trying to make a go of a career as a professional golfer. I was torn between two lovers, so to speak: golf and the law. And if you'll believe it, the law turned out to have more romantic appeal, as well as a more permanent beauty. Not to mention it's far better-endowered."

"But by practicing in the States," said Ballou, as they went into the clubhouse dining room, "you lose a lot of the romance and the glamour, don't you?"

"Not as much as one would think. For real romance and glamour, I missed my generation. I belonged in the 50 years from, say, Crippen to Stephen Ward. If I could have bookended my career with those two trials, I'd have gone to my grave utterly fulfilled, I daresay. Not that either of those were winnable cases, from the defendant's point of view."

Ballou knew which cases Hoo was talking about, and Hoo seemed to have assumed he would know – and this Ballou took as a high compliment. As they waited to order, they exchanged opinions on how Crippen could have been defended.

"How d'ye know about the Crippen case, Roger?" Effie asked, some minutes later, as she attacked her steak. "Ye're as bad as Hugh. Ye weren't contemplating a career as a barrister over in England when ye were a lad, surely?"

"No, but it was reading about all those English murders that made me fantasize about going in for law, when I was little," said Ballou. "Problem is, I was too lazy, and still am. I became a writer because I'm a lazy bastard. Writing's a racket. If you can do it, and if you can develop a steady client list, you can make a living at it without working all that hard. Not many people know that, lucky for me."

Ballou considered for a moment.

"Not to mention that I'm very much an introvert. That's why I spend so much time reading. I can handle myself socially – if kind of awkwardly – but I really am pathologically shy. That's why I'm a bachelor at my age, I guess."

"That's not the reason," Effie declared as though there were no arguing the point. "Ye're unlucky in love for the same reason ye can't play golf to save your arse. Ye just can't relax and enjoy yourself, and sooner or later ye panic, and the wheels fall off. Ye walk onto a difficult course like Mourning Wood, ye start out very well, then ye worry that ye're out of your depth, and ye start hackin' up the turf – just as ye did on the first hole, after that lovely tee shot. *L'audace*, Roger. *Toujours l'audace*! And a great deal of practice, which I believe ye don't get. Neither with the ladies nor with the golf."

"Maybe I don't practice golf as I should," Ballou replied, "but good God, I do nothing *but* practice on the ladies. I've been here not much over a month, and I'll bet you there's hardly a pretty girl in Wildenkill I haven't at least winked at. Probably a few ugly ones, too, just from habit."

"Aye, ye wink at 'em, and that's as far as ye get. Have ye made any progress with young Dora? Ye haven't been sending her flowers and love-letters yet, I should hope."

"I swear," said Ballou, "the whole town knows more about this non-relationship than I do. I've no idea how everyone stays so informed. Unless Dora's been talking."

"I've not seen her since our little swaree. Frances and I had quite the chat about her, though. Frances adores her, of course. But d'ye know, I can't stick her. Too good by half, she is. And too good for the likes of yourself."

"Do you mean I'm not a good enough specimen for her?" Ballou demanded – affronted, although Effie merely voiced what he'd been thinking all along.

"I mean ye'd never be happy with such a one. Ye'd be walkin' on eggshells, all the time, for fear ye'd disappoint her. But, ye'll do what ye'll do. Ye've asked her to the football, I suppose."

"How did you know?"

"She's clairvoyant," said Hoo.

"Clairvoyant your granny. Ye weren't there, at the bridge t'other night, Aoidh. I mentioned Van Devander's pipe band, and Dora was so full of enthusiasm, on about how she loved the football, and Roger sittin' there like an ox. I thought maybe, just maybe, he was bright enough to know she was lookin' for an invite."

"Well, not right at the moment," Ballou admitted. "But I did invite her, later."

"Nuff said, then. Now ye're on your own. Just bear in mind that it's a makeable putt. And now we can get back to murder."

"My love, if you will continue to hector Roger about his undoubted shortcomings," Hoo drawled, "there's likely to be murder done here and now, and I'll be obliged to represent the poor fellow in court after all."

"No, no," Ballou reassured them. "I try not to mind criticism as long as it's not entirely off the mark.

"But, listen, Hugh, you mentioned the Stephen Ward case. Do you know, that case – well, the Profumo scandal in general – was the first news item I ever followed, really paid attention to. I was all of six years old, just old enough to be able to read the papers, and Christine Keeler was the first girl I had a really serious crush on. Just from seeing her picture in the paper. And my Mom had the hell of a time trying to explain what 'prostitute' meant without having to give me the whole talk. Not to mention that I had to ask her why it was a crime to live off 'immortal earnings,' and did 'immortal earnings' mean that he'd never run out of money?"

"Aoidh, d'ye see a pattern emerging?" Effie asked. "He likes 'em slender and delicate, evidently."

"I've never met this lady you've been talking about," Mr. Hoo replied, "but if she's the least bit like Christine Keeler, save possibly for her physique, I'd be astonished. Miss Keeler was a... a malleable character. Impressionable, suggestible. The lady you've been describing sounds... well, very much the mistress of herself."

"But Roger sees 'em as equally unattainable," Effie argued. "And it's my belief that they're equally unsuitable. For different reasons obviously."

"I should have known better than to mention Christine Keeler," Ballou said. "But, seriously, Hugh, how would you have defended her pal Dr. Ward? Or could you have?"

"I could have got him off, I suspect. But just so you know, I had very much the same reaction to Christine Keeler. I was a bit older than you, of course: in my sixth year at Eton. I'd have been most reluctant to attack her on the witness stand. So I wouldn't have done. I'd have turned her into a defense witness, which would have been child's play. Then in my final plea, I'd have given 'em the old, 'You are not here to pass moral judgment on Dr. Ward as a man, but only to find on the specific charges... ' At any rate he'd not have despaired to the point of suicide if he'd had me on his case."

From that scandal, the discussion naturally flowed to other fine points of British history, to the Royal Family. It didn't surprise Ballou to find that Effie wanted to abolish the monarchy, while Hugh Hoo was a staunch royalist.

As Mr. Hoo signed the bill, Ballou considered that he'd better return the dinner soon – with Dora as his date, he hoped. Hoo nipped down to the locker room to collect his street clothes, Ballou retrieved his clubs, and they walked to the parking lot.

Ballou deduced that Effie had picked her husband up at the office earlier, for Hoo got into the passenger side of the Lexus.

"Wait a tick, Roger," said Effie, as Ballou was about to get into his car. She reached into her purse, whence she produced a package wrapped in a paisley silk handkerchief. She unknotted this to reveal a deck of cards. "Pick one."

Ballou drew the four of wands. The picture on it was of four long stakes – the four wands – stuck in the ground, with flowers strung atop them, forming a kind of bower, with a procession of celebrants approaching it from the background, holding bouquets of flowers over their heads.

"Excitement, anticipation, rejoicing," Effie remarked. "Often it means a new beginning of some kind. Or a ceremony. Perhaps your own coronation as King of the United States. Or some other kind of ceremony, Lord help ye. Night, Pip old chap." She took back the card, kissed Ballou on the cheek, and got into her car. Mr. Hoo waved goodnight as Effie started the engine.

Saturday, September 25

Just about the first thought that popped into Ballou's head when he woke up on Saturday morning was the fear that when he arrived at Dora's at noon that day, he'd find some other guy already there, and Dora telling him, "I was afraid moving the table might be a two-man job, so..." That delightful prospect stayed with him as he showered, brushed his teeth, dressed, broke fast, shat (with a nervous looseness, as he'd expected), realized that he'd forgotten to shave, stripped to the waist, shaved, and dressed again.

The weather was still more summer than fall, so he'd gone with tan chinos and a plain white button-down shirt – and because no jacket, he decided, no tie either. Then he looked in the mirror and decided that while his suspenders did make the trousers hang better, they undeniably made him look older and farmerish. However, the chinos were too big in the waist to wear with a belt: He'd be hitching them up every two minutes. So, he took them off, and put on the one pair of jeans he owned, which would do okay with a belt. But he hated jeans: stiff, hot, and (because they're designed to sit on the hips, not the waist) always feeling like they're about to fall down.

They'd look fine if he wore his leather jacket, but it was too warm a day for that. Ballou had a tan linen sport jacket, but when he tried it on, in combination with the jeans, it looked asinine. He thought about plain wool dress slacks, such as he ordinarily wore to work, but he didn't think they'd be right without a jacket and tie, not for football, and anyway they, too, were big enough in the waist to require suspenders. So, jeans and white shirt it would have to be.

It was still only 11:00, and the drive to Dora's house would take five minutes, tops, and Ballou didn't want to do anything that would get him dirty or disheveled, but he couldn't concentrate well enough to sit down and read, so he paced. He wandered the house, going from room to room, thinking. He wanted a smoke, but he almost never allowed himself to smoke until evening (to keep his usage down to a manageable level), and he didn't want to greet Dora with cigarette-breath, at least not until she'd got used to the idea.

Eleven-twenty. Ballou decided to write a poem about pacing. He sat down at the dining table and jotted a couple of lines, decided they sucked, wadded up the paper and threw it to the floor – then picked it up and walked it over to the wastebasket in the study.

Eleven-thirty. Ballou considered leaving early and picking up some chocolates or flowers for Dora, then decided that that would be fatal: the kind of overeagerness that would immediately remove him from contention. He continued to pace.

He remembered that the tickets were still on the desk in his study. He raced to the desk, pocketed them with a trembling hand, and sank into the study chair for a moment, holding his head as he thought all the standard "Oh, God, what if I'd... ?" thoughts.

Eleven-forty. He decided to bring his binoculars, too, and a couple bottles of water, just in case. And his cell phone, too, just in case. And pen and paper, just in case. These, he put in a knapsack, reminding himself to stand straight when he was wearing it.

Eleven forty-five. If he took a roundabout route, and drove very slowly, he could leave. Ballou braced himself, and started out the back door.

Eleven forty-six. Halfway to his car, Ballou stopped, remembering that he'd left his knapsack on the dining table. He went back to fetch it, and touched his shirt-pocket to ensure that the tickets were still there. He went to the bathroom and peed again, so he wouldn't have to later. He also put on his leather jacket after all, although it was supposed to get up near 75 that afternoon. ("You can never dress too warmly for a football game," his father had once advised, and besides, the jacket made him look tough.)

Eleven-fifty. Liftoff.

Even driving slowly, Ballou got to Valley Road at 11:55, and rolled the car downhill at about one mile per hour, pulling into Dora's driveway a minute later. Her Cricket was in the driveway, too, not in the garage, the door of which was closed. Ballou got out of the car slowly, walked back down the driveway to the sidewalk, entered the yard via the front gate, and walked toward the porch, thinking that if he knocked at 11:57 he'd be acceptably close to "on time." The fear stayed with him: There'd be some other guy there. His mouth filled with saliva in that familiar nervous reaction, and he tried to swallow, but couldn't, so he had to spit onto the lawn, checking first to ensure that Dora wasn't looking out the window, or anyone else watching for that matter.

And then it occurred to Ballou that no other car was evident near Dora's house besides hers and his, which probably meant no other man was there.

Ballou heard piano music through the open front window: Liszt's Hungarian Rhapsody No. 6, and not a recording, for at one point he heard an obvious mistake, followed by a pause and a repetition of the passage. The playing then proceeded almost perfectly. Dora played the trills midway through the piece; she had the right tempo going into the final theme, and Ballou stood on the porch, motionless, barely breathing. The piece picked up speed and volume as Dora rounded the final turn and headed down the home stretch – and she flubbed another note, and

Ballou was listening so intently that he could even hear her little gasp of frustration, but this time she didn't stop: she kept right on, and the climactic passage boomed out, getting louder and faster as Dora thundered across the finish line and struck the concluding chords.

Ballou waited just a second, and heard no other voices, so he called through the window, "Dora, that's *terrific!*"

"Roger, is that you? Just a minute!" From the angle at which he stood, Ballou couldn't see into Dora's house, but her voice came from near the window. Pegeen began to bark. "Oh, be quiet, Pegeen, it's only Uncle Roger!" In a few seconds, Dora came to the door and let Ballou in. Pegeen, appreciably bigger after only two weeks, didn't leap at him, but did sniff him and lick his hand.

"You got her trained now, huh?" Ballou said. Dora was wearing surgical scrubs and ballet slippers (her feet were tiny). But her face was perfectly made up, her hair tied back.

"Almost," said Dora. "Were you listening to me, out there? Oh, what you must have heard! I just never have enough time to practice, and I'm afraid it shows."

"Oh, no, it was great. I love Liszt."

"Then I hope you'll forgive me for what I was doing to him! Listen, Roger, you go sit down, and I'm going to kennel Pegeen out back, and then we can move that table if you're sure you don't mind. Pegeen, heel." Dora turned and led Pegeen down the hall toward the kitchen and, presumably, the back door.

From the entrance of Dora's house a hallway led to the kitchen at the back. To the right was a walk-in coat-closet and, between it and the kitchen, a small formal dining room. Immediately to the left was the entranceway to the living room; beyond that, if one turned left before entering the kitchen/dining area, another hallway led (Ballou supposed) to the bathroom and the bedrooms. In all, Dora's house was only a little bigger than Ballou's.

The living room, as Ballou knew it would be, was immaculate: not even any dog-hair that he could see. A baby grand piano stood by the front window, a doily and a vase of fresh flowers atop it. The walls were taupe with just a hint of dusty rose, the moldings eggshell-white, as were the chintz curtains. The oriental rug on the floor, predominantly dark red, had enough bits of purple and gold to let it work with the color of the walls.

Ballou supposed the occasional chairs and the love-seat – all of dark wood with upholstered seats and backs, and lace antimacassars – came from the late 19th century.

Against the wall opposite the window stood a pair of ceiling-high bookcases that contained coffee-table books featuring the works of Michelangelo, DaVinci, Turner, Grandma Moses, Gainsborough, and Schiele, among others, plus a great many children's books, old ones – some of them first editions, perhaps – including a set-bound complete works of Louisa May Alcott, and all of the Oz books: *The Wizard Of Oz*, *Ozma Of Oz*, *Rinky-Tink Of Oz*, and so on. A grandfather clock in the far corner completed the room.

Ballou's hands were icy. He didn't want to sit down, so he studied the spines of the books on the shelves.

"That's done," said Dora, returning. "Would you like some iced tea? Or soda, or orange juice? I'm afraid I don't have any beer."

"No, nothing, thanks. This is such a beautiful room. Now, where's that dressing-table you wanted me to damage for you?"

The whitewashed dressing-table stood on a spread of newspapers in the garage, with a matching wooden chair next to it, and Ballou judged it not heavy so much as bulky – although surely too heavy for a woman half his own weight. Ballou noticed that a portion of the back of the garage had been cut out, and a dog-sized door installed, presumably leading to the kennel out back. He could hear Pegeen moving about.

"I was thinking if we each took one end..." Dora began.

"Better if I just carry it," said Ballou. "You walk in front of me, pointing that end, like the prow of a ship. Your job is to guide it through the doorways. Got it?"

They went slowly. The mirror made the table dangerously top- and side-heavy, so Ballou had to hold tight and steer firmly. He feared first that he might accidentally kick the drawers (which were still on the garage floor); then that he might slip on the newspapers; then that he'd ding the table as they got it through the doorway that connected the garage to the kitchen (two doorways, actually, as between them, on either side, stood the back door and the base-ment door); then that he'd smash it against the stove or the kitchen table; then that there might not be enough room to turn the corner at the other end of the kitchen; then that his grip might slip and he'd drop it against the walls of that narrow hallway that led to the bedroom – and then, at last, the bedroom doorway remained as the final obstacle. That, finally, did take some manœuvring, but they managed.

"Now, let's just set it against this wall," said Dora, taking some of its weight and helping Ballou set it down for a perfect landing on the white pile carpeting.

"Oh, Roger, you are the *best*," Dora cried, stepping back from the table to admire it, and then to take the whole room in at a glance, as Ballou did likewise. "Oh, thank you!" She danced toward Bal-lou and lightly embraced him, darting away with amazing agility before he could even begin to hug back. Her smell, her touch, her hair tickling his neck, all for that briefest instant, resulted in a sort of electrical shock to Ballou's system; his body actually tingled, as though he'd swung a baseball bat against concrete. If Dora could be taught to punch, Ballou thought, she'd be a brilliant boxer. In, bang-bang, and out again, and never a glove laid on her.

Dora's bedroom looked even more Dora-like than the living room. The summer-sky-blue walls contained no suggestion of grey;

the ceiling and the lace curtains were an off-white similar to the carpet.

"If I ever have the time," Dora said, "I'm going to paint a sunrise on this East wall and the ceiling, with beautiful reds and oranges and yellows and greys, so I'll have that to greet me every morning."

The bureau, the windowsills and wainscoting, the door, and the closet door, were whitewashed like the dressing-table. The four-poster bed (stained dark mahogany, an odd contrast) was built unusually high, with a step set against the side of it for mounting and dismounting. On the dresser stood two leather-framed black-and-white photographs: one of a square-faced young man in an army lieutenant's dress uniform, who smiled frankly at the camera; the other of a young woman who had Dora's sharp cheekbones and chin, who gazed superciliously off to one side, into the middle distance.

"Those are from right around when they were married, I sup-pose," said Ballou.

"They look like fairy-tale characters, don't they?" said Dora. "Roger, could you excuse me for a minute? I want to change."

"Sure, but let me run and bring that chair from the garage first, and the drawers. You can't get dressed if you haven't any drawers."

"You're so clever," Dora called after him, as he headed down the hall.

Having retrieved the chair and drawers, Ballou waited in the living room, again not wanting to sit, and when she rejoined him Dora had changed into a white blouse (with a lace collar and a mabé pearl pin at the throat), a white cashmere cardigan, a tartan skirt, and high heels. She'd added a pair of pearl earrings, and her hair she now wore loose, center-parted, shoulder-length, gently waved.

"You ain't ugly none," Ballou remarked. "So. Let me show you my new old car."

*

Somehow, Ballou managed to drive to Kees Schermerhorn Memorial Stadium without any *faux-pas* that he could notice. He remembered to open and close the passenger door for Dora before getting into the car himself. He didn't make any wrong turns. He had no trouble finding a parking place just a couple of blocks from the stadium. Dora gave him another of her huge smiles as they walked.

"It's so exciting!" she said, gazing up at him, and Ballou felt that indescribable wistful thrill once again. He yearned for her to take his arm. "Are we going to win?"

"I doubt it. Cornell's a much bigger school. Like, ten times our enrollment. I don't understand why we schedule them. No, it'll probably end up 56-0, or some kind of baroque number like that."

Clumps of four and six people, and the occasional couple – mostly students, but all ages well represented – now walked along with them in greater numbers, toward the stadium.

"At least if it's 56-0, it'll be a reasonable score for a football game," Dora remarked. "Not one of those ludicrous scores like 25-11, with lots of safeties and missed extra points. If the score can't be easily arrived at with sevens and not too many threes, it offends my sense of order."

"Cornell's brought their band with them," Ballou remarked, as they heard drums and brass getting louder, the nearer they got to the stadium. "They've got one of the best bands in the country, by reputation anyway." They could see the Cornell band, in their red jackets, standing in formation outside the stadium; they played "I'm a Barbie Girl."

Also outside the stadium, Ballou spotted Martin Wandervogel, with several of his students, filming the scene. Their cameras appeared to be concentrating especially on several students handing out leaflets. Martin's son Curtis and Charlotte Fanshaw's thin, freckled eldest daughter were participating, although as far as Ballou knew the girl was still in high school. A couple of the other leaflet-passers did not look like college students, either. They appeared older, and somehow foreign – Ballou couldn't put his finger on how he could tell, but they were definitely "not from around these parts" – and he recognized the type from his own college days, when the University of Wisconsin's Marxist organizations would import professionals to lead their demonstrations. Watching the action, off to one side, stood Firenze Q. Tanquiz, drinking out of a red Dran-O bottle.

"Change the name!" the agitators shouted as they handed out their leaflets, trying to be heard over Cornell's band. "Change the name!"

"Stop demeaning Native Americans!" cried Charlotte Fanshaw's daughter, shoving a leaflet at Ballou. "Oh, hi."

"Hi," Ballou replied. "Right, we met at the Tea Garden, didn't we? How is your mother, by the way?"

"Fine. She's in Chicago this weekend, doing signings." The girl went back to handing out leaflets.

Ballou and Dora read the leaflet together:

WOULD YOU ROOT FOR A TEAM CALLED THE VAN DEVANDER N****RS?

**DEMAND CHANGE!
STOP THE USE OF
RACIST TEAM MASCOTS
HERE AND EVERYWHERE!**

Contact parzival@vandevander.edu
www.stopsportsmascotracism.org

The other side of the leaflet featured an indignant essay in the same vein.

Ballou glowered. "Now, this pisses me off," he told Dora. "Excuse my French, but it does. People going around looking for reasons to be offended, so they'll have another excuse to mind other people's business. It just infuriates me."

Dora looked at him gravely. "You obviously have strong feelings about this."

"You know what? Willful ignorance offends me. Stupidity offends me." Ballou knew his eyes were getting that look in them again, but he couldn't or wouldn't stop himself. "If there were a real issue of racism here, I'd agree with these idiots. But there isn't. This is purely a manufactured issue that's been concocted by a few professional troublemakers and people who take a pathological enjoyment in being offended – and they often get their way, people like that, because they shout and threaten and whine louder than anybody else."

Ballou's voice rose, and his hands began to chop the air.

"And really," he continued, "all these people want to do is make sure that everyone lives they way they think they ought to live. And they want to suppress anything that doesn't suit their worldview, but mainly what they love is, they love disturbing other people. They love *starting* with other people. See, Dora, there are two kinds of people in the world. Some just want to be left alone, and some can't stand to leave you alone. That's what we're dealing with here, the latter type. Despicable people. Honest to God, I could kill them."

Ballou's eyes were blazing, and he knew it.

"My," said Dora.

"Maybe you agree with them?"

"Why, I don't know," said Dora. "I would hate to think that they were just taking this position out of a pathological urge, as you say, or because they were ignorant."

Ballou figured that this wasn't going anywhere good.

"After the game I'll explain to you why they've got no case at all, if you're still interested. I don't want to work myself into a frenzy yet – which I will do, I warn you."

"Oh, Roger, you're very scary when you get angry. I just don't know what to think! I've never seen you so emotional before!"

"Don't worry," said Ballou. "I don't actually get homicidal except on nights of a full moon."

The Cornell band now began to play its slow, stately *alma mater*, and Ballou, grateful for the distraction, sang along:

> Far above Cayuga's waters
> There's an awful smell
> Some say it's Cayuga's waters
> I say it's Cornell!

Dora laughed, and Ballou felt relieved — he'd got out of a pickle for the moment — and then felt worried again, for now he didn't know whether Dora was too afraid of him to ever feel an attraction, or whether perhaps she'd found his intensity titillating. The former, he supposed. Ending its song, the Cornell band snapped to attention, and with the drums tapping out the time they marched toward the stadium, walking with an odd rolling gait.

Dora and Ballou followed. Behind them, Ballou could hear someone — whether a man or woman he couldn't tell — singing "We Shall Overcome."

He looked over his shoulder and saw that it was Charlotte Fanshaw's daughter, singing in a tenor voice, a big voice.

"Damn," Ballou said to Dora. "She's got some talent. Wish she'd put it to better use. Now, I promised you a pennant. In fact we'd better buy a bunch of them, before those goddam agitators manage to get them outlawed."

Tables of food and merchandise stood next to each of the stadium's entranceways, and Ballou bought himself and Dora each a Van Devander pennant and a Van Devander sweatshirt.

"One extra-large, and... Dora, you're what, an XL or a 2XL?"

The sweatshirts, like the pennants, bore Willie Wilden's menacing portrait. Ballou bought a program, too, and an enormous chrysanthemum for Dora. "Want a hot dog or anything?" he asked.

"Oh, I love hot dogs!" Dora replied, and Ballou wished that he could stop himself from reading suggestions into anything anyone ever said. He got four of them, and two large Cokes. Loaded with merchandise, walking carefully, they proceeded.

They had armchair seats, on the aisle, not too far up. The Cornell marching band had taken the field, playing the theme song from *The Prisoner*. The Van Devander cheerleaders – and, yes, Kelly Curley was one of them – executed tumbling stunts in front of the stands. The crowd broke into a low cheer, as the two teams of football players streamed out of a passageway under the stands and toward their respective benches: the Big Red in red pants and helmets and white jerseys; the Wildens in orange pants with a purple stripe, purple jerseys with orange trim and white numbers, and purple helmets with an orange V on the side.

"I've got two students participating," Ballou remarked to Dora. "See the third cheerleader from the right? The one with the curly hair? She's one of my poetry students. And number 73, there, I have to deal with him twice a day, in both my classes."

"Tim Dance," said Dora, checking the program. "Tackle, history major – and a poet! That's an interesting combination. Are they good students?"

"Too soon to tell, but they both seem okay. You know what was great, though? Both of them showed up for class yesterday dressed up. Miss Curley had her cheerleader's uniform on, and Mr. Dance had a jacket and tie, just like kids used to do in high school, before a basketball or a football game: the athletes and the cheerleaders would dress up, remember? To remind everyone to come to the game. I never saw that in a college before, though, until yesterday. I thought that was way cool. But I guess it would be considered too corny in most places. And I'll bet it's just the kind of thing that would outrage our president."

The Cornell band marched off the field, playing the "*Internationale.*"

A tattoo of snare drums, and a low whine of air escaping from the drones, and the Van Devander pipe-and-drum corps – about 15 musicians in all – marched onto the field, striking up *"Cabar Feidh."* They wore the standard short black kilt jackets, hair sporrans, shoulder plaids, and kilts.

The band segued into "Scotland the Brave," "Wings," and "Mairi's Wedding." Ballou scanned the stadium to see whether he recognized anyone else. Michael Brooke, a lone male amongst a small clutch of black girls, sat in the student seats down front. Tonia Kampling sat with this crowd too – so white, by contrast to the other girls, that she looked almost spectral. She sat on Brooke's left, talking animatedly and occasionally plucking at his sleeve. The black girl on Brooke's right glared at her in annoyance, and Ballou sensed that Brooke, too, was uncomfortable with Miss Kampling's attentions. He nodded to her from time to time, then smiled apologetically at the girl on his right, who was certainly the prettier.

In another part of the student section, Ballou spotted Lee Grossbaum, wearing a shocking-pink angora sweater that set off her black hair and light skin perfectly. She sat with a blond boy who seemed very attentive to her, and Ballou felt jealous – even with Dora sitting next to him. Miss Grossbaum looked around, caught sight of Ballou, and smiled and waved in a rapid, window-wiping gesture. It was so in keeping with her sweater, that way of waving – so heartbreakingly girlish, so redolent of stuffed toys and gum-wrapper chains – that Ballou felt a little swelling in his breast. He waved back – making a difficult but instantaneous choice between letting Dora see that he was noticing another girl, or snubbing Miss Grossbaum. The boyfriend seemed to send him a flash of hostility, and put his arm round Miss Grossbaum's shoulders as they both turned back to the field.

"Is that another one of your students?" Dora asked. "She's beautiful."

The starting lineups were introduced, a trio of pipers played the National Anthem – as he stood and faced the flag, Ballou saw that a Wildens banner flew to the left of Old Glory, just like at Runs' used-car lot – and the two kickoff squads formed up, Cornell to receive. The fans had sat back down, but now a stooped old man near Ballou, dressed almost entirely in Van Devander-logoed apparel – jacket, sweatshirt, cap, sunglasses – hollered, "Everybody up! Everybody up for the kickoff!" He motioned "get up" with both his arms. His tone sounded more indignant than enthusiastic.

Cornell returned the kick to its own 25-yard-line.

"Ladies and gentlemen," intoned the PA announcer, as the two teams huddled, "on behalf of Head Coach Rudy Grouwinkel and the rest of the Van Devander Wildens, we remind you that Schermerhorn Memorial Stadium is a smoke-free facility. We ask you to support the team in a positive manner. Any racist or sexist comments directed at players or officials will not be tolerated, and are grounds for removal from the stadium."

In less than five minutes, Cornell drove down the field for a touchdown.

"We might be lucky if it's only 56-0," Dora said. "They're so much bigger than we are. Their blockers are just pushing us all over the field."

Cornell's players were bigger, but erratic. They didn't score again for the rest of the quarter, and early in the second quarter the Wildens returned a punt to midfield and began driving. When they made first-and-10 on the Cornell 28, the Van Devander rooters in the stands began chanting, accompanied by the bass drum of the pipe band:

Oo-ga-cha-ga!
Oo-ga! Oo-ga!
Oo-ga-cha-ga!
Oo-ga! Oo-ga!

"Oh, dear, there they go with a display of racism!" said Ballou. "Isn't it shameful? How insensitive! How demeaning! How can they live with themselves? Why isn't something done about it?"

Dora smiled.

"But, seriously," Ballou went on, "look how much fun everyone's having, being Wildens! And I don't expect any of us will go out lynching Indians after the game, or denying them services. Okay, now I'll shut up."

"Oh, Roger, you're a funny fellow!"

Van Devander drove to the one-yard-line, scored on a rollout pass, and kicked the extra point to tie the score.

Cornell still couldn't move the ball. Another exchange of punts, then Van Devander intercepted a pass and returned it to the Cornell 20 with a minute left in the half.

Oo-ga-cha-ga!
Oo-ga! Oo-ga!
Oo-ga-cha-ga!
Oo-ga! Oo-ga!

But two foiled running plays and an incomplete pass later, the Wildens had to settle for a field goal. Still, they were up 10-7 at halftime.

"I doubt it'll hold up," Ballou commented as the two teams trotted off. "You're right, they're so much bigger than we are. They're bound to wear us down."

The Cornell band resumed the field and played another brief set, then the Van Devander pipes and drums prepared to take over.

The pipe-major, a wizened little man with white hair, strutted to the front of the formation.

"*Attain – SHAAAAA!*" he screamed. Drums rolled, drones buzzed, and the corps marched forward, playing "The Soldier's Return," and segueing into "Granny Duncan."

"That's the 'Crimean Long Reveille,'" Ballou told Dora. "It's a medley of seven tunes, played in exactly the same order, to commemorate an incident in the Crimean War, when a piper alerted his regiment to a surprise attack by the Russian army by playing whatever songs came into his head, just to wake everybody up."

"Why, Roger, you know everything! You have such a *huge* hippocampus!"

Ballou tried to think of a rejoinder, but decided it wouldn't work if he replied, "And that's not all I've got that's huge." Instead he replied, "I could be making it all up, you know."

The band struck up another tune. "I believe that one's called 'The Green Apple Quick-Step,'" Ballou remarked.

The game was exciting only because it was close. Clearly neither team was any good. Late in the third quarter Cornell put together a drive, and scored another touchdown a few minutes later, and with a quarter to play the Wildens trailed 14-10, and they looked tired. They got the ball twice, deep in their own territory, and never got it past their own 40. Cornell held the ball longer on its possessions, but couldn't score either. With three minutes left on the clock Van Devander punted again, and Cornell returned it almost to midfield. Two plays later, the Big Red made another first down, on the Van Devander 40 – with 2:10 to play.

"That's the ballgame," Ballou remarked. Well, we made 'em sweat a little, anyway. Could have been a lot worse."

"No, it's not over yet," Dora insisted. "We've got all three of our time-outs left."

"Yeah, but we'll have to use them on each of the next three plays. If they get one more first down, we won't be able to stop the clock."

Cornell picked up three yards on an off-tackle; Van Devander used a time-out. A plunge into the line gained another three yards for the Big Red; the Wildens called time again. Third and four, on the 34, with just under two minutes to play.

"We're sucking wind," Ballou commented as the teams huddled. "If they can't pick up four yards on the next play, I'll be very surprised."

"They don't even have to do that," said Dora. "If I weren't sure I could get the first down, I'd lose a few on the next play, to get a better angle for a punt. Then I'd coffin-corner it, and we'll be stuck inside our own 10-yard-line with no time-outs."

The two teams lined up, and it looked like a run. The Cornell fullback took a fake-handoff into the line – and the Cornell quarterback dropped back a couple of steps and passed into the flat.

"*Nooooo!*" Ballou cried. "He's a goddam idiot!"

A Van Devander linebacker darted in front of the intended receiver and picked off the ball as neatly as if he and the Cornell quarterback had rehearsed it. Ballou, Dora, and the rest of the crowd leapt to their feet, roaring in amazement, as the interceptor ran it back to the 40, the 50. He had one man to beat – but couldn't. He was hauled down at the Cornell 40.

"What a bunch of dummies!" Ballou screamed. "That's Cornell; they're supposed to be halfway bright! What possessed him to throw that thing?"

"Their coach probably called that play," said Dora. "What could the quarterback have done?"

"He could have blown it on purpose! He could have scrambled for 10 seconds and then let himself be sacked! That's what I'd have done! Stupid! Stupid, stupid, stupid! But what the hell, we'll take it!"

The Wildens, on first and 10, ran a "give," with the blockers faking one direction and the ballcarrier going the other, and it fooled Cornell completely: a 23-yard gain; first and 10 on the Cornell 17. With 1:36 left, Van Devander still had one time-out.

Oo-ga-cha-ga!
Oo-ga! Oo-ga!
Oo-ga-cha-ga!
Oo-ga! Oo-ga!

"Don't pass," said Ballou to himself. "Just don't pass."

An off-tackle slant gained nine yards, and Van Devander huddled quickly.

Oo-ga-cha-ga!
Oo-ga! Oo-ga!
Oo-ga-cha-ga!
Oo-ga! Oo-ga!

Van Devander lined up for the next play with three wide receivers and one set-back. "Oh, no," moaned Ballou. "Oh, don't worry," said Dora.

For once, the Wildens' undersized players had the advantage. They were quick, at least. All three wide-outs raced toward and past the goal line; each one juked his man out of position and stood wide-open as the ball looped into the air and came down big and soft and right into the arms of the man stationed in the back right-hand corner of the end zone.

Touchdown. Extra point. Van Devander 17, Cornell 14. One minute and 10 seconds left.

Cornell couldn't return the kickoff past its own 20. Two plays later an option pass was intercepted. The Wildens' quarterback took a knee on the next two plays, and ran the clock out.

Dora was laughing, hopping up and down. Down on the field, Kelly Curley and her colleagues turned cartwheels, and the pipers struck up "The Black Bear." The old man who'd ordered them to stand for the opening kickoff hollered, "Rose Bowl! This year it's the Rose Bowl!"

*

On their way back to the car, Ballou and Dora were almost trampled a couple of times by gangs of students who tore past them, shouting. Somebody brushed hard against Dora, and she stumbled; Ballou caught her arm before she could fall. When they got to the car, Dora leaned against it, her eyes closed.

"You okay?" Ballou asked.

"Just tired," she said. "I've been working too hard, as usual."

Ballou opened the passenger door for her, and she got in, sitting down as heavily as a 100-pound woman can, leaning back against the headrest. Ballou walked round to the driver's side, got in and started the engine.

"Roger, I'm not sure I'm going to be able to make the bridge tonight," Dora sighed. "I overbook myself, six days out of seven at least, and I never get enough sleep, and if I don't go home now and sleep for a few hours, I'm not going to be able to get up at 4:00 in the morning to take care of business. I'm sorry. You're just going to have to give everyone my regrets."

Ballou had been intending to suggest going someplace for tea, which would have kept them occupied until it was time to go to the Leahys' house for bridge, so his immediate reaction was a tremendous and sudden letdown – but in the next instant, he felt immensely flattered. Dora could have begged off the football game, after all, so that she could go to the bridge, instead of vice versa. The idea that Ballou's company might have been more valuable to Dora than an evening with the whole crowd was almost enough to make him not care that he was going to have to take her straight home, now. He got the car moving.

"You've always been like that, right?" he asked. "Kind of a workaholic, I mean. Ever since you were little, I'll bet."

"That's not a bad thing," Dora replied. "It just catches up with me sometimes." They rode in silence for a few seconds, then Dora gasped a little in recollection.

"My cake!" she exclaimed. "The one I made for the party tonight. Roger, I hate to ask you, but…"

"I can take it for you, sure," Ballou replied.

"It's a Gâteau St. Honoré. It's in my kitchen. You'll have to carry it very, very carefully; it's so fragile."

Ballou pulled the Cadillac into Dora's driveway. Between them, they got her cake into the Cadillac's front seat.

"And remember to put that chrysanthemum in some water before you turn in," Ballou reminded Dora, as he walked her back to her front door. Dora opened it and went inside; Ballou held the screen door open, uncertain as to whether he should follow her. She turned to face him.

"Thank you for a perfect day, you sweet man," she said, with a huge smile, and as she'd done the night they'd met, she offered Ballou her hand to shake.

Saturday Night

Ballou (bringing with him Dora's cake and his own curried chicken salad) found the Leahys' house with difficulty. He'd been told to take 9W north for about three miles, then turn right onto Old Sand Road – which was one of those poorly marked side roads, just about impossible to see after sunset, and it had long ago been paved, so it wasn't sandy at all, and Ballou ended up going right past and having to backtrack.

Old Sand Road, narrow and winding, led up a steep, wooded hill on which only a few houses had been built. The Leahys', which sat at the top of the hill, was surprisingly modest: a white, two-story building, smaller than the Quaggas' house, Ballou judged, and hard to see from the road because of several large pine trees in the front yard. It had a double-width driveway, and Ballou recognized the Hoos' Lexus already parked there, as well as Donald Quagga's Buick. Frank Leahy greeted him at the front door, looking grim.

"I'm afraid I've got some sad news," he told Ballou. "Frank O'Dell has died. Last night or this morning, probably the former. One of his neighbors found him."

"Oh, damn, Frank, I'm sorry. Should I…"

"No, come on in. Everyone's here anyway. There won't be any bridge, but we decided we'd let everyone come over and help us toast the old man."

"He went off easy, apparently," Leahy continued, as Ballou entered the foyer. "His next-door neighbor always phones him at some point during the day, just to be sure he's still there, and this time she called around two, and he didn't answer, so she waited a while and called him again, and still nothing, so she let herself into his house – they'd exchanged keys, see, so they could look out for each other – and she found him dead in the hallway outside his bedroom, as though he'd just keeled over his way to bed. He was dressed, so it must have happened shortly after I'd dropped him off last night."

They got both Ballou's and Dora's contributions into the kitchen without mishap. Lois Leahy, Frances Quagga, Effie Hoo, and another woman Ballou hadn't met sat around the kitchen table. Lois had evidently been weeping. She got to her feet and embraced Ballou, her eyes downcast in an expression of sorrow that Ballou sensed was not insincere, but perhaps somewhat studied. Effie and Frances likewise got up and kissed Ballou on the cheek, not speaking.

"Roger, I would like you to meet Carrie Plankton," said Lois, indicating the fourth woman. "She is a trustee at Van Devander, like Frank."

"Carrie is Van Devander's first alumna," added Leahy. "We didn't go co-ed until 1960, when she was Carrie Armbruster, so she heads the roll of infamy."

"I've heard about you," said Carrie Plankton, rising and shaking hands. "You're the one Faye Bannister calls the Missing Link." Ballou looked astonished, and he was: not at the information, but that Mrs. Plankton would tell him, and at the way she told him.

"You don't think that's funny?" Mrs. Plankton asked. "I think it's hilarious! She doesn't mean it badly; that's just her way. She thinks you're old-fashioned. You know how she is, always kidding."

"Oh… yes," Ballou agreed. "She's a caution."

"Roger, all the men are in the library," said Leahy, "and that's where most of the booze is. Come along, I'd like to show you a book that Frank O'Dell gave me when I finished college, that you'd get a kick out of."

Donald Quagga and Hugh Hoo were in the library; so was a balding, insignificant-looking man – he looked like Dick Van Patten, Ballou thought – whom Leahy introduced as Buford Plankton.

"We're chock full of educational bigwigs tonight," Leahy remarked to Ballou. "Buford, here, is the principal of Wildenkill-Verstanken High School."

"Good to meet you," said Mr. Plankton, very somber of face. "I'm sorry it has to be under these circumstances."

"Help yourself to whatever you like," said Leahy, indicating the liquor cabinet. He took down a large, slim book from one of the shelves and handed it to Ballou. "Here, Roger, take a look at this."

It was an old book, although well kept; the dust-jacket was only a bit brown and cracked along the edges. The front bore an early, primitive picture of Willie Wilden. It was called *The Tatler, 1773-1923: 150 Years of Van Devander Humor.*

"Look at the inscription, Roger."

Ballou opened to the fly-leaf, where a feminine hand had written:

> For my darling husband, on his graduation, You are my knight in shining armor!
> Ever upward! All my love, Kathie.

"That book was presented to Frank O'Dell by his wife, on his graduation with Van Devander's class of 1923," Leahy explained. "They'd got married when he came back from France, and she'd worked as a telephone operator, to support him through college. The *Tatler* is Van Devander's annual humor sheet. As old as the school itself. Some of the items in that book date back to before the Revolution."

Ballou leafed through it. The book contained cartoons, vignettes, paragraph-long jokes, comic verse – the standard college-humor stuff, some of it satirizing contemporaneous events, but most of it self-referential and thus incomprehensible to anyone not a dedicated historian of the college.

The items ran in chronological order; the pictures and the language showed a steady progression from Colonial times, to the early days of independence, to Napoleonic times, the Civil War, the Victorian era, and on up to the end of World War One and the beginning of the Roaring Twenties. The earliest items included wry references to cultural differences among Indians, whites, and blacks (who apparently were also admitted to the school from its earliest days), but these had practically disappeared by the early 19th century.

"That book," said Leahy, "has more history of the school than you'll find in any one volume. Frank O'Dell gave it to me when I graduated, and I'd like to hand it down to you, to commemorate your joining the faculty. If you'd like to have it."

"Are you sure you want to part with it? It's invaluable."

"I want to make sure it goes to someone who can appreciate it. Lois and I have no kids, and Frank's daughter Biddy has no connection with the school. So I'd like you to have it. Frank liked you a lot. He told me so after you met him the other day. Although he called you Robert. He said to me, 'Frank, that young man is exactly the kind we want at Van Devander.'"

Ballou looked skeptically at Leahy, and smiled on one side of his face. "If he said that, he was trusting his intuition way too much."

"He thought you were a keeper," Leahy replied. "So keep the book in good health – Robert – and be worthy of his prediction."

"Thank you." Ballou felt like he ought to make some little speech, but nothing occurred to him.

"That reminds me," said Quagga, "have you tracked down Biddy yet?"

"I called her apartment in Manhattan, and her maid said she's in Paris," Leahy replied. "She had an e-mail address, and phone, for the people Biddy was staying with, and I called over there and got the answering machine which was in French of course, which I don't speak but about two words of, so I left a message in English, and I sent an e-mail for her to call me – I didn't want to leave her a message that her Dad was dead, you know – so I guess she'll call me when she calls me. I hope she was about to come home anyway; this is a hell of a way to end a vacation. She always hated Wildenkill. Got out as fast as she could, came back as little as possible."

"Did she and Frank not see much of each other?" Quagga asked.

"Not a lot," said Leahy. "Biddy was conflicted about him, I'd say. And he was, too, about her. On the one hand he was certainly proud of her. Very, very proud of her. On the other I think he resented her. For not settling down and giving him grandchildren. By the same token, she may have resented him. Remember, her mother had to work, when she was growing up, until Frank O'Dell had passed the bar. The first few years of her life, Biddy spent more time with my family than with her own. She and I nearly grew up as brother and sister. And then she felt that Frank begrudged her her own career, in a way. I think that's a bum rap; sure, he had misgivings just as any man of his time and place would have had, but he certainly never held her back or discouraged her."

"Well, you were a good son," said Plankton.

"I tried to be. I don't mean Biddy wasn't a good daughter. She always did her duty by him. I was more what he wanted, though. I was happy to stay here in Wildenkill and build a nice little practice. And he adored Lois."

Leahy drained his highball.

"It's sad to see it all going away," he went on. "Lois and I, and Biddy, none of us have got long. Pretty soon nobody'll be left to remember the world we grew up in. But I guess every generation has had that complaint."

"I suppose it strikes more deeply when you don't have any children of your own," said Plankton.

"That was our choice," said Leahy. "And it wasn't easy. You know, in the 1940s, you just didn't hear of couples choosing not to have children. And it had never occurred to me, until I married Lois, that I might not have any. But the deciding factor was that we had a mixed marriage. If Lois were a white girl, I suppose we'd have had children. But mixed-race kids don't stand a chance. Nobody's going to care that they're half-white: they're always going to be a nigger or a Chinaman. They'll be outcasts to both their parents' families, and they'll grow up not knowing who the hell they are. So in my case, it was a matter of giving up children or giving up Lois. And I never regretted the choice I made."

Ballou made a point of not showing any reaction. But Plankton looked meaningfully at Hoo, who looked a little discomfited at being called on to comment

"Effie and I got married rather late in the day," said Hoo. "It wasn't an issue."

"Lucky bastard," said Leahy, winking at Hoo. "Anyway, you fellows all top up your drinks, and we'll have one for Frank O'Dell."

They all did as instructed, and Leahy held up his glass.

"Here's to a man who never screwed anyone, and died before he knew what hit him," he said. "I wish the same for all of us."

"Hear, hear," said Hoo.

"And now let's eat," said Leahy.

They trooped into the kitchen and filled up their plates while the four ladies looked censorious, as though they thought the men ought not to be eating at a time like this. But Effie eventually got up and served herself, too, and then Mrs. Plankton. Frances and Lois took only a very little of everything. They all moved to the dining room where the table was large enough for everyone to sit

down. The Coronation Chicken that Ballou had brought got strong
reviews, delivered in decorously muted voices.

"Say, where is Runs this evening?" Frances asked. "And where is
Dora? I never even noticed until just now!"

Ballou explained that Dora sent her regrets – and then he
realized that he too had clean forgotten about Runs. Again came
that awful sensation in his guts. Could Dora have been faking her
exhaustion after the game, so as to get rid of Ballou and have the
evening clear for a booty call? A ridiculous notion, and Ballou
knew it. But still, where was Runs?

"No doubt Runs invited Dora to the football, earlier this week,
and she had to tell him she'd already been asked," said Effie. "And
the poor lovelorn Indian brave couldn't bear to show up here
tonight, assumin' he'd see the two of ye as a courtin' couple right
before his face."

This was a new idea, and Ballou had to admit it wasn't impossible – or at any rate, not impossible that Runs had heard about his
and Dora's date one way or another, and that he'd reacted to the
news as Effie suggested. Ballou himself might have done the same
had the situation been reversed.

"Oh, of course, that must be it," said Frances with good-natured
sarcasm. "Somehow I can't see anything fazing Runs. Up to and
including a nuclear attack."

"He'd find a nuclear attack far less depressin', I daresay,"
Effie replied. "The strong, silent types pay a penalty for bein'
so."

"Effie, my love, you're weaving a fantasy," said Mr. Hoo. "Runs
is probably right when he insists that you're an Indian."

"Can ye blame me, when the reality is that he's probably just
got a bloody headache? Ye notice it doesn't occur to me that he
might have an engagement with anyone else."

"He's interested in cars, and bow-hunting, and gambling, and
that's about it," said Leahy. "I bet he had a hot date with a trans-

mission tonight – and then maybe a midnight rendezvous with a coon or a muskrat."

"You don't suppose he's in any trouble, do you?" asked Frances. "Francis X, you know him better than the rest of us."

"Highly unlikely," said Leahy. "He's kept his nose clean for 15 years now. He knows what's at stake."

"Our firm defended Runs in court once," Leahy explained to Ballou. "It's no secret. It was shortly after he came to this part of the country. He was living in an old VW bus and dealing meth-amphetamine out of it. The court appointed me to defend him. He could have gone away for a long time, but I plea-bargained my ass off. I'm not at liberty to give you all the details, but let's just say that with one thing and another, he didn't end up doing any time, although a few other people did.

"He got nine years suspended, and it was just lucky that there was an old gas station going for cheap in a bankruptcy sale. That's now Runs' used-car lot. I bought it for him and hired him to run it, so he'd have a job, to comply with the terms of his sentence, and over time he bought me out, and gradually added to the land, and built up his business. And he's worked hard. I give him credit. Not that he makes any fortune, but he employs people, and he turns a profit."

Leahy sighed a little, and laughed.

"Frank O'Dell was just about beside himself when I was appointed to that case." he went on. "From envy. He loved criminal law. It wasn't his specialty, and there was no money in it for him, but he used to jump at any criminal case.

"In any event, Runs is under obligation to me, and he knows it. If he ever decides to go back to that other life, he'll clear out of this town and do it someplace over on the other side of the Rockies. So as not to embarrass me. But he's not going to do that. Mind you, he's not going to be joining the Rotary Club anytime soon, either – although he could if he wanted to."

"He should," said Quagga. "His stories might make the luncheons halfway bearable, if anything could do that."

"This is why I have nothing but contempt for people who think drugs ought to be legalized," Plankton declared. "If he hadn't been caught, he'd still be dealing that garbage, if he hadn't gotten killed by now. But because he got caught he got the opportunity to turn his life around, and now he's a useful member of society."

"I'm not sure," said Ballou. "On the one hand I do agree with you that he probably would have kept on dealing drugs, but if his life got better it's because Frank was willing to give him a vigorous defense, and then helped him out – gambled on him – to an amazing degree. Most court-appointed attorneys would have given him nothing but the back of their hand, and he'd have got three-to-nine in Attica – if he was lucky – and by now he'd be a career convict. Frank, that's about it, right?"

"I probably took better care of him than some lawyers would have," Leahy conceded. "And I've always been a pretty good horse-trader. It's true, Buford. Runs would have gone to prison if anyone else in the district had been assigned to his case. As for what I did for him afterwards, I just had a hunch he was a good risk."

"Moreover," said Ballou to Plankton, "if you want to put street dealers out of business, what's the quickest way to do it? I say legalization. If you can get a fix at the Duane Reade on the corner just as easily as you'd buy a tube of toothpaste, the street dealer's finished. He won't be able to compete on price; he won't be able to guarantee his product. Why would anyone buy from him? And since drugs will then be cheaper, violent crime will go down, because nobody needs to mug or kill anyone for a fix."

"Maybe you haven't had much direct experience with drug-users," Plankton countered. "I have. I'm the principal of a high school. We've tried everything to keep drugs out of our kids' hands. We have a very strong anti-drug policy. We have mandatory testing for any student who wants to participate in extracurricular activities. Anyone caught with drugs in school is out, period, no exceptions. And despite all our efforts, I see way too many kids get into serious trouble – permanent trouble – on account of drugs. Crack, crank, cocaine, heroin, ecstasy, you name it."

"Wait, let me understand." Ballou looked perplexed. "You seem to be admitting that your policies aren't eliminating drug use, and maybe not even reducing it. So even if it doesn't work, you're going to make criminals of kids who might have smoked a little weed, make them take a piss-test when they sign up to play in the school orchestra – and maybe one day, somehow, this policy will suddenly become effective?"

Plankton turned his head slightly and gave a little exhale of annoyance. "And what kind of message would it send to our kids, if we acted like we didn't care?"

"That's not quite what I said," Ballou corrected him. "Care all you like. There's a difference between that, and treating every kid like a suspected criminal. Good God, what kind of a message are we sending them now?"

"Boys, boys," Lois remonstrated. "This is not the time or the place. We need to talk about something more cheerful. It is a sad enough time already."

Ballou and Plankton both shrugged, and each rolled his eyes at the stupidity of the other, and a grim silence reigned for a few seconds before Leahy announced that he was ready for dessert. "I want to try your girlfriend's cake," he said to Ballou.

As they ate, Ballou recounted the football game – and the demonstration that had preceded it. "Don, that gives me another idea for a column," he added.

"That'd work," said Quagga. "Who'd I get to rebut you, though? That's not Charlotte's subject. I suppose I could call her daughter. I could ask this Wandervogel, or maybe Dr. Bannister, and I'm sure one of them at least would be glad to take you on."

The party broke up earlier than it ordinarily would have done. Ballou gave Plankton a big forced grin as they shook hands, to suggest no hard feelings.

"Oh, Roger, I nearly forgot," said Frances. "We brought you back your plate, from last time. It's in the kitchen. And let me give you Dora's plates, too, so she won't have to wait to collect them." (Her smile turned conspiratorial as she added this last.)

As Ballou drove back down Old Sand Road, he reviewed the situation. He wanted to check on Dora, but that would be stalking. No, it would really only be stalking if anyone knew about it.

All he wanted to do was drive by Dora's house to look for a strange car parked nearby, or lights on in her house. But how would he know whether a certain car belonged on that street or not? And even if it didn't belong to one of her neighbors, mightn't it belong to someone visiting one of the other houses? And no conclusions could be drawn from her house being dark, if dark it turned out to be: It might mean she was asleep; it might mean she was out; it might mean she had a visitor and they were both in the dark.

Besides, how was Ballou going to drive down Valley Road to Dora's house, and not be noticed? His car wasn't inconspicuous. He could kill the lights as he turned onto Valley Road and go very slowly past Dora's house, but that'd attract even more attention, if anyone were out and about. Besides, since Dora lived on a dead end, he'd have to pull into her driveway and back out again, to get home: suicidally risky.

Take the car home, then walk to Dora's? He could still be spotted. And what would he be doing (a passerby might wonder), casing Dora's neighborhood at night?

What would be cool, Ballou thought, would be to creep through the woods at the back of Dora's house, to observe her house from a covert. That, he could probably do safely enough – but he still wouldn't learn anything conclusive about what was going on inside

Dora's house unless he were to get close enough to peep into the windows, which would be crazy.

Crazy and wrong, too: He supposed he ought to take that into account. Not to mention that if he made any kind of noise in the woods, Pegeen would be sure to raise holy hell, which would wake Dora up, which wouldn't do her any good – nor him, if she looked out the window to see what the fuss was about.

He could drive by Runs' lot. He knew Runs was a night worker. But if Runs weren't there he could be anyplace at all. And if he were there, did Ballou really want to drop in for a little visit and thus let Runs know that he wasn't with Dora? Fuck that, Ballou decided. If Runs really were eating his heart out about Dora – as Effie had suggested – then let him.

Monday, September 27

Ballou just managed to keep himself from e-mailing Dora on Sunday. At one point when the temptation had nearly overwhelmed him, he wrote a haiku, putting the scrap of paper in his shirt-pocket as a crackly reminder. The haiku read:

> Not if you want to
> Get into her panties, Sir.
> Wait a couple days.

So he waited until Monday afternoon to e-mail her that he had her plates, and could he bring them over that evening? He didn't get a response for a few hours, by which time he of course had worked himself into still more worries, mostly along the lines of "I must have done something to gross her out and now she's so revolted that she won't even respond, or speak to me again. What could it have been, though?" But he stayed at his desk in the Liberal Arts building, marking papers and researching a couple of freelance articles, until about six, when her response finally popped up.

DORA: Very busy all week. Would it work if I came by your place this evening just to pick them up? Won't be able to stay at all I'm afraid. Around 7 or 730?

BALLOU: You could but I hate to make you shlep. Want me to deliver them?

DORA: Would work better if I picked them up. Hope that's OK.

Thus, perplexed, Ballou sat waiting on his porch swing that evening. He'd left the plates inside, figuring that if he kept Dora outside on the porch she'd wonder how many bodies he was hiding.

Dora had on a plain grey wool skirt and a mauve blouse, buttoned up to the collar, and a blue paisley silk scarf worn under her collar bolo-style, fastened with a gold slide. She had Pegeen on a leash, and a large plastic storage tub under her other arm.

"Hey, good-lookin'," Ballou called as she neared the porch. "Not you, Dr. Fox; I was addressing Miss Pegeen. But I'm pleased to see you, too." He squatted down and hugged Pegeen.

"You two make a perfect couple," said Dora. "Roger, I brought you something. We had a baby shower to cater today, and I kept back a few sandwiches and that was my dinner a few minutes ago – and this can be yours, too, if you haven't eaten yet. I put in some deviled eggs, and some chicken and ham salad sandwiches, and there's various cakes and cookies, too."

Pegeen began sniffing at the tub.

"No, dear, this isn't for you," said Dora, handing the tub to Ballou as he stood up.

"My God, thank you," Ballou exclaimed. "Feels like a week's rations, at least."

"Well, I know you eat like a man."

"Yes, there's this big fat guy, just itching to get inside my body. And you're not helping to keep him out. This is great!" Ballou opened the door. "Come in, Pegeen, and bring your human."

"Believe it or not, these are all clean," he told Dora, indicating the plates stacked on his coffee table. "Neither Frances nor Lois bothered to wash them – you know what a couple of slobs they are – but I did!"

"I'm kidding," he added, for Dora looked at him as though she assumed he meant it. "What are you drinking? Will you have a martini with me, or a glass of sherry, or beer, soda, tea, anything?" Ballou was barely able to get this sentence out without stumbling or spitting. He felt far more nervous than he'd felt at the football game.

"Oh, Roger, I wish I could. I can't stay. I've got all this reading to do – I swear, I've been studying medicine twice as hard since I cut back my practice – but maybe you'd like to come walk with us for a little while?"

That, Ballou judged, was better than nothing. He excused himself to put the tub of food in his fridge, and just as he entered the kitchen, a Black Demon appeared, hovering in the air about his head.

"Hey, you know what?" the lone demon demanded of Ballou. "She's probably looking around your living room making a big long-ass list of all the different ways your house sucks. You didn't know you'd be committing suicide, letting her see this place?"

"Roger, I should introduce you to my neighbor, Mrs. Ellerkamp," Dora suggested, as Ballou returned from the kitchen. "She cleans houses in my neighborhood, and I've heard she's absolutely scrupulous. And very reasonable."

"See?" the Demon whispered. "Toldja! How grossed-out is she now, eh, Rog?"

Ballou forced himself to smile at Dora. "I'm a bachelor; what can I tell you?" he replied to her. He picked up Dora's plates and tucked them under his arm. "Lead on."

They walked more or less in the direction of Dora's house, but roundabout, taking detours here and there. Ballou told Dora about the abortive bridge party and about Frank O'Dell, whom she'd never met.

"And of course people asked after you," he added. "And Runs was absent too. He wasn't serenading you outside your window that night, was he?"

"If he was, he wasn't singing loudly enough," Dora replied.

"He's in love with you and you're not giving him enough encouragement. You're breaking the poor guy's heart."

The Black Demon, flying slowly alongside at Ballou's shoulder, snickered.

"Oh, Roger, don't be silly! I know Runs likes me, but I don't believe he thinks of me *that* way. He really is such a sweet man, and he's a wonderful friend. And he's actually a very good date. A perfect gentleman. He took me mushrooming with him, once, right after he'd sold me my car. We went into the woods and picked, oh, just pounds and pounds of morels. I still have a lot of them in my basement; I'll have to bring you some. And he took me to an Indian casino once, which isn't really the kind of thing I like to do, but it was interesting. And we bowled that day, too. We were both so bad!"

They walked in silence for a minute or so.

"Were you ever married, Roger?"

Ballou almost dropped the plates. Did Dora want to know because she was interested in him "*that* way," or was she just curious? And how to answer it without revealing the fact that nobody had ever wanted him?

"No, not even close."

"Why not? I'd think you'd have legions of women beating down your door."

"Maybe one or two have knocked. But never all that hard. Of course, I've known one or two girls I thought I would like to marry, but they weren't the ones who did the knocking."

Ballou heard wings flapping impatiently behind him. "Yeah-boy," said the Demon. "'I don't want to ruin our friendship,' or 'I'm just not ready for a relationship right now.' That's what they all told you, right? Tell her about that. That'll get her nice and hot!"

"I daresay you were married, at some point," said Ballou.

"Yes." Dora made a serious-sad little *moue*. "To my college sweetheart. We dated all through college, and got married when we were both in medical school, and eventually we set up a practice together."

Ballou had to absorb the blow, although he knew intellectually that it could not possibly have been otherwise: She *had* loved someone else enough to marry him, and probably enough to do all kinds of kinky shit in bed besides.

"And I gather it lasted quite a while?"

"A long time. But, well, he decided he wanted... other things out of life."

Ballou just stared at Dora, stumped.

"Must not have been easy for you," he said at last.

"No, it wasn't. Especially since we had a joint practice. There was a bit of acrimony. And I wasn't quite myself for a little while."

"Oh, I'm sorry." Ballou was about to reach over and put a hand on Dora's shoulder, but it would have been clumsy and contrived. He was not a toucher by nature; he knew he would be doing it only because he'd read somewhere that it was the thing to do – the "casual touch," according to the manual – so he kept his hands to himself.

"And that brought you up here?" Ballou asked.

"Among other things. I told myself that I had an opportunity to try something else – so I took it. And now I had better head home and get back to work – and I've made you carry my plates all this way for me, too, haven't I? Here, let me take them."

"Certainly not," said Ballou. "Not while people can see us."

They reached the top of Valley Road, less than 100 yards from Dora's house. Ballou searched his mind desperately as they strolled downhill.

"Listen," Ballou said as they went up Dora's front walk and mounted her stoop, "do you like to ride? I found a stable not too far off, just a couple of miles south of Catskill, on 9W, and they have trail-rides, and I haven't been on a horse in years, and I thought it might be fun to go there this weekend. Like maybe Sunday afternoon, after you've delivered all your stuff to the Tea Garden. We could get brunch, and then go for a ride. Would you like that?"

"Oh, Roger, I can't, this weekend. I'm going to be completely booked. And then next weekend I've got company coming up from the city. But that sounds like such fun! Maybe another time. You'll have to go, though, and bring me a report."

This was the killing blow: sudden and final. "Company coming up from the city" could mean only one thing: boyfriend. Intellectually, of course, Ballou knew it could mean something else, but realistically he knew it could not. Or perhaps he preferred to believe it could mean nothing else, the better to torment himself. Whatever his mental processes, he felt himself going physically weak, felt the ghastly weight of hopelessness plummeting into his belly.

Ballou wanted to reach out and touch Dora's face, draw her to him and kiss her, one soft kiss of defeat, of surrender, of desperate regret: a kiss that once bestowed, could never be repeated.

Exactly. The price of such a violin-playing gesture would be the immediate death of any hope he might have left. To that vestige of hope, Ballou decided in an instant, he would cling. Instead of reaching for Dora, he brought his right hand to his heart in an exaltedly heroic style.

"Upon mine honor," he said, stammering slightly, "I shall gallop my steed up hill and down dale, and tell you all about it over the bridge table."

Dora laughed, and Ballou decided not to prolong the interview. He gave Pegeen another skritch, and was about to bend down and get a kiss from her, but then he remembered that that would probably preclude any chance of kissing Dora, if by some miracle she were to let him know that she wanted him to.

But petting Pegeen had brought him a step closer to Dora, almost touching her. Ballou inhaled deeply.

"Mmm, that's nice," he said. "Your perfume." He straightened up very slowly, keeping his face just inches from her hair and inhaling again.

"Why, thank you," said Dora.

"No, thank *you*. All that food. You rock!" Ballou saw the opening and almost without thinking to do it he put his right arm round Dora's shoulders and drew her close. He deliberately let his face go past Dora's to make it clear he wasn't going to try to kiss her, and under that implicit condition Dora returned the one-armed embrace, although very lightly, and Ballou could not get his other arm around her because of the plates.

He had a sudden and horrible idea of what he might do: He would step back, and with comic deliberation say, "Excuse me," set the plates down next to Pegeen, straighten up, say, "Now then, where were we?" and go in for a proper two-armed hug – and Dora would shrink back from him, arms out to push him away, whispering, "Roger, no!"

Of course it never happened; he never did get the chance to try it. Dora simply stepped back, smiling still, and took the plates from him. "Thank you again for carrying them," she said. "And for the company. E-mail me."

As Ballou walked back up Valley Road, the sound of flapping wings grew louder. A second Black Demon materialized, then a third, a fourth, and at last the whole complement had assembled, circling Ballou's head and chattering. Ballou walked faster and faster, but of course they kept pace with him all the way home.

"Why, why, *why* did you do that?" one of the Black Demons demanded.

"Oh, give the dumb bastard a break," said another. "He didn't do any harm."

"Oh, yeah? Now she knows he's into her, dipshit!"

"Like she didn't know that before?"

"Okay, but there are ways and ways! You play it *cool*, for Chrissakes, you don't jump on a girl like that. Hell, put a toad down her back, pull her pigtails, make fun of her, bust her balls! That's how you tell a girl you like her! If you want her to be interested."

"Hey, she hugged him back!"

"Oh, yeah, and she was sure enthusiastic about it – only, not. I was just surprised she didn't shove him off her! That's what usually happens."

"Oh, shit, yes!" cried a third demon. "Remember that girl in pre-school? God, that was rich! And then that time in second grade, when he passed that girl the 'I love you' note?"

"Ha! And remember that girl in high school? He tried to kiss *her*, too, remember? I wanted to curl up and die right then. It was never gonna get any better than that!"

"Yeah, hey, Swift Boy, why didn't you try to kiss this one?"

"Yeah, on the cheek anyway."

"Cheek schmeek! You kiss her right on the lips and nothing tentative about it! You kiss her like you *know* she's gonna kiss back! Otherwise she's gonna get skeeved and push you off. Which I'm really surprised she didn't do, this time. Maybe she had a little cold, so she wasn't so grossed-out by the smell."

"What the fuck, are you crazy? If he'd tried to kiss her at this point, that would have *mega*-blown it!"

"Oh, who gives a fuck? He's blown it anyway – like he ever had anything to blow. It's *so* academic! He never had a chance; are you kidding? With someone like her? He's got a face like a pig! And he'll make a hundred grand a year when horses talk!"

"Forget it. Her boyfriend's coming to town. And he'll be going to town. Hey, I wonder what she sounds like when he's got his big dick in her."

"Oh, c'mon, you can't be so sure it's a boyfriend."

"Bullshit! If it had been her parents, she'd have said, 'my parents.' Ditto with a sister or a brother. Even if it was, like, an old girlfriend, she'd have said, 'an old girlfriend.'"

"Yeah, and when she said, 'Maybe some other time,' man, that spoke volumes! If she'd been interested, she'd have suggested a time."

"Nah, chicks never do that."

"Never do that if they're not interested, that's true."

"What's with giving him all that food then?"

"Being polite. He took her to the game; she's gotta do something nice in return, because she's Little Miss Perfect. And now, they're all square and she doesn't owe him any social engagements or anything. Besides, it was that, or throw the shit out."

"What do you suppose the boyfriend's like?"

"Probably a doctor, like her, or something rich. Venture capitalist of some kind, maybe. Or some big-time lawyer. Got a nice big square jaw, too; I bet he's not working on a double chin like Roger. Probably real thin, too. Oh, and that reminds me. Hey, fatso! Go easy on those sandwiches! Don't eat 'em all at once!"

"Hey, he's not *that* fat."

"Oh, *there's* a compliment. Not *that* fat."

"Look, I'm telling you, she likes him! She's not gonna fuck him this week, but she *likes* him."

"Yeah, sure, she likes him the way she likes anyone who isn't a downright asshole to her. She's polite and gracious and friendly to everyone, just like her mother taught her to be. Doesn't mean she wants him touching her."

"Well, would you?"

At this point, Ballou heard the simian screeching in his ear, felt the claws scrabbling up his back and shoulders, the one bony hand gripping him by the hair, and the hard, steady slaps against the side of his head commenced.

Tuesday, September 28

Luke Bonney, Jr., a wiry 15-year-old, stood in the kitchen, wrestling with the top of a jar of homemade marinara sauce, trying to break the vacuum and open the jar without having the whole thing explode on him and getting tomatoes all over the kitchen. At the same time he kept his eye on a big pot of water – knowing that a watched pot never boils, but the thing was right in front of him on the stovetop so what else could he do: pretend it didn't exist? – and calculating how many sausages to fry.

Luke guessed there'd be seven for dinner. His sister Bonnie didn't eat meat, and she was making Matilda not eat meat although Matilda would if she could. Sometimes Mom ate meat and sometimes not – and he figured he'd better make enough for Martin Wandervogel and Zeke, too, since Martin was picking Mom up at the Albany County Airport, where she was arriving from a book-signing tour. Martin and his kid had shown up unexpectedly at dinnertime the week before last and everyone had had to go short. Martin ate the way you'd expect a fat guy to eat, and that kid of his didn't eat much but you had to put something on his plate.

Luke usually handled jars well, but this one was tough. He whacked the jar lid with the dull edge of a table knife and twisted again, and at last the lid gave way with a sigh and a *glop*. Luke poured the contents of the jar into a saucepan, and drummed the knife on the worktable, chanting, "Chka-pow, chka-pow, chka-chka-pow-pow!"

Bonnie came into the kitchen, made a face at the sausages, and stood at the sink, gazing out the window into the back yard.

"Yo, guess," said Luke.

"What?" she snapped in her deep voice, obviously in a world-hating mood.

"I told that guy Roger Ballou about what happened today. After I mowed his lawn this afternoon. And..."

"You *what?*"

"Calm down! He wants to help you out!"

"And how can he do that? And how could you tell *him* about *my* problem? How could you tell *him* about *any* of our family's problems?"

"Everybody's gonna know in a day or two anyway," Luke pro-tested, as they heard the front door opening and the voices of their mother and Martin Wandervogel, and the noisy feet of Wandervo-gel's younger son. "And he said he wants to write about it."

"What'll you do if Mom finds out you told him that?" Bonnie hissed. "He writes for the newspaper! If he writes about it..."

"If he writes about it, why is that bad?"

"Because he hates our mother, Luke, are you stupid?"

"Who hates me?" asked Charlotte Fanshaw brightly, as she entered the kitchen. "A new one? Or an old one?"

"Roger Ballou," said Bonnie with a sniff. "Luke mowed his lawn after school today."

"He saw my ad," Luke explained. "You know, the one I put up all over town? He called here on Sunday night, and he sounded all surprised when I said 'Fanshaw-Bonney residence,' and he said maybe he had the wrong number, he was looking for Luke Bonney, Jr., so I told him Fanshaw was your name and Bonney was us kids' name – so yeah, I mowed his lawn. He paid me."

"Oh, that's funny!" cried Charlotte.

"But guess! He's got Old Betsy!"

"No!"

"Yeah. He showed me his car and asked me if it used to belong to us, and yeah, it's fixed up a little but it's Old Betsy. He told me he bought her from that Runs guy."

"Oh, my gosh," Charlotte said softly, looking a little sad. "I guess I never thought of anyone else driving it. And him of all people. Well, okay. How was he? I mean what did he act like?"

At this point Wandervogel's little boy burst into the kitchen and collided with Charlotte's legs, bounced off her and began an odd dance, whirling about and lifting his knees high, singing, "Ba, ba, ba, ba, ba, ba." This went on for a few seconds before Charlotte went to the doorway and called into the living room, "Martin, could you please come and collect Zeke? Luke is trying to cook in here." It took some seconds before Wandervogel entered the kitchen, and meanwhile nobody knew how to quiet Zeke – and when Wandervogel did arrive, all 300 pounds of him, the room became almost too crowded for anyone to move.

"Sorry, Miss Skinny," Wandervogel said to Charlotte. He scooped the child up in his arms. "C'mon back into the living room, Zeke, and let these people make dinner."

"*Nooooooooooo!*" Zeke howled, kicking, as Wandervogel carried him out.

"Are Fatty and Stinky staying to dinner?" Luke asked.

"Luke!" Charlotte tsk'd. "Yes, they are."

"Don't call him Stinky," Bonnie added. "He's just a little boy."

"Yeah, and he stinks," said Luke. "If he'd pee in the toilet, first time every time, he wouldn't." Zeke's protests continued from the living room, only slightly muffled by the kitchen door, and in a few seconds Charlotte's youngest child, Abel, entered by that door, shaking his head.

"Can't hear myself think in there," he complained. He looked at the worktable next to the stovetop. "Hey, sausages. Cool!" Bonnie rolled her eyes.

"Mom," Bonnie said, "could we please go someplace quiet to talk? Something happened at school today. They took my part away from me."

"Let's go out back," Charlotte suggested, opening the back door and stepping onto the stoop. Valerie, the Irish setter that was dozing at the other end of the fenced-in back yard, woke up at the sound and ran over to them, wagging her tail, as Bonnie followed her mother into the yard.

Both Luke and Abel glanced intermittently out the back window as they prepared dinner. They worked silently for several minutes, Luke piercing the sausages and laying them in the hot frying pan, dumping the spaghetti into the boiling water, and stirring the simmering pot of marinara, while Abel poured supermarket-made coleslaw from its plastic container into a serving bowl, and grated the cheese.

"Did Mattie set the table?" Luke asked, turning the sausages.

"Somebody set it," Abel replied. "Mattie's up in her room; you want me to go ask her if it was her?"

"You want a sausage up your ass?"

"What, yours? You'd like that, wouldn't you, you homo. Say, look at Mom!"

They observed through the window that their mother had assumed what they called "the Mom's-Going-Bananas look." As she listened to Bonnie, Charlotte's lips pursed and her eyes narrowed, her brows puckered downwards, her jaw worked slowly, and her fists clenched.

"Man, you can almost see the smoke coming out her ears," said Abel.

"I hope she doesn't do anything weird," said Luke. "Garlic bread out of the oven, please?"

Luke drained the spaghetti into a colander in the kitchen sink and rapped on the window, motioning his mother and sister to come in and eat. Abel placed the garlic bread on a wooden cutting board, covered it with a tea-towel and took it to the dining room, then re-entered the kitchen and picked up the bowl of coleslaw.

"Summon Fatty and Stinky, Dead Dick-Eye," said Luke, "and inform Miss Matilda that the shit's on."

"Ar, Cap'n," said Abel.

Bonnie re-entered the house, her mother right behind her. "We need to move on this tonight, before anything else happens!" Charlotte was saying. "I'm going to call Frank Leahy right now. We need to have a suit filed, an injunction, whatever it is we need to get, before it goes any further."

"Mom, please don't do anything crazy," said Bonnie. "Don't embarrass us. Can't you just call Mr. Plankton and talk to him first?"

"Oh, I'm just sure he'd do whatever I asked him to," Charlotte scoffed. "We need to call the newspapers too. Tonight."

The argument stopped temporarily as Luke handed his mother the platter of fried sausages and Bonnie the bowl of sauce and the grated cheese to take into the dining room. He took the big bowl of spaghetti himself.

"Mom!" cried Matilda, entering the dining room from the other end. Charlotte set the sausages down on the table and she and her younger daughter embraced. "I've been upstairs, writing," Matilda said. "Been writing every day while you were gone. I'll let you see some of it pretty soon."

"That's fine, Mattie," said Charlotte. She noticed the table set for seven, with a booster chair at one place, and she smiled a little. "How did you know Martin and Zeke would be staying?"

"Love is in the air," Matilda replied.

"Oh, don't be silly."

Wandervogel entered the dining room with Zeke, who was sucking his thumb.

"You shouldn't let him do that," Charlotte told Wandervogel as they sat down. "Abel sucked his thumb and he ended up needing braces."

"Yeah, dude, and they hurt," Abel said to Zeke.

"He'll stop when he's ready," Wandervogel replied testily. "He's a very bright boy. He'll know when to stop."

"Yeah, he's a genius," Luke muttered to Bonnie.

"Shut up," Bonnie said. She defiantly took the chair next to Zeke, which was ordinarily Luke's place.

"Thank you," said Luke.

They passed the food around. When the platter of sausages came to Matilda, Bonnie shot her a meaningful look, and Matilda, gazing longingly after it, passed the platter to Luke without taking any. Luke helped himself, then stood up and reached across Bonnie and Zeke to hand the sausages to Wandervogel. "See, I won't even make you touch the plate," he told Bonnie. Abel, who had started eating, cut off a portion of his sausage, and when Bonnie wasn't looking he dropped it into the napkin on Matilda's lap, under the table. Matilda pretended she had to sneeze, brought the napkin to her face, and got the morsel into her mouth. A moment later, Luke made a similar donation.

The phone rang, in the kitchen, and Bonnie – who sat farther from the kitchen door than anyone else – jumped to her feet.

"It's dinner, Bonnie," Charlotte protested.

"I should get it," said Bonnie, squeezing past Luke's chair, then Matilda's. Matilda discreetly folded her napkin over the bit of meat that lay in it.

"In case it's Curtis," said Luke.

"I do *not* like *Curtis*, you *dork*," Bonnie roared. "I'm sorry, Martin," she added at once. "I didn't mean it like that. You know what I mean." Clear of the table, she darted into the kitchen.

"She'll be a while," Luke muttered to Matilda. "Want a sausage?"

"Not yet," Matilda whispered. "If she's gone more than a minute I will."

"Mom, what were you getting so worked up about a while ago?" Abel asked, before Luke could stop him.

"Aw, Abel, you know," said Luke. "We all know."

"Yeah," said Abel, "but I want to hear Mom tell it."

"Well, and Martin doesn't know," Charlotte said. "Okay, well, Martin, I told you that Bonnie got cast in the school musical, last week…"

"May I speak with Bonnie Bonney, please?"

"This is."

"Miss Bonney, this is Roger Ballou. We've met a couple times, you'll recall. I'm calling because your brother Luke mowed my lawn this afternoon, and we were talking after he'd finished and he told me about the incident involving your school play, and I thought this might make an interesting piece for *The Wildenkill Advertiser*. Is this a good time to talk? Am I interrupting your dinner?"

"No, it's okay," Bonnie replied. "I don't know if I want to talk to you about this, though. You and my mother don't exactly like each other, do you?"

"If there's a story here, I'll call you and read you your quotes, so you can be sure it's on the up and up," Ballou promised. "Fair enough? There might not even be a story. I still have to run it by my editor."

Bonnie thought for several seconds. "Okay." She sat down at the kitchen desk.

"Okay, so what happened? Luke told me, but I need to get it from you."

"Well. I was cast in the school musical. We're doing *H.M.S. Pinafore*."

"This is at Wildenkill-Verstanken Consolidated High School?"

"Yes."

"And you were cast when?"

"It was announced on Friday."

"Good. Go on."

"Well, I got the part of Ralph Rackstraw." Bonnie could hear Ballou's keyboard clicking as she talked. "Do you know *Pinafore?* Okay, so Ralph Rackstraw is the leading tenor part, right? And I have a tenor voice. Not an alto, a real tenor. I sing with the boys, in choir. So the drama coach, Mr. Menshevik, he cast me as Ralph Rackstraw, and I was, like, ecstatic, 'cause that's such a great part.

"And then I get to school on Monday, yesterday, and there are rumors around the school that some of the parents had been calling Mr. Plankton – that's our principal – and they were protesting having two girls... Well, you know, there's Josephine, the female lead, and my friend Miffany Quagga is playing her, and I'm the male lead... I guess some of the parents... you know...

"Anyway, then some of the kids started teasing me and Miff, you know, about being lesbians? And we're not! We're so not! She's got this really cool boyfriend and everything? And then they started telling us to kiss each other? And stuff like that? And Miff is like, laughing about it? Almost like it's kind of cool, you know? And I know it's not supposed to bother me, but it does, and...

"Anyway, this afternoon Mr. Menshevik talked to me and he told me that Mr. Plankton had told him to re-cast the play. He – Mr. Plankton – he said I should play Little Buttercup the Bumboat Woman, and this other boy should play Ralph. And I can't play Little Buttercup, because I've got totally the wrong voice for her!"

"Did Mr. Plankton say specifically why he was ordering this change?" Ballou asked. "Or did your teacher tell you why?"

"He said... Mr. Plankton felt that it would be 'sending a mixed message' if a girl played Ralph," Bonnie replied.

"Did he elaborate on what he meant by that?"

"I don't know. He didn't say it to me. That was just what Mr. Menshevik told me. He was, like, furious. He said he was going to quit. And he said he was going to go to all the newspapers about it. Did he call you?"

"No, he sure didn't. You know, the *Advertiser* is only a weekly. If he were going to the press, he'd probably start with the dailies, like the *Freeman*, and maybe the New York City and Albany papers. Do you have this guy's phone number? This Menshevik?"

"Hang on, let me look in the book," said Bonnie. "Are you going to interview him too?"

"Of course. Him, Mr. Plankton – I know Mr. Plankton a little, so I'm sure he'll tell me his side of it – and maybe you could give me the names of some of the other cast members? I can talk to your friend Miffany when I call her father to pitch this story to him. And of course I'll ask Mr. Plankton to give me the names of the parents who complained to him, if any actually did."

"Oh, they did," said Bonnie. "At least Mr. Menshevik told me that Mr. Plankton told him so. And a couple of people called Mr. Menshevik too."

"Then maybe I can talk to them. Now, have you decided what you're going to do about this? Have you talked it over with your parents?"

As Bonnie continued talking with Ballou, Charlotte related the same story in the next room, with considerably more heat.

"... so anyway, I'm going to call our lawyer, just as soon as we're done eating, and sue the school, and this principal, and anybody else we have to, to get their attention," Charlotte concluded. "I am *not* going to stand still for this."

"Nobody's asking you to, Skinny," said Wandervogel. "But I'd hate to see you spending your money on legal fees. You should find someone who'll file suit on your behalf. I've got some connections."

"You mean like the ACLU?"

"Maybe them, and maybe some other people," said Wandervo-gel. "Do me a favor and hold off for a day or two, and let me look into this."

"I don't want to hold off! I don't want to wait till the show is already in rehearsal and my daughter doesn't have the part that's rightfully hers!"

"Give me till tomorrow, anyway, Skinny, okay? I've got lots of ideas about how we can deal with this and save you some money besides. Matter of fact, I have a feeling I can turn this to your advantage financially, without your having to sue anyone."

"Martin, I'm not interested in making money from this!"

"No, of course not. Of course not. I see that. But still, let me look into a couple of things for you."

"Da!" cried Zeke. "Bafroom!"

"Yes, go," said Wandervogel.

"You come wif me," Zeke demanded. "Toidy monfterf."

"Isn't that something?" said Wandervogel to the table at large. "Zeke thinks there are monsters that live in the toilet, and if he flushes they'll wake up and grab him. So I have to come to the bathroom with him and stand guard. It's amazing, isn't it, how cre-ative he is? Come on, Zeke." He and Zeke left the table and headed down the hall to the john.

"Oh, so what?" Abel asked. "I thought there were monsters in the toilet when I was little, too, but I didn't have to have anyone hold my hand. I just ran out of there as fast as I could, once I'd flushed."

The phone rang again in the kitchen, and they could hear Bonnie answering it.

"Let's see," said Luke. "She just had a fight with Curtis, and hung up on him, and now he's calling back to apologize, I'll bet." Matilda giggled.

Charlotte Fanshaw's face squinched up into a theatrical mask of misery; her face reddened, tears coursed down her cheeks, and she emitted a horrible keening moan.

"Mom, what?" Luke asked.

"Oh, nothing, apparently," Charlotte sobbed. "Except that I've been out of town for ten whole days and nobody bothers to ask me anything about my trip, and what might have happened and..."

"Mom, we talked to you on the phone every night!" Matilda protested. "We're sorry. Tell us about it. We really want to hear. We bet lots of people came to hear you, right? Which bookstore did you like best? Really, Mom, we're sorry. We just got sidetracked with what happened to Bonnie."

Charlotte sniffed, and blew her nose.

"Better get started, Mom, before they get done in the bathroom," Luke advised. "Or Martin will want Zeke to dance for us again. So, like, what's the coolest thing you did in Chicago?"

"I should wait," Charlotte said, blowing her nose again, "until Bonnie is off the phone. Her food's getting cold."

"She can nuke it," said Luke. "I unfroze one of your pies for dessert, okay? And we've got ice cream too."

The front doorbell rang, and Matilda got up to answer it. "That'll be Emmeline," she said. She was back, bringing with her not just Emmeline Quagga but Miffany too, just as Wandervogel and Zeke returned from the bathroom.

"Hi, you two," said Charlotte Fanshaw to the Quagga girls. "You're just in time for dessert."

Unlike her blonde sister, Emmeline Quagga was dark-haired and pale, very slender, with large lustrous eyes that usually conveyed a deep, lyric sadness. "No, thank you, Charlotte," she whispered, mustering the faintest ghost of a smile. "Mattie and I are working on a short story together, and I can't write at all if I eat too much."

"That's strange how people are different," Charlotte replied. "I can't write at all if I'm hungry. I had an eating disorder for years, you know. When I was your age. You should be careful of that."

"Em never eats anything," said Miffany. "She wants to waste away romantically like the Brontës. Anyway, is Bonnie around? I just came over to cheer her up, if I can."

Luke, as he did when either of the Quagga sisters was visiting, began to show off, in this case drumming on the table with the forefingers of each hand, in an Afro rhythm, *bum*-ta-dum, *bum*-ta-dum. "Ma ko saaaaaaaa," he stage-whispered. He began to chant, "Ma-ma-ko-ma-ma-sa-ma-ko-ma-ko-sa, ma-ma-ko-ma-ma-sa-ma-ko-ma-ko-sa..."

Zeke, hearing the beat, shouted, "Da! I wanna danf!" Luke, horrified that his drumming may have given Zeke the idea, stopped at once, but it was too late: Zeke was off his chair and running in a tight circle, knees pumping high, as Bonnie burst back into the room, obviously excited.

"That was the Associated Press I was talking to!" she exclaimed to the room at large. "It was... not the first call, but then somebody called right after that and it was a reporter from the Associated Press and they were asking about this *Pinafore* thing! I guess Mr. Menshevik gave them our number." She noticed Miffany and Emmeline. "Oh, hey. What's going on?"

"The Associated Press?" Charlotte asked, her voice rising. "Bonnie, that's great, but we should work out a statement right now in case anybody else calls."

"*Mommmmm!*" Bonnie moaned. "I can handle it! Really!"

"I know you can," said Charlotte, "but we want it to be just right. I should call Frank Leahy to see if he has any advice. Maybe legally there are things you shouldn't say. Oh, but we don't want to tie up the phone, in case another reporter calls."

"Use my cell phone," said Miffany, handing it to Charlotte, who took the phone and headed into the kitchen, with Bonnie following her. Zeke was now attempting *pirouettes* and *jetés*, bumping into the walls.

"Bad enough he smells like pee," Luke whispered to Abel. "He's gonna grow up to be queer, too, only no guy'll want to get near him." Miffany shrieked. Luke hadn't intended for her to hear him, but his heart soared.

Wandervogel looked startled. "What? What?"

"Oh, nothing," said Miffany. "Your little boy's so cute, that's all."

From the kitchen, they could hear Charlotte's voice, getting louder and more strident as she apparently tangled with someone on the phone.

"What do you mean, you don't think we can sue?" she demanded. "We can get an injunction or whatever you call it, at least! We can make them give her back her part! *Don't tell me to calm down!*"

Bonnie re-entered the dining room, fleeing the kitchen, and pushed past everyone toward the other door, averting her face. They could hear her running upstairs. Matilda cringed. "C'mon, let's go up to my room," she said to the Quagga girls.

"Not I," said Miffany. "I wouldn't miss this if Leonardo DiCaprio was up there waiting for me naked."

"Then I'll call another lawyer!" Charlotte cried from the next room. "If you're going to sit still for this, I'm not. *What kind of a lawyer do you call yourself?* Don't you have any social conscience *at all?*"

She burst back into the dining room, handing the cell phone back to Miffany with such force that the girl almost shrank from it.

"*Ooo!*" Charlotte cried. "People make me *sick* sometimes!"

"I told you, Skinny, just wait until I've talked to some people," said Wandervogel. "You need to sleep on it anyway. You were getting hysterical in there."

Charlotte's face, already showing considerable anger, transformed in a fraction of a second. Wandervogel actually paled as he saw it shift into the image of some half-human feral creature: her teeth bared, her eyes dilated like those of a leopard attacking.

"Don't you dare dismiss my anger that way!" she hissed at Wandervogel. *"Don't you dare blame my womb for what I'm feeling!"*

Wandervogel shrank back in his chair, which squeaked under his weight. Luke and Abel glanced at each other, and would have laughed if only they hadn't been within their mother's sight. Miffany and Emmeline Quagga stared open-mouthed, Miffany appearing shocked but amused, Emmeline dismayed. Matilda clasped her hands across the back of her head, pressing her forearms against her ears. Little Zeke stopped dancing, and hid behind his father's chair.

"Wait, what?" Wandervogel asked. "I didn't say anything about... about your..."

"That's what 'hysterical' means!" Charlotte's voice rose again, and her face went crimson. "It comes from the Greek word for womb, and when you call a woman hysterical you're completely belittling her feelings and blaming them on her... her *monthlies*, or *whatever you might call it when a woman's not around!*" Behind Wandervogel's chair, Zeke began to sob.

"I will *not* allow that kind of talk in my house! I think you'd better leave."

Zeke let out a long, low howl that sounded like genuine terror. Charlotte gasped, and her facial expression softened at once. She went behind Wandervogel's chair and crouched down to Zeke.

"Oh, honey, I'm sorry. I'm sorry, Zeke. I didn't mean to scare you," she said. "You know I wouldn't hurt you." This seemed to mollify Zeke; at any rate he quieted.

"I guess we had better go," said Wandervogel, rising slowly from his chair and speaking very softly, as though he'd just been physically beaten up. "Come on, Zeke, we can get dessert at home."

"No!" Zeke snuffled. "Want devert."

"Oh, stay for dessert," said Charlotte, calmer of voice, but still glaring at Wandervogel. "I'm sorry, Martin. That word sets me off, though."

Wandervogel started to say "I can see that," but thought better of it and sat down without another word, looking at the table.

None of the girls wanted any dessert, and at length Matilda coaxed Miffany and Emmeline upstairs. Luke and Abel kept exchanging surreptitious grins as they ate, but they said very little. The two adults would not look at each other. Even Zeke was silent, and he left a lot on his plate, which Abel took charge of.

Wandervogel and his son got up to leave. Charlotte walked them through the living room to the front door, Luke and Abel trailing behind to see if anything else would happen.

"Thanks for dinner, Skinny," said Wandervogel to Charlotte.

("I cooked it, you fat fuck," Luke muttered to Abel, who blew snot out of his nose holding back the laugh.)

"Zeke, tell Charlotte thank you for dinner."

"Fank you."

"You're welcome, Zeke," said Charlotte.

"I'll call you tomorrow when I know who to contact about this... uh, Bonnie's play," said Wandervogel.

"Thank you," said Charlotte, in a frostier tone than she'd used to Zeke.

"Don't I get a thank you for picking you up at the airport?"

"Yes, of course, thank you for that, too." Charlotte made no move to embrace him or even shake hands. "We'll talk tomorrow."

Father and son walked through the front doorway, down the porch steps, and into the darkness, toward their SUV. Just before Charlotte closed the front door, Zeke's voice drifted back, quite clearly: "Da, you fucked up!"

Luke and Abel guffawed, and punched each other; Charlotte looked at them as though trying to decide how to react.

"It's no loss, Mom," cried Abel. "He'd have squished you in bed, like a bug."

Charlotte stared at her son for a moment, then gasped and emitted an unearthly screech of laughter, collapsing against a wall, slapping her thighs with both palms at once, tears rolling down her cheeks again.

Wednesday, September 29

"No, Miff, I'm sorry, but I told Ballou I just don't see it as a story for the *Advertiser*," Donald Quagga told his daughter. It was early in the evening of the following day, and he was sitting in his living room with his pipe and a pre-dinner bourbon. Miffany paced, sipping Coke, and she frowned, looking away from him. "I told him to lay off it and just finish that piece he was working on before, about the Wildens."

"Dad, this is because Mr. Plankton's a friend of yours, isn't it?" Miffany accused. "You don't have to be too hard on him – but I would if I were you! Go after those parents who complained! Can't you just hear the wind whistling through their earholes?"

"Miff, I'm not in the business of showing up my friends," Quagga replied. "Plankton's already mad at me because Ballou called him up on his own, this morning, and told him he was pitching the story to me. So Plankton called me, and I had to calm him down, and then Ballou and I hollered at each other over the phone for about 15 minutes. I like Ballou most of the time, but he's got a few things to learn about diplomacy and humility."

"He's also *right*."

"I agree with you about 99 percent. But the *Advertiser* is not taking a position on it. Period."

"Oh, fine," snapped Miffany. She glowered out the window for a few seconds, then continued, in a less angry tone. "But I don't get it. Are you telling me that if somebody's your friend, he can do whatever he wants and you're not going to criticize him?"

"I'm not saying that at all. But in this case, what good would it do? I did advise Plankton to reconsider. But I'm not going to use my paper to embarrass him in public. Especially not when my daughter is an interested party."

Miffany sighed in exasperation. "They gave Bonnie's part to Barty Ashen. He's the only other tenor who can sing at all, and he isn't very good. Not to mention he's shorter than Bonnie and he's only a junior and if you want to know the truth he's more of a girl than Bonnie will ever be!"

"Give him a chance," said Quagga. "That part will make a man out of anybody. Don't be too sure he'll get it, though. If Charlotte Fanshaw doesn't sue over this, I'm even dumber than you think I am."

"I couldn't help overhearing," said Frances Quagga, entering the living room from the kitchen. She had a glass of sherry in her hand. "Dear, you have to admit, Buford's making an ass of himself."

"Yes, he is, and I'm not going to call everyone's attention to it," Quagga replied.

"And it's not like girls haven't been playing boys' parts in high school plays for... I bet for centuries!" Miffany argued. "There are never enough boys. We've got five or six girls playing Able Sea-men, and nobody said anything about that! And Mr. Menshevik taught us that boys played all the girls' parts in Shakespeare's plays – when Shakespeare was alive."

Quagga chuckled. "Even if you could find enough boys to do an authentic Shakespearean production, I can just imagine how all the sniggering little Beavises and Butt-Heads in your school would react to it," he said. "That was probably on Plankton's mind too. I'll bet he was more worried about that, than about a few idiotic parents."

"Miff, honey, could you please help me in the kitchen with something?" Frances asked. She had gone slightly pale, and she knocked back the remainder of her sherry in one gulp, which brought the color back to her cheeks. Mr. Quagga, knowing that this was a pretext, looked after them with a sad and weary expression. He too took a big swallow of his drink, and tried to go back to the magazine he'd been reading before Miffany had entered the room.

"Honey, just watch that stew for a minute, and stir it now and then," said Frances, as she commenced washing a colander of lettuce in the kitchen sink. Her hands jerked suddenly, and she nearly upset the contents.

"Mom, are you okay?"

"Oh, it's just time for the big talk," said Frances, looking out the kitchen window, unable to make herself look at her daughter. "I know you and Greg have been... well, seeing each other for a while – and I don't want you to feel you have to tell me anything about it, not unless you want to. But he's the first boy you've seemed at all... serious about. So I made an appointment for you with Dr. Eisenbarth tomorrow after school, and he can talk with you about a prescription for... for whatever you need, if that's what you and he decide you need, and maybe fit you for a diaphragm too, for extra insurance."

Frances shuddered just a bit, and continued looking out the window. Miffany looked amazed, and made as if to say something, but no words came.

"It doesn't make any difference whether your Dad or I approve of it," Frances continued. "When it comes to that... sort of thing, you're going to do what you're going to do – or not, which I'd prefer, but there it is. I'm just asking you to... well, take precautions. If you and Greg aren't doing anything, that's great as far as I'm concerned, but I want you to be prepared, if, you know, if it ever... if it becomes an issue in the future. I can come with you tomorrow, or you can go on your own. But do please go."

Miffany still said nothing.

"I hope I'm not embarrassing you. But I had to say something. You see that, don't you?"

"Thank you," said Miffany. "We're not... Greg and I aren't... but thank you. Yeah, I'll go, if you want me to. But... could you come along? And just sit in the waiting room? That way if somebody sees me, they won't assume I'm... pregnant or whatever."

"That's exactly what I was thinking. I didn't want you putting on a black wig and going to Planned Parenthood, or anything. This way, we can pretend we're both going in for the usual ladystuff." She laughed, and looked at Miffany at last, but her hands were still trembling.

"Really, thanks," said Miffany. "I know you don't care for Greg..."

"Oh, no, dear, that's not true. He's... a little rough around the edges, I guess, but I don't mind him. He's just... well, he's a boy. But you know that. No, he's nice. But, you know, if you were having his baby, at this point in your life, I might have a different attitude."

"Don't worry," said Miffany, with just the least bit of an eye-roll. "That is *so* not going to happen."

"That's what they all say," replied Frances, tearing up the lettuce leaves and dropping the pieces into a salad bowl. "That's why we're having this talk. And listen, honey, I want you to promise me something. Once you have that... that stuff... *use it*. Okay? Keep the diaphragm in your purse."

"Mom!"

"Well, *do*. Girls get pregnant because they think, 'It doesn't matter just this once.' Or they have this idea that if they're carrying that stuff around with them, it means... well, that they're not nice girls. And that's very foolish."

"And that's another thing," Frances went on. "I hope you understand that your Dad and I *don't* think you're foolish. We both think you're very smart and grown-up and responsible. And we want you to stay that way."

"Well, thanks," said Miffany. She considered for a moment, watching as her mother sliced up a tomato with a huge Julia Child knife. "Why aren't you giving me the big talk about condoms, then?"

"Check the stew, dear. Because for one thing I'm sure you know more about... about... those things... than I do. I expect you get it drummed into your head at school all the time. If they're not testing you for drugs, they're telling you you'll die of AIDS if you don't use a... a condom. For another thing, I could preach to you until Kingdom Come, but I know perfectly well you're not going to use them all the time. Maybe you should, but you won't. Everybody hates them, and sooner or later you'll decide not to bother. Look, dear, I know you *know* all this stuff already. I'm trying to actually do something practical. Rather than preaching at you."

Mrs. Quagga mechanically picked up a cucumber, and took up the knife to slice it into rounds, then she saw what she was about to do, started, and put the cucumber down quickly.

"Oh, my God," she said. "Let's talk about something else, shall we?"

*

Fri Oct 8 1999 11:58 AM Eastern Daylight Time
FROM: rballou@vandevander.edu
TO: dquagga@wildenkilladvertiser.com

Settlement Seen In High School Suit
By Roger Ballou, contributing editor

Sources close to the case say that the lawsuit recently filed by several parents of students at Wildenkill-Verstanken Consolidated High School against the Wildenkill-Verstanken School District, high school principal Buford Plankton, and each member of the Wildenkill-

Verstanken Board of Education, may be headed for a quick settlement.

Counsel for both sides told *The Wildenkill Advertiser* at press time that according to the terms of the proposed settlement, the defendants will admit no wrongdoing, but have agreed to institute a diversity training program at the high school, provided by a consulting firm, Modern Diversity Systems. In addition, the upcoming high school production of *H.M.S. Pinafore* will, as originally planned, feature student Bonnie Bonney in the leading tenor role of Ralph Rackstraw.

The suit was filed Wednesday in the Supreme Court of Bumppo County on behalf of several Wildenkill-Verstanken students who claimed that their civil rights had been violated and a hostile climate created when principal Plankton ordered a re-casting of *Pinafore*, substituting a boy for Miss Bonney and assigning Miss Bonney to a soprano part.

"We believe that this was the best outcome we could expect," said Hugh Hoo, attorney for the school district. "The school was looking – as any responsible school would – for a solution that would satisfy all parties, and we feel that we found one."

"We were never after the school district's money," commented James Dolciani, founding partner of New York City-based Dolciani, Wootton, Beckenbock & Chinn, which represents the plaintiffs. "We were after justice, and a settlement that would prevent another such regrettable incident from occurring. Both sides agreed on that. Once we established that common ground, with good will on both sides, we reached an easy settlement."

"I'm delighted that my daughter has her part back," said co-plaintiff Charlotte Fanshaw, mother of Miss Bonney. "That's all I choose to say."

"Of course I'm glad I got my part back," said Miss Bonney, "and I'm so glad they included diversity training in the settlement. I think our whole society needs it."

"I'm interested to see what the training will consist of," principal Plankton told the *Advertiser.* "I'm sure it will work out for the best."

"I'm a little tiny bit disappointed," admitted Bartholomew Ashen, the Wildenkill-Verstanken student who had been tentatively cast as Ralph Rackstraw. "But I hated to get the part that way, and Bonnie is such a wonderful singer, so I'm happy for her and I know she'll do a great job. Break a leg, Bonnie!"

Fri Oct 8 1999 12:18 PM Eastern Daylight Time
FROM: dquagga@wildenkilladvertiser.com
TO: rballou@vandevander.edu

Thanks for the fast turnaround, Roger. It's a sensitive matter, as you know. I didn't want to run a full investigative piece such as you originally proposed, but as long as we have the chance to scoop the *Freeman* re the settlement (which no doubt they'll report next week), we might as well run with this. I congratulate you on getting everyone to talk – especially Charlotte and Buford. As you've written it, I don't see how they'll have any bones to pick with you, or me. And good for you, calling that Ashen boy. Anyway that's that. Frances and I are off to the City for one of our theater weekends. If you're wise you'll get out of Dodge too: It's peak foliage season, so it'll be nothing but tourists this weekend and next.

Saturday, October 9

Old Mrs. Ellerkamp from across the street had let herself into Dora's house at nine, on Saturday morning, changed the bed-linen, mopped, dusted, swept, and straightened a house that didn't need any work done to it as far as she could see, but she went beyond what she supposed Dora expected of her, polishing the piano and the other furniture, carefully wiping each of the perfume bottles in Dora's bedroom, taking care to leave every item on every flat surface exactly where it had lain before she'd picked it up to clean it. Dora, arriving home from the bakery at noon, praised her effusively.

"It was nothing," said Mrs. Ellerkamp, in her slight German accent, as Dora paid her. "I don't know why you wanted me to come in here. You have it already so perfect."

"Oh, but I've heard such good things about you," Dora replied. "And ordinarily I clean house myself, but there just isn't the time this week. I might not be able to use you very often, but..."

"Every bit helps," said Mrs. Ellerkamp. "I like to make a little extra now, to save up for Christmas. You are having company today? Boyfriend?"

Dora blushed.

"Oh, I am sorry, I did not say that."

An electronic version of *"Für Elise"* twittered, and Dora scrabbled in her purse for her cell phone.

"Hey, little angel."

"Daddy! Hi!"

("I will let myself out," whispered Mrs. Ellerkamp, moving toward the front door. Dora gave her a big smile and a little wave, and mouthed, "Thank you!" as she left.)

"How's everything? You at that bakery of yours?"

"No, I just got home. Just a couple of small parties this afternoon, and I'm letting my staff take care of them."

"And then you're up at four tomorrow morning to start all over again, right? Honey, you might as well be in the Army!"

"Yes, isn't it awful? But I'm loving it. I really am. And this is just the nicest town. The foliage is supposed to hit its peak in just three or four days, and I can hardly wait!"

"Yeah, but then winter comes. And that's one thing Mommy and I don't have to worry about in Guadalajara, thank God. What brings you home so early today? Don't tell me. He's coming up for a visit, right? How are you two getting along now?"

"Oh, Daddy, I don't know." Dora walked around her living room, re-inspecting Mrs. Ellerkamp's work. "I haven't seen him since I left the city, you know. But, we've been in touch, of course, and he seems to still be very much in love with poor little me."

"And you with him? Not so much, I guess, right?"

"Oh, what can I tell you? I guess I wouldn't have moved up here if I really loved him. That's what I keep telling myself. He's just the sweetest thing, and he's so dear to me, but I need my space — for now anyway. You know, he's... he has so many really wonderful qualities, but he can be so... manipulative. Or he tries to be. It's mixed up. I just... I don't know if I love him. And I should know, I guess, at my age. I do admire him, so much, and I can't deny I'm flattered by how highly he thinks of me."

"Well, honey, you've got to follow your heart. And if your heart isn't leading in his direction, don't force it to go that way. But it does sound like you could do a lot worse than this fellow. He worships you – at least to hear you tell it – and that'd be an improvement over the last one, anyway."

Dora checked the kitchen, then went down the hall and inspected the bathroom.

"Daddy, please. I'm sure Jesse did worship me, once. And I'm sure he still does in his way."

"Do you hear from that jerk, lately?"

"Why, Cuhnul, suh, how you talk!" said Dora in a burlesque Southern accent.

"I can't help it. I doubt I'll ever get over how that boy did you. God damn it, if there's one girl who should be everything any fellow could want, it should be you!"

"Well, that just goes to show you. The heart has its reasons, of which reason knows nothing." Dora, now in the bedroom, stepped out of her high heels, mounted the step next to her bed, and lay crosswise on the coverlet, stretching and gazing up at the ceiling as she talked. "Yes, I did. Last month. Apparently they're pregnant.'"

"Ech. I'm sorry I brought it up. We should change the subject before I tell you how I really feel. Anyway, I know you want to get ready for your guest. You want to talk to Mommy for a minute?"

*

Late that afternoon, around 6:00, Roger Ballou drove toward the Motel 6 on the outskirts of Faber, Pennsylvania, about 175 miles southwest of Wildenkill. He'd decided, earlier in the week, to drive out to Faber College on Saturday to see the Wildens play their next football game, against the Faber Mongols, and to stay overnight and do some drinking, so he wouldn't be tempted to go snooping around Dora. Besides, he wanted to give the Cadillac a run.

Much to Ballou's surprise – and to the surprise of a few dozen Van Devander students with whom he'd sat, in the visitors' cheering section – the Wildens had outdone themselves again that afternoon, against an excruciatingly inept Faber team. They'd won, 38-6, and should have scored several more times at that. Ballou's student Lee Grossbaum and her boyfriend – Stan Something-or-other – were among those who'd made the trip, and Stan had apparently gotten over his jealousy enough to chat with Ballou during the game.

"I got some buds here," he'd told Ballou, as the game wound down. "My cousin's at Delta Tau Chi. We're gonna go bend a few later. Want to come with?"

Ballou had agreed to catch up with them that evening, and so, after the game, he headed to the motel for a brief lie-down and a shower before meeting the crowd at one of the student bars later on. He supposed he'd better prepare for a long night.

As he'd been almost certain would happen, the chubby blonde teenaged girl at the motel check-in desk smiled cheerily and said, "Okay, Mr. Ballou, yes, here's your reservation, and we've got you in a non-smoking room, just like you asked for!"

Ballou leaned on the desk and theatrically held his head in his hands.

"No, dear lady," he moaned. "I reserved a smoking room. Smoking, smoking, smoking. I made that crystal-clear when I called the other day. I eat cigarette sandwiches for breakfast, understand?"

"No problem! I'll just change that forya!"

"That's a relief," said Ballou. "I figured you'd tell me that was the last available room, and I'd be out of luck. What with it being a football weekend and all."

"No, we don't usually get filled up on football weekends. The Holiday Inn does, downtown, and all the bed-and-breakfasts do, but we're kind of the last resort."

"No pun intended, I hope," said Ballou. The girl looked blank. "I'm surprised," he went on. "I like Motel 6s. And I hate bed-and-breakfasts. Give me a place where you can get wasted in your room if you want to, and watch whatever you want on the tube, and wander out to the ice machine in your underwear. That's my speed."

"Well, that's whatcha got," said the girl. "Oh, no, wait. I'm afraid we don't have any smoking rooms open, after all."

Ballou's eyes dilated, and he inhaled sharply.

"Oh, no problem," the girl said again. "I'll keep you in your non-smoking room and you go ahead and smoke, and nobody'll notice since the door's on the outside. Here's an ashtray." She handed him one, and a card-key.

"You're a doll," said Ballou. "Grow up soon, and marry me."

*

"We should give Pegeen her walk now," said Dora to the man sitting in the passenger seat, as she pulled the Cricket into the driveway of her house. "She's probably going crazy from being in the kennel all day. Then I can show you the house, and get dinner ready, and then..." she laughed, "then the night is ours. Isn't this a pretty area? I'm so glad you took the train. The drive from the Hudson station is one of my favorites. You can really enjoy the trees."

"Yes, it's great," said the man, who was tall and long-legged. The top of the man's head bumped against the edge of the car's front door-frame as he emerged, and he patted his thick thatch of pepper-and-salt hair into place as he stood up, then straightened his cream-colored fisherman's sweater. Dora got out and opened the trunk, and the man removed his suitcase.

"Let's stop off in the bedroom first, though," he said, winking. He had a lantern-jawed, rugged face, quite handsome, deeply lined but youthful on the whole, and a smile that showed long white teeth.

"Well, we have to put your suitcase there, anyway," said Dora, as she unlocked the front door. "But I'd better give Pegeen her little workout before we do anything else; she's been locked up since five this morning." They entered the house. "So, here we are."

*

Frances Quagga, naked, hair flowing loose, stretched contentedly in the big bed in the Hotel Roosevelt. The Quaggas had at least an hour before they needed to get ready for the theatre. Mr. Quagga, similarly attired, stood across the room, at the ice-bucket, re-filling champagne glasses. He walked back to the bed and Frances sat up; they raised their glasses to each other and sipped.

"Getting a little flat," Quagga commented.

"Mmmm," Frances concurred. "I can't do anything for the bubbles, but maybe I can make something else rise again."

"Dear, I'm not in my twenties anymore. But we'll just see what we'll just see." Quagga lay down, and Frances snuggled close, caressing his face and wrapping one of her legs around his.

*

The sun was setting as Runs-Away-Screaming pulled his pickup truck off of Route 32 and into the dirt parking lot of the High Five, a brown log house with a neon Rheingold sign in the front window. The reek of stale beer wafted through the screen door. Runs didn't go in, but walked around the building to the back, to a yard covered with hard dirt where four men sat on crates, playing yahtzee. Two of them were his employees, Shank and Pruno. Pruno's pit bull, Mrs. Poopington, dozed near her master. Another dozen or so youngish to middle-aged men and women were watching the game, or talking, drinking beer, some standing, some seated at a long picnic table. A cloud of smoke from cigarettes, doobies, and barbecuing meat hung over all. Most of the men were lanky, tattooed, moustached, and ponytailed. The women mostly wore jeans and t-shirts or sweatshirts; most of them were bony, lipless, sunken-eyed, and wore their limp, dull hair in mullets, although one of them wore a long cotton print dress and had long, wavy hair parted in the middle and hanging nearly to her waist. A couple of the women were more heavily built. One of the larger ones had her peroxided hair up in a 60s-style beehive, and wore a flowered blouse, showing a lot of cleavage.

"How," said the peroxided woman, raising her hand palm outward and giggling.

"And how," said Runs. Shank passed him a doobie, and Runs took a long, blissful hit.

*

"Thank you for coming, Charlotte," said Martin Wandervogel, as Charlotte Fanshaw stepped into the foyer of his house. "Here it is, my little nest."

"It's huge," Charlotte exclaimed. "Don't you and Curtis and Zeke lose each other, in this big house?"

"Well, sometimes. Curtis has a little apartment of his own, down in the basement, so I hardly ever see him, and Zeke's with his mother, now, for the next month or so. Joint custody, you know, it sounds nice, but it can be a real hassle. And I do miss him."

"Awww," said Charlotte. "It's selfish of me, I know, but I'm glad I got to keep my kids. Luke wanted them, or rather he pretended he wanted them. I should have told him, 'Okay, take them,' just to see him back down."

Charlotte took in the immense front room at a glance. It had evidently not been cleaned in some time. Books and film equipment and a few of Zeke's toys lay scattered about, some objects in the fireplace.

"I picked up a little," Wandervogel explained. "But we're a bunch of guys here. And my students are in and out all the time. It's so exciting to watch them learn. I really feel like I'm contributing to society when I see how dedicated they are, and how eager they are to excel at their art."

"I'm afraid my soon-to-be-ex took a lot of the cabinetry, and most of the good china," Wandervogel said as they entered the dining room, "but I did what I could, here."

A white lace tablecloth was laid – a bit lopsidedly – over the dining table, which Wandervogel had set for two, with real silverware (tarnished) and crystal wineglasses.

"I'm not much of a cook," Wandervogel admitted, "but I make a pretty mean goulash. And I got some French bread, and we can whip up some kind of a salad. Ever had bull's blood? It's a Hungarian red. Very underrated. And then I want to hear all about your signing this afternoon. It was Poughkeepsie, right?"

"Yes, it was," said Charlotte. "And yes, I'd love to try some wine. Only… do you mind if I give these glasses a quick rinse first?"

*

"Does she howl and whine like that every night?"

"Why, no," Dora replied, "but then she's usually not in her kennel at dinnertime. She's usually right here by my chair, just as ladylike as can be, waiting for me to give her a little snack. She knows we're eating without her, poor thing."

"Well, I'm sorry," the tall man said, with a slight sniff. "But you know I'm allergic. Besides," (he flashed his white teeth again) "better to have her whining out there, than outside the bedroom door a little later."

*

"Dear?" Frank Leahy called. He had finished loading the dinner dishes into the dishwasher. "Dear, where are you?" He walked down the hall, toward the library.

"In here, darling," Lois replied. And in the library she sat, reading a magazine. Leahy stood in the doorway, grinning at her.

"C'mon up to bed," he said.

"But, Francis, it's still early!"

"Yeah, but I want to fuck you."

*

"Death, ill-dignified, crossin' ye," Effie Hoo noted. "And the five of cups, before ye, ye notice. Clear enough, that. Crisis brewin', and inertia's your enemy. Fast action saves ye, like as not. And beneath ye, the Emperor. A corporate entity at the base of the problem, and broken friendships may result."

The Hoos sat in their library, at a chess-table, where Effie had laid out a tarot spread. A table-lamp illuminated the cards; otherwise the room was dark.

"I suppose that would be a new bit of litigation coming up," Hoo mused. "Can't imagine what it would be, however."

"There's your answer: King of Cups, reversed. Ye don't know the man yet, save perhaps by reputation, but ye will soon. But look here: The Chariot, in this position, indicates that it may be a matter of all this goin' on around ye, ye see – not touchin' ye directly so long as ye hold fast and stay in control."

"I say, that's good news."

*

"He's not that bad of a teacher," remarked Curtis Wandervogel, as he tuned his guitar. He and Bonnie Bonney sat in the dark, in a picnic shelter at the currently deserted Mourning Wood golf course. "I get the impression he doesn't know much about poetry, but at least he keeps us busy."

"I still think he's a jerk," said Bonnie. "Obviously he's got something against women in general." Curtis played a couple of notes on his guitar, and Bonnie echoed them on her flute. Bonnie began playing a simple waltz tune, and Curtis picked it up and played along, keeping the rhythm as Bonnie improvised.

*

"Bring me a Bombay martini, very dry, up with a twist, please, and then bring me the biggest steak you've got, rare," said Ballou to the waitress at Blue Magoo, the bar in downtown Faber where he'd finally caught up with his students. He now sat at a large tableful of Faberites and Van Devanderians together. The students had already got a start on the evening, and several pitchers of beer stood on the table, empty or nearly so. Stan Something-or-other sat next to Ballou, on his right, and on the other side of Stan sat Lee Grossbaum. On Ballou's left sat a good-humored student in a Faber sweatshirt, with a grown-out crew cut and an aggressively friendly cocky-rich-kid manner.

"Martini and steak! You da man!" cried Cocky Rich Kid, slapping Ballou on the back.

"Well, Sir," said Ballou, gravely, "I've discovered that if a man's setting out to drink, it's best to eat a very large piece of fatty meat early in the evening. That way you can get a little fucked-up if you like, but it's not going to inconvenience you as much. You won't get out of control; you won't puke; you won't have as bad of a hangover the next day."

"Aw, shit, where's the fun in that?" Cocky Rich Kid demanded. "Say, what's up with your goddam football team, anyway, guy? We kick your asses every year, and today you turn around and do that to us? I don't get it!"

"Willie Wilden has been chewing on some magic mushrooms, no doubt," Ballou replied. He glanced over at Lee Grossbaum, who looked angelic in her fluffy white sweater, her wavy black hair framing her face, which Ballou could now see was faintly freckled. She held her beer glass with both hands, and when she drank from it a line of foam stayed on her upper lip, which made Ballou want to reach over and kiss it off. She caught his glance, smiled at him, ducked her head, and giggled. Stan Something-or-other was shouting to someone across the table and appeared not to notice.

*

Emmeline Quagga was over at Mattie Bonney's place, and even if she did come home early she'd have better sense than to go down to the basement rec room if she saw Greg's car in the driveway, so Miffany and Greg had as much privacy as they ever had.

*

"It worked out exactly as we'd expected," Wandervogel said to Charlotte, as he pushed their empty dinner plates out of the way, to the other end of the table, and prepared to slice up the lemon meringue pie Charlotte had brought. "The school board caved in as soon as the lawsuit hit them, and we got just what we wanted."

Wandervogel sat up straighter and huffed a bit with self-satisfaction, like a huge heavy bird flourishing its neck-feathers.

"With all my various ventures," he explained, "it pays to have a firm on retainer. That way I can get them to pitch in whenever I see any kind of social injustice that I feel I can do something about. That's so important, to be able not only to perceive some social ill, but to be prepared to step up to the plate and do what I can to cure it. Such as homophobia and sexism, in this case."

"It sure is," said Charlotte. "Let me put these dirty plates in the sink before we have dessert, okay?"

"Another thing I wanted to bring up with you tonight, Charlotte: Now that your ship seems to be coming in, financially, have you thought about how you're going to put that money to work for you? I'd like to tell you about a company that's certain to grow very fast, and that actually grows by pursuing social justice for oppressed peoples. Now, you may think that's impossible, but..."

*

Frances hardly ever smoked – except when she was in the city. Now she and her husband stood in front of the Helen Hayes Theater. It was intermission.

"I think I'll have one of those too," Quagga said, taking one of his wife's unfiltered Lucky Strikes. Frances, holding her cigarette between the very ends of her fingers, tilted her head back and blew smoke upwards in a straight, steady stream.

"You look just like a fashion model from way back, maybe the 1930s," Quagga said. Frances wore a sharply tailored black dress and jacket with fur-trimmed cuffs. She continued to look up at the sky.

"Pensive tonight, are we?" Quagga added.

"Just worried about Miff," Frances admitted. "Wondering where she is and what she's doing. I hope we did the right thing. I'd hate to think I put ideas into her head that weren't there before."

"If you did," said Quagga, "you'd be world-famous, as the first parent in history to have done so." He lit his cigarette.

"I heard a story once," he continued, "about a man of about my age and build – although maybe a little taller than I am – who had a remarkably beautiful daughter. He loved her dearly, of course, and he was terribly protective of her. He rarely allowed her to date – and only boys whose families he knew and thoroughly approved of.

"Well, one fine day his daughter comes to him, very wrought up, and says to him, 'Daddy, I've got something terrible to tell you. I'm afraid I'm in a family way.' And her poor father takes a few seconds to absorb the blow, of course, and at last he says, 'Thank God. I didn't know how much longer I could endure the suspense!'

"We did right, Frances, I'm sure of it."

*

Bonnie had been rhapsodizing non-stop for several minutes, making up the music as she went along, and was getting a little out of breath, but a deer, off in the distance, had been walking across the golf course and had stopped, seeming to look at Bonnie as she played her flute, and she told herself that the deer had stopped to hear the music, and that it would run off if she didn't keep playing. So she kept playing. She wondered why Curtis wasn't trying to make out with her – and wondered why she didn't want him to.

Curtis had given up trying to keep to her rhythm. As Bonnie got more and more creative, he could only put in a chord here and a chord there, and after a bit he stopped playing and just listened. He knew he ought to be trying to make out – she wasn't a bad-looking girl, and he liked her – but he didn't want to. Not with the situation as it was. She'd probably assume his dad had put him up to it. He, too, gazed off at the deer.

*

"Oh, Francis, what has got into you?" Lois squealed with delight, as Leahy flipped her over onto her belly. "You have so much energy!"

"No more than usual," said Leahy, on his knees, sliding into her.

*

Dora started to sit down next to the tall man, on the love-seat in her living room, then she hesitated. He was sitting near the middle.

"Move over a little," she said.

"You're not going to sit on my lap tonight?" he asked, gazing at Dora and sliding over maybe three inches. "I've missed you."

"Not yet," said Dora, sitting. "I have to get used to being with you again."

The tall man reached over with his far hand, his right, and took hold of Dora's left. He kept looking into her eyes, saying nothing. Then he leaned over, and aimed a kiss at Dora's lips. She turned her face slightly, offering her cheek. The man straightened up, looking sorrowful, and sighed.

"Dora, we've got to talk about the elephant in the living room," he said. "I've tried to understand. I mean, your career and your marriage blowing up one after the other – I didn't want to make life any more complicated for you. But it's been tough on me, you know, and I thought maybe when you said I could come up here you meant you were ready to..."

"Oh, Steve," Dora whispered, returning his gaze. "I don't know. It's all so confusing for me. I guess I felt that we had to take a break from each other. So I could be sure. And I don't know if it's right between us yet. Or if it ever will be."

Steve drew himself up a little, but did not break his gaze or let go of her hand. He tried not to change the expression on his face.

"This isn't what I was expecting," he replied.

"It's hard to explain," Dora said. "I love how you feel about me. I've always loved how you feel about me. I love how you look at me. And I know I wouldn't have gotten through... *that*... without you. You've been the most wonderful friend; you were there when I needed you most, and... and later on... well, when I understood how you felt about me, I was so sad and so alone, and I fell into it..."

"But now you're telling me that you never really cared for me after all. And now that your case is settled, you're going to just flush me away, like so much shit?"

"Oh, Steve, please, don't talk like that. You know that's not how I feel."

"Or maybe you want to just leave me in some kind of limbo, while you wait for someone better to come along? Or maybe you... maybe you just kept me around to make you feel better, and now that you're all okay, I'm dispensable?"

"Steve, no."

Steve looked away from her at last, sighing.

"You and I..." He shook his head. "You and I are man and wife, if ever two people were. I've always believed that, and I believe it now. Dora, I love you. I love you more than anyone has ever loved anyone. You know it; you can't not know it."

"I do know you feel that way, Steve. And it means so much to me. It really does. And I kept hoping... I kept waiting to feel the same for you as you do for me. But I don't know that I ever will."

"So for all the time we were... sharing a bed... and talking about getting married, all that time you never loved me? I don't buy that. I know you loved me."

"In my way I did, and I do. And for a while I tried to tell myself that I felt that spark – but I never really did. Oh, Steve, we should have some brandy for this conversation. Excuse me a minute." Dora got up and went into the kitchen.

*

"The doctor told me to start taking the pill on my next period," Miffany told Greg. "Meanwhile we have to use this."

Miffany and Greg, both naked, lay on the couch of the basement rec room, each with shoulders reclining against the opposite arm of the couch, legs entwined, almost crotch-to-crotch. Miffany had extracted a plastic case and a small tube from her purse.

"Now, watch," she told Greg, giggling. "I've never done this before, and you'd better know how it's done, too." She removed the diaphragm from its case, and held it up to the light to check for tears or punctures.

*

Shank and Pruno had both gone into the High Five for more beer, leaving Runs alone at the picnic-table where the three of them had been sitting and talking. He looked over to where the slim woman with the loose hair and the long dress stood, about 15 feet away; picking at a plate of ribs and talking with nobody in particular. She looked maybe 45, and she was beautiful-ugly, Runs decided. Nose too big, and enormous blue eyes too deeply set. She was dark of hair and skin, and Runs guessed that she, too, had some Indian blood. He tried to catch her eye, as the heavy woman with the blonde beehive sat down next to him.

"Hey, Big Injun," the heavy woman said.

"What up, Momma?"

"Want to take me for a little moonlight drive?"

Runs again looked over at the dark, slim woman – who looked back at him, too, curiously.

"No moon tonight, Momma," Runs growled. "Besides, you're too dangerous for me. Wouldn't trust myself that far."

The heavy woman guffawed and punched his arm.

The dark woman had turned away and was talking with a man Runs didn't know. Runs sat hoping that she would glance back in his direction, but she did not.

*

Lois had picked up the remote on the bedside table, and switched on the TV; her husband was looking at a Louis L'Amour novel, not actually reading it, as they both lounged in the bed. Lois began switching the channels, evidently frustrated.

"What are you looking for, dear?" Leahy asked.

"*Perry Mason*. I have forgotten what channel it is on, isn't that crazy?"

Leahy stared at his wife. "Dear, that show hasn't been on in more than 30 years," he said.

Lois stared back at him, equally astounded. "Really? Then I wonder what I was thinking." She continued flipping channels. Leahy's brows knit. He put down his book and watched her pushing the remote button, again and again and again.

*

"Not too many investors have heard of Modern Diversity Systems yet," Wandervogel told Charlotte. They still sat side-by-side at the dining table. "We intend to make a big marketing push to potential investors starting a little later this fall. I'm telling you about it now to give you a chance to get in on the ground floor, when the stock price is still very low. Because..." (here Wandervogel looked bashful) "well, I like you, you know, and I'd like to see you comfortably set up, if you can do it by investing in something that'll really help the human race. And MDS is one investment you can count on to do that."

"Well, thank you, Martin. I have a couple of old friends who know a little something about investing – I certainly don't know anything about it – and if it sounds like a good idea to them, I'll invest something."

Wandervogel drew himself up sulkily. "Consult them if you have to," he said, "but you'd better be quick about it, because this is one of those investments you really should get in on now, or your profit is not going to be as great after the stock price has already gone up. But, I'm sorry. I shouldn't be talking business on a Saturday night." He smiled again and refilled their glasses with bull's blood.

Wandervogel reached over and patted Charlotte on the knee. "I'm really glad you could get away," he said. "We haven't had the chance to talk, I mean, really talk, alone, and there's so much a guy can learn from you."

Wandervogel caught Charlotte's left hand in his right and pressed the ball of his thumb against hers, each of his fingertips against hers, so that their hands were up at shoulder-height, pushing gently against each other. Wandervogel gazed deeply into Charlotte's eyes, and she giggled.

*

Dora had had a little more brandy than she was used to, but Steve was drinking at better than double her rate – and yet he didn't appear at all drunk, save that he was losing animation and affect as they talked. Dora yawned, and shifted in her seat.

"I'm boring you," Steve remarked. "I'm sorry. I was a lot more exciting when I was keeping you out of jail." Dora had no time to react beyond a slight start, and a quick intake of breath, before he added, "I'm sorry. God, I'm sorry, that was a cheap shot."

"It was. There was never any chance I'd go to jail and you know it."

"The Devil got hold of my tongue," said Steve. "Really, I'm sorry."

"I know you are," said Dora. "But I really had better go to bed now. I have to get up at four, you know. Although you can sleep as late as you want to, and I'll be back here at about 10:30, and then we can go to brunch."

"I could use a little bed," said Steve, forcing himself to smile again and letting his hand rest on Dora's knee as he gazed at her.

"I'm going to take the day-bed in the study," said Dora.

Steve's jaw dropped. "No!" he gasped.

"I'm sorry, Steve."

*

"Moi, je déteste le football," Lee Grossbaum was telling Roger Ballou. She switched to English. "I only came because he asked me to. I wish he'd grow up." Stan Something-or-other had left their table about a half-hour before, to visit a tableful of Faberites across the room, and since then Ballou and Lee had remained next to each other, drinking beer and speaking French. Lee was majoring in French, she'd told Ballou, but he found her accent atrocious, and her vocabulary was heavily laced with "Franglais." Their heads were close together so they could hear each other. Ballou looked over, and saw that Stan and a couple of other students had stood up, pitchers in their hands, apparently having a chugging contest.

"Regardez ces clochards!" Lee added, with a sweep of her arm that knocked over an empty glass. "They're, like, out of a really bad movie." She took Ballou's cigarette from between his fingers, and puffed on it inexpertly, not inhaling. "Anh. God, look at him. He totally emb... (she suppressed a small belch) embarrasses me."

Just as she said this, Stan's knees buckled, and he sat down heavily on the floor. A couple of Faber students hauled him to his feet and helped him into a chair.

"That man needs to get his priorities in order," Ballou commented. "If I had you as my date, I'd hope my friends would be impressed enough already, without my having to show them how much beer I could drink."

Lee laid her head on Ballou's shoulder. Ballou took back his cigarette, dragged on it, and put his cheek against her hair. She looked up at him, obviously inviting him, and Ballou bent his head down and kissed her, open-mouthed, and she responded. After a long, long kiss, they broke away, and Lee stared into Ballou's eyes, cupping his face in one hand.

"You're so sexy," she whispered. "You're so smart, and so handsome, and *sooooo* sexy." She kissed him again, hard. "My pookins," she whispered in his ear. "Are you my pookins?" Ballou didn't respond, but held her tight, teasingly brushed his lips against hers, then slid his tongue into her mouth again.

"Oh, *duuuude*!" crowed Cocky Rich Kid, next to him, "You are totally gonna get your dick sucked tonight, dude!"

*

"*Saturday Night Live* is on in a minute, dear," said Leahy. "We can try that, see if it's gotten any better."

"What is that?" asked Lois. "Do I know it?"

"Channel four, dear."

Lois pressed the remote, then got out of bed, going to the closet for her red silk kimono, singing softly:

Observe his flame,
That placid dame,
The moon's Celestial Highness;
There's not a trace
Upon her face
Of diffidence or shyness:
She borrows light
That, through the night,
Mankind may all acclaim her!
And, truth to tell,
She lights up well,
So I, for one, don't blame her!
Ah, pray make no mistake,
We are not shy;

We're very wide awake,
The moon and I!
Ah, pray make no mistake,
We are not shy;
We're very wide awake,
The moon and I!

"Francis?" Lois looked at her husband, surprised. "Francis, are you crying?"

"Just hay fever, dear."

*

Martin Wandervogel leaned over, eyes closed, and thrust his face against Charlotte's, presenting his blubbery lips. Charlotte gave them a little peck and tried to make up her mind whether to kiss him again or draw back. Before she could, Wandervogel's mouth bore down on hers a little harder, and she opened her lips by way of experimentation. His beard scratched, but he didn't smell unpleasant. She decided he was neither a good kisser nor a bad one. He kept kissing, and Charlotte responded, a little harder.

*

Runs drove away from the High Five. After he'd gone a couple of miles, he turned onto a dirt road, a road that led into the woods, past some abandoned shacks, placed some distance from each other. One of these shacks had burned down years ago, and the land around it was overgrown with volunteer trees and weeds. Runs parked his truck and killed the lights; he stepped out of the truck into almost total darkness. From under a tarp in the bed of his truck he took a bow and a quiver of arrows.

He wandered through the brush, making very little sound, coming to a creek that ran behind the burnt shack. On the other bank of the creek lay more brush, and forest. Runs squatted on the bank of the creek and watched the water.

On the opposite bank he saw two shiny eyes: a possum, looking at him, then scurrying away.

He thought about the dark woman he'd seen at the High Five. She'd been looking at him, but she'd never come near enough to him to talk, and he'd not been able to think of a way to approach her. He reconstructed her appearance in his mind, remembering all her features one by one and forming them into a whole. Runs thought about the big woman with the beehive, too – for just a moment, a little resentfully.

Off to his right he heard a rustling. He turned his head toward the noise and saw, maybe 50 yards away, what looked like a 10-pointer. Very slowly, Runs drew an arrow from his quiver, and even more slowly he straightened up, raised his bow, and nocked the arrow – but the buck must have heard or smelled something, because he withdrew into the darkness as quickly as he'd come. Runs didn't mind; he hadn't been sure of a clear shot anyway.

*

Charlotte Fanshaw put her hands on Martin Wandervogel's shoulders and slowly pushed him back.

"It's just too soon, Martin," she whispered. "Not that I'm not enjoying this. But we're going to have to take it step by step. Besides, I should get home. I don't like to leave the kids overnight."

"Okay, Skinny," Wandervogel replied, sitting up. "Whatever you say. Whenever you're ready." He thought. "You know, you could go home, and then sneak back here again, when they're all asleep. I wouldn't tell anyone."

"It may come to that," Charlotte said.

*

"He's completely gone, dude," Cocky Rich Kid remarked to Ballou. Across the room, Stan Something-or-other had slid off his chair and sprawled full-length on the floor, inert. The Faberites around him were guffawing; two of the less-drunken ones tried to lift him by the armpits and legs. "Let's get him to my car," one of them suggested. "We'll take him to the house, let him sleep it off."

Lee Grossbaum was snuggled against Ballou, half-asleep, one hand on his chest. Ballou felt all right — not drunk, he decided, just a little fuzzy — but he was tired.

"Baby?" he whispered.

"Mm?"

"We need to get out of here. You're in bad shape, and I'm not as young as I was."

Lee sat up. She focused to a certain extent: just enough to catch sight of Stan being carried out. She looked like she was trying to pull herself together and go after him; then she sat back in her chair and leaned against Ballou again.

"That dumb shit," she said, slurring her words. "I have totally had it with him. Let him take care of himself. He's been ignoring me all night anyway."

"What can I tell you?" said Ballou. "We need to get you someplace, though. Sober you up a little. Are you hungry?"

"God… no. Wanna sleep."

"Were you and Stan planning to spend the night someplace?"

"We were jus' gonna drive back. But I guess thass not such a good idea, huh?"

"I guess not. Listen, he's not going anywhere till morning, that's for sure. We could find out where they're taking him, and take you there, too."

"Don't wanna sleep in a frat house," Lee grumbled. "Not with a bunch of drunk guys around, and not with *him*."

"Well, I hate to propose this, but you could stay in my motel room. We don't have to do anything but sleep."

Lee had buried her face in Ballou's sleeve, and now she looked up at him, smiling a little. "Yeah. Help me up."

Luckily the waitress was right there. Ballou asked for his tab, handed the waitress half again that amount in cash, and got Lee to her feet. They started toward the door, Lee not very steadily, Ballou looking at no one.

"Old Dude! You are *da man!*" Cocky Rich Kid shouted after them. "You da *dawg*! You da *shit!*"

Ballou had left the Cadillac only a block away. He let Lee into the passenger seat, then took a few deep breaths of the night air, to clear his head. He felt pretty sure that if he went carefully, he'd be in no danger of getting pulled over. Lee dozed off during the drive, awakening when Ballou had pulled into the motel parking lot, parked, and shut off the engine.

"Nice night," Lee remarked, in a clearer voice than before, getting out of the car. "But, oh, I'm dah-*runk*."

"No wonder. I didn't know a little doll like you could hold that much. The room's up those stairs, there. Can you walk?"

"Oh... sure."

Ballou had to walk behind Lee on the stairs, ready to catch her, for she wore high-heeled boots, and the pointed toes kept catching on the risers, making her stumble.

"Think you're gonna be sick?" Ballou asked, as he got Lee inside the room.

"Yeah. Maybe."

"Okay, then I don't want you to go to bed yet." Lee stumbled toward the bed, but Ballou caught her round the waist, and held her up. "If you lie down right now, you'll be sick, and you'll feel even worse in the morning." He manhandled Lee toward the bathroom.

"Here's what you do." Ballou searched his toiletries kit, and produced a bottle of aspirin. "I'm giving you four of these, and a glass of water." He sat Lee down on the edge of the bathtub, handed her the pills, and the water, and watched her consume all.

"Okay, now drink another glass of water," Ballou commanded, taking the glass from Lee and re-filling it. "Chug-a-lug." She complied. "Now, can you stand? I'm gonna leave you alone here for a while, and I want you to sit on the toilet, and pee, and drink water. Just keep re-filling your glass, and peeing, got it? Drink and pee. After a few minutes you'll start feeling a little better. When the room has stopped spinning, and you feel like you can stand without getting dizzy, then you can come to bed and lie down. Not before."

Ballou filled two glasses with water and set them on the sink, within arm's reach of the toilet. He filled the third glass for himself, and took it into the bedroom, where he removed his shoes, took a flask of brandy from his overnight bag, and flopped down on the bed. He propped a pillow against the headboard and lounged, smoking a cigarette and alternately sipping from his flask and the water glass.

He was starting to doze off, maybe 20 or 30 minutes later, when Lee emerged from the bathroom, her jeans pulled up but the waist-button and the fly hanging open. She had the plastic ice-bucket with her.

She walked, steadily enough, to the other side of the bed, set the ice-bucket on the floor, and sat down on the bed, pulling off her boots and her sweater. This done, she fell back, lying perpendicular to Ballou, her head touching his leg. She closed her eyes and mumbled.

Ballou got out of the bed, walked around to Lee's side, slid his arms under her, and half-lifted her, drawing back the covers and moving her so that she lay lengthwise, a pillow under her head.

Lee tried, without getting up, to get her jeans off: she pushed at them but they were new and tight, and she couldn't raise her backside enough to slide them off.

"Get 'em off me," she murmured.

Ballou did – forcing back the temptation to accidentally-on-purpose take her panties with them – and removed her socks, leaving her in her underwear. The undershirt was almost sheer, and he could see the outline of Lee's small breasts; the areolae were small as well, but with thick, prominent nipples. Three or four black hairs grew between her navel and the waist of her panties; a few more protruded from under each leg-hole.

"There you are," Ballou told her. He pulled the covers up to her chin.

"Mmmm," Lee responded, stretching and flexing her feet. "Nice." She smiled, her eyes closed. She rolled over on her side and began snoring softly.

Ballou paced back and forth in the small room, shedding his clothes. He considered various options. Waking her with a kiss, removing her undershirt and panties, and simply taking her. Getting into bed next to her and snuggling close, maybe playing with her breasts, so that she'd feel his presence, wake up, and respond. Letting her sleep for a couple hours, and maybe bagging a nap himself, and then having at her a little later. Cuddling with her and hoping she'd take the initiative eventually.

By the time he'd got down to his birthday suit, he'd ruled out those possibilities. He got back into his side of the bed, as far from Lee as he could, and jacked off. This took some time because he was tired and crocked, but he figured he had better do it. Lee slept on.

*

The tall man rolled over in the huge, high bed. He opened his eyes; he could see through a chink in the window-curtains that it was still dark. From the bathroom immediately next door, he heard the shower. He could, he thought, walk in there right now and surprise her; she'd be naked... and then he decided against it because maybe he might get another chance, someday, after all, if... But he couldn't imagine an "if." He couldn't even hope for one. He heard the water shut off, and he began to sob into his pillow.

He heard the bathroom door opening and closing; a moment later the bedroom door opened, very softly, and Dora entered the room almost noiselessly.

He stayed completely still, his face in the pillow, pretending to be asleep, waiting for Dora to climb into the bed next to him and snuggle up.

He heard a bureau drawer open, slowly, and Dora taking clothes out of it, very softly sliding the drawer shut, going through the same procedure with another drawer, opening a closet, collecting something, shutting the closet as softly as possible. He heard her moving toward the bedroom door, and the door opening and shutting again, so gently, and her footfalls fading down the hall.

The tall man pounded his fist into the mattress, over and over.

*

Notwithstanding his precautionary activities of a few hours before, Ballou woke at about nine in the morning with a monster hard-on. Lee had barely moved during the night. She was still asleep, over on the other side of the bed, breathing slowly and heavily.

Ballou thought about nudging her awake – quite by accident – and letting her see his condition. She might be inspired to do something about it. Which would feel terrific, but that kind of a hard-on – the "piss-hard" – has to be let down, and the bladder attended to, before anything else can comfortably happen. It wasn't worth the risk, Ballou decided.

Ballou slid out of the bed, and by the time he'd done his morning duties and emerged from the bathroom in clean shorts and t-shirt, Lee was sitting up, rubbing her eyes and rolling the kinks out of her neck.

"You want a shower?" Ballou asked. "I don't have a spare toothbrush, but you're welcome to use mine, if it's okay with you."

Lee tried to speak, but only an inaudible whisper came out. She cleared her throat, loudly and at length. "Did we... last night... we didn't do anything, did we?" she asked.

"If we had, I'd hope you would have remembered."

Lee tried to laugh, but the laugh turned to a cough. She did smile, though.

"I'm sure I would have. You kiss good, I remember that." Lee thought for a moment. "I'm sorry. I led you on."

Ballou sat next to Lee on the bed, stroked her hair, and gave her a little peck on the forehead.

"No, you didn't, not at all," he said. "I wouldn't have let it happen. Not last night. And now I'm hungry." Ballou prodded Lee in the tummy, and she grabbed his arm and giggled. "Go get a shower and then we'll get breakfast."

*

"Well, aren't you going to *ask*?" demanded Miffany Quagga. She and Emmeline sat on the sofa in the Quaggas' TV room, watching *Gomer Pyle* on TVLand. Miffany ate Kix out of the box and drank milky coffee. Emmeline, sitting next to her, slowly and carefully peeled a lemon with a paring knife and ate pieces of the peel, chewing them thoroughly.

"It's your business," said Emmeline, staring at the TV. "If you need to tell me, you'll tell me."

"Fine, then," Miffany snapped.

"Okay, if you really really *really* want me to ask, I'll ask," said Emmeline, languidly rolling her head back and stretching. "Does it really make such a great big difference if he's not wearing a rubber?"

Miffany tsk'd, rolling her eyes, and offered the box of Kix.

"No, thank you," said Emmeline.

"Oh, go on, have a Kick," said Miffany. "Miss Anorexia."

"I do *not* have anorexia. I eat."

"Have one lousy Kick." Miffany extracted a single little ball of cereal and held it out. Emmeline took it and popped it into her mouth, and let it dissolve.

*

The tall man, wearing latex gloves, had gone through the closets and drawers in Dora's bedroom, and now he started on the desk in the second bedroom, which Dora had set up as a combination study and consultation room. This was a room he had no business being in, so he listened hard, as he worked, for any sound that might warn him of Dora's return.

So far, only the Van Devander pennant displayed above her bedroom mirror, and the Van Devander sweatshirt he'd found in her bedroom bureau drawer, seemed at all incongruous to him. The papers in her office desk he'd seen before, when he'd conducted similar searches in her old apartment in the city, save for some documents connected to her catering business.

At the very end of his search, in the last desk-drawer he examined, he found the thick stack of baronial envelopes, each with his own calligraphy on the outside: ornate, swooping handwriting in blue-black ink. These were tied together with a blue silk ribbon. About 50 of them. He'd written those letters to Dora, on an average of one every other day, since she'd moved out of the city.

And now no more, he told himself. He could never write to her again. Dora would not have bought the pennant and the sweatshirt for herself.

*

"Okay, practically speaking, we have two choices," Ballou told Lee as she combed and brushed her hair. "First, you could just ride on back to Wildenkill with me, and to hell with your boyfriend. Second, we could drop you off someplace here. Maybe at his car, if you can remember where he parked it. Or do you know where that frat house is, where they said they were taking him?"

"I'm sure I could find it," Lee replied. "Not sure I want to."

"Well, please yourself. On the one hand, it might not be very nice to just leave him here. On the other, no guarantee he'll be in condition to get you home, even now."

"Plus some of my stuff is in his car. I can drive it if he can't."

"Okay. And consider whether you want to be seen being brought back to Van Devander in my car. I bet everybody knows my car by now. I don't mind, but…"

"No, you're right. I don't want to see him again, though. Oh, God, I do, and I don't, you know?" Lee looked into her purse and brought out a compact.

"Hey, no makeup."

"Huh?"

"Whatever we decide to do, you were out all night. You weren't anyplace where you could do your hair and makeup. Understand? You didn't stay in no stinkin' Motel 6 with one of your professors, you dig? Bad enough you've had a shower. I should have thought of that."

"Oh," said Lee. "Right. Say, are you still gonna call me Miss Grossbaum?"

"In class, you bet."

"How about out of class?"

"Out of class, too, if there's anybody listening."

"Okay... *Roger.*" She pointed to the box of tissues on the bedside table, on the side of the bed where Ballou had slept. *"Donay moi oon foy de Kleenex, s'il vous plait."*

"Une feuille de Kleenex," Ballou corrected her, handing her the box. *"Une."*

"Oo... oon."

"Keep your lips just like that, but say, 'eee,'" Ballou instructed. *"Une."*

"Very good. Again."

"Une."

"Okay, now '*feuille*.'"

"Foy."

"No, do it in three parts. 'Feu.' Set your lips like for '*une*,' but say 'eh.' Feu."

"Feu."

"Good. Now, 'feu-ee.'"

"Feu-ee."

"Now 'yeu.'"

"Yeu."

"Feu-ee-yeu. Feu-ee-yeu."

"Feu-ee-yeu."

"Now all together, real fast, in one syllable. *Feuille.*"

"Feuille."

"Perfect. Again. *Feuille.*"

"Feuille."

"Miss Lee Grossbaum, you're gonna have a beautiful accent before long."

"What are you, Henry Higgins?"

Ballou checked out of the motel, and he and Lee drove to a McDonald's and got each an Egg McMuffin and a coffee to go. They drove to the Faber College campus, and Lee got out of the car a block or so away from Fraternity Row.

"I'll tell him I slept in his stupid car," she told Ballou. "I'll also tell him goodbye – once he gets me home. Oh, and wait a sec."

Lee got back into the car, wrapped her arms round Ballou's neck, and kissed hard. Ballou kissed back, holding her, and inhaling. She smelled of soap, smoky bar, and girl.

Ballou didn't watch her walk away. He headed out of town. To his amazement, the Black Demons did not appear.

*

"Bartholomew, I'd like you to meet my special friend, Stephen DeGuiche. Steve, Bartholomew is the assistant manager here, and the headwaiter."

"Nice going at your age," said the tall man, looking up from his menu, flashing his teeth at Bartholomew.

Bartholomew smiled gamely at the tall man, and said, "I'm really glad to meet you. Dora's one of my very favorite people. Now, you better take good care of her!"

When they'd ordered, the tall man asked Dora, in a soft, even voice, "Since when are you a football fan?"

"Why, since always. You didn't know that? Well, no, you wouldn't have, since there's no college football in the city except Columbia."

"Found a nice guy to take you to the games here?"

"Yes, in fact. Would you like to meet him? We could stop by his house, or call him and ask him over for tea."

"Dora, you're really going out of your way to hurt me, aren't you? Are you enjoying this?"

Dora lowered her eyes, looking mildly reproachful.

"I'd like to cook for you tonight, Dora. If you'd like that. Like I used to."

"I don't want you staying at my house tonight. I'm sorry. This was all my fault. I shouldn't have let you come up here. It was a big mistake. I'll show you my bakery when we've finished here, and then I want to show you the shop right next to mine – he makes the most beautiful hardwood furniture and cabinetry, all by hand – and then we can drive back to Wildenkill and walk around town this afternoon, or drive around the country if you want to – there's this wonderful gift shop over in West Hurley that you'd love – but I need to take you back to the train this evening."

Stephen DeGuiche's face started working, and he swallowed.

"I'm going to come back one day, Dora," he choked. "And one day I will marry you. And that's all there is to it."

*

"Great shot, Hugh," said Leahy, on the tee of the par-three seventh hole at Mourning Wood. Hoo's tee shot had settled two feet from the cup. "Stiffer than a 14-year-old dick."

"One day," said Effie, "he's going to hit one into that bunker on the left, and he'll never get it out, for he'll have forgotten how to hit out o' sand." Her own ball lay in that very bunker.

"That's why I married a teaching professional, my love," said Hoo. "I shall watch your technique on the next shot with the eye of a vulture." They stepped back and watched Leahy tee up. He had to take a driver, on account of his age, and even at that the ball stopped 10 yards short of the green – but safe on the grass, at least.

"If I can't get up and down from there, I'm canning it forever," said Leahy, staring out after his ball. "Effie, there was a time when I took less club than you on this hole. If this is what growing old is all about, then fuck it. Your turn, dear!" This last was to Lois, and the foursome walked 50 yards ahead to the ladies' tee.

"Take your five-wood, and just swing slow and straight," Effie Hoo advised. "Lois, I see your game improvin' every time we play. Ye hit the ball very cleanly, for a beginner. Today's the day ye make your first par. I can feel it."

Lois took her club, pegged her ball up, and without any pre-shot routine, not even a waggle, she swung with a long, high, stiff-armed action. The ball didn't go very far in the air, but it flew straight and bounced true, well onto the green, about eight feet from the pin. "Oh, my God!" cried Lois. She squealed, and danced in a circle, holding her club aloft.

"Dear, did *you* hit that?" Leahy demanded.

Lois hopped into the air and into Leahy's arms, laughing. "In two years, Effie," she cried, over her husband's shoulder, "I will be giving you lessons!"

*

"I'm afraid Dora exaggerated a little, if she told you I make every-thing by hand," Harrison Lockwood explained in his hearty, breezy voice. "I have a power lathe, of course, and quite a few other power tools, but it is done mostly by hand. All the detail work is."

Harrison Lockwood was a bit older than Stephen DeGuiche, but probably not by much. His prematurely white hair and short, well-kept full beard and moustache added some years to his appear-ance. The beard couldn't conceal the deep dimples that appeared when he smiled. He looked very fit under his denim jacket. He could have been a folksinger, or a naturalist, or a union organizer – or an actor playing a folksinger, a naturalist, or a union organizer.

"Steve, isn't this amazing furniture?" Dora asked. "Look around and see if there's anything that would work in your apartment. I'm sure Harrison could ship it to you."

Stephen DeGuiche nodded, but said nothing. He had been progressively less responsive during brunch, and during the visit to Dora's Bakery and Catering.

"I can just see this chair in your library," cried Dora, indicat-ing a solid, heavy armchair stained almost black, with intricately carved finials on the backrest. "I actually saw Harrison working on this, a couple of weeks ago. How long did it take you, in all, Harrison?"

"Oh, long enough," said Lockwood. "I really have no idea. You lose track of time, when you have something like this to work with. Steve, come over here and look at the grain of the wood in this chair; maybe you'll see why Dora admires it. It's not really the workmanship. My job is just to embellish what nature has given me to work with."

"Mm," said DeGuiche, grudgingly approaching the chair.

*

Among the spam and the business-related e-mails on Ballou's computer, when he arrived home and logged onto the Internet early that evening, was a message from leegee@vandevander.edu:

Roger...
Got back safe. I had to drive. Stan could hardly see. Hes history. Thanks 4 all you did 4 me. See you in class tomorrow. Dont worry. I'll act like nothing happened. (GRIN) I wish something had! MWAH!!!
Lee

Ballou thought for a minute or two about whether he should reply at all.

Dear Lee:
I'm glad you're safe home. Take good care and I'll see you in class.
RB

He thought about adding something to the effect of, "If you ever need someone to talk to..." but decided that that would be not just superfluous but creepy. So he didn't. He changed the "Dear Lee" to "Hey, Lee," and sent it.

Monday, October 11

The Wildenkill Advertiser October 9–15, 1999

Anti-'Wildens' Agitators
Should Find Another Hobby
By Roger Sullivan Ballou

For the past several years, and somewhat more loudly than usual just lately, certain groups and individuals have been lobbying against the use of American Indian-oriented mascots for sports teams, on the grounds that such names as Indians, Braves, Red Men, Redskins, etc. are somehow insulting to Indians generally. These agitators deserve no more than to be laughed out of court and admonished to find a hobby other than looking for reasons to be offended.

For centuries, sports teams have been taking the names of various people or animals. U.S.C are the Trojans; Michigan State are the Spartans; Notre Dame are the Fighting Irish; Idaho are the Vandals; Ole Miss are the Rebels, Indiana are the Hoosiers. In each of the above cases, the team took the name, presumably, for two reasons:

(1) Those particular people are fierce in battle, or otherwise virtuous and worthy of honor;

(2) If your team takes the name of a certain group of persons – or of an animal, for that matter – some of that group's fighting spirit, which you admire, might magically rub off on you.

Are we to believe that any team that calls itself Indians, Braves, Fighting Ilini, Chippewas, Aztecs, is calling itself that for any reason other than to honor the nominated group? Would any team name itself after a people it wished to denigrate? Would a team call itself the Pedophiles, for instance? the Klansmen? the Poopie-Butts? Has such a thing ever happened, anywhere, in the history of professional or serious amateur sports?

(This weekend, the Van Devander Wildens' football team played the Faber Mongols. Are we to assume that Faber College intended to insult people with Down's Syndrome? Oh, dear, now that I've suggested it, no doubt they'll be pressured to change their mascot, too!)

But, some folks might respond, it's not so much the name that's degrading, as the personified mascot, or the ceremonies surrounding the names: Chief Wahoo of the Cleveland Indians; Nockahoma of the Atlanta Braves; the Braves fans' chant and gesture known as the "tomahawk chop." Okay, let's look at them one by one.

Chief Wahoo is merely a logo of a smiling Indian. Since when is smiling, or being an Indian, or both, inherently offensive? Nockahoma (employed as a mascot in the 1960s and '70s, but since decommissioned because he was deemed politically incorrect) sat in a tipi near the Braves' bullpen, whence he would emerge to do a victory dance whenever a Brave hit a home run. How is this morally different from the antics of any other dancing mascot, of which hundreds must exist all over the country? As for the tomahawk chop, while it certainly looks and sounds silly, is it any worse than other organized gyrations of other groups of fans?

And how about our own Willie Wilden? True, in the images displayed on Van Devander's pennants and sweatshirts, he appears to be not the most impressive physical specimen of all time, but his aspect is undeniably courageous, aggressive, and doughty.

Implied, if not explicitly stated in complaints about these team mascots, is the notion that Indians are some sort of superior beings – a transcendentally noble race – who ought to be treated with awe and veneration over and above that accorded to people whose ancestors didn't arrive on the American continent as long ago. Also implied is the suggestion that any race that has been as savagely treated as the American Indians have been, ought never to be spoken of in any way that might be considered light-hearted.

If extraordinary respect is what Indians demand, that's what they're getting, when a team names itself after them! As for citing past and present sufferings as an argument against mascotism, consider that the Rebels of Mississippi were killed in great numbers, and their country devastated, in a brutal war; the Trojans (of Troy, not of Southern California) were slaughtered to the last man, their women blinded and imprisoned. If it comes to that, what are we doing calling teams the "Eagles" or the "Bison," when those animals have been hunted nearly to extinction?

Speaking of nomenclature, I suppose I should explain why I refuse to use the term "Native American" when speaking of Indians. It is because that term, applied only to Indians, implies that they are more native than I am. I was born in this country. How much more native do you want?

Every American is descended from someone who came to the Americas from someplace else. We have never found evidence of any great apes in North or South America. That leaves the inescapable conclusion that the first Americans came here from another continent, most likely from Asia via the Bering Strait. Today's Indians are the descendants of immigrants as surely as I am.

We all know that Indians are called Indians because Columbus and his men, when they landed on Hispaniola in 1492, thought they had reached the out-lying islands of India. (Thus, that archipelago to the southeast of the continental United States is known as the West Indies.) So, American Indians were called Indians by mistake; what of it? It's not the first time that something or somebody was given a name that stuck, because of a misunderstanding. If a more politically correct term be desired, I at least insist that it be an improvement in accuracy.

In my observation, only a few people of American Indian blood – almost invariably white people with remote or fictitious Indian ancestry, at that – refer to them-selves as "Native American." The great, great majority of Indians I have known call themselves "Indians."

American Indians, as a race, have a rich history, many virtues, and good reason to resent the treatment their ancestors endured while people of other races were settling this continent. However, not on that account will I concede that they deserve to be treated with any greater degree of humorless reverence than that which we accord, say, the Fighting Irish.

*

Time To End Racism At Van Devander
By Dr. Faye Bannister

At the beginning of the year, when several students and faculty came to me with a complaint about Van Devander College's sports team mascot, I had to admit that it wasn't a matter I'd thought about much before. I should have. Two weeks ago, when I heard that a demonstration took place outside Kees Schermerhorn Memorial Stadium to protest the use of that mascot, I was delighted. Not a moment too soon, I thought.

It's high time we put an end to this kind of racism – here at Van Devander, or anywhere else that a people is insulted, dehumanized, objectified, mocked. Using Native Americans as "mascots" (and what an awful, ugly, paternalistic word that is, when you think about it) gives certain people an excuse to regard them as less than people. It encourages them to perpetuate every negative stereotype about Native Americans: that they're drunks, lazy, bloodthirsty, and maybe even cowardly. Even when a Native American team mascot isn't portrayed as a clown (and how rare is that?) he's at best portrayed as a "noble savage." Maybe brave, but not the equal, culturally or mentally, of the Anglo.

Native American team mascots are almost always objects of ridicule. Take the Cleveland Indians' uniform, for instance, which includes a picture of an idiotically grinning Native American, obviously drunk. Even teams that just use the name, without a mascot, are offensive. I cannot believe that in the United States of America we have a professional football team called the Redskins. Why not the N – rs, or the Wetbacks?

Van Devander is one of the worst offenders, with its "Willie Wilden" mascot. He's physically malformed, he's brandishing an instrument of death and destruction, he's stereotypically naked except for a loincloth, he's screaming incoherently (and I can't help assuming that the people who designed the logo figured he was probably drunk, too), and some people might get the impression that he's yelling from a safe distance, implying cowardice.

Not to mention the name "Wildens." I understand that's what the early Dutch settlers called the Native Americans. Obviously it means "wild ones." As though the Native American civilization was somehow less than the European one. They're animals, you see, not even people. That's the stereotype we perpetuate, as long as we tolerate a nickname like that.

And for God's sake, we use it even more offensively in the name of our town! Wildenkill! What would the reaction be if a town named itself Jewkill, or Womanrape? I am amazed that nothing has been done about this, but I intend to let the people of this town know that Van Devander College is not going to stand for it.

I can't change the world overnight, but I intend to change a few things, in my own little corner of the world, and there's no time like the present to start. Accordingly, I've ordered new sweatshirts, t-shirts, banners, pennants, and other logoed merchandise – minus the offensive picture of Willie Wilden. This will be available for sale at the next home game – Homecoming. Our fans will be encouraged to bring in their old shirts and banners – those that have Willie Wilden's picture on them – to exchange them for a rebate coupon good toward the purchase of the new merchandise. Moreover, the banner that depicts Willie Wilden will be removed from the football stadium.

That's just a start. As for the team name, according to the rules of the college, it can't be changed by me – only by the trustees. I intend to propose to the Faculty Senate that they should adopt a resolution demanding a name-change, and I'm confident that it will pass. I hope that they'll suggest a more humanitarian, peaceful name. I welcome suggestions – and maybe we can adopt the best of them as an unofficial nickname, which will become the de facto nickname whether it's ever adopted by the trustees or not.

(We're playing Williams College at Homecoming, and they're called the Purple Cows. Why can't we do something fun, like that, instead of the racist, hate-mongering mascot we have now?)

Also, starting with Homecoming, a certain cheer – apparently a malicious parody of what some people would call a Native American war chant – will be considered a racist remark. We have a rule in place, that clearly states that racist or sexist remarks constitute grounds for removal from the stadium, and that asinine cheer strikes me as about as racist as they come. It's hate-speech, pure and simple. Security personnel have been instructed to remove anyone from the stands who uses it.

I don't like to micromanage, so I don't have any plans, as yet, to abolish Van Devander's cheerleading squad. But I will point out that it encourages the sexual objectification of women. A forward-thinking school like Van Devander is no place to encourage looking up women's skirts. Our athletic department should consider itself duly warned that it may be creating a hostile environment for our women students. And they should consider what they ought to do about it.

As for changing the name of this town to something other than Wildenkill, I can't do much about that – yet. But what I can do is call for our students and faculty to get involved in the local government – to run for office, or support candidates who have enlightened, forward-thinking attitudes, who can turn this into a true "city for the people."

I have fallen in love with this town and this school. Many of Van Devander's students and faculty have, too. We want to cure it of its institutionalized racism and elitism. We can't do it all at once, but even the longest journey begins with a single step. Join us.

*

"Mr. Dance, have you got a minute?" Ballou asked his student as the afternoon's Expository Writing class was dispersing. "If you're running to another class, maybe you could stop by my office later."

"No, now's good." Ballou and Tim Dance fell into step and walked down the corridor toward the English faculty's offices. Dance was bigger than Ballou but still on the small side for a tackle. Not much chance of his playing football after college.

"How does the rest of the team feel about this?" Ballou asked. "About Dr. Bannister banning that cheer, and trying to get rid of the name, and all that?"

"I haven't talked to any of them," Dance replied, as they walked into the faculty room and sat down in Ballou's cubicle. "I just heard about it today, but I can ask around."

"Well, does it bug *you*?"

"It's the cheer thing that pisses me off," Dance replied. "I don't care about the name or the logo or whatever, and besides I'm a senior so I'll be gone by the time they officially change it. But I like that cheer, man. Professor. It identifies the team. You know, like when we played at Harvard, last year, they got the fans singing 'Fight Fiercely, Harvard!' And we have the 'oo-ga-cha-ga.' It's not much, but it's ours.

"And you know, when we have the ball, and we're driving, specially if it's late in the game and it's close, like against Cornell a couple weeks ago, and you hear everyone going 'oo-ga-cha-ga,' and, man, the hair starts standing up on the back of your neck, and there's nothing else like it. I know I'm not good enough to even get a look from the NFL. This is as close as I get to the big time. And I like that cheer, man. Professor. So does it bug me? I'm just fuc – I'm furious at her, if you want to know."

"Gonna do anything about it?"

Dance shrugged. "Don't know there's much I can do," he replied. "I'm not leading a strike by the football team, if that's what you mean."

"Hell, no," said Ballou. "But maybe we can brainstorm a little. Be great if we could come up with something."

Five minutes after Dance left, a knock came on the doorframe of Ballou's cubicle. Ballou looked up to see Stan Something-or-other, who looked mighty crestfallen, although sober. Ballou motioned him to the seat Tim Dance had vacated.

"I need to talk to you about Saturday night," Stan told him, keeping his voice down. "Lee won't talk to me anymore. And one of the guys we were with on Saturday said he saw her leaving that bar with you, and..."

"She won't talk to you? Don't tell me she refused to ride home with you."

"She drove us back yesterday. And she didn't say a word to me, and then when we got back here she just said, 'Don't bother calling

me again,' and took all her shit out of my car and walked away. And
I called over to Ohmygod and they won't take my calls, and she
won't even look at me when I try to talk to her..."

"Wait," said Ballou, perplexed. "You called over to *where*?"

"The Jewish sorority house. Omega Omicron. Only everybody
calls it Ohmygod Ohmygod. Because of... you know, it has kind of
a reputation. I mean, it doesn't, but the girls there are mostly real
stuck-up, so the guys they won't go out with are always making
up stories about them, you know, and... Look, does she have some
kind of thing going with you?" Stan's voice rose a little at the end,
and he snapped his head up and looked Ballou right in the face,
but he didn't appear to offer any menace yet.

"Oh, dear, did somebody tell you that, Mr. ... Stan?"

"No. She said she slept in my car. But then after we got back
here yesterday and we split up, I remembered that she couldn't
have, because I always lock that car, and I *know* I'd locked it Saturday night because I always do, and I know she didn't have the
keys. And everybody saw her leaving that bar with you."

"Well, she did," said Ballou. "She had no idea where you had
gone. She saw you being carried out – we all did – and she decided
she didn't want anything to do with you in the condition you were
in. I offered to find her a motel room, but she asked me to take
her to your car. She said she was going to make sure you didn't try
to drive it while you were drunk. She insisted on waiting for you,
which was noble of her, and more than you deserved, under the
circumstances. If she's decided to drop you, maybe she had a good
reason."

Stan looked perplexed, and then a thought hit him. "Yeah, but
why would she say she slept in my car? How could she say that?"

Because she's not bright enough to remember that she couldn't
have, Ballou said to himself.

"How the hell do I know?" Ballou replied. "For all I know, she
didn't. Maybe she told you that to spare you the knowledge that

she'd ended up sleeping on the hard ground, or just walking around all night, while you were doing whatever you were doing."

Stan buried his face in his hands and slowly rocked back and forth in the visitor's chair.

"Well, damn it, Stan, you should have taken better care of her. Not that it's my business, but a guy can't expect to get as drunk as you were, in front of his girlfriend, and still have her wanting anything to do with him."

Stan raised his head and glared at Ballou again.

"Are you sure you didn't sleep with her?"

"What can I tell you? You won't believe me unless I say I did, and I'm not going to lie just to satisfy you. And if you have to ask that kind of a question about anybody, maybe it's an indication that she's had enough of you. It's your business what you do, but if I were in your position and really wanted to get her back, I'd write her a letter apologizing for my behavior and begging her forgiveness."

"I told her I was sorry."

"Stan, you'd better learn this now: To get along with a woman, you have to get used to saying 'I'm sorry' over and over and over again, because she won't listen the first time. And even if you say it a hundred times she might not pay any attention to it. And even if you weren't wrong, and even if you're not sorry, you're still going to have to say it. Look, frankly, I'm pretty sure you've blown it permanently. And I know because I got myself into the same kind of fix a couple of times, when I was in college."

"You did?"

"What, you think I was born old?"

Stan held his head in his hands again.

"How am I supposed to trust you?" he asked Ballou at length. "How do I know you're not telling me that because you want her for yourself?"

"That's not something I can prove, is it? You don't have to take my word for it. Try to get her back."

"Then why are you telling me I blew it?"

"That's hardly information you didn't have before."

Stan rocked to and fro in his chair.

"There's gotta be something I can do."

Ballou shook his head. "There are things you can try," he conceded. "Let me tell you what I did, in your situation, so you'll know not to repeat it, because I promise you it doesn't work. I apologized, and I begged her forgiveness, and I asked her for another chance. And that was my fatal mistake."

Ballou thought for a few seconds before going on.

"Look, you probably blew it permanently," he told Stan. "But if you've got any shot at all, your only hope is to send her a letter – no flowers, no candy, no nothing else, just a letter – in which you say you're sorry for your behavior, you know that it was inexcusable, and you know that the relationship must end as a result of it. And then you say something like – hold on." Ballou turned away from Stan and began typing on his computer.

"'Although I know I can never see you again,'" Ballou declaimed as he typed, "'I hope to have your forgiveness, for I will always bitterly regret my behavior to one I admire more than she will ever know.' Or words to that effect. And then that's *it*. You got it? That's *it*. Period. Ask for *nothing,* other than forgiveness. Don't ask to see her, don't ask for any token, just take 100 percent of the blame, and walk away, and never initiate any further contact. That's your *only* chance, and it's a very slim one." Ballou hit "print," and handed Stan the piece of paper that bore the message of surrender.

"What you should have done," Ballou reflected, "from the point of view of keeping the relationship, is you should never have apologized in the first place. Anything like that ever happens again, with some other chick? Your best play, the next time you see her, is to say not a damn thing about it, just act like you weren't even thinking about it. And if she gets on your case, just say something like, 'Gee, what are you bothered about?' Let her get as mad as she wants. Let her yell at you, whatever – but whatever she does, just act like you can't believe she's making such a big thing of it, and plain refuse to play along with the idea that you did anything wrong."

Stan looked up at Ballou, half-believing, sheepish.

"Too late for that. I already said I was sorry."

"Okay, and from the perspective of moral correctness, you did right. From the perspective of getting her back, you didn't."

"How not?"

"You apologize for something like what went down the other night, and you're handing her a degree of control. Now you've got to crawl and beg to get her to take you back, and she won't find that very attractive, will she? So she'll hook up with some other guy whom she hasn't yet seen in that position. Bottom line is, she'll forgive you a lot faster for being a drunk asshole than she will for being a wuss."

Finally, Stan looked more than a little angry. "You mean you're a wuss if you apologize when you were wrong?"

"No! But in some situations you'll be *perceived* as a wuss. But look, now that you've already apologized and can't take it back, the next best thing is to do it over, in a kind of a strong, manly style. But like I say, don't count on it. It's your only shot. You could just ignore her completely. The best way to fascinate most girls is to let them think you don't give a shit. But that takes incredible self-control, which most guys don't have, if they're emotionally invested."

"Yeah-no, you're right, I'll write that letter like you said," Stan replied, in a resigned tone. "I can't let her go. You just don't have any idea what she means to me. God, she's the most beautiful… she is, isn't she?"

"She's very pretty," Ballou conceded. "Anyway, I hope I've helped. I'll just repeat, do *not* ask her for anything. That's crucial."

Saturday, October 16

.

"The short pitch shot is all about touch, ye see," said Effie Hoo, as Ballou finished hitting the last of several dozen practice balls onto the chipping green at Mourning Wood the next Saturday morning. "It's like any kind of aiming-and-throwing process. With practice, ye develop a sense of the force and speed ye'll require to make the ball travel X number of yards, or even feet. Your short pitch should be the first thing ye practice, when ye break your clubs out in the spring, because if ye have that sense, that touch, ye'll save a half-dozen strokes, every round."

"Thanks," said Ballou, returning his wedge to his bag. He wore his Willie Wilden sweatshirt with a sweater under it. It was a grey, drizzly day, definitely fall weather. "And now, Madame, we're off to Kees Schermerhorn Memorial Stadium. If you don't feel like passing out leaflets with us, I'll just give you your ticket, and you go ahead and take your seat."

"I'd not miss it," said Effie, "although I haven't handed out literature since I was wee, when my uncle stood for Parliament. Labour, of course, which I expect would be anathema to yourself."

"Your expectation is realized," said Ballou.

"I'd not have agreed with ye on this issue, before readin' your column," Effie admitted as they walked to Ballou's car. "Ye argued sensibly, though. Did ye organize this wee demonstration yourself?"

"Certainly not. The idea came from one of the football players, in fact. He blasted an e-mail to as many students, faculty, alumni, and townspeople as he could contact, suggesting that they show up at the stadium with Willie Wilden t-shirts and sweatshirts, if they had them. He mentioned it in both of my classes, too, although of course I didn't comment one way or the other. In the e-mail he put it to us as, 'Let's protect our dear old friend, Willie Wilden.'"

As it was well before kickoff-time, Ballou got a parking place just a few yards from the stadium, where he could see that two small groups were already gathering just outside: the pro-Willie Wildens and the antis, so far only four or five of each. Ballou and Effie joined their group, and each took a handful of leaflets – presumably composed by Tim Dance, who presumably was warming up on the field – urging people to write to the Board of Trustees and the Faculty Senate and urge them against any changes the team name or interference with the use of its mascot's image. Contact information was provided.

So far, hardly anyone was there to hand the literature to. The two groups stood at a distance, covertly eyeing each other. Bonnie Bonney was there once again, but never looked in Ballou's direction. Martin Wandervogel and several of his students – including Ballou's student Tonia Kampling – were filming. Wandervogel and Ballou caught each other's eyes, and both glared and looked away.

Fi Tanquiz showed up, carrying not only his Dran-O bottle, but a sign that read:

DON'T WANT YOUR WILLIE WILDEN APPAREL?
I PAY CASH, NOT REBATES!

"Where's the cash going to come from?" Ballou asked him.

"From... from my... my pocket," said Tanquiz. "They're offering $2 rebates on merchandise inside, if you turn, turn in a Willie Wilden shirt. I'm offering cash. I'm not going to pay out a cent, just watch. What's, what's the worst that could happen? Five people sell me their shirts? I can afford ten bucks. But I won't have to."

Little Chuck Tisquantum joined them, in a Willie Wilden sweatshirt with a pennant stuck down the back of it.

Apparently the anti-Wildens faction had not improved much on its high-water mark a few weeks previously. Its crowd this day reached a dozen or so, not counting the camera crew. The pro-Wildens group got bigger and bigger: five, 10, 20, then 30 people, mainly male students, and several adults who might have been alumni. Ballou was the only member of the faculty that he could see. The old man – the one who wore nothing but logoed apparel, who'd ordered everyone to stand for the kickoff at the opening game a few weeks ago – stopped by.

"What's all this?" he asked. Little Chuck Tisquantum explained it to him. The old man joined the crowd too, as they began to chant:

Ho-ho!
Hey-hey!
Willie Wilden's here to stay! Ho-ho!
Hey-hey!
Willie Wilden's here to stay!

Hey-hey!
Ho-ho!
Political correctness has to go! Hey-hey!
Ho-ho!
Political correctness has to go!

Fi Tanquiz whispered a suggestion to Ballou, who nodded. "Technically, it's 'Whom do we want?' said Ballou, "but it's best to be idiomatic in the circumstances."

"Who do we want?" Tanquiz hollered.

"Willie Wilden!" Ballou boomed.

"When do we want him?"

"Forever!"

The crowd picked it up.

"Who do we want?"

"Willie Wilden!"

"When do we want him?"

"Forever!"

"Rabbit season!" cried Tanquiz.

"Duck season!" replied 30 people, without missing a beat.

"Hey, there's Professor Cunn-i-*len*-zeez," said Fi Tanquiz. Professor Violet Menzies approached the group, wearing an antique raccoon coat against the chill. She walked arm-in-arm with the elderly French professor, Mademoiselle Macaque. The two women nodded to Ballou, Professor Menzies giving him a tiny one-sided smile.

"Violet, care to join us?" Ballou asked.

"We'll pass," Professor Menzies drawled. "I was always taught that a Southern lady doesn't demonstrate. Besides, I don't hold with this slogan-chanting. It discourages true discourse, the witty rebuke, the retort courteous. But y'all have our moral support."

"You please speak for yourself, Violette," said Professor Macaque. "I am opposed to *racisme*."

"Raison de plus, pour démontrer!" Ballou replied.

"Manifester," Professor Macaque corrected him. "To demonstrate politically, is *manifester*. *Démontrer*, that is, how you say, to show, to explain. This is *manifestation*."

"Manifestation, bien sûr. Merci pour me corriger," said Ballou, bowing. Out of the corner of his eye, he saw Michael Brooke walking toward the stadium, holding hands with the black girl who'd been sitting next to him at the game a few weeks before. Tonia Kam-

pling, catching sight of them, waved a little too enthusiastically and ran over to greet Mr. Brooke. Brooke's girlfriend shot dagger-looks at her; Brooke forced a smile. Miss Kampling talked rapidly at him, oblivious to the other lady's expression. Ballou was too far away to hear her.

"Violet, I just was reminded of something," Ballou said. "I need a little professional advice. I have a student who just will not participate in class. She hardly ever talks, and when she does she's so nervous and self-conscious that she can hardly say anything. And that, I could deal with, but she also has not submitted any poetry for class critique. That is, she'll hand in poems to me, but won't expose them to the class. What would you do in that situation?"

Professor Menzies snorted. "I'd shanghai the fragile little flower," she said. "You never promised not to discuss a student's poems in class if she didn't volunteer them, did you? So, pick one of her poems and give it to the class whether she likes it or not. Believe me, she'll start volunteering after that – rather than let you decide which of her poems get read in class."

She gave Ballou another nod, and she and Professor Macaque proceeded toward the stadium.

"That coat would've looked a lot better on the raccoon!" Bonnie Bonney shouted as Professor Menzies passed her.

"Die in a fire, you ugly girl," Professor Menzies replied conversationally, not breaking stride.

About 10 minutes before kickoff, the pro-Willie Wilden demonstrators formed a snake-line, hands on each other's shoulders, and made for the stadium, chanting the forbidden chant. Outside the entranceways, they broke up, since they had tickets in different parts of the stadium. Ballou observed that the new, unlogoed merchandise did not appear to be attracting any buyers.

"And where's Miss Sweetness and Light this afternoon?" Effie demanded as she and Ballou took their seats. "I'd have thought ye'd have brought her along, to impress her with your leadership skills. Or has she given ye the brush-off already?"

"She told me her busy season's going to run from now through the New Year," Ballou replied, "especially weekends. Which means no more football with her, I guess."

"So, that's it? That's the brush-off?"

"I've no idea. We e-mail a lot. Nothing big, just 'Hi, what's new,' or we tell each other funny stuff about our jobs."

"And I daresay ye're drivin' over to her bakery whenever ye have a spare moment. Ye're not able to keep away, are ye?"

Ballou bristled, inwardly, but he pretended to smile.

"Believe it or not, just once this week," he replied.

"Och, Roger, I'm not makin' sport of ye, not really. It must be hell to be a single man. No kiddin', ye must feel absolutely helpless every moment of your life, and I shouldn't wonder."

The stadium filled up nearly to capacity, with an optimistic crowd – no doubt partly because it was Homecoming, but partly also because Van Devander – unbelievably – had not lost yet that season. When Williams kicked off to Van Devander, the PA announcer recited the usual prayer of political correctness–with an addition:

"Ladies and gentlemen, on behalf of Coach Rudy Grouwinkel and the Van Devander Wildens, we remind you that Schermerhorn Memorial Stadium is a smoke-free facility. We ask you to support the team in a positive manner. Any racist or sexist comments directed at players or officials will not be tolerated, and are grounds for removal from the stadium. We especially ask that you refrain from any cheers or other expressions that might reflect negative stereotypes of Native Americans. These will be regarded as racist comments."

The crowd grumbled, and Ballou heard a few boos – but he also heard a few cheers, which infuriated him. On the whole the crowd was pretty subdued, as Van Devander failed to move the ball and had to punt – amazing to Ballou, because the Williams defense didn't appear to have any idea what it was doing.

"Williams' offense isn't much better, is it?" Effie remarked a few plays later. "They really do look like Purple Cows."

For a quarter, the two teams traded the ball back and forth: Williams inept, Van Devander listless. They played in near-silence, with only the occasional shout from the stands when it looked like a big play might develop – but none ever did.

In the second quarter, Williams, having pushed the ball to the Van Devander 40, made a field goal (which seemed to amaze the kicker himself, more than anyone else) to take a 3-0 lead. A few plays later, Van Devander fumbled deep its own territory, and while Williams couldn't advance the ball much farther, they added another field goal. At the half, Van Devander trailed, 6-0.

"I'm sorry this would be the game I brought you to," Ballou told Effie. "Not only is the team playing like shit, but since it's Homecoming, we'll have to sit through ten or 15 minutes of introductions of aged alumni before the band gets onto the field."

"Bear it with a becoming grace," Effie commanded.

The game, like the weather, continued drear and grey in the second half. Williams added another field goal.

Van Devander began moving the ball. They got it to midfield, then marched slowly, laboriously downfield – and still the crowd did no more than murmur. The pipe band's bass drummer ordinarily waited for the crowd to begin a chant, but this time hearing none, he began to play:

BOOM! (pause, pause, pause)
BOOM! (pause) BOOM! (pause)
BOOM! (pause, pause, pause)
BOOM! (pause) BOOM! (pause)

No response from the stands. But the drummer continued. On the Wildens' bench, the players and coaches – but not the cheerleaders, Ballou noticed – picked it up:

Oo-ga-cha-ga!
Oo-ga! Oo-ga!
Oo-ga-cha-ga!
Oo-ga! Oo-ga!

As the Wildens moved the ball inside the Purple Cows' 10-yard line, a few brave spectators (mostly alumni) – and, at last, the cheerleaders – joined in.

Oo-ga-cha-ga!
Oo-ga! Oo-ga!
Oo-ga-cha-ga!
Oo-ga! Oo-ga!

Not far from Ballou, two guards moved toward the old man in the logoed costume, who was chanting louder than anyone. Ballou, Mrs. Hoo, and several other fans formed a ring around the old man and began to chant, too, in the guards' faces.

Oo-ga-cha-ga!
Oo-ga! Oo-ga!
Oo-ga-cha-ga!
Oo-ga! Oo-ga!

Van Devander scored on the next play, and the crowd gave a real football crowd's yell – cheering for the team for the first time that day. Following the extra point, Van Devander kicked off, and as the teams huddled the PA announcer warned:

"Ladies and gentlemen, we remind you that certain cheers have been forbidden by order of our president."

"Up your crack, you kiss-ass wimp," screamed Fi Tanquiz from the student seats.

Williams could make no headway; they punted. Van Devander took over near midfield and drove for another touchdown – the crowd oo-ga-chagging all the way, this time, backed by the bass drum. Neither the guards nor the PA announcer said or did anything more about it.

Van Devander led 14-9 at the end of the third quarter, and the final 15 minutes were a rout, the Wildens scoring three times more to make it 35-9. The last score occurred when a Van Devander linebacker picked up a Williams fumble and ran it back 50 yards, mowing down tacklers all the way as the crowd leapt to its feet and roared. Effie let off an ear-shattering Highland yell, got Ballou in a bear-hug, lifted him a few inches into the air, and gave him a big wet kiss on the nose as she set him down.

Monday, October 18

Ballou saw the red message light twinkling on the phone on his desk, as he entered his cubicle after Poetry Workshop. He already felt rotten. He'd started class by producing copies of one of Tonia Kampling's poems, passing them out, and giving Miss Kampling the choice of reading the poem herself or letting him do it. Miss Kampling had stared at him, deep hurt in her eyes, like a small child who had just been terribly mistreated for no reason. As he'd read the poem to the class – and it was not a bad one – Miss Kampling actually covered her face with her hands. The criticism from the class had been tentative, as though each student were afraid of breaking her.

"It's good, Tonia," Michael Brooke had said. "Don't worry so much." Miss Kampling had gazed at Brooke adoringly and touched his arm, making him blush and stare at his lap.

As he sat down at his desk and began to play his messages, Ballou wondered whether he should have warned Miss Kampling that a critique was coming, and decided he probably should have, and that he'd probably withheld warning simply because he was a prick. He was pretty sure that instant karma was forthcoming.

"Roger, Faye Bannister. I need to see you in my office. As soon as you get this message. Immediately."

Ballou's guts turned to water. Had Tonia Kampling run right to Dr. Bannister's office to complain of his cruelty?

He walked over to the administration building. This time, at least, nobody was filming the interview, but once again Jack Hogenfuss was already sitting in the office. And this time Dr. Bannister was not smiling.

"Have a seat, Roger," she said, "and take a look at this." She handed Ballou a sheet of paper. "I got this by e-mail this morning, and so did a lot of other people. Apparently somebody blasted it to the whole school – the faculty and some of the students. I'd like to know what you have to say about it."

THE ONLY GOOD ONE IS ON OUR LOGO

What are Indians good for anyway? They're good for getting drunk, raping white women, scalping white men, and knocking white babies' brains out against a tree trunk.

When they're not doing that they're collecting welfare, gambling, and extorting money from the government.

These "noble savages" have a lot of nerve, saying that Indian sports mascots demean their race. When a sports team calls itself the Indians or the Chiefs or the Redskins or the Wildens or something like that, they're showing Indians a hell of a lot more respect than they deserve. Who wouldn't rather be a nigger than an Indian, any day?

Sherman and Custer and other great Americans should have finished the job!

– Roger Sullivan Ballou

"This is none of my doing," Ballou said.

"See, Faye? I told you!" said Hogenfuss. Dr. Bannister raised a hand to silence him.

"Do you repudiate it?" she asked Ballou.

"I didn't write this, and I don't agree with a word of it. I disown it completely. It's obviously somebody's attempt to satirize my position, but it doesn't even come close to doing that."

"Do you have any idea who might have written this?"

An idea, Ballou said to himself, but not a speck of proof.

"What was the e-mail address that sent it?" he asked.

"I didn't write it down," said Dr. Bannister. "Just a lot of random numbers and letters."

"I promise you it can't be traced to any e-mail account of mine. I have an AOL account, and my vandevander.edu account, and they're both password-protected, and I don't have the passwords written down anywhere. This could have come from anyone. It might be someone who's trying to get me in trouble, but if it is, he's doing... I'm sorry, Faye, *she or he* is doing a pretty clumsy job of it, since obviously I would have no reason to write such a thing. It might be someone trying to make a joke, but I hope you'll agree with me that it's not very funny. Either way, it's a pretty stupid person who's behind it, but that doesn't narrow it down much."

"Hmmm," said Dr. Bannister, steepling her fingers and looking wise. "You might be right. Or, have you considered the possibility that it might be someone who's on your side on... on this issue, and somehow got the idea that he'd be helping your cause with this kind of literature?"

"As far as I know," Ballou replied, "the people who are on my side – I assume you mean on the issue that you and I debated in the *Advertiser* – the people who feel the same way I do, feel that way because they like and respect Indians. Or because they *are* Indians."

Ballou was about to mention that Little Chuck Tisquantum, Jr. had been among the counter-demonstrators on Saturday, but thought better of bringing that incident up. He figured Dr. Bannister would, and he was right.

"I also understand that you participated in a racist demonstration outside the football stadium on Saturday, and in a racist display during the game. This has been noted, and I'm giving you an official warning against this type of activity. Any further infractions of this kind may result in suspension or dismissal."

"Really?" Ballou feigned astonishment. "A racist demonstration?" This time, Ballou decided to go ahead and use his eyes to full advantage. He leaned slightly forward in his chair and gave Dr. Bannister The Look.

"I suggest that you had better establish," he said, "in an open and legal procedure, that that demonstration was racist, or that it was anything but a perfectly legitimate defense of a school tradition, or that it was in any way disorderly, or prejudicial to the welfare of this school or to any student, or otherwise in violation of my contract or school rules. I also suggest that if you try to discipline anyone for cheering at a football game, you'll be opening up a major can of worms. Finally, if your accusation of racism ever goes beyond this room, you will take the consequences."

"Are you threatening me, Roger?"

"What on earth could I threaten you with? I'm rejecting your accusation, is all, and I'm advising you to be very careful what you accuse me of."

Ballou wanted to say a lot more but wasn't quite sure what he should say, or how. Pretty clearly, Dr. Bannister was having the same problem. They sat staring at each other for what might have been 10 or 15 seconds. Jack Hogenfuss didn't move, probably hoping that he'd been forgotten.

"Is that all?" Ballou asked.

"Actually, no, there is one other item, and that is this." Dr. Bannister passed Ballou another sheet of paper.

Mon Oct 18 1999 10:15
FROM: parzival@vandevander.edu
TO: rballou@vandevander.edu
CC: dquagga@wildenkilladvertiser.com
        hhoo@odelllawfirm.com
        effie.hoo@linkslessons.com
        fbannister@vandevander.edu
        editor_vandevandertatler@vandevander.edu
        editor_vandevanderian@vandevander.edu

Hi folks!

This picture was so sweet I couldn't help sending it over to you for a keepsake. Isn't it precious? Love blooms in the most unlikely places! Donald, this might look nice on the gossip page! Poor Hugh!

Best regards,
Parzival

Pasted into the e-mail was a slightly fuzzy but identifiable photograph of a laughing Roger Ballou getting embraced and kissed on the nose by Effie Hoo in the closing minutes of the football game two days earlier.

"Now, Roger," said Dr. Bannister, "your private life is your business, ordinarily. If you want to carry on with a married woman in private, I might not approve of it, but it wouldn't be my place to do anything about it. But if you're going to engage in public displays of affection on campus, at a school function, I suggest that you choose someone more... appropriate."

Ballou sat back and gazed out the window for a moment.

"Mrs. Hoo is my friend," he said, "and I took her to the game with the full knowledge of Mr. Hoo – not, as you say, that it's any of your business. When we scored our last touchdown, she grabbed me and gave me a little smooch, because she is that kind of a person. If you doubt me, I suggest you pick up that phone on your desk and call Mrs. Hoo right now. I can give you her number. Or why don't you call Mr. Hoo and discuss the issue with him? Or better yet, maybe you and I could discuss who this 'Parzival' is. I suppose you know that that's Martin Wandervogel. Maybe you'll talk to him about using a Van Devander College e-mail address to try to spread scandal. You might ask him about that other e-mail, too, while you're up."

"I'm not the least bit interested in who 'Parzival' is," said Dr. Bannister. "As for your explanation, I'm glad to hear it, and I'll give you the benefit of the doubt. Just be careful from now on. And you are officially warned for that demonstration."

"I dare you to use that against me," Ballou replied hotly, gripping the arms of his chair and leaning forward as though getting to his feet. Jack Hogenfuss started from his seat too, as though to interfere with a physical attack, but Ballou stopped him with a gesture. "If you try to mess with me over something like that..." (Ballou stopped himself, and returned his voice to a normal speaking tone) "you'll disappoint me." He rose, bowed slightly, and walked out of Dr. Bannister's office.

If there were a silver lining to that interview with Dr. Bannister, it was that Ballou now had another reason to call Hugh Hoo, and incidentally find out whether Hoo had seen the photograph, and whether he'd put the worst interpretation on it.

"My dear chap, I understand you've been romancing my wife," said the barrister as soon as he'd come on the line. "Or should I say, pitching the woo to Mrs. Hoo? Take her, Sir, she is yours. Look, as Effie would say, dinna fash yerself. She's explained it already, and I know exactly how it must have been. But what I wonder is this: This Wandervogel chap is not only trying to make trouble for you, or conceivably for Effie, or even for me, but he wants us to *know* that he's trying to make trouble. Letting us see who else he sent the picture to, as opposed to blackmail."

"That's not the half of it," Ballou said, and quickly but carefully recited his account of the mysterious e-mail blast, and Dr. Bannister's "official warning."

"At this point, I'm going to have to stop you," said Hoo. "This firm represents Van Devander, as you know, and that being the case, it would be inadvisable for me to speak to you on this matter any further, as it looks like litigation has become a real possibility.

"In fact, I must insist that from now on, our contact be entirely social. I'll be glad to tangle with you on the golf course or over the bridge table, at least until or unless you actually have to sue for wrongful termination, but... "

"That is what's going to happen, then, I guess," said Ballou.

"It's early times to be talking about that," said Hoo. "I wouldn't advise you to 'lawyer up' just yet, for I don't want you to be put to any needless expense. But oh, supposing something were to happen, and if someone were to ask me quite innocently about a good labor lawyer, I could recommend a name or two.

"For now, just keep your pecker up – but not around my wife, if you please! Speaking of which, we'll be seeing you on Saturday, *chez nous,* won't we? I'll give you a tip: wear dark clothing. Our house is a ghastly huge old haunted thing, and we usually have a good game of hide-and-seek after the bridge."

Ballou went home late that afternoon facing the probability that his decision to leave the city had been a disastrous mistake. Van Devander wasn't a big enough place for him and Dr. Bannister, and if she were signed to an unassailable contract, for three years, he couldn't count on being asked to stay longer than the one probationary year he'd signed on for – if he weren't fired sooner. So, would he have to move back to the city – no doubt to a much more expensive apartment than the one he'd left behind – in order to rebuild his writing business?

Plus, Ballou wanted to tell Dora the whole story — partly to impress her and partly to gain her sympathy — and he had no idea of how to do that to his best advantage.

Wednesday, October 20

Luke Bonney, Jr. was finishing raking the leaves that had fallen into Ballou's yard. Not that Ballou would have minded if the leaves had stayed there all winter, but he supposed some of the neighbors or some municipal authority might object, and now he was wondering – with his income apparently in jeopardy – whether he'd been extravagant, hiring someone else to do the job. But he couldn't bear the prospect of doing that back-breaking and incredibly boring work himself. As Luke dragged the filled polyurethane bags to the curbside, Ballou went into his house and came out with two Cokes.

"Here you go, Mr. Bonney Junior," he said, handing a Coke to Luke along with his fee. "Set a spell." Ballou walked back up the front porch steps and sat down in the swing, motioning for Luke to join him. Luke came up onto the porch but declined the swing, perching on the porch railing opposite.

"Can't stay long," said Luke. He guzzled Coke, and belched. "Have to get to rehearsal. My sister dragged me into that musical, too. I'm an Able Seaman. My brother's too young, or he'd be Abel the Able Seaman."

"And how's your mother's book doing?"

"Okay, I guess. She's still out of town a lot, you know, for those signings. And then she's got this new boyfriend she's with whenever she's in town, so I guess she's pretty busy with one thing and another." The boy grinned – a little lewdly.

"That filmmaker guy?"

"Yeah. And, you know, Bonnie hangs out with his son – the grown-up son – so sometimes that whole bunch is over at our place, and it gets kinda noisy. Only he gets upset – Martin does – when my brother and I aren't around, because he's always using Mom's computer. He claims his is broken, but yeah, right, I believe that. He just wants an excuse to come over. And he's always messing something up and going nuts. Sometimes he'll do stuff to the computer that I don't know how he did it, don't know what buttons he could've pushed. It's funny when it happens, though, 'cause he throws a tantrum, y'know, like a little kid."

Luke set down his Coke can, assumed a facial expression that was a fair impression of Martin Wandervogel's, and emitted a horrible groan, beating his fists on his knees. He jumped to his feet, pretending to bawl, as he kicked the porch railing again and again.

"Fuck!" Luke screamed. *"Fuckin' piece of fuckin' shit computer! Fuck! Fuck!"*

"Easy," said Ballou. "Don't break the railing. No kidding, he gets like that?"

"Yeah, and then he'll *order* me or Abel to fix it for him. Like it was our fault."

"Sounds funny as hell."

"It gets old."

"Then I daresay your mother will get tired of it too, eventually."

"I wish."

As long as Luke was there, Ballou could keep his mind off Dora. Once Luke was gone, there reappeared the stubborn feeling that he could not, would not wait until Saturday night at the

Hoos to talk with Dora. He sat in his study, working, for a couple of hours, researching an article and marking students' papers, all along asking himself, every few minutes, "Would she be at home now? Would it be a good time to call? And what would I be calling for? What would I say? Is it okay to call just to talk?"

At about seven o'clock, Ballou picked up his phone and punched in the first three digits of Dora's number, then put the phone back down. He didn't know whether she kept regular hours – what with her bakery – or not. She could be in bed. No, she wouldn't be. He picked up the phone and this time punched in five digits before desisting again.

He took a half-hour's walk – going in the opposite direction from Dora's house – returned home, tossed a salad, and put a potato in the oven to bake. He'd have a shower and a martini, and that would mean he'd have to sit down to dinner (that potato, that salad, and a small steak) at about 8:30, and then he might be full and contented enough so that he might resist the temptation to use the phone for the rest of the evening.

He took a long shower, put on his bathrobe, and limped into the kitchen – and the phone rang. Ballou scurried to the study, imploring whatever powers were out there to let him hear, "Roger? This is Dora. Would you like to come over here and make love?"

In which case, be-damned to the potato. Or, no! Better yet, he'd reply, "Sure, but you'll have to wait until I've had my dinner." He picked up the receiver, and forced himself to take a deep breath and let it out before hitting the "talk" button.

"Roger, it's Lee."

"Lee… ?"

"*Miss Grossbaum!*" Lee giggled.

"Oh, hi… Lee. I guess I can call you Lee when we're off duty. What can I do to you?"

"Are you busy?"

"Not really. Just got out of the shower. Just about to make a martini and have some dinner."

"Hey, you eat late. They serve us way too early at the house."

"You mean Ohmygod Ohmygod?"

"Yeah. I'm just lying around in my room. Nothing I want to see on TV. But I wrote more poetry this afternoon. I did my 20 lines for next week. Anyway, I just called because I wanted to see if you were okay. I heard about that e-mail. Well, actually I got a copy of it, and so did a lot of us. But I know you didn't have anything to do with it. And I don't think anyone thinks you did."

"I hope you're right." Ballou walked back to the kitchen, found his cocktail shaker, and took a half-peeled lemon from inside his fridge. "It's awfully nice of you to call. How are you doing? Are you okay?"

"Oh, I don't *knowwwww.*" Lee drew the last word out in a sort of whine. "I've just felt so uncomfortable since... since the other weekend. And you know, we never talked about it at all, and it just feels funny sitting there in class and acting like nothing ever happened... Like, I don't really want to talk about it? I guess there's nothing to talk about? I just... I'm just kinda down, y'know? And there's nobody here at the house I can really talk to. And well, anyway, I just wanted to hear a friendly voice. What's that noise?"

"I'm just breaking some ice cubes out of the tray. Can't make a martini without ice cubes."

"How do you make a martini?"

"I can talk you through it, if you like." Ballou cradled the receiver between his chin and his left shoulder as he set to work. "First you have to have your cocktail shaker ready, of course. Then you take maybe four ice cubes, one by one, and a soup-spoon, and you crack each ice cube with the spoon and drop the pieces into the shaker. Hear that?"

More giggles. "Yeah."

"Okay, now you add about a teaspoonful of dry vermouth. Some people who think they're real sophisticates say you shouldn't add any vermouth at all, but that's like eating an egg without salt. Okay, and now we put in the gin."

"Not vodka? I thought vodka."

"Only if you're an asshole or a girly-man. Nobody we would care to know would use vodka. Gotta be gin. Good gin, though. Like Bombay, Tanqueray, Boodle's. It makes a difference. And you have to use a lot. Like four or five ounces. A martini is supposed to be a big drink. I hate those bars where they serve you a martini in a glass that wouldn't do for Tom Thumb's piss-pot."

Lee shrieked in appreciation.

"And now," said Ballou, "you put the lid on the shaker and you shake it up good, for about ten seconds. Hear that?"

"Shaken, not stirred. Didn't somebody say that in a movie?"

"That's right. If you stir, your martini won't be cold enough. There are many ways to fuck up a martini, but there's no surer way than by not serving it cold enough. You sacrifice clarity, when you shake, because you aerate the mixture, but I think it looks better that way. Okay, now I'm going to the freezer to get the martini glass that's been sitting there since last night, getting frosty. And I'm going to strain the martini from the shaker into the glass. Hear it?"

"It sounds very sexy."

"That's the idea. A martini is an experience that goes far beyond mere drinking. Okay, now I'm taking this lemon, here – you can always spot a martini-drinker, because he's got a partially-peeled lemon in a Ziploc bag in his fridge – and I'm going to shave off about a two-inch strip of peel, taking *great* care not to cut into the fruit. If you get any lemon juice into the mixture, even a drop, it'll ruin your drink completely. Now I take the lemon peel and twist it over the drink, allowing the lemon oil to congeal in droplets on the surface, then I drop the peel into the glass."

"Don't you use an olive?"

"Some people do, but I don't. An olive gives you a slightly salty undertaste, which I don't like, and it displaces too much gin. Okay, now, some people prefer to take the initial sip of a martini while standing in the kitchen, but I prefer to carry the glass carefully into the living room and sit down before I take that first sip."

"Are you going into your living room now?"

"Indeed I am, and now I'm sitting down in my favorite chair, and I will take my first sip. Ohhh, *Christ*, is that good!"

"Oh, I can just see you!" Lee was laughing again. "That is so you! So... so *debonair*! You're so old-fashioned. In a nice way. But this is a bad time for me to be talking to you, isn't it? When you want to enjoy your martini."

"Oh, not at all. I don't get to go out to bars much, anymore, so I never get any conversation at cocktail hour. This is a nice little change." Ballou struck a match, and inhaled deeply on his first cigarette of the day.

"And now you're lighting a cigarette," said Lee. "I can hear it. Are you using that holder of yours? That is so cool!"

"Yeah, and I'm lovin' it," Ballou replied.

"They don't let us smoke in the house," said Lee. "I don't even smoke anyway, but I see other people doing it and they always look like they're enjoying it so much."

"We do. But you're a gum-chewer, right? And I bet you have a long chain of gum-wrappers, hung on the ceiling of your room."

"How did you know?"

"Just an inspired guess. So, anyway, you said you were feeling down? Anything you want to tell me about?"

"Oh, mostly that I lost a boyfriend. Not that I feel so bad about that, but it's lonely, you know?"

"What, he hasn't come crawling back to you?"

"He did. He told me all about how he talked with you about it — and listen, that's another thing. Thank you so much for not telling Stan all about... you know..."

Ballou only half-listened as Lee went into a long description of the letter that Stan had written her, apologizing for his behavior and withdrawing from their relationship; how he'd continued to try to see her; how she'd finally consented to a long but pointless conversation; how he had still sent her flowers the other day...

Mainly, Ballou was thinking. First, how likely was it that he was being set up with this conversation? Not very. He knew he was probably just being crazy. But he couldn't discount any possibility.

"Lee, let me ask you something," Ballou interrupted her, after a few minutes. "Are you mad at me? For not calling you after that weekend?"

"No!" Lee sounded genuinely surprised. "Why should you have called me? I thought you were mad at me! That's partly why I called tonight."

"No, I'm not mad at you at all. Give yourself a break; that's the kind of thing that can happen on a football weekend."

"I will. What's that banging?"

"I just got a frying pan out of the cupboard. I'm going to fry up a steak for my dinner."

"Ah!" said Lee. *"Vous mangerez un biftec, et quoi d'autre?"*

"What, you want to speak French now? I'm rusty as hell."

"I thought you were going to coach me on my pronunciation. But maybe I should let you eat, now."

"No, that's okay. But in private, we don't have to *vouvoyer* each other. I'm *'tu.'* And so are 'yu.' It'll force you to practice the 'ü' sound, anyway."

"Okay... *d'accord, si vous... si tu veux."*

They found the conversation much slower going once they'd switched to French, partly because Ballou was fixing his dinner but mostly because they each had to grope for a word now and then, or use the English word and ask for a translation. As Ballou ate, Lee read him a few poems she'd written in French. He thought they were bad but not terrible, and he kept that thought to himself.

Finished eating, Ballou dumped the dishes in the kitchen sink for another day, or another week. He got a beer from the fridge, and returned to the living room.

"You know," said Lee, continuing in French, "I had a funny dream last night. I dreamt that you and I had gotten married."

"Is that so? Hmmm. I suppose you could have done worse."

"Does that please you?"

"Well, you're certainly pretty enough for me."

A long pause.

"I wish I could kiss you again," said Lee, at last.

"Darn it, Lee, you're trying to get me in trouble, aren't you?" Ballou said this no more than half-kidding. "Are you recording this conversation?"

"*Noooooo,*" Lee replied, in such a tone as to imply that she wondered what Ballou had been smoking. "Should I?"

Ballou briefed Lee on his various run-ins with Faye Bannister, Martin Wandervogel, and Wandervogel's cohorts.

"For all I know, it was you who complained of me in the first place," he added, with a forced laugh.

"No, it wasn't me." Lee said. "It does sound like somebody's trying to get you in trouble, though."

"No shit. Which is why I'm kind of paranoid at the moment."

"Well, maybe I should have recorded this." Lee giggled. "I like hearing your voice. Would you kiss me if I was there?"

"Probably. Which is why I'm not inviting you."

"I can't get you off my mind," Lee said. "I just had to call you. I'm not helping anyone. Trying to get you in trouble, I mean."

"Well, they're going to get me with or without your help. But you're not doing yourself any favors, thinking about me so much. I'm nothing all that great."

"Awww. Yes you are. Roger? What are you wearing?"

"A goddam chastity belt. And a sheet-metal jockstrap."

"Ha-ha. No, come on. What are you wearing?"

"Just my bathrobe."

"Mmmm. I got into my pajamas while you were having dinner. I'm just lying on my bed now, talking to you. But I could take them off. If you wanted me to."

"What kind of pajamas are they?"

"Pink. Cotton flannel. They're nice and soft. They have white elephants on them. And I'm wearing pink fluffy slippers, too. Roger? If I took my pajamas off... would you take your robe off?"

Ballou took a last quick slug of beer, got up, and walked through the bedroom and into the bathroom, stripping off his robe and tossing it to the floor as he walked. He found a bottle of baby oil, returned to the bedroom, and lay down on his bed.

"I guess I would," he said. "But wouldn't you rather I took them off for you?"

"Go ahead," Lee whispered. "I want you to see me naked."

Saturday, October 23

"First, I shall explain the rules to the newcomers," Hugh Hoo announced. It was the following Saturday night, and they'd cut the bridge short, since there were 11 guests: two foursomes and one three-handed table, which is never much fun. They had congregated in the Hoos' rumpus room, at the back of the main floor of their old gabled house. Hoo wore black slacks, black sneakers, black socks, black gloves, and a black turtleneck — as did Effie, who now pulled a black stocking cap over her blonde hair.

"If you're wearing hard shoes," Hoo continued, "I suggest you take them off, the better not to be heard. The limits are the interior of the house, from cellar to attic — although good luck getting the attic door open and pulling down the ladder without anyone hearing you.

"We use the sofa in the front parlor as home base, because that room has three entries: from the foyer, which connects to the library and the upstairs; from the dining room, which connects to the kitchen and the back study; and from the rumpus room, here. That discourages the strategy of base-sticking, you see, which in any case is bad form, and none of us would do such a thing. And there is to be no hiding in the front parlor, so nobody can rush straight to base when the seekers have finished counting 100.

"The front parlor will be lit; the stairways will be lit so as to minimize the likelihood of falls and ensuing personal injury claims. The cellar will be lit but only with the main overhead light. All other lights will be turned off, and the curtains opened, so that we'll have only dim illumination from the moonlight outside. Considering there are so many of us, we should have two seekers, so they can develop a concerted plan.

"To be caught, a hider must be tagged by a seeker. None of this crying 'One-two-three on Roger,' or whomever. There must be a touch, and even the slightest touch by the seeker on a hider's person or clothing will suffice. But the seeker's own clothing doesn't count, excepting gloves. If it did, you could take off your belt and use it as a whip and gain three feet of reach. I thought of that, though I've never seen it done."

"You have an Eye-talian mind, Hugh," Frank Leahy commented.

"*Grazie*," said Hoo, bowing. "After you've counted 100, the seekers will set this kitchen timer for 20 minutes; when it goes off, all out are in free. But I advise you not to wait it out – this house is big, but it's not that big – and spend as little time in the hallways as possible, for it's there where you'll be caught."

"And no fair counting by binary numbers!" Dora cried.

"D'you know, that's one I hadn't thought of," Hoo admitted.

"If I'm cornered, can I take and bust a chair over your head, to keep you from tagging me?" Runs asked.

"Er... no," said Hoo. "No tactics that constitute a breach of the peace or other misdemeanors-at-law. However, I have seen some interesting crawling-matches, when someone's hiding under a bed. Come to think of it, Runs, considering your size, we should make a rule that we can't hide under beds when you're 'it,' for you'd never be able to come at us."

"Less'n I picked up the bed."

"Just so. Let's adjust the rules for the occasion, then, just to save wear and tear on the furniture. Anyone caught under a bed may be claimed verbally. And of course barricading is not allowed, nor is the locking of any door. The setting of traps and deadfalls is forbidden. So is the digging of Burmese tiger pits. The use of knives, firearms, sharpened sticks, poisonous chemicals, intestinal gas, fresh or tinned fruit, nuclear devices, germ warfare, other instruments of assault, are all strictly proscribed. Now, then: one, two, three..."

"Not it!" came the chorus, not exactly in unison.

"Lois, I believe you and I were the last two," said Hoo. "Off we go to the front parlor, and we'll commence counting a few seconds from now."

All through the cocktails and the buffet, Ballou had taken special care not to pay much attention to Dora, speaking to her only when she spoke to him, not sitting too near her, catching her eye and smiling only a couple of times in the course of the evening.

He'd got to the Hoos' a bit early that evening, before Dora, and as he'd sat chatting with the Hoos he'd started at the sound of any car in the street, and had literally felt faint when Dora finally arrived. He knew, from this, that he could not and would not withdraw from the pursuit.

If Lee Grossbaum ever called him again, Ballou decided, he would tell her kindly but firmly that the flirtation mustn't go any further – for her good as well as his – and that any relationship outside the classroom would be a grave mistake.

Here was Dora, and if Lee Grossbaum were beautiful and willing, Dora was... Dora was what he wanted. Or – he had to admit this nasty suspicion to himself – perhaps he only wanted the ideal.

Now, in the Hoos' enormous house, Ballou had a perfect opportunity to whisk Dora into some unexplored closet and try to steal a kiss – and under the circumstances he could do nothing of the kind. Indeed, he would have to stay well away from her. Even if quite by accident he were to bump into her in the dark, she would conclude that he'd been angling for it.

Straining his eyes, he watched Dora slip out of her high heels –
such tiny, perfect feet! – and leave the rumpus room and begin tip-
toeing upstairs. That meant Ballou would have to stay downstairs.
He felt his way to the library and found a big overstuffed easy chair
that had its back to the door. Ballou quietly sat in this, scrooged
down, bringing his head below the top of the chair-back and
drawing his feet up off the floor, and waited. Presently he heard
Mr. Hoo call melodiously, "Ready or not, here we come!"

Ballou tried to breathe without sound. In a couple of seconds,
he heard the library door open very softly – but it seemed to him
that it was too soon after Mr. Hoo's warning for him or Lois to have
got there. Then he smelled Dora. She had evidently doubled back
from upstairs and was still looking for a place to hide.

The library was almost entirely dark. Ballou could hear Dora
drawing nearer, then he could hear her setting her hand on the
back of the chair. Did she have the same idea Ballou had had?

Yes. She walked around to the front of the chair and started
to sit in it, but at the last instant she perceived the presence of
another body, and she leapt away, gasping as though she'd been
scalded. She overbalanced, and stumbled to the floor with a soft
thud and a little yelp. Ballou jumped to his feet, starting to help
her up, and just at that moment the library door swung open again
and Mr. Hoo trained his flashlight on the two of them: Dora sitting splay-legged on the floor and Ballou squatting next to her.
Mr. Hoo bounded over to them in two steps and lightly brushed
each of them on the arm with his hand.

"You two will be it for the next round, I'm afraid," he whispered.
"But pray continue. You still have nearly 20 minutes." He tiptoed
out of the library, leaving Ballou and Dora in the dark again.

Dora, still on the floor, was laughing soundlessly, her whole
body heaving, tears streaming down her cheeks. Ballou grimaced.
It occurred to him that a more courageous guy – a guy with the
audacity to actually go after Dora and win her – would have

followed her upstairs in the first place, would have pursued her in the dark and grabbed her playfully and not cared that she knew he was following her on purpose to grab her.

And this gave him the idea to force himself to laugh along with Dora — wheezing silently of course — and to lean forward on the balls of his feet so that he could place his hands on Dora's shoulders as though to steady himself as he laughed. Dora responded by lightly grasping his forearms as they rocked back and forth for a few seconds, laughing into each other's faces. Then at the same moment they stopped, and just grinned at each other, and Ballou had the notion that now, *now* was the time to pull her to him and kiss her properly — when a low but loud moan sounded from somewhere: from upstairs, Ballou thought. A woman's voice. The moan turned into a wild, frantic shriek.

"Francis! FRAAANNCIIIS!"

"I'm coming, dear," Ballou could hear Frank Leahy calling from somewhere. "Just stay where you are and keep talking, and I'll find you."

"I don't know where I am, Francis!" Lois cried.

*

"Dear, it's okay." Leahy had found his wife upstairs, and had helped her down to the front parlor, where the rest of the company was reassembling. "You're in Hugh and Effie's house. You've been here many times."

"Yes, Francis, I know. What is happening to me?"

Leahy looked at Dora.

"Has something like this happened before?" Dora asked.

"No, I don't think so," said Leahy. "Dear?"

Lois still looked bewildered, but she tried to laugh. "How would I know?"

"She's always been forgetful," said Leahy to Dora. "Ever since I've known her. Remember how I told you she can remember songs? But..."

"But I've never been able to remember whether I've put sugar in my coffee or not," said Lois. "Not even when I was very young."

"But lately..." Leahy started, then looked around at the Hoos, the Quaggas, and the others. "Maybe this isn't the time to go into it," he said. "Lois, we need to get you a drink."

"Yes, where is my booze?" Lois demanded.

"I'll get you one," said Leahy, moving toward the rumpus room, where the bar was. "Dora, come help me."

Effie sat Lois down on the sofa and looked over at her husband. The Quaggas looked at each other; the Planktons looked at each other; Runs looked at Ballou. None of them knew what to say.

"It comes and goes," Leahy told Dora, in the other room, as he filled a glass with ice, vodka, and pineapple juice. "Usually she's just like always, but every couple of days... and I'm not up on the difference between ordinary forgetfulness and... and Oldtimer's Disease."

"It's not my specialty," said Dora. "And I certainly couldn't do a diagnosis here and now. I'd advise you to just take her to her regular doctor, and get a referral to a specialist if need be."

"It's irreversible, isn't it?" asked Leahy. "Damn it, she's only 74! She's still a young girl! It's not fair!"

"You never can tell," said Dora. "We all have mental slips of various kinds, at any age. This could be nothing at all."

Leahy just shook his head.

Thursday, October 28

"Are you sure I'm not bothering you?" asked Mrs. Ballou.

"No, it's fine," Ballou replied. "I'm grading papers, but I could use a little break." (And this call will get me off the hook for a few weeks, he added to himself.)

"It's a very gloomy, rainy day here," said Mrs. Ballou.

"Then I guess we'll get that in a day or two. It's a beautiful morning here. Most of the leaves are down now, but it's still awfully pretty. I'm going to go for a drive in a little while, as soon as I've finished with these papers."

"Well, be careful. Keep your eyes on the road. I just read an article about how secondary roads in mountainous areas are the most dangerous."

Silence as Ballou counted ten.

"Are you taking anyone with you?" Mrs. Ballou asked.

"Yeah, I have a date with a married woman."

Mrs. Ballou gasped.

"Don't worry. I'm going horseback riding with my friend Frances Quagga. She's the wife of the guy I got my house from. A very respectable person."

"What happened to that girl you took to the football game? Did it not work out?"

"I'm seeing her this afternoon also," said Ballou. "See, another friend of mine – that Indian guy I told you about, Runs-Away-Screaming – he's throwing a big Halloween party at his used-car lot on Saturday night. And Dora – the girl I took to the football game – she e-mailed me the other day and asked if I could help her decorate his place, you know, for the party, and Frances got the same invite, so after we're done riding I guess we'll go over there."

"How did this Mrs. Quagga come to invite you out riding?" Mrs. Ballou asked. "And Roger, are you sure that's a good idea? Have you even been on a horse since you were a little boy? Be careful. Don't go any faster than a trot, and take a guide with you."

"I know, I know, you just read an article."

"Roger, why do you always…"

"Anyway she didn't invite me, I invited her, okay? Since you asked. So that we could gossip. That's what we do in a little town like this. And maybe she can tell me something about Dora that I don't know already."

"That sounds so calculating," Mrs. Ballou complained. "But I guess it won't hurt. Just don't go making any of your off-color references. Like you're always making when we talk."

"I'll make worse ones, okay?"

"I'm just afraid you *will*."

"I will if you want me to."

"Roger, please stop this. Listen, I want you to do me a favor. Call me after your Halloween party, okay? So I can enjoy it vicariously. You can call your old Maw in a few more days, can't you? That wouldn't be so awful."

Ballou clenched his teeth.

"Yes, of course I can," he replied. "But why not go out and look for a Halloween party of your own? You might actually prefer it to staying home."

"Oh, honey, if only I could make myself do *anything*."

*

"And yet you kept the habit, all this time," Ballou noted. He and Frances were trotting along a wooded trail, Ballou on a grey gelding and Frances on a bay mare, a couple of miles away from the stables where they'd picked up their horses. Frances wore high boots, jodhpurs, a short tweed jacket, and a black riding helmet over her hair, which she'd tied up in a chignon.

They'd started out at a walk, then Frances had speeded her horse to a trot, and Ballou had kept up with her – but when she'd decided to go to a canter and then to a full gallop, Ballou hadn't the first idea of what to do, except to hang on while his own horse followed the leader. And he'd stayed aboard, somehow – in fact, he'd discovered that he felt more secure astride a galloping horse than a trotting one – and could now say he'd galloped a horse, once in his life anyway. He'd probably faked it well enough that Frances couldn't have known that he'd had no idea what he was doing. Now, going at a slower pace, Ballou felt relieved – and a little smug.

"I'm so proud of myself, that I can still fit into it all," said Frances. "It's been... no, I won't tell you how long ago I bought it. I'm 25 and holding!" She winked at Ballou, who once again felt a little envious of Donald Quagga.

"We'd better get back," she added, "if we want to help Runs and Dora before it gets dark. How is that going, by the way? If you don't mind my asking."

"I can't say it's going at all," Ballou said, as they wheeled their horses around.

As they sometimes trotted, sometimes walked back toward the stables, Ballou told Frances about the almost-attempted kiss of a few nights before. "And of course what happened after that, well, that pretty much killed any further opportunity," he concluded. "And I called her on the phone Sunday; I'm afraid I used Lois as an excuse, you know, but that was all Dora could talk about, and I couldn't think of a tactful way to ask her, 'Uh… listen, were you wanting me to kiss you last night, or what?'"

"That's so awful about Lois," said Frances. "And if it's what I'm guessing it is, it's going to be even harder on Frank, I'm afraid. To watch someone whom he obviously loves so much just slowly fall apart, probably over years…"

"I guess I'll be spared that, at least, by never getting married," Ballou reflected.

"Oh, give it time," said Frances. "Just go slowly."

"I'd go at whatever speed was called for, if only I knew what to do next," said Ballou. "There's nothing I could do that wouldn't look like an obvious move – and it's like two kids pulling a wishbone. Whoever pulls, loses."

"Look, I'll watch the two of you this afternoon," Frances offered. "I'll tell you if I see anything."

"*Hola*, Kemo Sabay." Runs-Away-Screaming wandered over from the garage to the gas pumps to greet Ballou, who was filling the tank of the Cadillac. Frances had got out a few minutes before, before Ballou put the car through the wash, and was now over by the garage, talking with Dora.

"How's that beautiful gal runnin' for you?" Runs asked. "Perfect day for a drive, ain't it? Leaves are comin' down, but you know, for me, it's just startin' to get good. My favorite time of year's about a month from now, between Thanksgiving and Christmas, when it's nice and cold and gettin' dark early, and the trees are bare. Just makes you cry then, it's so beautiful."

"Looks like someone's been busy around here," Ballou noted.

Crepe ribbons in fall colors, chains of plastic autumn leaves, strings of cut-out witches on broomsticks decorated the wire fence around Runs' property. Here and there hung plastic skeletons and ghosts. Pumpkins of various sizes stood all over the lot: Ballou guessed at least two dozen, some artistically carved, and some clumsily so.

"Yeah, Dora organized a regular decoratin' bee today," said Runs. "You missed most of it. She brung over a big kit full of punkin-carvin' tools, can you beat that? Little knives and chisels and I dunno what-all, and she got me and Shank and Pruno to help out, and then Frances' two girls were by here with some friends of theirs, a while ago – skippin' school, you bet – and then other people would drop by, customers, and by God if some of 'em didn't stick around to carve a punkin or help put stuff up. Well, you know how Dora does. She turns that charm on you, and you'd do anything for her. Looks nice, though, don't it? You gonna be here Saturday?"

Bonnie Bonney rode into the lot on a bicycle, and pulled up next to Ballou's car. She carried a big black polyurethane bag over her shoulder.

"Hi, Runs," she called. "Oh, hi," she added, noticing Ballou. "Oh, my God, you really do have our car!" She stared at it.

"Don't worry," said Ballou. "I'm taking good care of her."

"Yeah, I know, it just seems so strange." Bonnie turned to Runs. "I brought some more decorations. And some smudge and a cauldron." She dismounted from her bicycle and rummaged in the sack. "Dried roses and marigolds," she announced, bringing them out. "They're traditional for Samhain." (She pronounced it "*sah*-wen.")

"That's the real name for Halloween," she explained to Runs, handing him the armful of flowers and bringing out the cauldron. "It's really a pagan holiday, you know. I'm going to bring a bunch of people on Saturday, if that's okay, and we can do some rituals."

"You just ritual up a storm, darlin'," said Runs.

"Do Native Americans have special rituals for this time of year?" Bonnie asked. "They must have, right?"

"Yeah, we go on a Vision Quest," said Runs. "We drink the white man's firewater and chew peyote till we see the true nature of the universe. Then when we sober up we forget all about it, so we have to do it again next year."

Bonnie looked perplexed.

"And we play a game called Squamish," Runs added. "You ever play Squamish?"

Bonnie shook her head. "I never heard of it."

"You're innerested in Injuns, and you never heard of Squamish?" Runs shook his head incredulously. "Hell, it's only the most sacred game the Injuns have. Bigger'n lacrosse, even. On special occasions, the whole village plays, or maybe one village plays against another village. The Injuns played it for the Pilgrims, at the first Thanksgiving."

"There's professional Squamish, too, right?" Ballou asked.

"Hell yeah. I played pro Squamish, years back. I was a starting Outside Grouch for the Cleveland Steamers."

"I remember that," said Ballou. "You guys made the finals of the Fibonacci Series one year."

"We sure did," Runs recalled. "We shoulda won that seventh game. Only we got penalized for a Dirty Sanchez in the final seconds, then the other team scored a durmish at the gun and beat us."

"Yeah, anyway," Runs turned back to Bonnie, "bring your momma, bring your friends, whoever you want. Ain't seen your momma since she sold me Roger's car, here. Yeah, bring everybody. We'll have a lot to eat. I got two great big bucks hangin' out behind the garage, and we'll roast a couple pigs, too."

"Eeew," said Bonnie. "I don't eat meat. That's so sad, killing deer. They're so beautiful."

"Darlin', they wouldn't look so beautiful if hunters didn't thin down the herd every season," Runs replied. "They'd starve to death, instead of dyin' quick. And that'd be after they'd overrun most of the countryside and started walkin' into towns because they can't find no forage. They'd be fallin' dead in your front yard."

Bonnie thought for a few seconds.

"But it's so awful to see people driving around with a deer tied onto their car," she countered. "It's, like, obscene almost."

"Well, how else do you get a dead deer home?" Runs demanded. "Set him up in the passenger seat, maybe stick a cigarette in his mouth, and let him bleed all over the upholstery?"

"I just don't understand it," said Bonnie. "People don't have to hunt. Maybe it was different for your people, way back, when they had to hunt to survive. I know, it's part of your culture and all…"

"Part of anybody's culture," Ballou put in. "Any race, any ethnicity. They've all hunted and raised animals for slaughter. It's hardly peculiar to Indians. Just like all cultures have fought wars."

"Oh, that's not so!" exclaimed Bonnie. "In school right now we're learning about the Hopi tribe, in the Southwest, and they were strictly agricultural and totally peaceful, never had any wars. Isn't that great?"

"Now, ain't that just like a girl, to be innerested in such a bunch of mollycoddles?" said Runs. "What's the point of bein' a damn Injun, if you don't get to have any wars?"

"*Whaaaat?*" said Bonnie, laughing to show that she was scandalized.

"Me thank-um Great Spirit every day for making me half a Cheyenne," Runs added. "At least Cheyennes were tough. My momma was a Wigwag, and they never fought anybody. I was embarrassed, as a kid, when I found out the Wigwags never raided any settlements or took scalps or did any of that fun shit. They were farmers; just plain sissies compared to the other tribes."

"You don't think that's a good thing, that they were peaceful?" Bonnie asked.

"Well, all's I know is, if you tried to do a movie about the Wigwags, it'd put a lot of folks right to sleep. The Cheyennes got into a lot of old movies, though, didn't they?"

"Can I leave the cauldron here, till Saturday?" Bonnie apparently had had enough of the debate. "Then I've got to get to rehearsal."

"Sure," said Runs. "Put it in my office."

"Poor kid's about as much fun as a toad at a bug-dance," Runs muttered to Ballou when she was out of earshot.

A few minutes later, Ballou had joined Dora and Frances, who were seated each on a short stack of tires, next to the garage, working on pumpkins.

"This is my second one this afternoon," Dora announced. Her pumpkin appeared to be a mask of Tragedy. Dora was carving tiny teardrops along its cheeks and filling them in with glitter-paint. She'd already carved the lines around the eyes and mouth to indicate despair: amazingly intricate work considering she'd cut clean through the shell for each line.

"I chose too big a pumpkin," she mourned. "If I'd chosen a smaller one maybe I wouldn't have messed up. It's completely asymmetrical." Ballou looked at it again: the carving looked exactly symmetrical to him, perfectly proportioned.

"If you're disappointed in that," he said, "I'm afraid to show you what I can do."

"Oh, I'm sure you'll carve a lovely pumpkin," said Dora. "Anyway it's not a contest."

Frances winked at Ballou.

Ballou picked up a pumpkin – not too big, not too small – and began studying it, trying to determine what kind of a face would look best on it. He thought to give it an orangutan's face, perhaps using its innards for hair. He took a pen out of his inside jacket pocket and began drawing lightly on its surface, and for a few minutes got so absorbed in this task that he only now and then listened to Dora's and Frances' conversation.

"… and of course I couldn't say anything about it if she were my patient," said Dora, and Ballou began to pay attention. "I couldn't tell for certain, and I'm not up on the latest tests. But from what I know, I'd be very surprised if it doesn't turn out to be Alzheimer's. And that means they can expect a slow but steady deterioration, over years. Lois is just lucky she's got someone who loves her as much as Frank obviously does. Imagine having to go through it alone."

"Companionship in old age," Ballou remarked. "I believe that's the only Biblically sanctioned reason for marriage, other than begetting children."

"Then I guess I'll be in trouble in the next world," Dora replied. "I got married at 22, and I can't remember ever wanting to have children."

"The companionship is a very important part of marriage, no matter what your age, or whether you have children or not," said Frances. "I think it's the best part."

"Well, I am companionable," said Dora. "If I can't say anything else in my own favor, I will say I'm companionable. And I have to admit it: Now that I've been single for a while, I've discovered that I miss being married. I really liked being married. I know you don't sympathize with that, Roger, since you're such a bachelor."

"I don't know about that," Ballou replied. "I just haven't had the benefit of your experience. Doesn't mean I'm entirely opposed."

And at that point Ballou was stymied. He might have said something on the order of, "Maybe I just haven't met my wife yet," but that would suggest that he was eliminating Dora from consideration. He might have said, "I'd get married if you were part of the deal," which would have been too far in the other direction.

He showed Dora his marked-up pumpkin and asked, "Does this look right? It's supposed to be an orangutan." Dora took Ballou's pen and with a few quick strokes corrected his drawing, making it much more accurately simian. Ballou was mortified.

"You did just fine," said Frances, as Ballou drove her home. They'd worked until dark, and Runs' lot held a riot of jack-o-lanterns ready to be lit up on Saturday. "You kept the conversation light, and you certainly didn't make any *faux-pas* that I could see.

The only thing I'd have to criticize is that you weren't flirtatious enough. You've got to put the idea into her head, and you weren't doing that. You've got to try a little harder."

"If I'm not trying, you're extremely trying," said Ballou. "I'm trying as best I know how; it's just not much of a best."

"She dropped a very broad hint," said Frances. "Saying she missed being married. And going on about how companionable she is. And she is."

"Maybe she was just saying it as she'd have said it to you if I hadn't been there. Maybe she's not as Machiavellian as we are."

"Roger, dear, nobody is that much of an *ingénue*. Not even Dora. Why not just tell her how you feel about her?"

"Oh, yeah, that'd work," said Ballou. "Dora, I must confess it: I've fallen madly in love with you! And I want you to fall equally in love with me! Whaddaya say?"

Frances grimaced.

"There, you see your own reaction?" said Ballou. "I'll tell you what she'd say." (Ballou tried to imitate Dora's tiny voice.) "'Oh, Roger, I'm so very flattered, I really am. You're so sweet. But I think we should just be friends.'"

"Oh, Roger, give yourself a chance!"

"No, listen, Frances, I've done exactly that, a few times, when I was a lot younger. And I got the same result, every time. 'I think we should just be friends.' Girls just don't go for that kind of tactic. Not unless they're already really attracted to the guy – and in that case, the guy almost never has to declare himself, because the girl does it for him. You always have to make it her idea.

"See, if I were to do that, I'd be putting her on the spot, right? In effect I'd be asking her to *choose* to be attracted to me. And attraction isn't a choice, you know that."

"Well, how do you know she isn't attracted to you already?" Frances asked. "Have you done anything to encourage her, really? You have to make the first move."

"I thought I had, honest to God," said Ballou. "I was trying to give her the message without scaring her off or grossing her out. And if she doesn't feel anything for me by now, I'm not going to *make* her feel it by telling her how *I* feel. Am I?"

"I'm not sure," said Frances. "Maybe you're missing what's going on. She talked about marriage in front of you. She – likes – you. Don't you get it?"

"Oh, sure, no doubt she likes me. I'm not sure she *likes* me likes me."

"Maybe she doesn't know that yet either," said Frances. "But maybe she does know it, and maybe she's as nervous as you are. I know that when I met Don, I was really attracted to him, but I didn't know how he felt about me – but when he let me know that he was genuinely smitten, I certainly didn't resist; it just made me – well, it tipped me over the edge and I fell in love with him!"

"Well, Don does have a presence."

"You think you don't?"

"Actually, yeah, I do – by accident. When I'm not thinking about it. It's all very well to say, 'Just relax and be yourself,' but if you're in a situation where you have to remind yourself to do that, you won't do it. It's like telling yourself, 'Don't think of a hippopotamus.' Anyway, Dora must know I'm smitten, as you call it, unless she's totally stupid – which she ain't."

"And if she does know it, I'm sure she's flattered like you have no idea," said Frances. "Maybe she wasn't ready before. Maybe she's slowly becoming ready."

"I'm not so sure. I don't know how girls' minds work, but guys – I don't know if you know this, but guys usually decide right away whether they're attracted to you or not. And if they are, they'll do something about it if they get the chance."

"Well, Roger, I'm attracted to you – but I'm not going to do anything about it."

Ballou almost swerved the car off the road. "*Are* you?"

Frances laughed, and put a hand on Ballou's arm.

"Calm down," she said. "I'm just saying that attraction does not happen instantly for... for girls. I wasn't attracted to you right away, but I became attracted when I got to know you. Mind you, I'm not any the less attracted to Don because of it. And maybe Dora is being cautious. I'm sure her divorce wasn't easy."

"Oh, she told you about that? Do tell! Like, sordid details. C'mon!"

"Honestly, Roger, she has never gone into any details. Just that she was married a long time. And no, she hasn't said anything one way or another to me about you."

Ballou shook his head. "Anyway, I'm not successful enough. I'm sure she can guess how much money I make. And any guy who's worthy of her would have to be at least as successful as she is."

"Oh, I give up," cried Frances. "If you're really so determined that you're not good enough for her, why are you bothering with her anyway? Why not just forget her? You've a whole campusful of 19- and 20-year-olds to choose from!"

"There's that," said Ballou. He pulled the car up in front of the Quaggas' house. Frances' younger daughter, the willowy, melancholy Emmeline, wearing a loose peasant blouse, sat cross-legged on the front lawn, gazing off into nowhere. She was evidently composing, for she had a notebook in her lap.

"Em, honey, can you see anything at all?" Frances called as she got out of the car. "And aren't you cold?"

Emmeline looked up at her mother in surprise; evidently she hadn't noticed the car approaching.

"Yes, I am," she replied, arching her head back, shaking her long straight hair, as though to show how much she enjoyed the cold air. "It's wonderful."

"You remember Roger, don't you, dear?"

"Raaaaah-gerrrrrr," Emmeline drawled, still leaning back, with her eyes half-closed. "Roger is poetry in a leather jacket." She sat up straight and looked right at Ballou, then went back to her note-book as though to jot down that metaphor.

Frances rolled her eyes, and gave Ballou a little nudge.

"Want to come in? Have a quick drink? Em, is Daddy home?"

"Mm."

"Is that a 'yes-mm' or a 'no-mm'?"

"Yes, unless he's gone out," said Emmeline.

"There's a word for that, Roger, isn't there?" Frances asked.

"Tautology."

"Tautology. Well, if Don's home, we can ask him about your little predicament. Maybe he can give us the male perspective."

"No!" Ballou kept his voice down, hoping Emmeline couldn't overhear. "God, no. It's funny. When you've just met a girl, some-how you don't mind talking to a guy about her. But later on, when you've had a couple dates, it's not the same. It's... unmanly, in a way. You can talk to another girl about it, because she's a girl, right? But if you talk to a guy about it, you feel like a wuss. Don't ask me to explain it to you. I'll have a drink, but not a word to Don about any of this."

Frances stood shaking her head for a moment.

"I'll tell you something you might try on Saturday," she said. She grabbed Ballou by the sleeve and spoke into his ear. "Dora has syphilis, and chlamydia, and... and pinworms. Keep that abso-lutely in mind, all the time you're at the party."

"I'm serious," said Frances. "Behave just as you'd behave to a dear friend whom you like very much – but who has awful com-municable diseases."

Saturday, October 30 – Sunday, October 31

By eight o'clock on Saturday night there was no more room to park inside the fence of Runs' lot, so quite a few cars, trucks, vans, and motorcycles were already parked on the shoulder of the highway. It looked like at least 60 people so far, milling about outside the garage, mingling, or strolling around and admiring the for-sale cars – and more people arriving. Smoke issued from an enormous barbecue grill, set up a respectful distance from the fuel pumps. Lights had been strung along the fence and the main building; jack-o-lanterns glowed here and there, all over the lot. Speakers had been set up, and Johnny Cash's "Ring of Fire" blared over the scene, carrying well out onto the highway. Ballou, walking uphill from the front gate to the garage, considered the illegal parking, the fires, and so forth – and guessed at some dozens of legal violations, one way or the other.

"But that's terrible," said Ballou's mother. "Why didn't the police do anything?"

"It would've been the Sheriff's department, rather than the police, since he's outside town limits," Ballou explained. "And I would guess that someone put in a good word with the Sheriff and asked him not to interfere, considering who-all was going to be there. The Leahys were there, the Quaggas, *le tout Wildenkill.*"

"That's terrible," Mrs. Ballou repeated. "They shouldn't have special privileges like that."

"Yeah, yeah."

"What was everybody wearing? What were you wearing?"

"Well, Mr. and Mrs. Leahy came as the people in 'American Gothic,'" said Ballou. "Mr. Leahy had the overalls and the pitchfork, you know, and Mrs. Leahy had the gingham dress and the apron. And Mr. and Mrs. Hoo – they're the Scottish lady and the Chinese guy – she was dressed up like the old Empress of China, the dowager, Cixi. She had one of those heavy embroidered Chinese robes from the 19th century, and a big black wig, and her face painted all white. And Hugh Hoo came as Bonnie Prince Charlie, with the kilt and the doublet and a broadsword and a powdered wig, really something to see."

"Who was Bonnie Prince Charlie? Was he a famous Scotsman, I suppose?"

Ballou explained who Bonnie Prince Charlie was. He gazed out his living room window as he spoke, observing the glorious bright blue Sunday morning that he felt too flummoxed to enjoy. And God forbid he should let his mother know why he was feeling that way.

"Anyway," he continued, "Mr. Quagga came as Canio, and Mrs. Quagga had a sailor outfit, like Nellie Forbush in *South Pacific.*"

"Who is Canio?"

"You know, the clown from *Pagliacci.*"

"Oh. I always thought the clown's name was Pagliacci." (Ballou did a long, theatrical eye-roll and a slow head-turn, appealing to the empty room to share his amazement.) "And what was your friend Dora? Was she there?"

"Yeah, she was there, but I hardly spent any time with her. She was pretty busy the whole evening."

"Well, then, what were you?"

"Alex."

Ballou wore heavy boots, white skivvies, an improvised plastic codpiece round his waist, a white shirt, and a bowler hat, and he carried a cudgel. He had pasted false eyelashes on one eye. Under one arm he carried a giant tin of Nut Clusters.

Three large trestle tables had been brought inside Runs' triple garage, two of them laden with food. At the unencumbered table sat Effie Hoo, in her imperial Chinese attire, doing a tarot reading for a middle-aged, uncostumed man with prematurely white hair, whom Ballou didn't recognize. Dora, dressed in a pale taffeta dress with an enormous floor-length skirt, laid out pies from a big cardboard box. Runs was helping her. Despite the cold, Runs wore nothing but loincloth and full war-paint – and a blue Civil War-style kepi on his head. His paunch obscured the loincloth somewhat.

Ballou thought about walking over to Runs and Dora right then and there, then thought better of it: He didn't want to appear to be horning in on their conversation, and he didn't want Dora to think that he was seeking her out right away.

Then he remembered. Syphilis, chlamydia, and pinworms. He straightened his shoulders and walked over to them, presenting Runs with the tin of Nut Clusters.

Runs peered at the tin, nodding critically. "Mmm," he grunted. "Crunchy Frog. Heap good!"

"You're Glinda the Good Witch, I guess?" Ballou asked Dora. Syphilis, chlamydia, and pinworms.

"You're so clever!" Dora cried. "She actually wore a pink dress in the movie, you know, but I just cannot wear that shade of pink. Luckily I found this cloth which is almost pink but actually looks good on me, and I had the pattern, too – the exact pattern from the movie. But who are you?"

Ballou explained. Syphilis, chlamydia, and pinworms.

At the next table, the white-haired man stood up, evidently having finished his reading.

"Harrison!" Dora called over to him. "Harrison, here's another of my friends I'd like you to meet. Harrison Lockwood, this is Roger Ballou."

Harrison Lockwood was about Ballou's size; as ruddy as Ballou was pallid; square-jawed and quite handsome. His big muscular hand squeezed Ballou's hard.

"Harrison's my neighbor, over in Verstanken," Dora explained. "He has the shop right next to my bakery. Roger, he makes the most beautiful wooden furniture and cabinetry! You should stop by there, the next time you visit me, and see what he does! I'm sure you'll find something there that's just right for your house."

"Yes, Dora and I have been neighbors for months now," Lockwood confirmed in his hearty, breezy voice, "but we hadn't had much chance to get acquainted until just lately, and she said I should come out here tonight and meet some of her friends."

"Roger's one of my very dearest," said Dora, smiling up at Lockwood and then at Ballou. "Just a wonderful writer. And a very good teacher."

Ballou felt like he might faint. It was possible, he knew, that he was just over-sensitive, but he felt in his gut that this guy was it. It wasn't anything he could discern in Dora's face — she always had that huge smile for everyone — or in her body language. He just had a sense — an inescapable sense — that Dora was showing this guy off.

"Did Effie tell you anything interesting?" Dora asked Lockwood.

"I'm amazed at what she told me," said Lockwood. His voice was a calm lake, now: slow, smooth, gently undulant, even when talking over the party chatter and the Johnny Cash. His gaze shifted from Dora's eyes, to Ballou's, to some point in the middle distance — a point whence he apparently drew his almost divine serenity.

Dora looked at Lockwood seriously, not replying.

"It's remarkable, Dora, how each of your friends is an artist in his or her way," said Lockwood. "And how each of them – again in his or her own way – is so spiritual."

"Oh, Harrison, there are two more people I'd like you to meet," Dora cried, touching Harrison's arm and looking past Ballou, out into the lot. "Frances! Donald!" She waved at the Quaggas, and tugged at Harrison Lockwood's sleeve.

"Actually I had been in his shop once or twice before, so I knew him a little already," said Frances, on the phone to Effie the following evening. "He seems nice enough, but I didn't get a handle on him. He does make impressive furniture. Apparently he's quite well known for it around here. Anyway I don't know if Dora just invited him as a friend, as she said, or if he was her *date*-date."

"My guess?" Effie replied. "They've not done the deed yet, but they're contemplatin' it. Mark me, even if they stop now, he'll get farther with young Dora than our friend Roger ever will."

"Oh, poor Roger!" Frances exclaimed. "I caught sight of him, just as Dora was introducing Harrison to us, and he looked like a crushed petunia. Although he was trying not to show it. I felt so sorry for him. But who knows? Maybe he's got nothing to worry about."

"Och!" said Effie. "I suppose it's possible that nothin' will ever happen between Dora and that Harrison creature. But far longer odds that anything could happen between her and Roger. I just don't see it. Roger's not good enough for her."

"Effie!"

"It's the plain truth! I'm not sayin' Roger's not a good man, if ye like that sort of a fellow. But he's a... a nebbish, as we say in the Highlands. D'ye see him as a consort for Dora? Do ye now, really? He's got no ambeetion, nor any real talent."

"I get the feeling that Dora doesn't care all that much about money, though."

"I couldn't speak to that, and anyway it's not a matter of how much money he makes. One can be a success without makin' a lot of money. No, it's not his earnin' power I'm talkin' about – I doubt this Harrison fellow has any more a year than Roger does – and it's not the social status or whatever ye want to call it. But a woman wants a man she can look up to, doesn't she?"

"Figuratively speaking in my case," said Frances. "But yes, we do, don't we? But Roger is... admirable, in his way. Why would she not look up to him?"

"Because – he – excels – at – nothing," said Effie, biting off the words one by one. "He might well be enough for a great many women, but Princess Dora requires a Prince Charming. Or to use another leeterary analogy, Dora might fall for either an Ashley Wilkes or a Rhett Butler, but poor Roger: Deep in his heart, he's only Charlie Hamilton."

"Well, this Harrison... Lockhart, Lovelock, whatever... he does make very nice furniture," Frances mused.

"*Voilà la différence,*" said Effie. "He's a master craftsman, with all the confidence that comes with that. And he's got that serenity goin' for him. That self-satisfaction, I'd call it. Which no woman can resist. Och, he's more than a match for our Dora. She might have more fun makin' a man of Roger, but she'll never find out."

Let him have her, Ballou tried to tell himself. Syphilis, chlamydia, and pinworms. But the thought sounded idiotic to him now. Sour grapes, and he knew it all too well.

"I'm going to mingle," Ballou announced to Runs, and wandered back outside the garage, away from Dora, Lockwood, and the Quaggas. He felt unsteady on his feet, as though he were getting up from being physically knocked down.

Several of Runs' friends stood in a group near the grill, passing a doobie around. Ballou recognized Shank and Pruno, also decked out in paint and feathers but looking somewhat less believable as

Indians, what with their droopy moustaches, and their fish-belly-white torsos contrasting with their tanned arms.

"Pruno, show Rog what you got out back," Shank said. "Bet he'd take one."

"Yeah, c'mon," said Pruno, motioning to Ballou to follow him out back, behind the garage. They had to walk past Dora and Lockwood, and Ballou kept his face averted as they did so.

The area behind the garage was unlit; Ballou could hardly feel his way along. Pruno brought out a flashlight and shone it on a big uncovered wooden crate. "Take a look in there," he said.

Ballou heard something moving inside the crate.

"Mrs. Poopington slung 'em Wednesday," Pruno explained. "Just three days old."

In the crate lay Pruno's brown-and-white pit bull, half-asleep. In a squirming pile, tiny puppies nuzzled at her belly.

Ballou squatted down and let Mrs. Poopington sniff his hand; she licked it, and he scratched her ears. Keeping one hand on Mrs. Poopington to reassure her, Ballou began to stroke the puppies, one by one. The least of them, which was black except for white front paws and a white muzzle, tried to suck his finger.

"Four boys and three girls," said Pruno. "That's the runt. She only got six titties, and he can't get a look-in, most of the time. I have to bottle-feed him." He picked up the puppy by the scruff and passed him to Ballou. "You know anybody lookin' for a pit?"

The puppy immediately started licking Ballou's face.

"Don't let him get too friendly," Pruno warned. "He'll think you're his daddy."

"Pruno's his daddy for real," Shank sniggered.

"He's all head and paws, ain't he?" said Pruno. "Here." He handed Ballou a little bottle of formula and a towel. "Careful he don't shit on you."

"A pit bull?" cried Mrs. Ballou. "Roger, are you serious?

"It's not for sure. It's way too small to leave its mother yet. And I haven't paid any money. They're nice dogs, pit bulls. I knew a lot of them in the city."

"Oh, but Roger, I've read so many articles about how dangerous pit bulls are…"

"And I bet you've never seen one, right? I bet you wouldn't know one if you did see one."

"But they're supposed to be almost wild, aren't they? Uncontrollably violent! That's what I've read."

"Not at all. They're very friendly, very loyal. But, yeah, they can be pretty fierce when they have to be, and you have a problem when you get some creep of an owner who teaches the dog to be mean. Some people do that. But when you raise them right, they're terrific. And they do take a lot of attention, Pruno warned me about that. They're a real handful, unless you train them early."

"Can you trust this… Bruno?"

"Pruno. With a P."

"The way you describe him he sounds like some kind of criminal."

"Well, obviously. Pruno is a kind of prison-made booze. I suppose he had a liking for it when he was in the joint."

"And you said his friend's name was Shank? Is that a prison word too?"

"Yeah, a shank is any kind of improvised stabbing weapon. A screwdriver, a sharpened toothbrush, whatever. Maybe this guy was handy with one."

"Roger, I really don't like the sound of the people you're getting involved with."

Returning from behind the garage, Ballou spied the old man who always came to the Van Devander football games, standing by himself some distance off, admiring an old Thunderbird. He wore his logoed outfit, as usual, and mirrored glasses.

Walking up the driveway, all of them dressed in long dark hooded cloaks, were the two Quagga girls, Charlotte Fanshaw's two daughters, and several other teenagers. Among them Ballou recognized Bartholomew, the waiter from the Brookside Tea Garden. Luke Bonney, Jr. was with them too, but in contrast to the others, he wore a Buddhist-style robe of bright saffron. Charlotte Fanshaw walked behind them, dressed as the Wicked Witch of the West, all in black with a black pointed hat and black wig, her face painted green.

"Ah, goot evening, veddy-veddy goot evening, *pro*-fessor *Ba* -lou," said Luke, with a ghastly quasi-Hindi lilt, bestowing a *namaste* on Ballou. "Have you heard the word of the Almighty Dalla? Yez indeed: Jesus saves; Moses invests; but only Dalla pays dividends!"

"And you are the Dalla Lama, I take it," Ballou replied.

"I wish you wouldn't make fun of that kind of thing," Bonnie said to Luke. "You're as bad as Mom." She glanced over her shoulder at her mother, for whom Runs was siphoning beer from a keg. Then she shot Ballou a brief unfriendly look and flounced away, re-joining her schoolmates.

"Quite a game this afternoon," Ballou said to the old man in the logoed attire.

"Never seen them play like that," the old man wheezed. "This'll be our first winning season since... maybe 1971 or '72. We're six-and-one, and we should win two of the last three, anyway, and we'll have an outside chance against Navy. I'm excited."

Charlotte Fanshaw passed near; Ballou nodded to her and smiled a little. Charlotte nodded back, and stared hard at the old man and his logos and glasses before walking on.

"Listen, Roger," the old man said to Ballou. "I really am curious about your poetry class. Just to see if poetry students have changed at all since I was teaching. I haven't been in a classroom in more than 20 years."

Ballou forced himself to act as though he'd known all along.

"You're welcome anytime," he said.

"You know what?" Llandor asked. "I'm afraid to. To talk to young poets again. I'd come in with good intentions, but I'd start ridiculing them and insulting them, and I'd intimidate them so badly that they'd never write another line." He coughed. "Not that that would be so bad."

"What brings you here? Do you know Runs?"

"We use the same bookie," said Llandor. "And I let him hunt on my land."

The red-haired woman who'd appeared in Ballou's office a few weeks earlier, to deliver Llandor's note, approached them, a filled paper plate in each hand. She passed one to the old man, and acknowledged Ballou with another of her mysterious smiles.

"Nice to see you again," Ballou said, but she did not reply except to bow slightly from the shoulders.

"I need to get me some of that too," Ballou said, nodding at their plates. "Excuse me." Once more he walked in the direction of the grill, where the Wicked Witch of the West was piling barbecued pork onto a bun.

"That looks good," Ballou said to her, "but I believe I'll try the venison. I never get it at home."

"I might have known you'd be a friend of his," said Charlotte.

"I'm not," Ballou protested. "We were just now getting acquainted, if it's any of your business. I guess he's not as reclusive as he's cracked up to be, is he?"

"I never said he was," Charlotte replied. "What I wrote was fiction. Remember?"

"Fair enough," Ballou admitted. He felt that he ought to do something to make the situation less hostile, rather than just walking away, but he couldn't think of anything to say that wouldn't make matters worse — and he'd already tried "How's the book doing?" a few weeks ago. Then he caught sight of Dora, standing maybe 10 yards away from him, with a platter of cookies in her hand that she'd apparently been offering to the other guests.

Harrison Lockwood, for the moment, was nowhere nearby. Dora's glance met Ballou's.

For just an instant, Ballou felt a rush of horror: Here he was, caught flirting (Dora might suppose) with another woman, and either she'd assume that he was less interested in her, Dora – and thus she'd gravitate all the faster to Harrison Lockwood – or, worse she would just plain not care. And then the horror dissipated, replaced by a feeling of hostility. All of a sudden, Ballou wished he really were flirting with Charlotte Fanshaw, so he could rub Dora's ski-jump nose in it – only, why would Dora give a shit?

Syphilis, chlamydia, pinworms. Ballou gave Dora a big smile and an enthusiastic "come join us" wave.

"Hang on, Charlotte," Ballou said. "It's about time I got a chance to introduce you two!" He almost crowed with mischief. "Glinda, I'd like to present the Wicked Witch of the West. Wicked, meet Glinda!"

The two women screamed in delight at each other's costumes and made as if to embrace but only mimed the gesture, since they both had their hands full. Ballou then introduced them by their proper names.

"Charlotte," he added, "Dora has been telling me how interested she is in your columns, especially the one where you talked about plastic surgery, remember? It so happens that Dora is one of the top plastic surgeons in the United States – as well as the best baker in the district."

"I don't know about that," said Charlotte. "I make a pretty mean apple pie."

"Why, then, we'll have to compare recipes," said Dora.

"Oh, there's no such thing as a pie recipe," Charlotte declared. "It's an art."

Nearby, Mr. and Mrs. Leahy chatted with Buford and Carrie Plankton, who were not in costume. Or rather, Mrs. Leahy was talking to Mr. Plankton, while Frank Leahy and Mrs. Plankton appeared to be arguing. Ballou strolled over toward them, and almost bumped into Harrison Lockwood.

"Oh, hi," said Lockwood. "Is that Charlotte Fanshaw you were talking with? I've always wanted to meet her. I'll get Dora to introduce me. Do you know Dora well?"

"Fairly." Ballou edged away from Lockwood, who had moved a little too close.

"She's really something, Dora, isn't she?" said Lockwood. Again, he didn't have to raise his deep, even voice to be heard above the music. "A spiritually rich person. What a remarkable life-journey she's had." He looked not at Ballou, not at Dora, but once again into the mysterious distance.

"Mm," said Ballou, and edged away again. Lockwood, apparently divining Ballou's discomfort, gave a sudden hearty chuckle and reached across his body to clap Ballou on the right shoulder with his own right hand, before walking over to Dora and Charlotte. Ballou wished he could wrench Lockwood's arm off at the shoulder and beat him to death with it.

"I didn't stay too long after I met Llandor," Ballou told his mother. "You know, always quit while you're ahead; always leave the party while you're still having fun. Add it up, I didn't score too badly, did I?"

"What do you mean, 'score'? That sounds awful."

Ballou sighed. "All I mean is, I got through the evening without any serious mishaps, and I met Llandor, which is kind of neat, and I've got a dog if I want one."

Ballou had not said a word to his mother about Harrison Lockwood. He'd avoided talking about Dora whenever his mother had brought her up. He didn't want to explain that he'd left the party early because he'd been afraid of what he might see.

Wednesday, November 3

On the following Wednesday morning, Ballou arrived at his Poetry Workshop class to find President Bannister seated in a spare chair, by the window, a few feet from the table where the students sat as usual.

"I've heard so much about your class, Roger, that I decided to audit this morning," she announced to Ballou, with another of her gingival smiles.

Ballou forced himself to smile back. "That's great, Dr. Bannister," he said. "But if you're going to audit, you'll have to consider yourself a student, and sit with the rest of us." He indicated an empty seat at the table. "And in this classroom, I'm Professor Ballou. Now, Mr. Taylor, you're up first."

"An appropriate expression," remarked Scott Taylor, passing around copies of a poem entitled "Flushing Sixty-Five." Taylor then began to read, slowly and with careful enunciation:

O Naked Prole!
Snog, egregos. A bod, no rows.
Look: milk! Ucch!
Jet her, Sir, chop-o!

The poem continued in this vein for three quatrains, followed by an envoi:

Not for you ones,
  sevens and elevens
Just thirteens and twenty-fours
Till sixty-nine.

"Comments?" asked Ballou.

"Well, it's all sexual and... and *poopie* references, isn't it?" noted Annette Schlegel. "It's very arcane, though, in some parts." She smiled, half-naughty, half-shy. "Maybe I just haven't led an exciting enough life to understand all of it."

"I like the way Scott mixes slang terms from different traditions, or I guess different bodies of slang would be a better way to put it," said Curtis Wandervogel. "Like, 'bod,' that's way out of date, but I think it was current in the 1960s and '70s, for 'body.' And 'snog' is British slang for, like, 'making out.' 'Egregos' is a mystery to me, though. I know 'egregious' is a word. Scott, you might want to check that."

Scott Taylor made as if to respond, but he remembered Ballou's rule, and didn't. Ballou nodded to him in appreciation.

"You know, I bet the author meant 'egregos,' even though I suspect it is an invented word," said Ballou. "In this case, we will have to ask the author."

"Yes, I meant 'egregos,'" said Scott Taylor. "It means what it means. In this context, it's a noun in the vocative case, following a verb in the imperative mood."

"Oh," said Curtis Wandervogel. "So, if it is an invented word, it sounds Greek, somehow. And 'chop-o,' I'm guessing that that's a version of 'chop-chop,' which is pseudo-Chinese for 'quickly.' Probably the author used 'chop-o' as an assonance or false rhyme with 'rows.' Or maybe he's representing the word *'chapeau,'* using that spelling to indicate an American pronunciation. So my interpretation is that Scott is paying tribute to the many cultural influences that have shaped the English language."

"But I don't get all those numbers at the end," said Michael Brooke. (Ballou noticed, for the first time, that Curtis Wandervogel and Michael Brooke wore identical sweaters this morning: pullovers with wide horizontal stripes of purple, orange, and white, the Van Devander colors.) "Sixty-nine, of course, probably sexual."

Tonia Kampling, sitting next to Brooke, shrieked out a nervous giggle, turned bright red, and tried to hide her head between her shoulders. Brooke glanced at her in exaggerated consternation.

"But, 'Not for you ones,/sevens and elevens,'" Brooke continued. "You don't know if he's saying 'you ones,' like 'you people,' or if he's referring to numbers one, seven, and eleven. Is he saying, 'You people don't work at 7-Eleven'?"

The speculation continued, and Ballou was delighted – first, that none of the students saw that the poem was a puzzle, which Ballou himself had begun to solve as soon as he saw what Scott Taylor meant by "Sixty-five" in the title and "Sixty-nine" in the concluding line. Second, because the students kept looking and looking for symbolism, and Ballou hardly had to say a word: so much for any accusations of "chalk and talk." Dr. Bannister, meanwhile, busily and conspicuously took notes.

"Dr. Bannister? Would you care to comment?"

"Oh, no, thank you, Roger. Your students are all doing such a good job. I'm sure I couldn't add anything. I'm very impressed with all of you." Dr. Bannister beamed at the class.

Tonia Kampling was next up for a critique: volunteering for the first time.

"Sherrie?" Miss Kampling whispered to Sherrie Zizmor. "Please?"

Miss Zizmor read Miss Kampling's poem to the class:

I follow you like a familiar

Wishing to absorb you, become you, complete you

Wishing flower open to the bee

Falling flying weeping in my dreams

But oh you're such a shit

But oh you're such a dear

Oh shit oh dear

Oh dear am I a dear,

Doe to your buck?

I buck I writhe in bed to think of you

"It seems to me that this poem is crawling with ambiguities and ambivalence," Ballou remarked. The class tittered, sensing sarcasm.

"No, I'm serious," he added. "The third line strikes me immediately. On its surface, it looks like a hackneyed, ordinary metaphor that doesn't relate well to the first two lines. But the exact wording that Miss Kampling has employed leaves it open to a number of interpretations, and therefore, in an odd way, it's interesting to me. But, Miss Kampling, I would find it even more interesting if you'd rhapsodized more on the idea you express in your first two lines before you give us that third line.

"Miss Zizmor, you had the benefit of reading the poem aloud just now; can you give us some insights?"

Throughout this last half of the session, Dr. Bannister continued to take notes; indeed her pen hardly stopped.

Ballou sat in his office for the rest of the morning, phoning various sources for an article on real estate investment trusts. Then he organized his notes, quickly cutting-and-pasting them into a logical sequence to form the bare bones of the story. Working through lunch, he wrote the lead, figuring he could certainly get the article done in two hours, after his Expository Writing class: in time to e-mail it to his client. He had time to step outside for a 10-minute walk around the common before that class was to begin – chastising himself even so for allowing himself that little break.

Faye Bannister remained on his mind. Her showing up to audit the poetry class could mean nothing good. Undoubtedly he'd committed two or three firing offenses, at least, in the course of that 50-minute session.

He walked across to the Student Union and was turning around to head back to the Liberal Arts building when Fi Tanquiz and another of his students, Albert Weems, emerged together from the side door of the Union and greeted him. Albert Weems was a short, very black young man with round thick glasses that magnified his eyes. He wore a striped pullover just like the ones Michael Brooke and Curtis Wandervogel had sported that morning.

"What's up with the sweaters?" Ballou asked, as they walked along. "Are some of you trying to start a fad?"

"Yeah, a g… gay fad," said Fi Tanquiz. "Albert's a member of the Gl… Gleefully Suck a Dick Society."

"Fuck you, Tanquiz," said Weems. "It's the Glee And Succotash Society," he explained to Ballou. "It's the men's glee club. We're giving a concert tomorrow night. So we have to wear these sweaters today, since most classes are Monday-Wednesday-Friday and we won't get as much publicity if we just wear them tomorrow."

"They're okay, if you like that kind of music," said Tanquiz. "You oughta go."

"It's the oldest glee club in the United States," said Weems, defensively. "It started in 1784. The only other club on campus that's older is the Red and White Christian Sodality."

"Albert knows everything about this school," Tanquiz remarked. "Although why he would want to I have… have no idea."

"Does the Sodality survive?" Ballou asked.

"In theory," said Albert Weems. "We've now got maybe 15 or 20 Indian students on the whole campus, and of those maybe two or three are real Indians, and I don't know that they're Christians.

I'm pretty sure the others are white kids who invented an Indian great-grandmother just to be cool. Or to qualify for minority status. I looked up the records once, just for fun, and the Sodality hasn't had any members since the 1950s."

"Y... you mean they were all castrated?" Tanquiz asked, as the three of them entered the Liberal Arts building. "They don't have any members? They could call themselves the N... the N... the No-Willie Wildens!"

Ballou herded the two students into the classroom ahead of him. On entering, he spied Faye Bannister once again – this time seated amongst the general population. Across the table from her sat Frank Leahy, who winked at Ballou.

"Thought I'd observe, Professor," he said.

"A trustee and a president in the same day? I'm flattered beyond description," said Ballou. "Dr. Bannister, Mr. Leahy, you're both new, so I'll explain the format of the class before we get started."

Ballou switched on the tape recorder. "Each week, each student is required to write one essay of between 600 and 1,200 words. The topic is up to the student, but each week I give them a very general idea. For example, I might assign the class to choose a habit or a proclivity that other people might regard as undesirable, and defend it. Or I might ask them to compare the virtues of something old and something new, such as board games versus computer games. I've also had them write a piece in which they tell the reader how to do something.

"This week, the assignment was to write an assessment of an historical character. You two newcomers are at a disadvantage, I'm afraid, because the two essays we're going to critique today were distributed to the class on Monday to be read beforehand. But I happen to have extra copies here." Ballou slid two three-page documents across the table to Dr. Bannister and Mr. Leahy.

"First up today is Mr. Tanquiz," he continued. "I'll call for a minute of silence, to allow the visitors to speed-read the text, and the rest of you can take that time to organize your thoughts. I want you to notice, for starters, that Mr. Tanquiz has used a classic and time-honored idea: the debunking of a hero, or a heroine in this case. That's easy to do, but difficult to do well. So as we go over this, I'd like you all to pay attention to the author's objective, and see whether he's accomplished it."

Devil's Advocate
By Firenze Q. Tanquiz

Very soon Mother Teresa will be made a Saint by the Roman Catholic Church as Saint Teresa of Calcutta. Don't bother to question this. It's a sure thing. But wait a minute. Just about all her life, she had practically everyone in the world agreeing that she was the most wonderful person ever born—maybe holy or super-human. I don't want to say she isn't, just to be an asshole. I want people to think about what they're praising when they praise Mother Teresa.

In a strictly religious sense, Mother Teresa may have been a saint. She spent all her life working for the Church and tending the sick, and I'm sure a bunch of bozos are going to jump out of the woodwork with stories of "miracles" that she performed. It doesn't matter whether those stories are true. The Church is going to promote her to sainthood because it's great public relations. But that's not her fault. Let's look at what she did.

Actually let's start with what she didn't do. Did she make any sacrifices, really? Did she do anything that was really hard to do? Anything she didn't want to do? Evidently she did exactly what she wanted to do with her life, and I don't believe she did it for others. She did it for herself.

What did she do, to get her jollies?

She encouraged deathbed baptism of Hindus. We're talking about baptizing people into a religion they didn't believe in, when they were unconscious or too sick to say no. Baptism is just some witch-doctor saying ooga-booga, but you don't do it to people without their consent. It's a desecration. It takes away any dignity they have left, while they're lying in their own shit.

She fought against birth control. In India, the most overpopulated country in the world. She knew that more birth control is the answer, if you want to get rid of crowding, starvation and disease. What she did was like if you claim you're trying to cure an alcoholic, and at the same time you're telling him it's God's will that he should drink. Multiply that by eight hundred million or whatever the population of India is.

She wouldn't allow anyone to adopt any child out of her orphanages, if the person had ever practiced birth control or had an abortion. She said, "such a person cannot love." She knowingly and on purpose kept children out of a home with parents – and I'm not talking about abusive parents, I'm talking about people who wanted these kids – and by doing that she kept them housed with her, which meant there was less room for other kids still out on the street. That's sadism.

And we hear all this crap about Mother Teresa's "humility." The phrase that gets repeated, over and over, is, "she washed the feet of lepers." So what does she want, a medal or a chest to pin it on? It's not like lepers can't wash themselves. Washing the feet of lepers was her way of showing off. I used to know eight-year-old boys who ate bugs, but nobody calls them saints. This is the same thing as how Gandhi used to walk around in a diaper. It's called, "I'm the humblest guy in the world and proud of it!"

And let's look at how much good Mother Teresa did, with all the money she raised. Did you ever see any pictures of her "Houses Of Hope" or whatever she called them? Most of them didn't have anything more than a space on the floor for their patients to die on. With all the money she raised, she couldn't build bigger and better places? She couldn't buy beds? Guess what? These awful places were advertising for her. She used them to guilt-trip the rest of the world. She used her patients for money.

Got that? She used her patients for money. She didn't give a rat's ass for those people, except as props for her fund-raising. And who knows where that money went?

Let's not fool around here. Mother Teresa was used by the Church, and she was glad to be used. She was a pin-up girl for the cheque-mailing dipshits who've always kept the Church in a fine old style. If she'd actually tried to get the Church to help fight disease and homelessness, the Church would have lost the wealth and power it maintains by keeping the masses as poor and stupid as possible.

What good did Mother Teresa do for humanity? She did sweet dick for humanity. She did a lot of good for the Church, I guess. But mostly she was just stroking herself.

I saw her funeral parade on CNN. When they carried her body through the streets, hardly anybody in Calcutta noticed. Why weren't there thousands of people lining the route of the procession? I don't know, but there weren't. Sure, people thousands of miles away adored her, because it's easy to just say, "Yeah, yeah, she was a great humanitarian." And if you said anything bad about Mother Teresa you'd probably be shot. But the people in India didn't seem to care about her much. Gee, why not?

Mother Teresa was the most repulsive geek in the world's crookedest carnival. If there's any cosmic justice, she's now indulging her love of self-mortification by star-ring twice a day as "the Amazing Coprophaga, Bride of the Burro" in some other-worldly Tijuana whorehouse.

"Mr. Tanquiz, this is quite a mouthful," Ballou remarked. "Who'd like to start?"

"I can't question the substance," said Albert Weems, "but I question the style. I know some writers think it's effective to write the way they talk," (Weems caught himself, and grinned) "and, yeah, I guess Fi did tone it down, at that, but still, this is too conversational, and you use terms like 'asshole,' and 'dipshit,' and 'getting her jollies,' that are just going to put a lot of people off, and are you sure you want to do that?"

"Good point, Mr. Weems," said Ballou. "This essay has the makings of a sort of musical piece. But you know what I think is its problem right now? It has the same tempo, the same volume, the same feel to it, all the way through. Mr. Tanquiz, you start angry and you end angry. You might not want to do that. You need to build to a climax, like a piece of music.

"You know how to tell a joke, right? You have to build up to the punch line. You have to start slow and easy. Same thing here. See, your last paragraph is the show-stopper. And one reason why it's so funny, and makes your point so well, is that it's so obscene. So it might be more effective if you started off in a quieter tone, then built your case against Mother Teresa more in sorrow than in anger. Set it up, take your time. Then with that last paragraph you knock the reader flat on his ass."

Leahy and Dr. Bannister stayed silent as the other students made their comments, Dr. Bannister taking notes and ostenta-tiously shaking her head once or twice: Ballou wasn't sure at what. He supposed she was just trying to intimidate him.

"Next up," said Ballou, "is an essay by Mr. Dance, here, which is entitled 'The Quiet End of a Noisy Man.' I'll mention to our visitors that Mr. Dance is a history major and our star offensive tackle, and he's eloquent on both history and football."

The essay was an assessment of the career of Alabama Governor George Wallace, the segregationist politician who flourished in the 1960s. The two visitors began to read. Ballou, knowing what was in the essay, watched Dr. Bannister reading, waiting for her eyes to dilate and an indignant look to cross her face – as he knew would happen, about halfway into the essay, where Dance quoted Wallace's infamous affirmation:

"Boys, John Patterson out-niggered me, and I'm not going to be out-niggered again!"

"Mr. Dance, you're a natural," Ballou said, kicking off the discussion. "I want you to buy yourself a bow tie and an ivy plant in which to drape yourself, and take root at some hoity-toity university, and shake things up a little."

Tim Dance gave a little shrug, and grinned.

Dr. Bannister raised her hand, looking prim and serious.

"I would be interested to know how your students feel about the author's use of the N-word in this piece." Her eyes shifted to Albert Weems for just a moment.

"Anyone?" Ballou asked. Silence, for several seconds. "Mr. Weems?"

"Whether or not the word is appropriate depends on the context," Weems explained to Dr. Bannister. "I don't have a problem with it. In this context."

"Well, if I'm going to be a student for today," Dr. Bannister said, "I have to comment on this, uh… Tim. You have to be very careful. Especially in view of recent events at this school. And as you go through life. There are certain words that it's just not a good idea to use. In any context. By using them, at all, you run the risk of creating a hostile environment that could surround anything else you do or say. And I have to add, Roger, that I'm a little surprised that you wouldn't say anything about this choice of words. Although I don't know, maybe I shouldn't be surprised."

"I don't forbid any words in this class," said Ballou. "I wonder why anyone would want to simplify our language, anyway. I say the more words we have, the more shades of meaning, the more ways to tweak a sentence one way or another, the better. After all, if someone offered you a box of 16 crayons, or a box of 64, which would you take? Dr. Bannister, have you ever read *Nineteen Eighty-Four?*"

"Of course."

"Then you'll recall that in that book, Orwell invented a futuristic form of English called Newspeak, and its purpose was to make it impossible to utter a politically incorrect idea. In the course of that book, one of the scholars working on a Newspeak dictionary says that Newspeak is a diminishing language, that it contains fewer and fewer words all the time – and that as words left the language, so would ideas. His idea was that eventually, Newspeak would eliminate the expression of any but the very simplest, most politically pure thoughts. I say we run the risk of creating a Newspeak in our own time, if we declare certain words too offensive to ever be uttered, in any context."

"Not a bad idea," Dr. Bannister countered.

Ballou grinned. "I wish you would add this class to your course-load next semester," he told Dr. Bannister. "I'd like to see you expound that position in a full-length essay. For the time being, this might be a topic for one of the rest of you to tackle, in one of your future papers. The question of whether ideas can or should be eliminated by revision of language. Or, more broadly, how language can influence society, or whether it should be made to. It's a very good point, Dr. Bannister, and thank you for bringing it up."

When Ballou dismissed the class, Dr. Bannister glanced at him out of the corner of her eye and remained seated, completing her notes, as the rest of the class started to rise.

"Well, Dr. Bannister, did you find anything to fire me for?" Ballou asked.

"Give me a day or two to think, Roger!" she replied. "Hah!"

"That was first-rate, Professor," said Frank Leahy, speaking to the entire room.

*

"I can't believe that Roger Ballou of all people introduced us," said Charlotte Fanshaw. She sat in Dora Fox's living room, watching Dora pour tea from an exquisite white-on-white Rosenthal teapot into cups of the same pattern. "What perfect cups!"

"And if you like what's in them, you can give Roger credit for that," Dora replied. "He brought me this tea. He's a dear, dear friend, and so much fun. But you haven't had good experiences with him?"

"Oh, nothing worth talking about. Mmm. Delicious tea. No, he's just... well, he's like a lot of people: in awe of Llandor, and so he has to attack anyone who attacks his hero. I understand that. I've been getting it from plenty of other people besides him."

Dora inclined her head slightly and said nothing; instead she began slicing the almond cake that Charlotte had brought.

"I was afraid it would be coals to Newcastle to bring you a cake," said Charlotte, "but I do like people to try my baking. I can't help it."

"And sometimes I get tired of my own creations," said Dora. "Why, this is mmmm!"

Charlotte, cup in hand, got up from her seat and walked about the room, examining the piano, the books, the what-nots.

"I always wanted to take piano lessons," she remarked. "I bought an old used piano for my children. But with one thing and another, I never took a music lesson in my life, and I've always regretted that. It must be wonderful to sit and play in this room."

"It is," said Dora. "It's very restful and soothing. Tell me, have you thought about it a long time?"

"Oh, since I was very little," said Charlotte.

"Since... oh, no!" Dora laughed. "I'm sorry. I didn't mean how long had you thought about playing the piano. I meant have you thought about the procedure for a long time?"

"The proce – oh, yes." At last they were back on the same page. "I guess I started thinking about it a few years ago, when I was still trying to keep my marriage together. I thought it might help, but we didn't have the money, and when my husband told me that he was... moving on... well, then I told myself not to bother since it wasn't going to do any good anyway, and then for a long time I wasn't dating anyone seriously and anyway I still couldn't afford it. But now that my ship seems to have come in financially, and I seem to be involved in what I hope will be a long-term relationship... at this point I'm just exploring the possibilities. I want to know what it will cost and what it will look like. I might do it as a Christmas present – both to him and to myself."

"What it will look like will depend partly on what you want, and partly on how much tissue we have to work with," Dora explained. "We could fill, if you wanted to go bigger, or we could do a reduction. I just want to stress up-front that I won't be doing the procedure myself, if you decide to have it. I've gotten completely out of surgery. But I'd be glad to give you a preliminary examination, and of course we could talk about any other procedures that you might want done – and then when you're ready, I'll organize everything for you and find you the best surgeons and so on. That's the direction in which I'm taking my practice now: consulting, rather than doing procedures."

"I thought that was where all the money was," said Charlotte. "In surgery, I mean. Is there a story behind why you got out of it?"

"No, no big story," Dora replied, laughing. "Just too stressful. Life's too short. I love to work with people – but I prefer to do it while they're awake."

"Was there a moment – an epiphany – when you said to yourself, 'I'm done with surgery'?"

"Not really," said Dora. She tensed a little. "Anyway, I can look you over and show you some of the procedures that are available. Another thing you might want to consider, since you've had four children..."

"Twat-tightening?" asked Charlotte, pleased with her own boldness. Dora gave a half laugh, half horrified gasp.

"I didn't mean that specifically," Dora replied, recovering. "It's one of a number of options to consider, depending on what you need and what you can spend."

"Do you have any 'before and after' pictures?"

"Oh, loads. In the other room." Dora rose. "Step into my lab-*or*-a-t'ry," she added in a Béla Lugosi voice, indicating that Charlotte should follow her down the hall.

As they entered Dora's office/examination room, Dora excused herself and checked her computer for new e-mails. She found two: one from rballou@vandevander.edu; the other from harrilock@hvc.rr.com. The subject line of rballou's was "Glee?" That of harrilock's was "Wood you?"

From the corner of her eye, Dora noticed Charlotte looking over her shoulder, and not being sneaky about it. Dora darkened the screen.

Thursday, November 4

"Poor Zeke," said Martin Wandervogel, as he and Charlotte Fan-shaw walked from his Montero across the faculty parking lot to Van Devander's Student Union. "He'd have loved to see Curtis perform tonight. I asked his mother if we could have him just for this evening, but she just wouldn't be flexible. But maybe it's a blessing in disguise. I don't know if he's old enough yet to sit through a two-hour concert, especially when it's past his bedtime."

"There'll be others," Charlotte replied. "There's something so magical about bringing children to a concert. Usually they're so fascinated by what's going on that they forget to misbehave."

"If you're lucky," said Wandervogel. The two of them entered the Union and walked upstairs to the second floor, to the main auditorium. There Van Devander's graduation exercises took place every spring, plays were produced, people got married, and various musical clubs performed. The seats were already filling up.

"We'd better sit up front," said Charlotte. "I didn't bring my glasses."

"Skinny, you shouldn't be so silly about your glasses," Wander-vogel replied. "If you don't like how they look, get contacts."

"They make my eyes red. I'd rather just be nearsighted."

Charlotte spotted Mr. and Mrs. Quagga, sitting in the second row, and waved to them. She led Wandervogel over to two empty seats directly behind them.

"It's good to meet you at last, Martin," said Quagga, when Charlotte had performed the introductions. "I understand I've published a letter of yours, pseudonymously. I'm glad to see that it led to the two of you getting acquainted."

"So, Charlotte," said Frances, "here we are at the same show, while our daughters are rehearsing together for another one! I can hardly wait; it goes on in just three weeks now, doesn't it? Is Bonnie having fun with her part?"

"She's loving it, thank you," said Charlotte. "Only she was so sorry to have to miss this, tonight. She and Martin's son Curtis are such good friends."

Quagga looked diagonally over Wandervogel's shoulder and waved to someone behind them. "Well, hello there, Roger! Dora!"

"Hey, Donald," said Ballou, letting Dora into the third row first, then stepping in himself and shaking hands with Quagga. "I should have guessed I'd see you and Frances here." First Dora, then Ballou, bent down to kiss Frances, and as Dora straightened up she gasped in recognition of Charlotte, who sat only a Martin Wandervogel away from her. She and Charlotte exchanged little squeals of greeting, and Charlotte introduced Martin to Dora. Charlotte then greeted Ballou, politely enough.

"Charlotte, how the heck have you been since Saturday?" Ballou inquired. "Martin, good to see you again!" Charlotte smiled at Ballou but didn't offer to shake hands, which relieved Ballou because it meant he wouldn't have to offer his to Wandervogel, either.

However, Wandervogel was an itch that Ballou could not leave alone. With Dora leaning forward to talk with the Quaggas, Ballou addressed Wandervogel across her back.

"This should be a great show," he exclaimed. "Martin, your son showed up for class yesterday wearing his glee club shirt, and when

I found out what it was about, I decided I'd have to show up and support him. Curtis is lucky, to be a singer as well as a poet. That's such a useful combination. Is he a tenor, a baritone... ?"

"A baritone," said Wandervogel, looking at the stage.

"Great," said Ballou. "Does he sing in a band, as well, or give solo performances? Now that I know he sings, maybe I can persuade him to set some of his poems to music!"

"He does that already," said Wandervogel, still looking away. "And he plays guitar."

"That's the instrument you'll learn first, if you're smart." Ballou was still grinning. "It's a major chick-magnet. Nothing beats a guitar."

"Hrm," said Wandervogel.

"Charlotte, why aren't we fighting anymore?" Ballou demanded. "I've given Don, here, a few more ideas for subjects on which you and I can debate, but he says you're not much interested in sparring with me after all."

Charlotte regarded Ballou superciliously.

"No, I'll leave the deep reasoning and the hair-splitting to you," she replied. "That's not what I write."

"Say, Charlotte, I was so glad to hear that your daughter got that part. I can't wait to see the show. Is she a serious musician? I mean, does she intend to make a career of it? I've heard her sing. It was... well, she was taking part in a political demonstration, actually, that's where I heard her, and she really does have an impressive voice."

Wandervogel continued to look askance, although glancing down at Dora now and then. Ballou glanced at her also, to make sure she was still occupied with the Quaggas, and he noticed for the first time — that is, he'd noticed it before but not remarked on it to this extent — that she was interacting with them the same way she did with Ballou himself. Whether talking or listening, she did it with absolute focus, with an intensity that flattered rather than intimidated. He certainly didn't blame Wandervogel for looking at her with interest; indeed it made him feel quite proud of himself.

"Is she looking to be a voice major in college next year?" Ballou asked Charlotte.

"I don't know that she's chosen a major yet," Charlotte replied. "She has a lot of interests. She likes to write, and she's very interested in women's studies."

"Any chance I'll be teaching her?"

"Well, she hasn't applied here. She's thinking about Mills, Barnard, Aurora, Wellesley, Santa Cruz, Berkeley…"

"Thank God!" Ballou exclaimed. "I mean, thank God you've got such a bright daughter. That's a real blessing."

As the two of them talked, Wandervogel turned in his seat and looked over Ballou's shoulder, hailing someone behind them. Ballou noticed this, and he heard and felt that person moving into their row, toward the seat on the other side of him. He turned and saw that Faye Bannister was about to sit down.

Dr. Bannister gasped at the sight of Ballou and recoiled, starting back so violently that she bumped the woman next to her, who was about to take the last seat in that row, on the aisle. The two of them almost fell over.

Ballou was delighted. "Dr. Ba – Faye! This is great. Sit you down! We're all here to root for Martin's son. He's going to steal the show, unless one of my other students does it for him."

Dr. Bannister looked around the hall for another pair of seats. Plenty were available, but mostly in the back or at the edges, and Ballou could almost hear her doing a quick mental upside-downside study on whether she should snub him so blatantly.

"You take this seat, you're taller," Dr. Bannister said to the friend she'd just jostled. That lady squeezed past to sit down next to Ballou, and Dr. Bannister took the aisle seat.

Ballou looked around the auditorium, which was now well over half-full: a bigger crowd than he'd anticipated. He noticed that the glee club – maybe a dozen young men in all, each wearing a purple, orange, and white sweater, white slacks, and white sneakers, each carrying a purple folder – were mingling here and there in the aisles, gradually forming into four threesomes, each in a different part of the auditorium. Two other young men and a young woman waited just below the stage with their instruments: drum set, rhythm guitar, and piano.

Ballou spied Lee Grossbaum, just entering at the back of the hall with a couple of girlfriends, and he immediately turned his head back to the stage, hoping she hadn't seen him. He prayed for the lights to go down, and in a minute or so they did, and in the almost total darkness a deep, amplified voice intoned:

"Ladies and gentlemen, for the two hundred and sixteenth year – the Van Devander College Glee and Succotash Society!"

From all over the auditorium, seemingly, sprang up a Swingle-style vocalise – no words, just syllables:

Dat – da-dat –
da-dat – da-dat-dat
dat-daaaa – vadavadava
dat-davada, davada
da, aaa, aaa, aaa

Ballou recognized it: the "South American Getaway" from *Butch Cassidy and the Sundance Kid.* As the lights slowly rose on the stage, the four groups of singers moved up the aisle toward it, singing all the way, mounting the stage via a short flight of steps at the front of it and standing on risers as a full ensemble.

The song sounded even better with all male voices than it had with the mixed chorus that had performed it in the movie, Ballou thought. A tenor handled the slow part that had originally been scored for a soprano soloist.

Accompanied by rhythm guitar and drums, the chorus performed Milton Nascimento's "Maria Maria" in the same manner – vocalise, not with lyrics – and Ballou saw Mr. Quagga raising his eyebrows and nodding in approval. The applause at the end was much more than polite.

The next number began with the basses – still in vocalise – giving a fast three-quarter-time rhythm as the baritones and tenors broke into Manuel de Falla's "Dance # 1" from *La Vida Breve*: not singing so much as playing their voices as instruments, imitating horns, trumpets, trombones, going louder and softer by turns, shifting their volume at amazing speed so that the whole chorus seemed to pulse. The drummer imitated castanets by playing the rim of his instrument, accompanying the vocals with a fast "clickety-click."

Halfway through the piece, the deepest basses switched into a thunderous quick-march, using their voices to imitate timpani, as the lighter basses took the parts of euphonium and tuba: a stately but inexorable charge of elephants, harassed by the staccato trumpet of the tenors, the baritones caught in the middle with their horns and trombones. Then the pace slowed, and the basses regrouped and came back in more softly; the tenors retreated and counterattacked; then the baritones hooked up with the tenors for a recap, and at last all joined forces for the whirling, breakneck-speed finale.

As the applause died down, Dr. Bannister whispered to her friend, loudly enough for Ballou to hear, "I had no idea this was a men's chorus. I would *not* have come if I'd known this was an all-male club. I feel *very* uncomfortable about this."

Next, the Society performed a short set of Jacques Brel songs, giving them a somewhat precious, old-fashioned collegiate treatment. At the end of the set, Ballou reached over and touched Dr. Bannister on the knee.

"Faye, about what you were saying before: I don't know this for sure, but someone told me this is a *gay* men's club. Not just a men's club. That's what I heard."

"Oh," said Dr. Bannister, nodding in comprehension and apparent approval.

Next, Michael Brooke took a star turn, stepping to the front of the chorus, twirling a bamboo cane, a battered porkpie hat on his head, his jaw outthrust in a cocky attitude. He sang "Inkadinkado," in the manner of Jimmy Durante. Some of the students in audience looked at each other quizzically, but they didn't seem to hate it.

"Dis is da greatest audience dis side of oblivion," Brooke growled, as the applause died down.

Next, Brooke sang "September Song" as a solo, the chorus providing background. He used his Durante voice, again, but softly, so that the audience had to pay attention. He did it without the mugging and swaggering, looking soulfully out above the audience as he sang.

And when he got to the part about the days dwindling down to a precious few, all of a sudden tears started gushing out of Ballou's eyes, streaming down his face, before he'd had any idea that they were going to come; it was too late to get out a handkerchief and pretend that he just had to wipe his nose. Ballou squeezed his eyes shut and held the handkerchief to his face. He was afraid Dora would notice – and afraid she wouldn't.

At the end of the song, Ballou couldn't applaud; he was still trying to get the tears under control. When at last he put the handkerchief away, he observed Martin Wandervogel looking at him out of the corners of his eyes. Dora put her hand on Ballou's arm – just for the briefest instant and ever so lightly. So she had noticed – but was that good or bad? Ballou thought to take hold of her hand – but hers were now folded in her lap, so it would have been a matter of seizing her hand, rather than just casually taking it, and he didn't try.

The chorus began a fast rhythm – *dum*, dum-da-dum, *dum*, dum-da-dum – and Brooke/Durante dropped his sentimental affect and resumed his tough, aggressive, strutty pose.

"Everybody's *talkin'* at me," Brooke sang, still in Durante voice, in a frustrated, angry tone. He couldn't hear a word they were saying, Brooke complained: only the echoes of his mind.

It was the best song of the set; it was sublime. Ballou's mood swung in a moment; he sat gaping, enthralled, as the chorus hummed like a string orchestra under Brooke's vocalizations, and through the recap. Ballou wished the song could go on forever.

"*Bravo!*" Ballou roared at the end of the song, leaping to his feet. In a few seconds, most of the audience joined him. Michael Brooke, flushed and smiling, had to take two bows.

As the applause died down, Ballou overheard Wandervogel muttering to Charlotte, "That's ridiculous. Durante never sang that song. And what is that kid, anyway – the good little House Negro?"

"But that's the point," said Ballou, knowing he should mind his own business but not able to help himself. "Durante should have sung it. That song would have been perfect for him, and this kid just showed us how he'd have sung it." Wandervogel shrugged.

"And furthermore," Ballou added, "what are you suggesting, calling Brooke a 'House Negro'? You mean he's some sort of race-traitor because he's not singing rap or Motown?"

"Oh, come on," Wandervogel replied. "He did everything but shuffle. And you're just pretending you didn't see it."

At intermission, Ballou and Dora strolled around the auditorium lobby with the Quaggas. Frances gave Ballou a wink and remarked, "It'll be all your fault, Roger, if Charlotte ends up getting married again."

"I hope she doesn't marry *him*," said Dora.

A little ways away, Charlotte and Wandervogel were talking with Dr. Bannister, who appeared to be leaving early.

As Wandervogel sat back down for the second half, he glowered murderously at Ballou.

"You're dead, you son of a bitch," Wandervogel hissed. "You
don't like me? That's your business. When you bring my son into
it, there's trouble."

"What the hell are you talking about?"

"Did you or didn't you tell Faye Bannister that this is a gay
group? Yes or no?"

"I didn't say it was a gay group. I said I'd heard that it was. I
don't know that. And my mentioning it had nothing to do with
your son. I've no idea whether your son is gay or not, and I don't
care."

"I've got a good mind to beat the shit out of you – after I've
sued the shit out of you."

Dora, between them, tensed – as though she anticipated having
to physically stop the two big men. Charlotte grabbed Wandervogel's sleeve. "Martin, not now!" she pleaded. The lights started to
go down.

To start off the second half, the Society did a set of pop/rock
songs in the style of medieval Spanish madrigals. Next, a bony
white-haired Scandinavian-looking boy with a monster Adam's
apple – Hjalmar Ek, the program said – sang a medley of Negro
spirituals in a big bass voice, with the chorus backing him: "Every
Time I Feel the Spirit," "Scandalize My Name," and "On My
Journey."

The concert concluded with a straight-ahead pop set: "You
Caught Me Smilin'," "Groovin'," and "Greetings to the New Bru-
nette" – and then a tall counter-tenor took a solo part on "Take a
Chance on Me."

He started out slowly, mournfully, wistfully; then the basses
came rumbling in under his voice like a pondful of bullfrogs,
speeding the tempo. In came the full complement of tenors and
baritones, singing the verses in a simple harmony.

Some of the audience began clapping along, on every fourth beat. Ordinarily that sort of accompaniment annoyed Ballou, but in this case for some reason it seemed appropriate, and he joined in.

The rendition had nothing tricky or fancy about it; it was simple and direct, performed with as much enthusiasm, as much élan, as the whole rest of the concert. The applause kept on and on, at the end, with whistling and stamping mixed in. The director, a small, tweedy-looking man with a beard, took a bow; so did the accompanists; the soloists all bowed again; at last, the crowd quieted and the ensemble performed two encores: "Oh, You New York Girls," and "The Battle Hymn of the Republic."

"That was morally improving, if you like," Ballou said, as he put on his topcoat and fedora. "How about we all walk over to The Old Log Inn for a beer or three? I'll buy the first pitcher." He addressed this not only to Dora and the Quaggas, but to Martin and Charlotte as well, just to see what would happen.

Wandervogel glanced at Charlotte.

"Oh, I can't be exposed to cigarette smoke," said Charlotte, with a simper that combined apology and moral superiority. "I'm sorry. Maybe we could go someplace for coffee and dessert instead?"

Ballou looked terribly disappointed. "I'm afraid I can't be exposed to caffeine and sugar at this time of night."

"I can't be exposed to anything," said Dora. "I've got to be up at four in the morning, so, Roger, I'm going to have to ask you to drop me off home before you do anything else. Or I can walk, easily, if you'd rather go for a drink or whatever."

"No, no!" Ballou had to work to keep his voice calm. "Your carriage awaits. We'll do the beer thing another time." He turned to Wandervogel. "And, Martin, believe me, what I said to Faye had nothing whatever to do with your son. I was just reporting to her something that I'd heard. Really. I promise you I meant no reflection on Curtis. That didn't even occur to me."

"You had some reason for telling Faye it was a gay group," Wandervogel snarled. "Why even mention it? If it was just a rumor you heard."

"Because," Ballou said, "Faye had her panties in a twist about it being an all-male club. One of my students had told me it was a gay club, and I thought it would sit better with her if I told her that."

Wandervogel shook his head.

"You're a piece of work, Roger. You're something else."

"I'm glad you think so."

The Glee and Succotash Society had descended from the stage and begun chatting and embracing and shaking hands with their friends and family. Ballou spotted Michael Brooke coming down the aisle, his arm around his girlfriend; they were laughing into each other's faces in exhilaration. A few yards away, alone, stood Tonia Kampling, gazing wistfully at Brooke.

"Mr. Brooke!" Ballou cried, stepping into the aisle. "That was about as much fun as I've ever had with my clothes on!" He grabbed Brooke's hand and pumped it hard.

"What Roger said," Frances seconded. "Even if I wouldn't have put it quite that way."

Ballou introduced Michael Brooke to Dora and the Quaggas, and Brooke introduced his girlfriend, LaVeda Flakes.

"Wait, you're *that* Roger Ballou?" Miss Flakes asked.

"He's okay," Brooke told her. Miss Flakes, not reassured, looked at the floor.

"We're all old enough that we can remember seeing Jimmy Durante on TV," Mr. Quagga said to Brooke. "You really brought him back to life."

Curtis Wandervogel was coming down the aisle, trying to catch his father's eye. Ballou saw him first, and congratulated him.

"Curtis! Come here!" Martin Wandervogel snapped. Curtis couldn't do so, because Martin and Charlotte had not yet emerged into the aisle, and Ballou, Dora, the Quaggas, Michael Brooke, and LaVeda Flakes were all standing between Wandervogel and his son, but Curtis looked nonplussed by his father's tone. Ballou and the rest of them stepped aside to let Martin Wandervogel move into the aisle.

"You, Roger, I want you to hear this too," Martin commanded. "Curtis, this guy here, this *Professor* Ballou, has been saying this is a gay group. Is it?"

Curtis looked at Ballou, astonished; so did Michael Brooke.

"That is not quite the case," said Ballou loudly to his students. "I want you to hear me explain the situation, instead of listening to this lying sack of shit."

"Oh, I'm a lying sack of shit?" Wandervogel huffed. "Who's the liar? Who's been spreading the rumor that this is a gay group?"

"You're misrepresenting the situation," said Ballou. "Now shut the fuck up and let me tell these fellows what happened." (It registered on Ballou that Dora was standing right there, but he couldn't have cared less that she was hearing him talk that way – and he noticed this, in the moment, and was amazed.) "Guys," (this to his two students) "do you know a kid named Fi Tanquiz?"

"Oh, that squirrely little dick?" Brooke asked.

"Yeah, him. I was talking with him and Albert Weems, yesterday – shit, Weems can tell you himself; let's ask him." Ballou looked around the thinning auditorium for Albert Weems, but couldn't see him.

"... Anyway," said Ballou, coming to the end of his story, "that's why I told Dr. Bannister I'd heard it was a gay group – and maybe now she'll leave you alone, instead of forcing you to go co-ed. Maybe it wasn't too smart of me to do it, but that's why I did it."

"Man, you are too much!" Brooke roared, wrapping a long arm around Ballou's shoulders. "Curtis, ain't he too much?"

Curtis laughed a little too loudly, a little too ostentatiously: not sure how to take it but going along with Brooke's reaction.

Wandervogel took a step forward and bitch-slapped his son — not hard, but that wasn't the point.

"Don't you *ever* take sides against your father in public, you little shit!"

All four women gasped. Ballou and Quagga looked at each other sidelong, hunched their shoulders, and grimaced. Curtis, after a second's hesitation, turned on his heel and strode back up the aisle toward the stage door. Brooke hurried after him, leaving his girlfriend behind. He caught up and put a hand on Curtis' shoulder, but Curtis shook it off and kept going. Wandervogel brushed past Ballou — bumping him — and headed for the front exit, Charlotte following.

Ballou, Dora, and the Quaggas stood still in the aisle for several seconds, looking first at each other, then, surreptitiously, at the retreating figures.

"Well!" said Mr. Quagga, sounding a bit like Jack Benny. "This was certainly the most stimulating glee club concert I can remember attending."

Thursday Night, Reported Saturday

"So, tell!" Frances commanded Roger Ballou, over the phone late on Saturday afternoon. "Has it happened?"

"Something has happened," Ballou replied. "Nothing good."

"Oh, dear! Well?"

"Well, I drove her home after the concert, of course, and as you might imagine we were talking about that little incident…"

*

"I do *not* like people like that," said Dora, as she and Ballou walked to the faculty parking lot. "Charlotte's quite a nice person after all, but that friend of hers…"

"Don't get me started on him," Ballou replied, but his mind wasn't fully on the conversation. He didn't even consider any possibility that Dora would invite him inside when they got back to her house – let alone invite him to make free with her – but he wondered just how he should handle the process of saying goodnight, this time, and how he could diplomatically ask to see her again. Or should he not bring that up at all, until a day or two later?

"Actually I've got to get started on him, to tell you the background," Ballou said as he let Dora into his car. He scurried round to the driver's side, let himself in, and started the engine. "You remember we saw him at the football game, a few weeks ago, filming that demonstration..."

"Oh, what an awful person he sounds like!" Dora exclaimed, literally shuddering, as Ballou finished his account. "It doesn't surprise me to hear all that."

*

"So, you have her definitely on your side," said Frances. "How soon are you going to see her again?"

"Well, there's the thing," said Ballou. "She started telling me all about how busy she was for the rest of the year..."

*

"I'm so glad you asked me to this concert because this might be the last free evening I'll see until January," said Dora, as they turned onto Valley Road. "I'm having a bit of a lull in business this weekend, so I'm going to take advantage of it and spend my evenings working on a presentation – because *next* weekend I'm going down to Washington for a medical conference and I'm going to be one of the speakers – and then after that, business is going to *really* get hectic leading up to Thanksgiving. I might have a slowdown for a week or two thereafter, or I might not – I have no idea at this point – but you can be sure I'll be going full-tilt for most of December and right through New Year's week, and I have to sleep sometime..."

*

"Well, that's not so bad," said Frances. "She's probably telling you the truth anyway. But you know, she has to have Thanksgiving dinner herself, somewhere, and Christmas dinner. Maybe you could find some way to get together with her then."

"Yeah, but it gets worse," said Ballou. "I haven't told you the punch-line yet."

*

"... and to top it all off," Dora concluded, as they pulled into her driveway, "my friend Harrison is going to be giving me lessons in woodworking, starting on Monday. I'm so excited! That's something I've always wanted to learn about, and I've never had the opportunity. I would so love to be able to make my own furniture, or at least make simple things like little decorations..."

*

"Ohhh," moaned Frances. "Oh, Roger. I'm so sorry."

"Yeah, that does it, doesn't it?"

"Not for sure. Maybe she's just interested in woodworking, and he's available to teach her, and that's all there is to it."

"Yeah, right, I'll believe that. Do you believe it?"

"Well, that's not the way I'd bet, I'll admit. He does have the advantage of seeing her every day, being right next door to her. And if he's actually giving her lessons..."

"Yeah. I'm dead."

*

"That's the guy you're going to marry, I guess," said Ballou, turning off the engine and forcing himself to grin at Dora. "The electricity between you two was absolutely palpable at Runs' party the other night. I bet poor Runs is heartbroken, right?"

"Oh, Roger, what are you talking about?" Dora didn't laugh or smile; she looked absolutely serious. "Don't be silly. It's just a little baby friendship right now. I'm not in any hurry to get involved with anyone anytime soon, believe me."

Ballou said nothing more. He knew he should have let the subject alone entirely, but it was as though he'd had to say something if only to spite himself. They got out of the car, and Ballou walked Dora to her front door. She turned her head well aside, clearly presenting her cheek but making no offer of an embrace. Ballou didn't have time to think or prepare; he just touched her cheek with his lips – quickly, dryly – and Dora had backed off before he could get his arms up to embrace her. "E-mail me!" she said.

Ballou walked back to his car and re-started the engine. In the back seat, hovering over his shoulder, appeared a Black Demon. It said nothing. It just slowly shook its head from side to side. Ballou backed out of the driveway and headed back up Valley Road, deliberately keeping Dora's house out of his field of vision.

"Yeahhhh," sighed the Demon at last. "Shit, huh?"

Monday, November 8

Ballou taught his Monday classes as usual, and behaved (he supposed) more or less normally, but gnawing at his guts – he could almost literally feel it inside his body – was the certainty that Dora and Harrison Lockwood would be together for at least some hours. When would she show up at Lockwood's shop for her first lesson? At what point would he put his arms round her arms and his hands on hers to guide the plane or the bench knife, and press his body against hers and lean his face down to hers for their first... ?

Following his afternoon class, Ballou took his Cadillac for a spin, not much caring where he went. He drove down to Kingston, stopped into a used-book store there, and found nothing that interested him. Storm clouds were coming in from the West, bringing an early dusk.

He took a detour on the way home, to Runs' lot, where he swept and vacuumed the car and put it through the wash. That done, he filled his tank, parked the car off to the side, and walked around to the back of the huge garage to visit Mrs. Poopington and the puppies.

"They ain't all nursin' all the time, now they're bigger, so that little runt gets his chance sometimes," Pruno told him. "He's near as big as the others, now. Bet he'll be ginormous once he's full-grown. What you gonna call him?"

"Haven't said I'd take him," Ballou replied. He petted Mrs. Poopington, leaving the puppies alone to nurse. The smallest one was a dark chocolate brindle, Ballou noticed, not black as he'd looked in the dark.

"You got that look of love, Bro," said Pruno. "That boy's stole your heart. Call him Brad. Brad Pit."

"Fuck no," said Ballou. "I'm not gonna name him after some loverboy actor who gets all the broads who'd never look at me. I'd end up resenting him. I could call him Zazou. You know, Zazou Pit. Or Pit the Younger. William for short."

Pruno screwed up his face in incomprehension.

"Crawley," Ballou decided. "Sir Pit Crawley. That's his name." Sir Pit Crawley had finished nursing, and Ballou picked him up and rubbed noses with him.

"Hey, if it suits you, it suits me," said Pruno. "I better get back to work." Ballou stayed behind for a few minutes to commune with the dogs, then walked back around to the front of the building, where Runs-Away-Screaming stood by the pumps, talking with a customer. Runs spied Ballou and gave him the "be right with you" signal. Ballou hoisted himself up onto the trunk of his car and sat, watching the cars go by on the highway.

"Coffee?" asked Runs. "Stay there, I'll bring it out. No sense sittin' around the office on a day like this."

"Your tastes in weather are contrarian," Ballou said.

"Me like-um cold cloudy day, if that's what you mean."

Runs came back with two covered Styrofoam cups and handed both to Ballou, who held them while the Indian settled next to him on the trunk of the Cadillac. The car gave a loud "whuff" as it sagged.

"Watch it," said Ballou. "Front end of this mother's gonna flip right over."

Runs lit a cigarette and took back one of the cups.

"So," said Runs. "You were workin' on her, and then she got innerested in this new guy?"

Ballou was horror-struck, as though Runs were a doctor confirming his own strong suspicion that his case was terminal.

"What'd she tell you about it?" Ballou asked, deliberately keeping his tone conversational.

"Me? She didn't tell me shit. I just seen her with that guy at the party, th'other night. Haven't talked to her since. Could be just my imagination; could be nothin' goin' on there at all, I guess. He had that way about him, though, didn't he?"

Ballou knew he showed fear and despair in his face. He wished he could be as constitutionally impassive as Runs.

"Kemo Sabay, I hate to bust your bubble," said Runs, "but she never thought about you any more'n she ever thought about me. 'Good friend' is all you'll get. You know what old Casey Stengel said, right? 'If it ain't happened by midnight, it ain't gonna happen – and if it does, it ain't gonna be worth it.' That little spark don't get struck on the fourteenth date."

They sat silently again for almost a minute.

"I got a dog to court her with," Ballou said, knowing as he said it how pathetic it sounded. "One of Pruno's. It should be big enough to take home by Christmas. And it'll be a friend for hers."

"Too late," said Runs. "It'll be a done deal by then. No gal wants to be alone at Christmastime. And this'n won't be; I can just about gahrantee you that."

The first raindrops hit Ballou's windshield about a half-hour later, just as he pulled his car into the detached garage at the back of his house, inhaling the cold brown paper scent of the two bags of groceries from Giant Foods that sat beside him in the passenger seat. Runs' pronouncement had closed the issue, in Ballou's

mind, but still he'd felt too stunned to grieve as he'd driven on to
Giant Foods. He knew the grief would return to him later. And
so would the resentment, the murderous, spiteful anger. For the
time being, though, a sweet sense of calm had come over Ballou,
as it usually did when he'd played his last cards with a woman
and lost.

The rain came down a little harder, as he walked from the
garage to his back door. The sky was fully dark. Ballou entered his
kitchen, turned on the lights, put the groceries away, went to the
bedroom, hung up his tie and sport jacket – and it was then that
he began to wish he could cry. He tried to. Couldn't. He swung his
right fist against the stuccoed wall of his bedroom.

"Fuckin' shit!" he screamed, pressing his hand between his
knees to dull the pain.

Muttering more curses, rubbing his damaged knuckles with
his left hand, he walked into the living room, and before turning on any lights he looked out the front window to see how the
storm was progressing. The rain was coming down harder now. He
turned on his living room lights and began to pace, still rubbing
his knuckles, trying to gather his thoughts – trying to think of
anything he could do that might be more constructive than pacing
in a circle.

It couldn't have been much more than a minute, if that,
before he heard the knock on his front door. Ballou stepped
to the front door, switched on the porch light, and opened the
door to Lee Grossbaum, wearing an ankle-length raincoat and
a wide-brimmed cloth hat that the rain had pushed low on her
head.

"I came by to give you my poems," Lee said. "Is it okay?"

"It's... sure, I guess..." Ballou stammered.

"Is this okay?" Lee asked again. "I was just going to put them
in your mailbox, here. I called and you weren't home, so I decided
I could use a walk anyway, but..."

"Come in before you drown," Ballou said. He held the door for Lee as she stepped into the front hall, taking off her hat and letting a few ounces of water pour onto the floor from its brim. Her long black hair tumbled down as she shucked off her raincoat; Ballou took it from her hastily and shook it out on the porch before shutting the front door.

"I wanted to give you my poems for this week," Lee repeated. "I didn't have them ready to turn in this morning in class, and I didn't want you to take credit away if I was late…" She searched in her bookbag and produced two sheets of notebook paper. "I thought about just leaving it in your office, but I didn't know if you'd get it…"

Yeah, Ballou said to himself, I believe you.

"Well, come on in and sit down till the rain lets up, anyway," he said aloud. "Let me find you a towel." Ballou darted into his bedroom and grabbed one from the linen cupboard, not letting himself think about what was going on. Lee was still standing in the front entranceway when he returned; she dried her hands and face, shivering.

"You'd better have some tea or something to warm you up," Ballou said.

With what looked to Ballou like a smile of victory, Lee walked into the living room and sat down in the middle of his couch. She wore a bulky black sweater, jeans, and sopping sneakers. She had no makeup on, and her faint freckles and disheveled hair made her look as though she'd just traveled forward in time from Ballou's own college days.

"And you'd better get those shoes off," Ballou said. "I'm sorry I don't have a fireplace to dry them over. I mean, I have, but I haven't used it yet. I don't have any wood. I should get some." Lee began taking her sneakers off. "Listen, if you need to hand your poems in a day or two late, I'm not going to cut your head off or anything. So anyway, can I get you some tea or something?"

Ballou grabbed the back of his head, as though to physically stop himself from babbling. His hand was freezing cold, and he could feel it shaking.

"Isn't it about time for you to have your martini?" Lee asked.

Ballou looked at the mantel clock. It was 5:30.

"It's before my usual time, but I guess I could have it now, if you'd like to have one with me."

"Oh, I don't want one," said Lee, still smiling up at Ballou as she removed her socks. "I'll take some tea if you have some. But I want to see you have your martini."

"Let's have tea first. By the time we're done, it'll be a little closer to a civilized cocktail hour."

"You have so many books," Lee remarked, getting up.

"Pick out something to read while I'm occupied," said Ballou.

Ballou went into the kitchen, noticing that his hands were shaking worse and worse. He fumbled the teapot, caught it before it could fall to the floor, juggled it, controlled it, and set it on the kitchen worktable.

"Here you go," Ballou announced, entering the living room bearing an ornate wooden tray on which he'd placed the teapot and flowered china cups and saucers. Lee had resumed her place in the center of the sofa, having chosen a big book of Charles Addams cartoons. Ballou placed the tray on the coffee table before her. "Oh, nuts, I forgot the milk and sugar. Hang on."

"Never mind," said Lee. "I like it plain. That looks so elegant!"

"It's all from yard sales," Ballou replied. He sat down – next to her, but not too close. "That's one of the fun things I've discovered since I moved to a small town. The way my dishes get broken, I'd be a damn fool to ever buy anything new." He poured tea. "Better get it down you while it's hot. Your health, Miss Grossbaum."

Ballou took a cigarette from a little enameled box on the coffee table and fitted it into a holder, hoping that Lee wouldn't notice how his hands were trembling. A muscle in his back seized up, and he had to shrug and roll his shoulders until it relaxed.

On Ballou's first attempt at striking a match, the matchbook popped out of his hand and skittered across the coffee table. He retrieved it before it could hit the floor, tried again, and this time managed to light his cigarette. He looked at Lee as though ironically inviting praise.

Lee giggled, and spilled a little of her tea – and only then did Ballou notice that her hands were trembling, too.

"Oh, look at me!" she exclaimed, and took a sip. "I'm just shaking all over! I... I'm sorry, it was hard for me to get up the nerve to come over here like this." She held out a hand, exaggerating the trembling.

Ballou took another drag on his cigarette, and felt a little calmer. He held out his own hand. "Steady as a rock," he announced. He advanced it so that his fingertips barely touched Lee's.

"It wasn't easy to get here," Lee said. "I went in all directions, just in case. And by the time I got here it was dark, so I'm sure nobody saw me. Nobody knows I'm here."

Ballou raised his eyebrows as much as to say, "Indeed?" He took hold of Lee's hand and squeezed it, and she squeezed back and raised his hand to her lips. Ballou let go her hand and touched her hair, and Lee leant into him, and they kissed long and softly.

"Mmmmm," Lee murmured. "This is dreamy. I love kissing a smoker."

"Well, have some more." Ballou took another drag, and they kissed again. Ballou wrapped his arms round her, one hand on her back under her sweater; he could feel a ribbed undershirt, and no bra beneath that.

They lounged on the couch, kissing, for what felt to Ballou like 20 minutes anyway. He started to worry. He hadn't been with a woman in years. If they ended up in bed, would he get it up all right? At the moment, he was too nervous to get hard. But Lee was at his fly, opening the package, and he let her, and when she started sucking all systems were go.

"Aren't you gonna show me the bedroom?" Lee whispered. She sat up, and with one swift move took off her sweater and undershirt. Lee was straddling Ballou's legs, and he sat up and faced her, caressing her naked shoulders. "Come on," he said, "let me up, and we'll move operations."

Lee was evidently not very experienced – or at any rate she had not learned much. Immediately, once they were naked in bed together, she tried to guide Ballou into her, and he had to tell her, "No, baby, not yet, we have a long, long way to go yet." He kissed Lee's face, her hairline, her neck, ran his hands over her breasts and belly, stroked her legs with his legs. He kissed her collarbones, her shoulders; he tongued her armpits. He sucked her nipples, turn about, and ran his face over her belly.

"Such a pretty tummy," he whispered. "Maybe I'll shoot all over it later."

"Mmm, yeah. Or on my breasts. I love that."

Ballou moved downwards, nuzzling her genitals.

"Roger, you don't have to. I'm not that crazy about it."

"Of course you're not. You've been dating little boys all your life. I'll show you how it's done." Lee sighed, giggled, and relaxed, and Ballou showed her.

"Now this," Ballou announced, "is the way to drink a martini." He and Lee half-sat, half-lay against the pillows: she drinking tea that he'd retrieved from the living room and re-heated; he sipping a martini and smoking another cigarette. Ballou felt wonderfully calm, amazed, proud of himself, and above all relieved. He hadn't bungled it at all, not in any way. He'd made Lee come four times (he'd counted) while going down on her, and she'd cried out and come a fifth time when he'd slid his cock into her. When he'd been about to come, she'd pulled him out and aimed him at her breasts, moaning and arching her body.

"So, tell me," said Lee, snuggling under Ballou's arm. "Who's the worst poet in our class? Besides me."

"You're far from the worst," said Ballou. "But I'm not going to tell you who's the worst; are you kidding? That'd be totally unprofessional."

"Oh. Well, yeah, I can sort of see that, I guess."

"I better feed you, after all that exercise. I could make us some bacon and tomato sandwiches. Unless you keep kosher, do you?"

"God, no. Except we have a kosher kitchen at the house. But, no, that'd be great."

"Or we could send out for pizza. I think the rain has stopped, so we won't be imposing on the delivery people."

"Oh, yeah!" Lee replied, sitting up. "What do you like on yours?" She jounced up and down on the bed. "I like mushrooms, and fresh garlic, and extra cheese. Do you like extra cheese?"

Ballou had put his robe on to answer the front door and accept the pizza, and Lee was wearing his Willie Wilden sweatshirt, which hung almost to her knees. They ate sitting cross-legged in the bed, chatting in a mixture of French and English, sometimes adding a little German.

"You should learn some Italian," Ballou suggested, closing the pizza box and leaning across the bed to set it on the floor. "Then you could rip up Giulio's poems in the original. Although he's actually a pretty good poet."

"Maybe," said Lee. "But he's a creep. He asked me out a couple times. Can you imagine?"

"I can't imagine you going for him," Ballou admitted. "But I guess you can't blame him for asking. And you've got to feel sorry for guys who... who aren't exactly fascinating to women. Because they're the ones who have to put their egos on the line, and do the asking, and they usually get shot down, and it must be hell for them after a while. A guy can end up totally hating himself, if he's constantly getting rejected. Because guys like that, they usually understand, on some level, that they're not attractive – but they usually don't know how to do anything about it."

"I don't see how you would know anything about that," said Lee. "You could have any girl you wanted."

Ballou almost told Lee she was full of shit, then thought better of it. He grinned at Lee, and looked down at her legs. He looked at the bottom of the sweatshirt, gathered round her thighs, and thought about how her legs had felt when she'd wrapped them round his back, before, and held him tight within her until he'd been about to come – and then he smiled at her again, and reached over and took her face in his hands and kissed her, then pulled her down under the covers and pulled off the sweatshirt, and she undid Ballou's robe and took it off him and they were naked again, and they both shivered a little because of their full stomachs, but that made it all the more delightful to feel their bodies rubbing together, and they laughed.

Ballou kissed Lee's face and neck ravenously, almost violently, sucking her flesh, as she moaned and squirmed, squeezing his chest muscles with her hands. He licked and sucked her armpits again, then flipped her over and bit her shoulders, her back, then he spread her buttocks and teased her anus with his tongue: Lee gasped in surprise at this, at first, but then breathed, "Ooooh," and gave in to it.

It took them a long time. Ballou had another shot in his locker, but it wasn't going to go off for a while. They sixty-nined for a few minutes, then Ballou couldn't wait any longer. He got atop Lee and entered her as they tongue-wrestled and held each other as though to crush their bodies into one; Ballou heard Lee's breath sobbing in her throat as he nuzzled her cheeks.

Ballou broke away from Lee, flipped her over again, and re-entered her horsy-style. Lee moved her torso back and forth as they rocked, rubbing her nipples against the sheet. "Pull out and come in my mouth when you're ready," she whispered, her voice jerking.

"Don't let me fall asleep," Lee murmured as they snuggled. "I can't sleep over. I can't be seen walking out of here in the morning."

"I guess not," said Ballou. "I sure wish you could." He pricked up his ears and listened. "Too bad the rain stopped." He stroked Lee's hair and her cheek, and pressed her face against his chest. "I wish we could just stay in this bed forever and ever."

"I'd wear your penis down to nothing," said Lee. "I can still taste you."

For some reason the last remark touched Ballou like nothing else Lee had said or done all night, and he held her all the tighter.

"I saw you at the concert the other night," Lee murmured. "That was such a beautiful woman you were with. And I was afraid she was going to get you if I didn't do something fast. You can't imagine how tough it was for me to get through the weekend, wondering if you were with her. I walked past your house twice but I was too much of a coward to knock."

"All's well that ends well," Ballou whispered. He reached down and ran his hand through Lee's pubic hair, letting his fingertips play over the outer edges of it, just above her hip joints. She took his hand and guided it between her legs.

"Could you make me come, again?" she asked.

Tuesday, November 9

Lee had left shortly after midnight – by the back door, proposing to cut through several back yards before emerging onto a sidewalk a block or two farther on – and it had been another hour before Ballou could unwind enough to turn out the light. A sharp banging on his front door woke him at about eight. Ballou rolled over and decided to ignore it.

A few seconds later, though, the banging was repeated, and a man's voice shouted, "Mr. Ballou? It's the police. If you're there please open up!"

The word "police" did what it was supposed to do: caused Ballou to leap out of bed, dash to the front door, and open it. There on his porch stood Chief "Yogi" Jorgensen and his partner, "Boo-Boo" Perdue.

"May we come in?" asked Chief Jorgensen.

Ballou had no reason not to admit the policemen. He had nothing illegal in his house, and he was sure Lee Grossbaum was of age... but could this be about her? Was she missing? Or found dead? Or was she claiming she'd been raped?

Ballou felt a ghastly tingle of terror all over his body. This was it. Even an accusation – as completely innocent as he knew he was – would land him in jail for weeks or months, would ruin him financially, would destroy his career, would reduce him to beggary or to living with his mother.

"No, I'm sorry," he told Jorgensen. "Unless I know what's what, I'm afraid I can't let you in without a warrant. We'll have to stand here and talk."

"Do you want to put some clothes on?" Jorgensen replied. Although the rain had long since passed over and it was a sunny morning, it was pretty cold – and Ballou was standing there stark naked.

For a moment, Ballou thought to defy Jorgensen and say, "No thanks. I'm fine the way I am; tell me what this is about." Simply because he wasn't going to let any damn policeman make it his business what he, Ballou, was wearing. But he realized at once that aside from pissing the policemen off, that move would be just plain idiotic, so he excused himself – saying, "Don't worry, I'm not running off" – and returned to the bedroom to get his bathrobe, noticing that the combination of cold and fear had shrunk his package down to an acorn and an empty sack.

"Can you tell me where you were between, say, two and five this morning?" asked Chief Jorgensen.

"Yes, I was right here. All night, from about 5:30 on."

"Anybody else who can prove that?"

"No."

"Are you sure?"

"Officer – Chief – what? Was I supposed to have been someplace else?"

"Well," said Jorgensen, "there was an incident early this morning. Right around three-thirty, four. It was reported that somebody planted a burning cross on the lawn in front of a house a couple of blocks away from here. This house has a mother-in-law apartment above the garage, and on the porch of the mother-in-law somebody also left a big bowl of... well, it looked like chitlins, actually, raw chitlins covered with ketchup and... fecal matter, and a piece of paper attached to it that said – excuse the language – 'nigger-lover's guts.'"

"And what has that got to do with me?"

"Well." Jorgensen looked away from Ballou and shifted his feet. Somehow Ballou sensed that this was a studied movement. "We have information that the person who lives in that apartment is known to you. We also know that she is... well, we don't know if *involved* is the right word, but she's friends with a bl – an African-American b – young man. Who we understand you also know. And we've heard that you've been involved in several race-related incidents on campus... "

"Just a damn minute. Who told you that?"

"Well, were you?"

Ballou briefly told Jorgensen about his article in the *Advertiser*, the demonstration at the football game, and the bogus leaflets.

"If you want to stretch a point, I guess you could call those race-related incidents," Ballou concluded, "but there was no racist behavior on my part, let alone anything anti-black. I'd still like to know who told you all this. Considering you got the call four hours ago, I suppose the person who called you gave you my name."

"I can't tell you that," said Jorgensen. "But that would be a reasonable assumption. But I'm sure you know how important it is that if you have any contact with her – with this individual – that you not do anything that could be even remotely taken as retaliation. Know what I mean?"

"Is this a student of mine?"

"It might be."

"Well, she's mistaken if she says I had anything to do with this."

"Another thing," said Jorgensen. "In the past couple of days, this individual received two threatening notes in the mail." (Jorgensen consulted his notebook.) "One of them said – again, excuse the language – it said, 'Every day, Nigger Lover, you should say goodbye to your nigger boyfriend like it was your last chance. When you least expect is when we plan to strike.' and the other said 'Your poetry sucks shit.'"

"Did she show you the letters?"

"Yes, we have them."

"Are they hand-written?"

"That, I can't disclose at this time."

"They can't possibly be in my handwriting," said Ballou. "Any of my students would have samples of my writing, though. If you find my fingerprints on them – you might, if the envelopes and paper were stolen from my office, but that's all I can think of."

"And that's another thing," said Jorgensen.

"Yes, of course. I'll present myself at the police station in… say, two hours, and you can take my fingerprints – and writing samples too, if you want. Fair?"

The moment he'd shut the door on the departing policemen, Ballou's felt his belly swell up, and his sphincter felt like it could give way in the next few seconds. He raced to the toilet and blew out approximately a cubic foot of gas and diarrhœa, gasping and groaning all the while. He remained seated on the pot, bent almost double, waiting for the second wave that he knew would come in a couple of minutes. Because he was, in effect, chained to the spot, he was able to concentrate his mind, and he ran over the situation:

- The only black students I know at all are Michael Brooke and Albert Weems, and I only ever see Brooke with a black girlfriend – and Tonia Kampling is always hanging around him, but she's not his girlfriend. Is she? And could she be the one the cops were talking about?
- I didn't do it. Not even sleepwalking could I have done it.
- Lee can vouch for me – or no, she can't, because she left about midnight. And I won't involve her. No way.
- I bet she'd lie for me, and say she was here later, but I won't ask her to.

- It's Wandervogel. Or one of my students, only I don't think I've pissed any of them off that bad. Or Faye Bannister herself, but no, that's preposterous.
- It's immaterial who did it, just so I can prove it wasn't me — or make it impossible for anyone else to prove it was me.
- People know who I am, especially on campus. Even at four A.M., someone would have identified me.
- The cops don't really think I did it. If they did, they'd have been more insistent, and tougher. They'd have tried harder to make me let them search the house.
- Could someone have been here, and left incriminating materials? Not in the house. But my yard? Empty kerosene can? Look around, and if you see it, don't touch it — because it certainly does not have your prints on it now.
- How about my office at the school? Same story. Someone could plant something there — it's an open cubicle — but again, it wouldn't have my prints on it.
- And if I tell those guys about the various ways someone might have set me up — using a pen from my desk or some such — they'll think either I'm paranoid, or I'm anticipating the evidence that they're bound to find on their own. And if the latter, they'll think I'm guilty as hell.
- If the cops come back here with a search warrant, they'll take my computer, with my whole career on it: my research, my articles, my lecture plans, all of it. Not to mention the computer at the school. I'll be finished. Every project I've got going right now, I won't be able to work on.

Ballou wiped vigorously, went naked into his study, and copied his entire Word program onto a CD-ROM. This, he took into the kitchen, and hid it in a box of cornflakes, pushing it well down into the cereal. He made a second copy, which he resolved to keep on his person at all times. Thus, worst-case, if the police confiscated his computer, he could buy a new one and load all the data onto it.

Leaving breakfast until later, Ballou showered, dressed, and walked to campus, intending to perform a similar operation on his office computer before reporting to the police station.

Walking along Elm Street, Ballou noticed a crowd gathered around a house some distance ahead of him. As he got nearer, he saw that the yard had been cordoned off with yellow police tape. The burnt cross – a small one, about thirty inches high, wrapped in charred rags – had not been removed. A TV crew was there. Dr. Bannister was there, talking to a reporter. Ballou wasn't close enough to hear what she said, and she apparently didn't notice him.

Martin Wandervogel and a couple of his students were filming the scene. Ballou had no choice but to walk right past them.

"Have you come by to admire your handiwork, Roger?" Wandervogel asked in his grand voice. "You've really outdone yourself, this time." Ballou looked straight ahead and kept walking without saying a word, but he knew he was being filmed.

An idea hit him. He turned, and walked back toward Wandervogel. He could see the fat man tensing, as though fearing a physical attack, and Wandervogel called to his camera crew, "Get this! Get this!"

Ballou stopped about six feet from Wandervogel and looked at him critically, a slight smile on his face.

"Martin, you look pale, and kind of haggard," Ballou said. "Have you been up all night, by any chance? And your shoes – gosh, they're pretty wet. Oh, I know, you've been standing on the wet grass all morning. And I know it would never have been you who actually did the work. Good luck with your film."

At his office on campus, Ballou again made two copies of his Word program. One of the CDs he put in his inside jacket pocket along with the one from his home office. The other, he took into Violet Menzies' cubicle – she was not in – and slipped it behind a cabinet, where most likely it would remain until Professor Menzies' death or retirement.

When Ballou arrived at the police station, Officer Perdue – all jollity, and assuring him that "We're just doing our job" – took his fingerprints.

"It'd be easier if you just let us take a look around your place this afternoon," he told Ballou. "We could ask a judge for a search warrant – and you could get yourself a lawyer, and fight it, I guess, but we'd get it sooner or later for sure. What say you just take us back there and show us around?"

At least the cops didn't take Ballou's computers. They didn't find any suspicious materials in Ballou's office, house, yard, or car – no kerosene, no rags, no racist leaflets – and they didn't bother to look in the box of cornflakes.

"You know, we have to check out every lead," Chief Jorgensen told Ballou as he and his partner left Ballou's front porch for the second time that day. "Could be someone's got a hell of a hard-on... er, got an awful grudge against you. Maybe that fellow you almost had the fist-fight with, a while back?"

"I prefer not to speculate," Ballou replied.

Ballou didn't have Lee Grossbaum's phone number – and he knew better than to call the Omega Omicron house phone – and he was pretty sure she would not call him that night. For one thing, at that stage of a relationship the woman starts expecting the man to call. For another, he guessed that she'd be going through the day-after angst at this point: a mild freak-out, an "Oh, no, what have I gotten myself into?" For a third, she had done the chasing before, and human nature would cause her to pull back, now, to let Ballou do the chasing if he would. So, he e-mailed her:

I don't have your phone number, but would like to talk with you. Call me; I'm here all evening. Or e-mail me your number.
XO
Roger

He struck out the "XO" before sending it. Lee did not call him, that day or evening, or e-mail him. Nor, Ballou told himself as he got ready for bed that night, would she ever. He had given her the willies, he supposed. He had a knack for that. Or maybe, in retrospect, she was disgusted with herself for bopping an old man.

Ballou lay in the dark, eyes shut, but wide awake. And Dora? What was he going to do about Dora now?

Well, how badly did Lee want him, if she wanted him at all? Supposing Lee had gotten spooked, or had only wanted Ballou once for fun in the first place: That would leave everything back where it was. And while Ballou was 99 percent sure that nothing would ever happen between him and Dora, he could not bring himself to dismiss the one percent. But if he really did have only a one percent shot with Dora – if that – he might as well focus on Lee, if Lee were up for anything further.

Given the choice between Dora and Lee, both equally willing and available, what then? Dora, he was pretty sure. How could any man prefer any woman to Dora? But how could he not want more of Lee? At least he knew what the sex would be like – and it was as good as he could ever hope for. Sex with Dora, he still could not quite envision, could not predict how it could happen or what it might consist of or whether it would even be worth it if it did happen.

Dora, with her perfect, antique-laden, clinically clean, no-smoking house, her constant toiling on projects at which she excelled (was there nothing she wasn't good at?), hardly ever sleeping: Could he live with that? And for sure, she'd get sick of Ballou's lack of accomplishment and ambition, his inability to make serious money, his general worthlessness.

Lee, too – if for different reasons – would probably find Ballou insufferable in the long term. She was barely 20 years old and still pretty much a girl, with girlish interests – Ballou hardly had an idea of what her interests were – and no doubt he'd drive her crazy before too long just by being what he was: a Henry Higgins, set in his ways, exacting of others, and not a man she would want to spend her life with. For now, Ballou supposed, he was Lee's strange fruit, naughty and dangerous. Soon enough, he'd be an old prune.

Ballou thought that epigram rather good. He sat up and spoke it into his cassette recorder before falling asleep.

Wednesday, November 10

Lee Grossbaum did call on the following evening, Wednesday. She sounded tongue-tied at first: When Ballou asked, "What's up?" she just said "Nothing much," followed by several seconds of dead air – during which time Ballou took care to note down the number of the incoming call.

"You missed class this morning," Ballou said. "Are you all right? Are we going to see you on Friday?"

"I guess so. I just couldn't come to class today. You know. I have to get my courage back."

Ballou didn't know what to say. It was probably only about ten seconds, but the silence felt like a full minute to him. Finally, he said, "I wouldn't mind seeing you again outside of class, you know." And immediately he regretted it, because it was both too eager a remark, and not eager enough.

Lee giggled. "I wouldn't mind either," she said. "When are you going to invite me to spend the night?"

"Oh, God, that's another thing," Ballou replied. "I'd be very surprised if I'm not literally under surveillance at the moment." He told Lee all about the investigation.

"Oh, Roger! I knew about the cross thing, but you? They think you did it? Listen, if you want me to, if I have to, I'll go to the police myself, and – "

"No, you won't. First of all it wouldn't do any good, because supposedly this incident took place after you left. And second, I don't want you to involve yourself. It'd be nothing but trouble."

"But I can tell them I was there all night – or at least late enough to… so that you couldn't have been anyplace else."

"No, please, Lee. It's nice of you, it's wonderful of you, but don't go lying for my sake. I didn't do it, and they have no evidence, and we've got to leave it at that."

A long pause.

"Roger, you are such a good man," Lee whispered. "I'm just aching for you, Roger. I am! I am!"

"Aw, you're a sweetie. I wish you could come over right now. But I guess it's going to have to wait a few days. Maybe this weekend. Listen, could you take a bus somewhere? Like, to Albany, maybe? I could meet you at the bus station there, and we could drive a little further on, like to Rome, Utica, Centerboro, and hole up in a hotel. Like from Friday night to Sunday afternoon."

"Ooooo!" Lee squealed. Ballou could almost see her bouncing up and down on her bed. "That'd be way nice. But, Roger? How about that lady I saw you with at the concert last week? Aren't you still seeing her? Won't she be disappointed?"

Ballou had to pause for a few seconds to prepare a response: He hoped Lee didn't notice.

"I don't know if you can say I've been 'seeing her,' the way that term is meant these days," he replied. "She's a friend, we spend time together, but I've got lots of female friends."

"I know you must have." Ballou caught just a trace of complaint in Lee's voice. "It's okay. I know you have other women. You could have whoever you wanted."

"I wouldn't say that," said Ballou. Lee had told him that twice, now. "But she's just a friend."

"I like it that you have so many women friends. It makes me proud of you."

Did she mean proud of him because he was a man whom women liked? Or because she thought he was a stud and she was proud to be one of his harem? Or was she trying to cover up her hurt at not being the only woman in his life? All these possibilities occurred to Ballou in that instant, but he had no clue as to which came closest to the truth.

Saturday, November 13

Dora had hoped to avoid Jesse entirely at the conference in Washington, but she knew he would almost certainly attend, and it would have been virtually impossible not to run into him. She had prepared herself for it. Still, it caused an actual physical weakness when she got into the elevator at the Watergate Hotel following the Saturday afternoon session and found herself standing next to him. He looked the same as ever: five-foot-six, slim but hard-bodied; his custom-made suit showing off his tight build; his hair – greying now – perfectly razor-cut. (Only a very few people would ever know that some of what he had on the top of his head was a transplant, and that he had once had considerable bagging under his eyes. Her work on him, Dora believed, was some of her best ever.) She shuddered ever so slightly and pretended not to see him, to buy herself an extra second to collect her wits.

"How are you, Dora?"

Dora forced herself to smile, and she pretended to read his name-tag.

"Why, Dr. Jesse Rifkind! I'm well, thanks. And you?"

"Fantastic. We're both fantastic." Jesse had pushed the button for a higher floor than Dora's, but he stepped out when she did. "Dora, could we talk for a minute?"

Dora stood still; she'd started toward her room, but thought better of it.

"All right, but only for a minute. I've got a lot to do, then I'm meeting someone for dinner."

"Aw, Dora, don't pull the Dora act on me, okay? I won't take up your valuable time. I just thought I should let you know, since I have you here. We're almost there. It looks like it'll be a Thanksgiving baby. A boy. We're just as excited as can be."

Dora felt a little faint, but she was pretty sure it didn't show.

"That's wonderful," she replied, summoning an even bigger smile. "I'm very happy for you." Neither could think of anything more to say, for a few seconds. "Thank you for telling me. You know I'll always wish the very best for you."

"I'm sorry, Dora, but I have to ask: What are you doing here at all? You're not…"

"I'm abiding by the terms of the court order," Dora said. "I'm not doing any procedures. I'm still a member of this organization, and I'm not going to let people think I've dropped off the face of the Earth." She paused, as though considering whether to go on, then did. "I'm also here to make sure you don't try to push me any farther under the bus."

"Why would I do that?" Jesse asked. "I'm trying to put it all behind me just as much as you are."

"My name might come up," Dora said. "And if anything gets said about me, I want to be where I can address it. And if there's any confusion about how the whole thing was settled, I want to be sure the correct information gets out."

Now Jesse looked affronted. "You were very lucky to do so well in the settlement," he said. "You'll have your career back in a couple years and it'll all be forgotten – as long as you keep quiet about it yourself. You had just better be careful that you don't keep this thing alive longer than it has to be – especially not by revising reality to somehow make me responsible for your mistakes."

"What's alive," said Dora, very softly and evenly, "is that you let me take the fall, and I need to make sure it doesn't continue."

"That's not how I see it," Jesse replied. "But obviously we're never going to agree. I was hoping we could forget about it long enough to just catch up, anyway. Are you free tomorrow for breakfast?"

"No, thank you," said Dora. "Jesse, it was good to see you again. Good luck to you. And to... Cynthia." (Dora dragged this name out just a bit, clearly sarcastically, and she was astonished at herself and a little ashamed of having done so.) "And to the little one." She extended her hand, and Jesse shook it. She waited for him to push the elevator call button, then she headed down the corridor, walked past her room, took a turn, and got out of sight. She stood, straining her ears, waiting for the "ping" of the arriving elevator, and the sounds of Jesse getting in and the door closing.

*

"You two make a wonderful couple!" called a scratchy, phlegmy male voice. Dora and Dr. Killius Jones, walking arm-in-arm, turned and looked about on the dark street to see who had spoken. An elderly drunk, hideously dirty, raised his pint of booze to them. "You look like you come out of a real classy old movie! God bless!"

"Thank you kindly, Sir," replied Dr. Jones, tapping the gold head of his walking stick against the brim of his black homburg, and he and Dora continued strolling back to the Watergate.

"We do, don't we?" said Dora to Dr. Jones.

Dr. Killius Jones, of the University of Cincinnati College of Medicine, had been Dora's mentor through medical school, and they'd kept in touch ever since. He was about 70; he looked like an older Cesar Romero, with a thick, backswept thatch of white hair and a rakish little moustache. He wore a black double-breasted suit, silver tie, and a black opera cape. Dora wore an ankle-length iridescent evening dress – neither exactly white, nor blue, nor violet

— and a wrap of white fox fur around her bare shoulders. A multi-strand pearl choker, centered with a large blue topaz, accented her throat. She wore her hair in a simple updo, with a little glitter in it.

"Very appropriate, that fur piece," Dr. Jones remarked. "A little fox for a little Fox."

Dora smiled, but Dr. Jones continued to perceive a certain melancholy about her, as he had all through their dinner.

"Dora, you're not your usual self," he said. "Something's been eating you all night. Would you like to talk about it?"

Dora sighed, considering whether she wanted to get into it.

"Oh, I'm just a little sad right now," she said. "I ran into Jesse earlier today. And I know I shouldn't let that perturb me, but it does, I can't help it."

"Yes, I should have guessed as much," said Dr. Jones. "I spoke to him myself, last night. He told me about his… blessed event. I suppose that would bother you, to hear about that. I know it was painful to me, too, many years ago, when Mrs. Jones remarried — even though we were not on good terms after our divorce. It is so sad — isn't it? — when they move on. I'm sorry."

"I still don't understand it," said Dora, and Dr. Jones could see a tear rolling down her cheek. "I know I shouldn't be thinking about it after more than two years, but I can't help it, I really can't."

"Considering he wrecked your career, I'd say you'd have to be crazy not to think about it." said Dr. Jones.

"That's not the story he'd tell, of course."

"Well, maybe a bottle of champagne, up in my suite, would be appropriate. We haven't had a good long jaw since you left school."

"Oh, we used to have the most wonderful talks!" Dora told him, laughing a little even though she continued to weep. "You absolutely got me through medical school, you know. It was like having a second father right along with me. And maybe I could use a little paternal counsel tonight. I'll come up for one glass, to toast my dear old friend."

Dr. Jones had one of the deluxe suites, high above Washington. He'd ordered Veuve Clicquot, and it was exquisite. Dr. Jones proposed, "Bye-bye to the blues."

"To happier times," Dora replied, and they drank, standing at the window, overlooking the Potomac.

"Are you getting along, Dora? I know you got kind of a knock today, but in general, are you coping? You can tell your Dr. Jones."

"Oh, Killius, I... really, I am happy. I'm having so much fun with the catering — it's just as high-pressure as surgery, let me tell you — and I have friends, and more of a social life than I had in the city. I'm afraid I got rid of Steve De Guiche — I told you about Steve, didn't I? I broke it off with him a month or so ago..."

"No! It sounded to me like he was perfect for you."

"He's sweet," said Dora. "Maybe a little too sweet. I was... well, I was vulnerable, and my tears were his music, so to speak, and I let myself fall into that relationship even though I realized fairly soon that he wasn't the one for me. And I keep telling myself that I would like to get married again, but I'm so afraid it will turn out the way it did with Jesse. I'm a good wife, Killius, I am. I'm fun to be with, at least I hope I am. But that wasn't enough."

"Find someone who's done the children thing already," Dr. Jones suggested.

Dora shook her head. "The baby may have been just an afterthought for Jesse," she said, after some consideration, "I know I sound catty, and maybe unfair. But that had never been an issue between us in the past. Maybe he decided he wanted a child partly so that he could justify everything else that happened, after it happened. But let's talk about something more cheerful."

She smiled at Dr. Jones, and all of a sudden she noticed that he was mooning at her, with the same expression she'd seen on the face of Steve De Guiche, and on the face of Jesse Rifkind years ago — and it struck her that not only had she seen that look many and many other times, from boys and men, but that she'd probably gotten it many times without having seen it. She'd never imagined she'd get that look from Dr. Killius Jones, and all of a sudden she wondered whether he'd been looking at her like that, without her noticing it, when she'd been in medical school.

Dr. Jones saw that she saw his look, and he dropped it. He cleared his throat as though trying to decide what to say – and then apparently decided to say nothing. He poured them each another glass of champagne.

"I almost forgot," said Dora. "About my presentation tomorrow, I hope I'm not imposing, but I had an idea – it's funny how I usually get my best ideas after a glass or two of champagne, but tell me what you think of this…"

They talked on for at least another hour. Partway through the conversation Dora had to excuse herself, and since she was running the water in Dr. Jones' bathroom anyway for purposes of delicacy, and since his toiletries kit was right there under her nose, she was unable to resist a peek.

The little bottle of Viagra she found stuffed well down inside the kit, and she counted only three pills left in it. The refill was dated only a month previously. Dora grimaced, and then burst out in giggles, only just getting her hands over her mouth quickly enough to stifle the noise. And then she felt a just a bit sad that perhaps her old friend had had cute ideas about this evening and that she was going to disappoint him – and she was also slightly horrified at Dr. Jones, perhaps disillusioned, but still above all amused, and a little mystified at why she was finding the situation so funny. She put the bottle back exactly where it had been, and rejoined Dr. Jones.

"Give me just another drop," she said, "and then I'll have to say goodnight."

Monday, November 15

<u>8:45 AM</u>

Brent Parris was 19 years old, over six feet tall, husky and slightly flabby, with sloping shoulders and an inflamed, acne-scarred face, much of which he hid under mirrored glasses and a Smokey Bear hat. He'd been a deputy in the Bumppo County Sheriff's Department for a year now, and was proud of it. In high school he'd been a member of the Youth Anti-Drug Police Auxiliary – the only member of that organization in Wildenkill-Verstanken Consolidated High School.

He had sometimes wondered why he had no friends – but he'd figured out why pretty quickly. It was because he was so much more serious than the other kids and didn't put up with any nonsense – so he concluded. But he had grown used to loneliness and had learned to like it.

This morning, he stood in an alley off Wildenkill's Main Street, at the side of the building that housed the law offices of O'Dell Leahy Hoo. He'd taken that position so as to keep an eye on both the front and back entrances of that building. By venturing a few feet toward Main Street, and holding his mirrored glasses in his hand with his arm extended, he could see a few yards down the street without being seen himself. This – seeing and not being seen – caused a physical thrill, the main symptom of which was a sudden and delicious urge to defecate. He fought it back, which intensified the sensation.

He knew Frank Leahy by sight – Leahy sometimes visited the Sheriff's office on business, and Parris saw him sometimes at the courthouse, too – and he was pretty sure that Leahy knew him. He'd resolved to take Leahy by surprise, just in case.

Leahy walked up Main Street, toward his office. Quickly, Brent Parris put his sunglasses back on and strode out of the alley, onto the sidewalk, to stand directly in the older man's path. Leahy stopped, looking not startled, but nonplussed.

"Good morning, Mr. Leahy," Brent Parris said loudly and clearly, touching the brim of his hat with his black-gloved hand in a half-salute. With his left hand, he thrust a large brown envelope against Leahy's chest. Leahy reflexively accepted it.

"You're served," said Brent Parris. "Good luck, Sir." He walked down Main Street in the direction whence Leahy had come, not looking back, holding himself very tall, swaggering so that the pistol at his hip would bounce just a little as he walked. He had several other sets of papers yet to serve.

8:55 AM

"You have reached the office of Roger Ballou. My office hours are Monday, Wednesday, and Friday, 11:30 to 12:30 and 2:30 to 3:30. Leave a message and I'll get back to you."

"Roger? Frank Leahy. Just to give you a heads-up in case it hasn't happened already. You're about to be served with a lawsuit. Don't panic, and don't worry. Just call me as soon as you can, or better yet drop by my office. I should be in all day, but if I'm occupied you can talk to Hugh. I'll try you at home and on your cell."

10:35 AM

Ballou had not stopped by his office prior to starting that morning's Poetry Workshop class. He'd left his house a little before nine, to have breakfast at Smitty's, and he'd sat there for nearly an hour and a half, marking papers, with his cell phone turned off, and he'd gone directly from Smitty's to his class. Lee Grossbaum had smiled at him as he'd entered the classroom, but just a little smile, with just the barest twinkle, and he'd smiled back but shifted his eyes away at once so that his smile had greeted the entire class.

Wanda Motski had just cleared her throat to read her poem when a sharp rap came at the door, and before Ballou could say "Come in," Brent Parris did come in.

"Professor Ballou? You're served. Good luck, Sir."

Ballou knew what "You're served" implied, but before he could think of anything to say to the deputy, Parris had turned and walked out of the room.

Ballou felt his hands going cold and numb; he almost dropped the envelope he'd been handed. "Excuse me for a minute, Miss Motski," he said.

Listed as plaintiffs in the suit were as many as 10 names that Ballou didn't recognize, all listed as students at Van Devander College. One of the names he did know: his own student, Tonia Kampling. The defendants were Van Devander College, Francis X. Leahy, Caroline Plankton, several other names that Ballou recognized as trustees, and several faculty members – including Roger Ballou.

"Miss Kampling... *you're* suing me... for creating a *hostile environment?*" Ballou's voice wasn't loud, but it had risen so high in pitch as to sound almost like a shriek.

Tonia Kampling had gone paler than usual.

"I... I didn't know it would be like this," she whispered. "It's against the whole school, not just you... and... and... and... I didn't *know* they'd come in here in front of everybody... and..."

"In what way have I created a hostile environment? For you, specifically?"

"She doesn't have to answer that," said Scott Taylor. "You're not a lawyer, you're not deposing her."

Ballou rounded on Taylor, but he bit back the "go fuck yourself, punk" that had formed on his tongue.

"You're correct, Mr. Taylor," he said.

"You *bitch*." This from Lee Grossbaum, hissed across the table at Tonia Kampling with such vehemence that the whole class started. Miss Kampling gasped, and stared down at her lap for a moment, then gathered up her books and bolted from the room, averting her face as she brushed past Ballou.

Ballou glanced around at his students. Scott Taylor still looked amused; Lee Grossbaum still looked outraged. The rest appeared dumbfounded or embarrassed.

"I guess we'd better just go ahead," said Ballou. "Miss Motski, I'm sorry about the interruption. Whenever you're ready."

Noon

"The game's afoot, my dear chap," Hugh Hoo exclaimed. "Here's rather a bit of luck. Now I can represent you after all. What larks we'll have with this case, I promise you!"

Ballou, Hoo, and Leahy sat around a table, drinking coffee, in a conference room at O'Dell Leahy Hoo. Having picked up Leahy's message right after class, Ballou had felt a little better – at least he had someone on his side, or so he hoped – but he still had no idea what course to take, except to get to the lawyer's office as fast as he could.

"Forgive me for not laughing," said Ballou. "I've just had everything I own in the world taken from me by a bunch of moronic politically-correct students – only I'll have to watch it go away gradually over the next few months, while I sell off everything to pay you or whomever else represents me. And my mother will probably insist on paying whatever I can't pay: Hell, she might insist on being the primary payer! And I'll end up living in a shelter and bagging groceries for the rest of my life!"

"Roger, this won't cost you a red cent," said Leahy. "You're an employee of the college, and their insurance will cover all your legal fees, most likely, because it'll be in school's best interest to defend you. And if the plaintiffs collect damages — which I have to tell you is not likely — the insurance company's going to pay that, too. Yours and the college's, and probably mine. But they're not going to get a judgment against us. No way that I can conceive of."

"But look at the specifications in the... the suit, if that's the right word for these damn papers here," Ballou persisted. "They cite me for distributing 'hate-literature,' and for sending harassing and intimidating letters to this student of mine, not to mention leaving a bucket of shit on her doorstep — and never mind that I didn't do any of that, but I still have to defend myself on those charges, and they're not part of anything I did in my official capacity. Not to mention that they're trying to get me for what I wrote in the *Advertiser* about Indian nicknames, and for taking part in that demonstration!"

"Oh, well, most of those points are absurd," said Hoo. "I'm astonished that their attorneys included them. As for the harassment and intimidation, that is something I've not heard about yet. Perhaps you'd better tell us about it."

"Well, Christ, for all I know there might even be criminal charges involved," Ballou said. He launched into the story, first of the bogus literature he'd been accused of writing, then of the police visit he'd received a few days before.

"There's this annoying little thing called evidence that they have to have if they're going to nail you on that," said Leahy. "It sounds like they don't have any. I gotta tell you, though, Roger, you're the dumbest white man I ever heard of if you let Yogi and

Boo-Boo search your place without a warrant. I know them, and they're not the type to frame an innocent man, but plenty of cops would. Don't you know that?"

"Frank is right," said Hoo. "From this moment forward, *stum*! Not a word to the police, not a word to anyone, and don't let anyone even think about searching your home or effects without proper authorization."

Ballou leaned forward in his chair, resting his elbows on the conference table, covering his face with his hands.

"I'm fucked," he said. "And Faye Bannister has probably fired me already."

"Oh, crikey, I hadn't thought of that," said Hoo. "Anyway she can't, not without proper procedure. She could suspend you, but I'd have to advise her against doing that. It'd prejudice the case if they tried to discipline you at this stage. In fact I had better call her right now to make sure she doesn't do any such thing." Hoo picked up a cordless phone from a side table and punched in a number. "Faye Bannister's office, please," he said.

"For now, really, I wouldn't worry," said Leahy to Ballou. "Your legal bills will be covered, and..."

"Yes, Hugh Hoo here," said Hoo into the phone. "May I speak with Dr. Bannister, please? Oh, well, have her call me, would you? Yes, that's H-O-O... "

"If I know Faye, she's lining up a press conference already," said Leahy.

"The more fool she, if she does," said Hoo, hanging up the phone. "One of us ought to run over there and stop her physically."

"I'm after reassuring Roger that he's got nothing to worry about, anyway," said Leahy. "Maybe he'll believe you, if you tell him."

"Quite right, Roger," said Hoo. "For one thing, you mustn't flatter yourself. These plaintiffs are obviously not out to get you personally. If they were, they'd have found a way to sue you and only you. No, they're after much bigger game. They're after the school. As for you and Frank and Carrie Plankton and the others being sued personally, this is obviously just one of those cases where they sue everyone in sight and hope to hit pay dirt somewhere – in the form of someone who'll be frightened into turning on his co-defendants."

Hoo paused for a moment, then went on.

"But that's another thing I don't understand: how anyone – any of the plaintiffs, or their attorneys – expect to realize any significant damages out of this claim. This case absolutely smells. Page after page of the most spurious, trivial claims. It's incredibly weak, hardly worth answering – yet obviously they hope to get something out of it."

"Maybe something other than monetary damages," Leahy added.

"D'you know, it's funny," said Hoo, "but the plaintiff's attorneys are the same firm that sued the Wildenkill-Verstanken school district just a few weeks ago. Dolciani, Wootton, Beckenbock & Chinn. You interviewed Mr. Dolciani yourself, Roger, you recall? And they're a Manhattan-based firm. Why are they so interested in a small town upstate? Or rather, why are so many plaintiffs in this small town so interested in engaging them?"

"Do you know anything about them?" Ballou asked. "Do they have any credibility? Maybe they're hoping the college's insurance company will settle, just like the school district did, to make them go away. Only when the school district settled, they didn't pay out any damages, did they? So there wasn't any big profit for anyone, not even for the lawyers."

"It is a mystery," Hoo agreed. "What could they get in a settlement? Five dollars per plaintiff, for mental anguish?"

"I don't know either," Leahy cried, "but we're gonna fuck 'em. Let's eat."

2:00 PM

"I welcome this lawsuit," said Faye Bannister energetically. She stood on the front steps of the administration building, in front of a microphone. Before her had assembled reporters and camera crews from the CBS and ABC affiliates in Kingston and the NBC affiliate in Catskill; Martin Wandervogel and his film crew; and a few newspaper reporters, including Frances Quagga for *The Wildenkill Advertiser.* Frances wore a sharply tailored wool overcoat of dusty rose, a strand of pearls round her neck, and a cloche hat on her head, under the band of which she'd placed a little card with the word "PRESS" hand-lettered in Gothic. A few curious students also hung about.

"I appreciate the fact that this suit was filed by people who are genuinely concerned about Van Devander College and about the state of education in this country in general," Dr. Bannister continued. "I understand that the lawyers representing the plaintiffs are hoping that more plaintiffs will join the suit, and I would encourage any student to come forward with any complaints they might have about the… the kind of atmosphere that may have been created up to now. I hope this matter can be settled quickly and effectively, and that we can satisfy the students' desires for a more diverse and politically sensitive society – at least here at Van Devander. I for one have been shocked and outraged by the insensitivity and outright racism and sexism that are displayed on a daily basis on this campus, and frankly I'm not a bit surprised that some of our students got fed up with it and decided to take it to court.

"I'm also concerned that no arrests have been made yet, in the recent case of racial hatred and harassment, and that some unknown person is still free to terrorize our students. For what it's worth, I urge the police force to get on the ball and arrest the guilty party and bring him to justice, and end this horror."

One of the TV reporters raised her hand.

"Is any disciplinary action being taken by the college against any of the defendants at this time?"

"I'm doing what I can," said Dr. Bannister. "As of this afternoon, one of the faculty members named in the suit is suspended – with pay, I regret to say – because he may be under investigation on criminal charges as well, and I'm afraid that until this matter is resolved, we can't afford to have him in a position where he might go on creating the hostile environment that he's been accused of creating. As for the trustees named in the suit, it would be up to the Alumni Association to discipline or remove them. But I would certainly urge the Alumni Association to examine their options."

Dr. Bannister took a dramatic pause and, assuming her gingival smile and holding her arms out in a gesture of benediction, continued:

"I've also appointed one of our faculty, Martin Wandervogel – hi, Martin! – to head up a Diversity Task Force, which I hope will be able to go some way toward alleviating at least some of the hurt that's been caused by the past conduct of a few bad apples. Martin, would you like to step up here and say a few words?"

Wandervogel, who'd been supervising his crew, stepped up to the microphone, looking deeply concerned.

"This is a job that I accept with all humility," he announced, "but I firmly believe that somebody has to do it. I was invited to join the lawsuit, as I believe some other members of the faculty were, but I declined because of my tremendous respect for Faye Bannister and because I was confident that she could rectify the situation without anyone having to resort to legal action. Of course I made that clear to the people who spoke to me, and I urged them to think twice before filing this suit, but apparently they felt strongly enough about it that they went ahead with it. So, now, all I can do is attempt – in my small way – to help Faye realize her vision for this school, and help create a welcoming, nurturing environment."

Wandervogel paused dramatically, and scanned the audience.

"Minority students, and I'm talking about African-Americans, gays, women, and Native Americans – and I myself am Native American, so I can feel a particular empathy – minority students have been *marrrr*-gin-al-iiiiiized… and made to feel *other*… and generally de-*meeeeeeeaned*… to a degree where common morality is outraged…"

Wandervogel went on for about four minutes. As he spoke, he nodded at Frances to show that he'd seen her hand raised, and finally he invited her question.

"Nice hat," he added, before she could speak.

"Thank you," said Frances. "This is such an exciting development. What nation are you affiliated with?"

"What… nation?"

"Yes, you mentioned that you're a Native American. What nation are you affiliated with? What tribe?"

"I'm a… a Cherokee, uh… one… sixteenth, on my mother's side." (Wandervogel celebrated the successful conclusion of the sentence with a little tilt of his head.) "And of course I'm personally offended by the continued use of a Native American as a team mascot at this school, as you'll see if you go to the website I've set up, www.stopsportsmascotracism.org. I've made quite a study of the marginalization of Native American and other minority students here at Van Devander. It's obviously been going on for a very long time – after all, Van Devander is more than 200 years old, so you can imagine. I frankly wonder if we've seen any progress at all since they first started admitting non-Anglos to this school."

"Do you happen to remember when that was," asked Frances, "when they started admitting non-white students here?"

"I'll have to look that up, Frances. But I'll get back to you."

2:24 PM

Ballou, having again not had time to stop by his office before his Expository Writing class, had not learned of his suspension. Thus, while the press conference raged outside (and outside his awareness), he'd gone ahead and taught a class that technically he had no business teaching. Walking to his office-cubicle after that class, dreading what he might find on his voice-mail and e-mail, he spotted Curtis Wandervogel coming down the hall toward him. He didn't recognize Curtis for a moment, because the young man had stuffed his long hair under a baseball cap. Curtis darted toward Ballou and touched him on the arm.

"Professor, listen a second."

"You didn't hear this from me," Curtis muttered. "I'll deny it. But listen. Modern Diversity Systems. Got it? Modern – Diversity – Systems. Write it down, don't forget it."

4:15 PM

"You back again already, Kemo Sabay?" Runs-Away-Screaming demanded, as he strode over to the gas pumps. "I swear that pretty gal drinks up a tankful every couple days."

"Yeah, she's thirsty," Ballou replied, replacing the nozzle in its cradle. "Took a little road trip this weekend, and boy, she sucks up the fuel."

"True dat," Runs conceded. "If she gives you 10 miles to the gallon, she's doin' good. You had a perfect weekend for a drive, anyway. Nice and cold and rainy. Good to see the sun today, though, just for a change."

Ballou grunted.

"S'matter? Life's kickin' your ass? On a pretty day like this?"

"You've no idea," said Ballou. He told Runs about the lawsuit.

"And then this kid," Ballou continued. "The son of our friend Captain Wonderful as you call him, out of nowhere he comes up to me in the hall this afternoon and tells me to check out this company called Modern Diversity Systems. Well, what they are – Modern Diversity Systems – apparently they're a good-sized consulting firm that specializes in so-called diversity training for businesses, schools, various types of institutions. Now, I suppose it's conceivable that they might have something to do with this lawsuit, but how could this kid – this Son of Wonderful – why would this kid know that, unless..."

"Unless his old man was behind the suit," said Runs. "Only why's the kid on *your* side?"

Ballou told Runs about the slapping incident at the Glee and Succotash concert.

"That'd do it, boy," Runs reflected. He thought for a moment more. "Listen, if you want to find out about this Modern Diversity Whoozis, why don't you call my brother Two Dogs? He's a whatchacallit, a stock analyst, lives down in Alabama, and he knows all about just about any operation in the world. He's with a company called Goldstein-Powell – his white man's name is Dodge Powell. You could look him up, easy enough."

"Wait!" Ballou exclaimed. "Dodge Powell? From Birmingham? I know Dodge Powell! I've never met him personally, but I've talked on the phone with him several times, when I've been working on one article or another. Sure. He's a good talker. I would never have made the connection, though. Would never..."

"Never have guessed he was kin to me?"

Ballou, from his conversations with Dodge Powell, had always pictured him as chubby, blond, and pink-faced.

"Ain't seen him or talked to him in years," said Runs. "Him and me, we took pretty different paths in life. No bad blood, so far's I know, but we just never were much innerested in keeping in touch. You can tell him I said howdy."

"I better run on home," said Ballou. "Alabama's an hour behind us; still time for me to catch him this afternoon. I'll just go say hi to Sir Pit Crawley, real quick."

5:15 P.M.

"You a friend of ol' Jimmy Dan?" Dodge Powell's voice was high, hoarse, breathy, and distinctly Southern; in fact he sounded very much like President Clinton. Ballou, on the other end of the line, tried to revise his mental picture of Dodge Powell, imagining now a dark-skinned, black-haired man perhaps nearly as immense as Runs-Away-Screaming, perhaps with shorter hair slicked back in a pompadour, perhaps wearing chinos and a short-sleeved sports shirt, sitting in a slightly cluttered office in the firm of Goldstein-Powell in Birmingham, Alabama.

"Small world, ain't it?" Powell continued. "How is that ol' sumbitch, innyway? What's he doin' with himself?"

Ballou told him how he knew Runs, and about Runs' business. Powell chuckled.

"Him and his names. When we were kids, I used to call him Big Chief Nasty-Ass of the Nowipum tribe. I don't think that was his favorite, though."

From this information, Ballou gathered that Dodge Powell was older than Runs, and probably just about as big, and thus able to tease his brother without fear of getting beaten up.

"Okay," Powell drawled. "Modrin Dye-versity Systems. Lemme tell you about them. So happens they're a pretty interesting bunch. And they're a little bit mysterious, so it's no wonder you didn't get much information from their Website. MDS is a consulting firm, a boutique consulting firm. Not as big as, say, McKinsey or Andersen, and not as generalized."

"Basically they specialize in political correctness, don't they?"

"That's about right," said Powell. "MDS runs seminars in sensitivity training, diversity training, anger management: all that nice liberal shit. They also make movies, videos — what they call industrial films — that they sell to corporate clients. Their clients tend to be large corporations, schools; I've even heard of one time when they were hired by an entire municipal government. And they ain't cheap. And besides their seminars and that, they're also in the business of selling books and videos, and logoed merchandise.

"Like for instance I hear tell that if a school, say, has got a controversial team mascot, like an Indian or an endangered animal like a whale, MDS will contact that school and pressure them to change the team name, change the logo, and buy all their new logoed merchandise — sweatshirts, coffee mugs, what-have-you — from MDS's manufacturing branch. They're quite an organization. Real nicely diversified, as befits the company name."

"And they're pretty well known in the business world, are they?" Ballou asked. "I'd not heard of them at all, until I did an article about a lawsuit against our local school district, maybe a month ago..."

"See, that's their *modus operandi*," said Powell. "They are not really a high-profile company, because their business is stealth. Stealth and opportunity. Well, and creating opportunities, sometimes. Now, Roger, this is off the record, okay? This is between you and me, and even at that I gotta be real careful what I say."

"Understood."

"Lemme give you a theoretical," said Powell. "I'm not saying that any specific company actually does anything like this, but let's say it's possible that a company *could* do this. Let's say, just for argument, that a company's major investors are able to in-*fil*-trate various entities around the country. Schools, businesses, what-have-you. Supposing they were to go into these companies and act as provocateurs, stirring up complaints, stirring up lawsuits — or threats of lawsuits — on the grounds of sexual discrimination, racial discrimination, creating hostile environments, and whatever else you got. Well, now, that corporation, or that school, even if it's done nothing wrong, it doesn't want any of the publicity attendant upon being sued, you follow me?"

"So, the corporation will settle out of court, to make it go away?" Ballou asked.

"Bingo. And as part of the settlement, the plaintiff's attorneys will recommend that they hire this company, which'll provide all the necessary training to be inflicted on the alleged offending parties. And you know: a client here, a client there, and it adds up to some serious money for Modern... for that company."

"And I suppose these lawsuits are usually bogus?"

"I couldn't speak to that," said Powell. "I reckon some of 'em are more meritorious than others. The point is, the defendants in these cases are not gonna fight. Most usually, in that sort of case, you're guilty no matter how innocent you are, and even at best you're up to your ass in legal fees. It's way cheaper, in the long run, to hire this theoretical consulting firm to get you certified as sufficiently sensitive and P.C."

"And how do you know so much about this company?" Ballou asked.

"Why, because I specialize in publicly held consulting and financial services firms, and it's conceivable – just conceivable – that this firm went public just a few weeks ago," Powell replied. "Then, of course, the original investors could sell out and be real well set up – no matter how the company does in the future."

"And would the original investors include a guy named Martin Wandervogel?"

"Well, of course, when they were a private company, they didn't have to disclose much, but that'd be a good guess. He's listed as a director – and not just as a movie director, either. And it'd figure he'd be involved in an operation like this."

"You know him?"

"Why, hell yes I know him. At least I know his films, some of 'em, and he's got a reputation in the investment world. Not a sterling one, I'd have to tell you."

"Is he a crook?"

"Oh, I don't have any evidence of that," said Powell. "But they tell me he's a smooth talker. A real good fund-raiser. Good at doing things with other people's money. Nothing illegal or unethical about that, of course. That's the backbone of commerce, always has been. But let's just say he's made enemies, here and there, because his investors don't always do as well as he does."

6:30 PM

"Lee, it's Roger." Ballou hadn't been able to help it. He knew it was risky to call Lee – he wasn't sure whether it was possible to tap a cell phone, but he guessed it would be easy enough – and it might make him look weak or desperate in Lee's eyes if he called her looking for commiseration about what had happened that morning. On the other hand, whom to call for that kind of comfort if not a girl-friend? – if that was what Lee was, now. And to not call her would have been caddish in his own eyes, if some other guy had had a similar weekend and then not called on the following day.

"Roger," Lee breathed. "Are you okay? What's happened?"

Ballou told her as much as he could recollect of his conference with the lawyers, and added, "I've been doing some research on my own, that I can't talk about right now, but it looks favorable."

"I'd like to kill that Tonia Kampling," said Lee. "I know why she's doing it. She knows she's not pretty enough to attract someone like you. She's probably had a crush on you all semester, and since she couldn't get you, she had to... you know, *get* you."

"That's funny," said Ballou. "I always had the impression she was sweet on Michael Brooke."

Lee snorted. "Yeah, she is, him too. But he's another one she can't get because she's not good-looking enough, or interesting enough. He can do way better than her."

"But wait," said Ballou. "In all fairness, I'm not sure she's the one setting me up. I bet she's being used. Maybe someone she knows has been harassing her, to get at me through her. I don't even think she put the cops onto me – or if she did, it's because someone else put the idea in her head."

"I'm not so sure," said Lee. "You're not a girl. You don't know how our minds work. Guys... well, guys are jerks. Except you, of course. But guys are pretty much all jerks. Girls, though – they're mean. And you're just starting to find out how mean."

"You're not."

"You haven't made me mad yet."

That stopped Ballou for a moment.

"I hope I never do," he said. "Listen, Lee, you tell me how you think we should handle this. I don't want this to wreck what you and I have, and I hope it won't. But..."

"Yeah, we're going to have to cool it for a while," Lee replied. "You're going to be all... I don't even know the word."

"Preoccupied."

"Yeah. And we can't be sneaking around to see each other. I love seeing you, Roger, you know that, don't you? But we do need to back off – just for a while. If you got caught with me, now..."

For just a moment, Ballou felt relieved that Lee had come to his conclusion on her own – relieved that he wouldn't have to reason or negotiate with her. Then he felt a little angry – and apprehensive – that she'd arrived at it so readily.

7:00 PM

And that put Dora back into Ballou's mind, not that she'd ever been entirely out of it. Even during the weekend just past, with Lee never more than a few feet away from him – and even at times when he was enjoying Lee's company the most, indeed maybe even especially at those times – Ballou hadn't been able to help thinking of Dora: sometimes wistfully, and sometimes through the voice of a Black Demon, berating him:

"Have you *no* constancy? Don't bother answering that. Just how seriously can we take you, when you say you care for *anybody*? Don't bother answering that, either."

Ballou had rationalized. His last conversation with Dora, he was pretty sure, had confirmed his position as a pal – a position from which it's almost impossible for any man to advance. She was out of the picture, and thus this weekend with Lee had been in no way a betrayal, nor a sign of fickleness. Nor could his previous and perhaps ongoing infatuation with Dora in any way constitute any unfair behavior toward Lee. Which of us has not had attractions that never came to fruition, yet never entirely disappeared?

Still, Ballou valued Dora's esteem highly enough to go to some trouble to keep it – and thus he would have to contact Dora at once. He supposed she was back from Washington by this time, and he didn't know whether she watched the local news or read the *Kingston Daily Freeman*, but if she heard about Ballou's exploits in the media before he'd had a chance to present his side of it…

He could call her – but how would he sound, if she hadn't yet come home and he left a message to the effect of, "Dora, I'm in trouble. I need to talk. Please call me"? But he couldn't just show up and knock on her door. There was no help for it: He'd have to risk a phone call.

But she was at home, and she said, "Of course, come over. I can't promise you any useful advice, but I'll listen. We can take Pegeen for a walk."

So Ballou put on his fedora and his camel's-hair polo coat – it was fully dark outside and the temperature near freezing – and headed out the door. He walked, taking a little detour, avoiding the Quaggas' house for reasons he couldn't quite articulate.

<u>7:30 PM</u>

"That's a wonderful outfit, by the way," said Ballou, as he, Dora, and Pegeen walked toward the forested area behind Dora's house. Dora was wearing a loden cape with a jeweled pin on the collar, over a textured, tailored rust-colored suit and a flowered blouse of light green, blue, gold, and burgundy.

"It's all about accessorizing," Dora explained. "The gold and the topaz and tourmaline in this pin relate to almost anything else I might be wearing, so it brings everything together."

"Guys have it easy," Ballou observed. "White shirt, solid tie, jacket, and I'm good. But I guess it would be fun to put yourself together like that. That's one thing I miss about living in the city: I could have more fun with clothes when I wore a suit every day."

"Well, why don't you still? If you like wearing suits. I've never seen you in one but I'm sure you wear them very well."

They stayed close together in the dark woods, emerging at the edge of another road at the bottom of a hill.

"The question," said Ballou, "is whether I'm going to have a job that'll require a jacket of any kind. I just came over to tell you what's going on. Because if you heard about it from other sources, you might not have too good an opinion of me anymore – assuming you do now."

"Why, you know I have a very high opinion of you, Roger."

This made Ballou straighten up and walk a little taller – and only then noticed that he'd been slouching, contrary to his usual posture, probably for many hours. He told Dora the whole story: the fifth time he'd told it that day.

"Roger, that's incredible. I can't think of another word to describe it. Well, appalling, maybe."

"I don't know how it's going to turn out," Ballou said, "and I'm pretty sure that even in the best case, I'll be wiped out, financially. I mean destitute. It's scaring the hell out of me."

"I'm sure you can trust Frank and Hugh. If they tell you there's nothing to worry about, there probably isn't. But I'm sorry to see you going through this. You don't deserve it."

Ballou wanted to take Dora's hand, but he knew better. He scrabbled in his mind for a witty reply and found none.

"Let's get back," said Dora, "and you can come inside and have dinner. I could make us an omelette."

Ballou felt a charge go through his whole body; he recognized it. It was like the first time a girl had ever said to him, "You don't have to go home tonight, do you?"

8:00 PM

"Quite a little excitement at the school today," Martin Wandervogel announced at Charlotte Fanshaw's dinner table. He, Charlotte, and her children had sat down a little on the late side because Bonnie and Luke had been at *Pinafore* rehearsal.

"Some of the students got fed up and took their grievances to court," he explained. "I was pretty sure it would happen – you know, people tell me things – and now there's going to be some changes. And we've gotten rid of your friend Roger Ballou, at least temporarily."

"Good," said Bonnie. "I think he's some kind of Nazi."

"Aw, come on, Bonnie," said Luke. "He tried to help you, didn't he?"

"He fakes integrity pretty well," said Wandervogel before Bonnie could answer. "He has a fairly convincing surface manner, so that if you don't know the circumstances he can come across as a stand-up guy. Those are the ones you have to watch out for. No, he's disingenuous.

"Ballou likes to go around offending people, and then when he offends them, he pretends like he doesn't know how or why they should be offended. He's a classic passive-aggressive. I feel sorry for him, as a matter of fact. He's probably a very unhappy person, and wants to make everybody else just as unhappy as he is."

"Like when he invited me and Martin to have a drink after that concert," Charlotte elaborated. "He was just doing it to make us uncomfortable."

"Okay, but what'd he do to get sued for?" Luke asked.

Wandervogel listed the grievances. "He claims he didn't write the e-mail, and that he didn't harass that girl," he added. "But I don't see how he can prove otherwise."

"Does he have to prove it?" Mattie asked, almost whispering. "Don't they have to prove he did it?"

"Who else could have harassed her?" Wandervogel demanded. "Who else would have reason to? Anyway we've got him out of that school, and the trustees are probably scared to death right now."

"I'm going to use your computer for a few minutes, Skinny, if you don't mind," he added, rising from the table. "I need to send a few e-mails before it gets too late."

Charlotte had two computers in her house: one in her study, and one in the basement. That wasn't enough for her and four children, and she'd promised them that a third one would be forthcoming now that their ship had come in. (Two new phone lines – one for the downstairs computer and another for the promised third computer – were supposed to be installed that week, but for now "Internet time" had to be allocated, and it often led to skirmishes.) Luke and Abel glanced at each other.

"It's okay," said Bonnie to Luke. "Come on downstairs and we'll work on 'A British Tar.' Mattie, you can play the piano, and Abel can sing the Bosun's part."

"After you've loaded the dishwasher," Charlotte reminded them as she cleared the table.

9:00 PM

"Noses are quite fun," Dora told Ballou. They sat at her dining room table, eating off her Rosenthal china. Ballou was painfully conscious of every movement he made as he ate – especially when dealing with bread, since for some reason even his most painstaking technique ended in another few crumbs falling onto the tablecloth, whereas the area around Dora's plate remained immaculate.

Ballou was so fascinated by Dora's tiny fingers, by the chewing action of her cheeks, by her lips – just seeing her open her mouth to take a bite made him feel a little wobbly – that twice so far, he'd had to remind himself to stop staring and keep eating.

"The thing about noses," Dora continued, "is that you can be pretty sure of how they'll turn out – if you have a good surgeon. And it can be so much fun to work with the patient and determine what kind of nose she wants. Of course you can't always give her exactly what she had in mind, but you can get it close, and sometimes absolutely perfectly."

"Do different types of noses go in and out of fashion?" Ballou asked. He began to feel a bit looser, just because the conversation was absorbing him.

"You know, they do," said Dora. "Just in the past decade or so, I've noticed a trend to bigger noses, and that's partly because of Princess Diana, but also partly because of TV and computers."

"You're kidding."

"No, not at all. People are becoming used to seeing celebrities on a small screen, instead of a big one. You've noticed that in comic strips, in the newspapers, the people are all drawn with exaggerated features? That's because their features would almost disappear if they were drawn to scale. And conversely, if you see a big nose on a movie screen, it looks terribly large, and a very small nose looks just right. So, 40 or 50 years ago, women would request just a little teeny nose."

"But now," said Ballou, "with the smaller images shown on a TV or computer screen, the larger features appear to be more attractive."

"Exactly. Julia Roberts, just for one example, would not have been considered all that beautiful in the 1930s. Because of that huge mouth."

"But now that TV screens are getting bigger, are we going to see a trend back to smaller features?"

"That remains to be seen, but it wouldn't surprise me."

"So, noses are your favorites?"

"Oh, no. No, they're the most fun, but my real specialty is blepharoplasty. That's eyelids. They're the hardest to get exactly right, and it's also the area where there's still a lot of work to be done. Blepharoplasty hasn't been perfected to nearly the degree that rhinoplasty has."

9:15 PM

His nose should pant and his lip should curl
His cheeks should flame and his brow should furl
His bosom should heave and his heart should glow
And his fist be ever ready for a knock-down blow

His attitude!
His attitude!
His at —

The anguished roar from upstairs made all four children jump. There followed a furious stomping of feet, then the sound of their mother's fast tread above them as she moved through the kitchen to the top of the basement stairs. Luke and Abel grinned at each other.

"Luke?" Charlotte called. "Could you come up here a minute, please? Martin's having a little trouble with the computer again."

Entering his mother's study, Luke saw the sight he'd grown used to seeing: Wandervogel, purple in the face, gripping his scalp with both hands, hunched down in the swivel-chair in front of the computer, rocking back and forth rhythmically, and whimpering softly. He glared up at Luke.

"It's doing it *again*," Wandervogel growled accusingly. "Fucking piece of fucking shit!"

Wandervogel had clicked on a Website that had triggered an endless stream of pop-ups, proliferating faster than Wandervogel could close them.

"No need for you to come in, Charlotte," Wandervogel said hastily, getting up from his chair. Charlotte was standing in the doorway of the study.

"I can fix it," said Luke. "No big problem, it'll just take a few minutes."

"I don't have a few minutes," Wandervogel snapped.

"Sh-sh," said Charlotte. "If Luke says he can fix it, he can. Why don't we just go for a little drive? I'm sure it'll be okay when we get back."

"But..."

"Come *onnnnn*, Martin. You can tell me all about what happened today." Charlotte winked at Wandervogel and fisted him lightly in the ribs.

Luke, alone, commenced dealing with the popups – but slowly. He heard Wandervogel's Montero starting up in the driveway, and he began to explore.

9:30 PM

"It seems like with some of these people, you could have made all kinds of changes," Ballou remarked. He and Dora still sat at the dining table, but Dora had moved her chair closer to his so they could look together at the photographs in an immense leather-bound album she'd fetched from her study. "Did you ever have a patient who was on the run from the law?"

"No, never – that I know of," said Dora. "And if I had, I would have found some way of refusing to treat him. I did once have a patient who was in the federal witness protection program. His picture isn't in here, for obvious reasons."

"Ever get the urge to cross a patient up? Maybe give her a big long chin and a nose the size of Texas, that meet in the middle? Or give her just one eye in the center of her forehead?"

"It wouldn't be possible in the first place," Dora replied. "You have other people in the room with you."

"But wasn't that what happened in *Arsenic and Old Lace*? The crazy surgeon keeps changing the bad guy's face, and eventually cuts him to look like Boris Karloff?"

"Well, you have to suspend your disbelief to enjoy that part," said Dora. "Would you like to hear me play the piano? I never get the chance to play for anyone anymore."

9:45 PM

Bonnie and Mattie continued to practice downstairs, Bonnie singing and Mattie accompanying her on the piano. Luke, still in his mother's study, heard Abel come upstairs and then go up to his bedroom. As quietly as he could, Luke ran up to the second floor.

"Abel, c'mon down to the study a minute," he said, standing in Abel's doorway. "Keep quiet."

"Look at that," said Luke, shutting the study door. "I've been snooping his e-mails. I just forwarded a bunch of them to my own address, so I've got copies."

"Who's this 'Serafina' he's writing to?" Abel asked, reading. "And what's 'effy-meral' mean?"

"Eph-*em*-er-al," Luke corrected him. "I just looked it up. It means 'lasting for only a short period of time.'"

"'My relationship with Charlotte is dess-*tyned* to be... eph-*em*-er-al,'" Abel read aloud. "'I have to stay with her now for politi-cal reasons and in any case I can't get seriously involved with anyone until my divorce is final, but please don't think that she can mean anything to me while you're in the picture. You and I have found something special and wonderful in each other despite our difference in ages which is really not that much because you and I are both very old souls... ' When did he write this?"

"Look at the date," said Luke. "Yesterday. There's others." He reached over Abel's shoulder and clicked open another e-mail, this one addressed to "Xcallaber."

"'I can hardly say that Charlotte is my sexual ideal,'" Abel read. "'Her breasts sag and she's Stretch-Mark City which is understandable since she's had all those children, but it doesn't make her very attractive. And those loud theatrical fake orgasms...'"

"Hate to say it, but I can sort of imagine," Luke commented.

"'... what is it anyway with these...'" (Abel sounded it out slowly) "'pee-ree-men-*op*-a-yoo-sal women? They drive you crazy with their moods and their sexual ag... aggressiveness that would be attractive in a young woman but is just pathetic when they reach a certain age. The best you can say about that type is, "They don't tell, they don't swell, and they're grateful as Hell." I have to admit I was... in-fat-u-at-ed with her at first but that emotional type of woman can drain you in a very short time.'"

"Whoever 'Xcallaber' is, it's obviously a guy he's writing to," said Luke.

"How many of these are there?" Abel asked.

"A lot. I haven't looked at them all yet. They go back weeks and weeks. Say, when was the first time he and Mom did it? If you had to guess?"

Abel considered. "Maybe a month ago? Wait. It was a Saturday night, because remember, he came over here after that football game and told us about how he saw that Ballou guy kissing that old lady, and Mom was laughing her ass off? And then they went out to dinner and she came back here and then she snuck back out around midnight and came back around four in the morning. So, yeah, a little more than four weeks ago, now."

"So let's look at the day or two after that," said Luke. "He was probably bragging about it to this Xcallaber guy, and maybe to the rest of the world if he's anything like most guys I know. Scroll down to October 17th, 18th."

10:00 PM

"Pull in here at the school!" Charlotte urged Wandervogel as they neared Wildenkill-Verstanken Consolidated High School. "Let's park, like teenagers!"

Wandervogel sighed, quietly enough that Charlotte didn't seem to hear him, and pulled into the parking lot. Charlotte scrambled over the seats and into the bed of the SUV. "Come on!" she urged. Wandervogel took a couple of seconds to weigh the costs and benefits of admitting he wasn't in the mood, and decided he'd better go along. Being much bigger, he had to get out of the vehicle and climb in from the back.

"What's the matter?"

"I've explained, I'm not comfortable when the woman initiates it. And besides, this is a very confined space."

It was: Wandervogel could not stretch out at full length, and he worried that his legs might cramp.

"Fine," snapped Charlotte, rolling over and gazing out the window. "I would think you'd be more into it, considering what happened today."

"Oh, all *right*," Wandervogel grumbled. If a man can flounce while unbuckling his belt, Wandervogel did.

10:05 PM

"'Charlotte and I are very lucky to have found each other,'" Abel read. "'We celebrated our love for the first time last night'... Uiiiiich!"

"He wrote that to a *guy?*" Luke demanded.

"No, a lady, gotta be," said Abel. "See? 'christinadoll.' That's a lady's handle."

"Yeah, I guess," Luke conceded. "Anyway, what are we gonna do? Should we show Mom all this?" Luke leaned over Abel's shoulder again, hit "forward," and sent the e-mail to his own address.

"I don't know," said Abel. "Think she'd want to know?" He opened another of e-mail, this one addressed to "nksdv."

> Nat:
>
> Cut and paste the copy below, send it to a safe address, then shotgun it from there to everyone on my Van Devander mailing list. This should get the ball rolling.
>
> THE ONLY GOOD ONE IS ON OUR LOGO
>
> What are Redsticks good for anyway?
>
> They're good for getting drunk, raping white women, scalping white men, and knocking white babies' brains out against a tree trunk.
>
> When they're not doing that they're collecting welfare, gambling, and extorting money from the government.
>
> These "noble savages" have a lot of nerve, saying that Indian sports mascots demean their race. When a sports team calls itself the Indians or the Chiefs or the Redskins or the Wildens or something like that, they're showing Indians a hell of a lot more respect than they deserve. Who wouldn't rather be a nigger than an Indian, any day?
>
> Sherman and Custer and other great Americans should have finished the job!
>
> – Roger Sullivan Ballou

Abel stared. "That Ballou guy is using Martin's e-mail?"

"That's weird," said Luke. "But that settles it, right? Like, maybe for some reason Ballou sent this to Martin and asked him to spread it around for him? But that doesn't make any sense. Why would he ask *Martin* to do it? Or maybe Martin found out about it and decided to get Ballou in trouble for writing it..."

"But he wouldn't do it that way," said Abel. "He'd just tell everybody, 'Hey, look at this e-mail I got from that Nazi Ballou.'"

"Riiiiight," Luke reflected. "Unless somebody else was pretending to be Ballou and sent it to Martin, and Martin thought it was real... but then he'd have the e-mail address that he got it from in the first place!"

"So you think Martin made it up himself?"

"That wouldn't be so weird," said Luke. "Remember how that kid, that What-Was-His-Name, wrote all those love-letters with your name on 'em, when you were in fifth grade?"

"Yeah, only he didn't make his Rs like I make mine, so it didn't work."

"We gotta show Mom this, don't we?"

"I dunno," said Abel. "I bet Bonnie would tell us not to."

"You think? Yeah, maybe. Mattie would tell us to tell Mom, though."

"Could it get Mom in trouble?"

"No, that e-mail wouldn't," Luke said, "and do we want Mom going around with a guy like that?"

"Better print 'em out, anyway," said Abel. "Are you going to show that to Ballou?"

"Oh, shit," said Luke. "Mom would love that. But he's getting sued for it. We can't let Martin frame him – if that's what's going on. But I guess we have to let Mom see it first. I *gotta* tell him – Ballou – but how I tell him is gonna depend on what Mom does."

10:15 PM

"*Oooooh!*" Charlotte had clambered on top of Wandervogel and was trying to stuff him into her: no easy matter because of his belly and because of the tendency of his penis to retract into his body cavity for protection.

"Oooooh, I love it!" she gasped, humping against him. "Oh, *God* I love it!"

Wandervogel gritted his teeth. He didn't much care whether he got hard or she shut up – just so long as one or the other happened quickly.

10:30 PM

Ballou was dying for a cigarette. And for a drink. He hadn't had either all day, since this visit to Dora had precluded his customary martini. He hadn't liked to ask if there were any booze in the house, and once Dora had offered to play for him it would have been ridiculous to have said, "Great, but first I need to step outside for a smoke."

Dora had started with one of Satie's *Gymnopédies*, to get warmed up, then a Rachmaninoff prelude; then she played Beethoven's *Moonlight* Sonata all the way through. She'd responded with just the least smile and a little nod when Ballou had applauded the Satie, and the same following the Rachmaninoff. During the Beethoven, Ballou supposed that she'd forgotten he was in the room. Her face would grow stern, even coldly furious (an expression Ballou had never seen on her before) when she struck a difficult passage. She attacked the music, running it down like prey.

The way most pianists play "Solace" (probably obedient to the composer's directions) it sounds labored, like the tread of a four-legged giant whose legs change length, turn-about: one of the four being shorter than the others. But Dora played it in her own way, at an excruciating, tantalizing slow tempo – slower, no doubt, than even Joplin himself would have played it – de-emphasizing the tango undercurrent by soft-pedaling the left-hand notes. She began improvising, going over old ground and turning up new stones; this went on for almost ten minutes.

As he clapped, all of a sudden, a huge yawn crept up on Ballou and he fought it back, his eyes watering from the effort.

"Oh, Roger!" Dora exclaimed. "I'm sorry to be boring you. I know you must be exhausted after a day like this."

"No, no. Please, take it as a compliment. You're a doctor; you should know that when someone yawns, he's actually interested, and trying to keep his brain active. Or whatever I've got for a brain."

But Ballou really was tired. He didn't want Dora to invite him to spend the night, for he probably could not have performed. He didn't even want to try to kiss her. He just wanted to go home and sleep. This realization relieved him enormously.

"That was fantastic," he said. "But I have to admit I'm shot, and I'd better let you get some rest too."

"It was so sweet of you to come over and tell me everything," Dora told Ballou, as she got up from the piano. "It means a lot to me that you value my opinion so much."

Ballou held out his right hand, palm down. Dora grabbed it and pulled him to his feet.

"You're so tired. Let me drive you home. It's no trouble."

"No, thanks. I do my best thinking when I'm walking by myself at night. And you've done enough for me for one evening."

"What are you going to do?"

"I'm not sure. I'll just get out there and be a tough guy. Gotta be a tough guy. Thank you, Dora. Thanks for everything."

Dora helped Ballou on with his overcoat, and put her left hand in the crook of Ballou's right elbow as she walked him to the front door: a sympathetic touch, Ballou judged, rather than an indicator. Then she gave his arm a little squeeze with both of her arms. Ballou leant down to kiss her on the cheek, this time remembering to wet his lips beforehand. Dora allowed it, with a little giggle, and released Ballou's arm rather quickly, but not in such a way as to convey regret or distaste.

Ballou almost lost his footing as he walked down the path to Dora's front gate. He waited until he'd gotten to the top of Valley Road, where it intersected with Herkimer, before lighting a cigarette.

Tuesday, November 16

"You're not in a hurry to get to class, are you?" asked Chief Jorgensen, the next morning. He and Officer Perdue stood at the head of the outdoor staircase that led to Tonia Kampling's little apartment. "We've got some news for you, if we might come in for just a couple minutes."

"Sorry it took so long," said Jorgensen, as the two policemen sat down in chairs made of metal tubing, at the oilcloth-covered table in Miss Kampling's kitchen. "We don't have all that sophisticated testing equipment at the Wildenkill police station. We had to send the materials over to a lab in Kingston. We got the results back on Friday afternoon, but we figured we'd let you enjoy your weekend before we came bothering you again. You have a nice weekend?"

Tonia Kampling looked paler than usual – perhaps only because it was still early in the morning and she'd just finished washing and dressing when the police arrived. She hesitated, as though she found the question peculiar coming from a cop.

"Yes, I did, thank you," she said after a few seconds. She looked back and forth at Jorgensen and Perdue, whose expression was less friendly than the Chief's. "Can I offer you some peppermint tea? That's all I drink, I'm afraid."

"No, thank you, Tonia," said Jorgensen. "We just wanted to stop by and tell you where we are in the investigation, because we're sure you want to see it wrapped up and the guilty party brought to justice just as much as we do."

Miss Kampling made no reply, but sat down at the table, opposite Jorgensen and next to Perdue.

"First of all, we have a pretty good idea that as we'd suspected all along, the person who sent you those letters is in all probability the same person as left the... the materials on your doorstep, and the same person who burned the cross on your lawn.

"Of course, we got no fingerprints from the cross or the bowl. And on the envelopes, we found that there were a good many fingerprints – yours, of course, which we'd expected to find, and others which might belong to postal employees and anyone else who might incidentally have handled the envelopes."

Chief Jorgensen smiled indulgently, as if to reassure Miss Kampling. Officer Perdue, however, continued to stare at her, his elbows on the table, his hands forming a steeple in front of his chin, tapping his fingertips together slowly and rhythmically.

"Obviously," Jorgensen continued, "the perpetrator wore gloves while preparing the letters, because – as I say – the envelopes had several sets of prints on them, as of course they would have, but there were no prints on the letters themselves. So of course that put us right up a stump, you follow me? Only Boo-Boo, here, he had an idea, didn't you, Boo?"

Officer Perdue shifted his gaze away from Miss Kampling and looked down at the floor, diffidently.

"Well, it was just a little thing that made me curious," Perdue mumbled. Chief Jorgensen clapped Perdue on the shoulder.

"Don't listen to him, Tonia, he's just modest. That 'little thing' might've just cracked the whole case. Tell her, Boo."

"Well, I just wondered," said Perdue, looking Miss Kampling in the eye again, his expression getting a little harder. "No fingerprints on the letters, right? Well, that'd be natural, if the perpetrator was wearing gloves. And of course your own fingerprints would be on the envelope from when you picked the letters up and opened them – looks like you used a letter-opener – but what struck me funny is this: There were no fingerprints on the letters *at all!* Why weren't your fingerprints on any of the letters themselves?"

Silence. Tonia Kampling looked astounded, and her eyes shifted away from the two policemen.

"You knew what the letters said," Perdue continued. "Funny thing, though, that you knew what they said yet you apparently never took 'em out of the envelopes. I just could not figure that one out, not for the life of me."

"And you know, Tonia," said Chief Jorgensen, "when Boo-Boo mentioned that to me, I couldn't figure it out either. How *could* you know what those letters said? Unless maybe you'd read 'em, somehow, *before* they got into the envelopes – and then just plain *forgot* to put your prints on 'em before you called us."

Miss Kampling sat immobile in her chair, staring at Jorgensen with a look of terrified appeal that probably all cops have seen.

"Something else, Tonia," said Jorgensen. "That bowl of pig's intestines and... feces, that was left on your doorstep? You know, it's a funny thing, and even I hadn't known this, but did you know they can actually extract human DNA from feces? They can, though, isn't that something? And those lab people, well, supposing they matched the DNA from the feces with the DNA from the spit that was used to seal these envelopes..."

"But they couldn't." Almost at the moment she said it, Miss Kampling realized her mistake; her eyes widened and she started to inhale violently, then suppressed that reaction.

A long silence.

"How do you know they couldn't?" asked Jorgensen, in an almost tender tone. "I swear, you must be psychic. I didn't say they did do a DNA match, remember. I just said 'suppose they did.'"

More silence.

"Anyway, that was what the lab results showed," Jorgensen continued. "They couldn't collect any human DNA off the envelope's seal. Probably whoever sent it wet the seal with a sponge. Moreover, they told us that while you can extract human DNA from feces, for some reason you can't match it to the DNA you'd find in a person's hair, or skin, or blood, or saliva. The... the substances in the bucket would have to be matched to another stool specimen."

"What do you expect we'd find," Perdue broke in, his voice surprisingly harsh, "if we took you down to the county jail and had one of the matrons stand over you while you provided a stool specimen? D'you think we'd find anything that might interest us? Young lady, if you have anything to tell us – anything at all – now's the time. You come clean with us now, and chances are we can help you. Want me to tell you what'll happen, though, if you don't tell us the truth right now?"

"Take it easy, Boo-Boo," Jorgensen remonstrated.

"I'm just trying to give it to her straight, Chief," Perdue retorted. "Young lady, you are looking at felony charges here. Do we understand each other? You know what felony means? It means prison. Years in prison. You want to know what prison does to a young lady like you? Want me to paint you a picture?"

*

Martin Wandervogel held court several afternoons a week at a large table in the cafeteria of the Student Union. On that afternoon, five of his students – two boys, three girls – were sitting with the film professor as Ballou approached. None of them looked in Ballou's direction.

"Martin," said Ballou. "I'd like to chat with you, if you could spare a few minutes. About this case that's come up."

Wandervogel's expression changed from hostility to a sort of solicitous concern.

"Gosh, yeah," he said. "That must have been tough for you, getting hit with that suit. Listen, if you want to talk about it, I'm here to help. I hate to see one of my colleagues in trouble. Even if you and I do have our little differences. Only thing is, this might not be the right place to do it. I believe some of the people at this table are involved in the case, and it might not be right for you to be... uh..."

"It's okay," said one of the young men, getting up and gathering his books. The others followed, one female student giving Wandervogel a lingering smile as she left.

"I'm not even sure you're supposed to be here," said Wandervogel, as Ballou sat down in the chair at his immediate left. "You're suspended, I understand."

"I can't say I've been formally notified of that. I've heard rumors to that effect. But the Union's open to the public."

"Well, Roger, what can I do for you?" Wandervogel asked. "This is a bad situation for anybody to be in. And I have to tell you frankly that if you're guilty, you ought to man up and take your punishment. But I'm not vindictive. It doesn't give me any pleasure to see you in this kind of trouble, believe me. I have a feeling that if you make the proper apologies for your conduct – of course, that harassment of that poor young woman, that's another matter."

"I'm sorry to disappoint you, but I didn't do that. I have a good idea who did."

"I've got a rock-solid alibi for that night, for your information," Wandervogel retorted. "Someone who'll testify in court, if necessary. And I wonder if you can say that. Roger, I feel sorry for you. Really. You're a... a *pitiable* person. Gosh, you must be about the loneliest guy in the world."

Wandervogel stared levelly at Ballou, to let the insult sink in. He looked off into the middle distance, then focused on Ballou again, and went on.

"I know what it's like," Wandervogel said. "I've been teaching at colleges all over the country, for years, and yeah, you come into a new job, where you're in a position of power and authority, and you know that some of your female students are going to admire you, look up to you, and the temptation to take advantage of that situation can just overwhelm you. You can't wait to get your hands on some of those sweet young things. Believe me, I know.

"But I know that it doesn't always work that way, for everybody. Sometimes a certain individual just doesn't have… I don't know, the charisma I guess you'd call it, to pull it off. And I guess it must be awfully frustrating. It can *eat* at you, can't it? And you're sitting there all alone at home, wondering why you can't make out like some of the other instructors can… and at the end of the day you've got to take out your frustrations on somebody, don't you? It's human nature, Roger."

Wandervogel gave Ballou a comradely pat on the arm. Ballou forced himself not to recoil. Wandervogel sighed, and shook his head.

"Tonia told me," he continued. "She told me you were paying her some attention, and that she just wasn't interested, and that she was very uncomfortable with it, but that you just weren't getting the message. And she was at her wit's end, Roger, trying to figure out how to handle it. You know, Roger, she's a shy girl. She's not assertive. She just couldn't bring herself to tell you to just leave her alone – but I guess you eventually got frustrated when she didn't respond, and… you know, Roger, it's too bad that you're so alone in the world. Maybe if you'd had someone to talk to about it…"

"You can comfort yourself with that fantasy all you want to," Ballou retorted. But he was horrified. If Tonia Kampling really had been weaving a detailed story about his having come onto her…

"I don't believe she really said anything like that to you," Ballou added, "and if she did, she's very much mistaken."

"I guess it'll be her word against yours, then," said Wandervogel. "But I know what she told me."

The two men sat glaring at each other for several seconds.

"Roger, why did you come in here to talk with me?" Wandervogel assumed a stern, authoritative expression. "Did you hope I'd be able to get you out of this somehow? That maybe if you came to me, I could talk to Tonia and maybe smooth it over for you? Oh, Roger, that'd be really improper. Especially now that this lawsuit is ongoing. I believe they call that tampering with a witness. And if I were to report it you'd be in really serious trouble. But as one colleague to another – as a *fayyy*-vor from one colleague to another – if you were to make a clean breast of it to me..."

"Have I asked you for anything?"

Wandervogel thought, trying to reconstruct the conversation.

"Did I even mention any student's name to you?" Ballou persisted.

"Then why are we talking?"

"Actually, I wanted to bring up a different case," Ballou said. "I know you've become friends with Charlotte Fanshaw..." (Wandervogel straightened in his chair, almost literally preening.) "and you're also friendly with her daughter Bonnie. And I got to thinking about that legal action that the two of them were involved in, a few weeks ago, with regard to that play at the high school."

"What of it?" Wandervogel's expression didn't change.

"Well, you know, that case was settled out of court. And it's a funny coincidence that the law firm that represented them – represented Charlotte and Bonnie – is the same bunch that's representing the students in the suit against me. Another funny coincidence: One of the conditions of the settlement was that the high school had to hire a company of which you are a director. Modern Diversity Systems."

Wandervogel flushed. He opened his mouth to speak – but before he could, he spied, from the corner of his eye, Police Chief Jorgensen entering the cafeteria and striding toward their table.

"Well, Roger," said Wandervogel, laughing with relief, "looks like you'll be spending tonight in jail after all. Maybe I can get Charlotte to bake you some cookies."

"Just look at this!" Chief Jorgensen exclaimed. "The last time I saw you two gentlemen together, I thought I'd have to call out the SWAT team! And now here you are like two old pals!"

Under the circumstances, Ballou had no reason to think anything other than that Jorgensen had come to arrest him. At lightning speed, his brain began instructing him:

Sit up straight. Stand up straight when he tells you to stand. Ask him to cuff you in front. Whatever happens, keep your dignity. Keep your head high. Don't hide your face. Don't ask him to sling your jacket over the cuffs.

"Professor Wandervogel, I wonder if I could have a word or two with you," said Chief Jorgensen. "I'm sorry to interrupt you gentlemen, but it's kind of important. Professor Ballou, maybe you could excuse us?"

Ballou's jaw dropped. He had heard, but he didn't believe his ears sufficiently to make himself comply.

"Oh, before you go," said Jorgensen, "I should tell you you're off the hook, with regard to that cross-burning incident. We've arrested the young lady, that Tonia Kampling. And she's confessed to setting up the whole thing herself. The letters and all. She apparently sent them to herself. She's cooperating with us."

Now it was Wandervogel who went pale, but Ballou, staring dumbfounded at Jorgensen, didn't notice.

"She's a confused young lady," said Jorgensen, shaking his head. "Apparently she's been under a lot of stress, what with one thing and another. Not doing too well academically, we understand, and she was... frustrated in a romantic relationship, too, I guess you'd call it. And somehow it seems the pressure was just too much for her, and she had a sort of a meltdown."

"I've seen this... this type of erratic behavior before," Jorgensen continued. "It's not all that uncommon among college students, I'm sorry to say. And it can manifest itself in all kinds of strange ways. Although usually it happens in January, closer to Finals Week. Anyway, that's about all I can tell you at this point. We spent most of this morning questioning her, and I guess she'll be arraigned tomorrow. For false statements, malicious mischief, and so on. Meanwhile she's in the county hospital. For observation."

"County hospital?" Ballou echoed. "The psych ward?"

"Just for observation. She was... well, she'd start laughing inappropriately, and so on. We didn't know what to make of it."

"But she's always like that," said Ballou. "I'm not sure she's crazy, just nervous. And maybe socially inept."

"Well, it seemed safer to put her in a hospital – and less unpleasant than the county jail, I'm pretty sure. Which is where she'll go soon enough."

Numbly, Ballou picked up his briefcase and stood.

"One more thing," said Jorgensen to Ballou. "She wanted me to tell you she's sorry she got you involved. She said she wanted to create an incident, but she didn't mean to get you in trouble. You can believe that or not, I guess."

"But... but jail's no place for her either," Ballou stammered.

"If you have any questions, I'll be in my office bright and early tomorrow morning at seven," Jorgensen said.

Ballou took the hint. He was shaky on his feet as he walked away from the table, and he noticed it. He was outside the building before he could remind himself that he hadn't thought about where to go next. It took him nearly a full minute to remember that he had better inform Frank Leahy and Hugh Hoo immediately.

*

"What's this about, Officer?" asked Wandervogel as Chief Jorgensen sat down, in the chair to Wandervogel's right.

"Chief," Jorgensen corrected him. "Probably nothing, at this point. This young lady, this Miss Kampling, she's one of your students, I understand. Now, we have to keep in mind that she's... well, as I said, she's confused. Didn't always make a lot of sense, when we were questioning her. But she did say – as I was explaining to your buddy Roger just now – that it'd been her intention to create an incident, a racial incident. I gather that for one thing, she was kind of attracted to a young African-American man, and she thought that might be a way of getting his attention. That was one thing she told us. The other was that she was trying to do you a favor."

"Me?"

"You're making a film, I understand. About the... the political situation here at the college?"

"Well, it's a documentary," said Wandervogel. "The central character is Dr. Bannister, the president of the college. I'm trying to show what it's like for a progressive woman to take over the leadership of a college that's full of outdated ideas, and I'm showing her efforts to bring the school into the twenty-first century – which is upon us." Wandervogel smiled as though in self-congratulation.

"Did you ever tell this young lady that you wished a racial incident would happen on campus?"

"I don't need to wish for them; they happen every day. Just look about you."

"Did you tell her that you'd like to see Roger Ballou fired?"

Wandervogel leaned back in his chair, looked Chief Jorgensen right in the eye, and chuckled expansively.

"Chief, this is obviously a Henry the Second situation."

"I'm afraid I don't understand."

"Well," Wandervogel explained, "if you'd studied your English history, you'd recall that back in the tenth or eleventh century or so, I forget which, the King of England, Henry II, was having a disagreement with... with one of the high-muck-a-mucks in the church, a man named Thomas à Becket. Anyway, he said something like, 'Who will rid me of this turbulent priest?' He was just blowing off steam, but one of his knights took it seriously, and actually murdered this Becket.

"We've probably got the same situation going on here. I probably said something like, 'Roger Ballou should be fired' – because I don't like him, I'll admit. He's a racist and an incompetent teacher. And maybe this young woman decided to help the process along. That's all that occurs to me."

Jorgensen took out a notebook and consulted it.

"While we were questioning Miss Kampling, she said, quote, 'Professor Wandervogel told us' – that is, she said you said this to a group of your students – "'It'd be great if there were a really serious racial incident while we were making this film.'" Do you recall making a statement like that?"

"Of course not."

"Well, I guess we'll have to check that out," said Jorgensen, shutting the notebook and getting to his feet. "Thanks for your help on this, Professor. We'll be in touch." As Jorgensen turned to leave, he almost banged into Charlotte Fanshaw.

"Excuse me," Charlotte said to the policeman, not looking at him. "Martin, we need to talk." She sat down in the chair that Jorgensen had just vacated, and put a small pile of printed-out e-mails in front of Martin Wandervogel.

"My children saw these," she said, very softly.

Wandervogel glanced down at the papers.

"My children saw these!" Charlotte shrieked, slamming both her fists down on the table. Every pair of eyes in the cafeteria turned to view the action. Chief Jorgensen, at the exit, wheeled around and watched, wondering whether to intervene.

Wandervogel sat and stared at the papers for what might have been 10 seconds.

at the Tea Garden and Frank said you'd be there too, and I guess some of your baking will be there as well.

At this point Ballou had been about to tell Dora that he still had an unclaimed ticket for the last football game of the season, that Saturday – five days before Thanksgiving – but then he wondered whether it would be wise to be seen there with Dora, where Lee might see them together again. Then he remembered that Lee didn't even like football – and in any case, Lee knew he spent time with Dora – so he went ahead and added the invitation.

Then, before sending the message, he realized that he owed Dora considerably more than an e-mail and an offer of another football game, and that it'd be much more suitable to print out the message and take it to a florist. But here it was about five in the afternoon and he didn't know where Dora was or where she'd be, and he felt he had to contact her that day one way or another. He tried to think of some more gallant gesture that could be brought off within the next hour or two, but nothing came to him. Flowers tomorrow, maybe, he decided, and he sent the e-mail.

And should he call Lee, or e-mail her? He thought not – at least not with all the details. He felt that Lee would neither understand nor approve, if he said anything that suggested sympathy for Tonia Kampling. Besides, Lee had been the one who'd suggested that they cool it. It would be up to her to heat things up again.

By seven that evening, of course, Ballou started to worry because he had not yet heard back from Dora. By nine, his agitation was so bad that he considered breaking down and sending Lee an e-mail after all. A large martini only took the edge off his nerves: He was occupied with the notion that Dora had probably not gone home at all, but was spending the night with Harrison Lockwood. He had a substantial glass of brandy after dinner, then a second: partly to celebrate the indescribable relief at no longer

being in great danger of losing his job and his money, and partly
to drown out the near certainty that Dora was currently doing at
least as much for Harrison Lockwood as she'd done for Ballou the
night before.

At midnight, an e-mail finally appeared:

> Dear Roger:
>
> Thank you for telling me all that you know, and you're
> more than welcome for last night. I'm just glad I was able
> to comfort you a little, and I'm so glad it's working out. I
> knew it would. Your feelings about your student just illus-
> trate what a kind person you are. I'm afraid I can't see you
> until Thanksgiving Day because as you can imagine I am
> snowed under just getting everything coordinated for that
> holiday weekend. But I certainly will see you then! Sleep
> well!
>
> Dora

This told Ballou nothing — not even whether she was alone —
but at least it appeared that Dora was vertical. And not particularly
perceptive, Ballou thought, if she considered him a "kind person."
He turned off the computer without responding, and went to bed.

Wednesday, November 17

Roger Ballou had decided to show up to teach his Poetry Work-shop class, just to see whether he'd encounter guards posted at the classroom door to keep him out. He saw none, nor anything else out of the ordinary. He walked into his classroom on the dot of 10:30 to find Professor Menzies standing in his place.

"Well, here's our guest lecturer," she told the class, picking up her notebook and starting out the door. "I was a little afraid he wouldn't show up, but only a little."

Meanwhile, on the steps of the administration building sat Fi Tanquiz. He'd been waiting there, with his recording equip-ment, for a couple of hours – along with three TV camera crews, Mrs. Quagga from the *Advertiser,* some kid he didn't know from the *Van Devanderian* (the campus paper), and several other reporters – from the *Freeman* and other papers, Tanquiz guessed.

"H-... here she comes," Tanquiz cried, jumping to his feet.

Dr. Bannister glowered at the sidewalk as she approached the building; she apparently hadn't caught sight of the welcoming committee. As the reporters stirred themselves and began moving toward her, she looked up in surprise. She hesitated, and made as if to turn aside and go into the Liberal Arts building instead, but then she thought better of it and continued walking toward the reporters, forcing a smile.

"Hi, kids," she called. "Not looking for me, I hope!"

"Any comment on yesterday's arrest?" asked one of the reporters, as they swarmed around her.

"Are you planning any disciplinary action against the student?" asked another.

"Did you know that Roger Ballou showed up to teach his class this morning?"

"One at a time, one at a time!" Dr. Bannister stopped, holding her hands up in surrender. The reporters formed a semicircle around her – cameras, recorders, and pens all going. "Sorry I'm a little late getting in this morning: I was in conference with the school's attorneys, and I'm confident they're working everything out. I don't know how much else I can tell you."

"Well, how... how..." (Tanquiz belched loudly in mid-stammer) "How much do you know?"

Dr. Bannister set her feet, straightened her posture, and began to recite the statement she'd been composing on and off since the previous night.

"Yesterday evening, along with the rest of you," she said, "I learned that a student at Van Devander College had been arrested for allegedly concocting a false incident which had become part of the basis for a lawsuit against the school, its trustees, and some of its faculty. I trust that the matter will be dealt with by the justice system, and the administration of Van Devander College will have no further comment on that case."

"Do you stand by your earlier statement that you welcomed the lawsuit?" Frances Quagga asked.

"Well, Fran, certainly I'm sure its intent was to try to benefit the school in the long run. I got the impression that the students who sued the school were not trying to collect damages so much as they wanted their grievances redressed. And to that extent I was in sympathy with them all the way."

"Is the student who was arrested going to be disciplined by the school?" asked the reporter from the *Van Devanderian*.

"Frankly, I hope not," said Dr. Bannister. "I'm also hoping that any criminal charges against her will be dropped. If the police press charges in this case, it might inhibit any other individual who experiences real harassment from coming forward with a complaint. I hope she can be allowed to become a productive student again. I'm sure she's been through a lot without my adding to her problems."

"Max Nix, of the *Freeman*. Dr. Bannister, is the suspension of Professor Ballou going to stand, in view of the evidence that he may have been set up by a prankster?"

"Well, Max, I haven't decided that yet. I have to say that's not one of my big concerns at the moment. Roger's being paid; let him enjoy his vacation! Ha!"

"F-Firenze Q. Tanquiz, WVDV radio, t-tape for broadcast. H-how many sweatsuits do you own, and how often do you change them?"

Some of the reporters laughed, and Dr. Bannister chuckled sportingly.

"Well, Fi, I put on a clean one every morning. If you want to see me in different colors, buy me some new ones."

"If I bought you a cheerleader's uniform, would you wear it?"

More laughter.

"Well, maybe I'd wear it in solidarity with the exploited members of the cheerleading squad. Ha!"

"Seriously," Tanquiz persisted, "are… are you surprised at who got arrested for this?"

"Well, of course I assumed it would be a white male." Dr. Bannister giggled again. "That's the kind of thing they do."

"Faye, are there any plans at present to hire Modern Diversity Systems to deal with the various tensions on campus?" This from Frances Quagga.

"Well, Fran, that company's name has certainly been suggested to me," said Dr. Bannister. "We're hoping to introduce some kind of diversity training very soon, and we'll be considering several options. I'd have to refer you to Martin Wandervogel, who's heading our Diversity Task Force."

"Is it true that five of the 10 students who are party to the lawsuit are Professor Wandervogel's students?" asked Mrs. Quagga. "And that the other five are 'special non-degree students' taking one course each?"

"I have no idea," said Dr. Bannister, no longer smiling.

*

Violet Menzies didn't bother to show up to "teach" Ballou's Expository Writing class, and none of his students asked him whether he was still officially suspended. Fi Tanquiz advised Ballou, "Professor, listen to my show tonight. You should dig it."

*

"Fiiiii Tanquiz! Dynamite – joooooock!"

The invariable promo jingle was followed by a recorded sound-bite of Faye Bannister's voice: "Of course I assumed it would be a white male. That's the kind of thing they do."

"Thank you, Dr. Bannister," came Fi Tanquiz's voice.

"That's the kind of thing they do," the sound-bite repeated. "That's the kind of thing they do."

A throbbing techno tune began playing, and Tanquiz had synchronized the sound-bite perfectly in time to the music:

*"Of course I assumed it would be a white male – that's the kind of
thing they do*

That's the kind of thing they do
That's the kind of thing they do
That's the kind of thing they do
Of course I assumed it would be a white male
That's the kind of thing they do
That's the kind of thing they do
That's the kind of thing they do

That's –
That's –
That's-that's-tha-that's –
That's the kind of thing they do
That's the kind of thing they do
That's the kind of thing they do
That's the kind of thing they do

Over and over the clip ran, that night. Tanquiz played the
song a half-dozen times more in the next three hours. He inserted
the sound-bite, or parts of it, before and after station promos. He
conducted "interviews" with Dr. Bannister.

"Dr. Bannister, what do you consider the most important duty
of a college president?"

"I have no idea."

"Dr. Bannister, what was your first sexual experience?"

"Well, of course I assumed it would be a white male. That's the
kind of thing they do."

Ballou, listening, wasn't sure what to make of this. It did sound
like Dr. Bannister's voice, all right. He picked up his phone and
punched in Frank Leahy's number.

"Frank? Roger. Listen, tune your radio to 99.8. Don't ask questions, just do it."

*

At just about the same time, Charlotte Fanshaw was on the phone to Donald Quagga.

"Don, I'm going to send you a new column that I want you to run this weekend in place of the one I sent you on Monday. Please. It's very important. I'll have it to you in just a couple more hours."

*

The Wildenkill Advertiser November 20–26, 1999

'Diversity' Specialists Target Wildenkill Area; Profit For Prof May Result
By Frances Quagga, managing editor

Well, Gentle Readers, what a "Ten Days That Shook The Campus" this has been for Van Devander College!

On November 9, it was reported that a Van Devander student, Antonia Kampling, had been visited by one or more persons who burned a cross on her lawn and left a bucket of feces and a threatening letter on her doorstep (preceded by a series of other threatening letters through the mail).

That was followed, this past Monday, by a lawsuit filed by several Van Devander students (including the above-mentioned "victim") against the college, its trustees, and some faculty, charging that in various racist and sexist ways, the defendants had created "a hostile environment" at Van Devander, injurious to the plaintiffs.

The following day, Tuesday, Van Devander police arrested Ms. Kampling on charges that she had fabricated the racial incident. The day after that, Dr. Faye Bannister, president of Van Devander College, expressed surprise at the arrest, stating, "I assumed it would be a white male. That's the kind of thing they do."

Since then, Ms. Kampling has been released on bail and has returned to her parents' home in New Rochelle pending further disposition of her case. Dr. Bannister has issued a public apology for her remarks and withdrawn her suspension of Prof. Roger Ballou, one of the defendants in the lawsuit.

Yesterday, in Bumppo County District Court, Judge Ernestine Orlick granted a motion by the defendants' attorney, Hugh Hoo, for summary dismissal of the civil suit.

One might suppose that all of that would be quite enough excitement, especially with Thanksgiving impending. Ah, but think again!

Now, it appears that the desire to drum up business – and not high-minded idealism – may have been behind the late and unlamented brouhaha. I shall present you with a series of facts that may at first appear to be unconnected – but, Gentle Readers, bear with me!

• The plaintiffs in the suit were represented by a Manhattan-based firm, Dolciani, Wootton, Beckenbock & Chinn: the same firm *mirabile dictu!* – that recently represented several students and their parents in a discrimination suit against the Wildenkill-Verstanken Consolidated School District arising from the casting of a musical.

• DWB&C (as we'll call it for the sake of shortness) has been involved in several discrimination lawsuits in the State of New York – including the one against our school district – in which, as part of an out-of-court settlement, a San Francisco-based consulting firm called Modern Diversity Systems (MDS) has been hired to provide "diversity training." This training takes the form of such courses as "Painting A Rainbow," "Look-sism And Diversity," "A Politically Sensitive Work-place," "Appreciating Multiculturalism," and other such courses as might indicate a degree of social engineering.

• DWB&C has represented the plaintiffs in three discrimination suits in New Jersey, which also were settled by the hiring of MDS.

• In the state of California, the *Advertiser* has dis-covered, MDS has been hired as part of the settlement of eight discrimination suits in the past two years. In each case, the plaintiffs were represented by a San Francisco-based law firm: Howard, Fine & Besser.

• Martin Wandervogel, a visiting professor at Van Devander, is a director of MDS, which became a publicly traded company on October 20.

• Of the ten students listed as plaintiffs in the suit against Van Devander, five are registered in one or another of Prof. Wandervogel's classes.

• Each of the other five is registered at Van Devander as a "special, non-degree" student. Each of those five is newly registered this fall. Each is over 23 years of age. Each took up residence in the Wildenkill area within the past three months. Three of them share an apart-ment; all five live in buildings owned by – guess who! – Martin Wandervogel!

• The lawsuit against Van Devander College came on the heels of the publication of a racist pamphlet, allegedly written by Prof. Ballou and distributed to Van Devander faculty and students via e-mail. Prof. Bal-lou has denied authorship, and Wildenkill Police Chief

Christian "Yogi" Jorgensen has told the *Advertiser* that the pamphlet was almost certainly originated by – wait for it, darlings! – Martin Wandervogel!

"We don't know that this hoax, or practical joke, or whatever you want to call it, rises to the level of a crime, and at this time we don't plan to arrest Mr. Wandervogel," Chief Jorgensen added, "but the investigation is ongoing."

Prof. Wandervogel, contacted by the *Advertiser* on Thursday, had this to say about the e-mail:

"It was a joke, for God's sake. It was so over-the-top that no sane person could possibly have taken it seriously. Ballou thinks he's so tough, but he squeals like a little girl whenever someone yanks his chain a little bit."

Conceivably, even with the dismissal of the lawsuit against Van Devander, demand for diversity training may persist. So far, however, neither Dr. Bannister nor Prof. Wandervogel has volunteered to submit to it.

Stay tuned, darlings!

*

Van Devander Can't Afford Bannister
By Roger Sullivan Ballou

This past week, a student at Van Devander College confessed to sending threatening letters to herself and creating what looked like an incident of race-based harassment. The student, Antonia Kampling, will likely be expelled from Van Devander and criminally prosecuted. She could be punished under New York's "hate crimes" laws – which in my opinion would be a reaction out of all proportion to the offense. But what will happen to the president of Van Devander College, Faye Bannister?

At a press conference on the day following Ms. Kampling's arrest and confession, Dr. Bannister was asked whether she was surprised at the outcome of the investigation. Her reply:

"I assumed it [the culprit] would be a white male. That's the kind of thing they do."

Yesterday (Friday), Dr. Bannister issued the following statement:

"I apologize to anyone whose tender sensibilities may have been offended by what I said. It was an attempt at humor that some people pretended to take literally. I certainly didn't mean it seriously, because that's the kind of stereotypical thinking that I've been fighting throughout my career. I have received e-mails from men who were offended by the comment, but I've received just as many if not more from women who agree with it. In retrospect, I have to admit it was inappropriate."

Hmmm.

"... the kind of stereotypical thinking that I've been fighting throughout my career"? Did I hear that right, Dr. Bannister? Whence came those stereotypes in the first place? And I can't help observing that someone who would make a remark like that about white males is obviously not busting the seams of her sweatsuit to fight that kind of thinking.

Suppose Dr. Bannister had said, "I figured it was going to be a black guy because we all know what they're like." One wonders whether anyone would have considered such a semi-apology sufficient. Anyone think she'd still have her job right now?

I believe Dr. Bannister all the way, when she says she's been contacted by women who agree with her comment. Her attitude isn't original to herself. It's quite fashionable within the world of "progressive" academia – and the more shame to that community. That certain scholars and pedagogues – who should know better – can replace one set of bigoted ideas with another, and then pat themselves on the back for their advanced, enlightened views, is more than sad. It's disgusting.

What should Van Devander College do about Dr. Bannister?

I hesitate to recommend termination. Anyone can make a boneheaded remark from time to time. But there are boneheaded remarks, and then there are statements that clearly display the speaker's attitude, however she might otherwise try to camouflage it.

I don't doubt for a moment that this is how Dr. Bannister really feels about white males. If that's how she feels, she has no business being a college president – unless she's presiding over an institution that intentionally and openly teaches such values.

The question is this: Does Van Devander College – a school with a tradition of colorblindness that dates back to 1773 – wish to be represented by, and molded by, such a president?

I hope not; I pray not.

I don't say Dr. Bannister should be deprived of her income, nor forced to undergo "diversity training." Either of those remedies would violate her unalienable right to form and hold her opinions. But she should be required to fulfill her three-year contract at Van Devander in a non-executive position, where she can nurture her moronic ideas without befouling the entire school with them.

*

Living Life
Charlotte Fanshaw's Column

Cleaning A Man's Toilet

Having been a single mom for a few years now, I've become accustomed to the fact that boyfriends come and go. I'm not used to it – you never do get used to it – but accustomed.

I recently went through another breakup. I've had worse ones. In this case, the relationship had barely had time to get off the ground – although certainly my hopes had risen higher than they should have. I try to take at least one life-lesson away from each of my relationships, and something that might make me feel a little better about myself. The first is easy. The second, I have to search for sometimes.

Most children have to be nagged to clean up after themselves. But my children are neat, all four of them. They get it from their father, I suppose. Certainly not from me. "Mom, you're such a slob," my eldest child Bonnie sometimes scolds me, and she's not wrong. I just will not clean the hair out of my brush every time I use it, and sometimes if I'm in a hurry I'll leave a little makeup-smeared tissue on the bathroom sink. My ex-husband used to complain about it before Bonnie was old enough to.

My most recent boyfriend at least boosted my ego a little bit in the bathroom department.

I got the first indication that maybe I was clean and neat compared to some people the first time I used M's upstairs bathroom – not the guest bathroom downstairs, but the one off the master bedroom – and I picked up what I thought was a raisin from the bathroom floor.

It wasn't a raisin.

After that, the yellow grout between the tiles held no terror for me. That, at least, I had seen before. (By the way, that doesn't come from bad aim, as a lot of women assume, but from the splashback.)

The black mold around the fixtures was another story. I'd seen black mold before, of course, but nothing like at M's place. I wasn't able to tackle it first thing that morning. I was still in that place in the relationship where I couldn't quite admit to my children that I was staying overnight with a man, so I was sneaking out at midnight, sneaking home before dawn, only to find out just recently that all four of them had known all along what I was up to. But the next afternoon, I was over at M's house in my worst clothes.

The bathroom mirror was a revelation. It's a fact of life that some men get boils on their shoulders, and women just have to learn not to mind them. And I guess the temptation to pop them overwhelms some people. But it doesn't look nice when they're splattered on the mirror and left to dry.

I'll spare you a description of what I extracted from inside the rim of the toilet bowl. There was a lot of it. And a lot of flushing. And a lot of crying "Eeeew!" But I got it clean. And M thanked me. He even promised he'd try to keep it that way. Then he said, "Actually,

I kind of need to baptize it right now." And he sat down then and there, and he did.

That was not a new experience for me. I've been married. But I wasn't married to M yet, so I excused myself.

"Oh, come on," he called after me, "stay here and talk."

"I can hear you in the hall," I answered – and I could.

"Skinny, would you come in here?" he asked after a few minutes. "I want you to come look at this and tell me if it looks unusual to you."

I guess I must have hesitated.

"Awww, come on! Just look! What's the big deal?"

Somehow if it's a baby, that's a fair question. A grown man is something else. But I looked, eager-to-please as I am. And in fact it did not look unusual, except for its size.

"Could you smell it for me, and tell me if it smells normal to you?"

Again, for a moment, I couldn't force myself to move.

"Oh, go on, it's cool. I just, you know, I worry about that stuff."

So I did. "It seems fine to me," I said, and I flushed.

"Oh, Charlotte, no!" M cried, waving his arms, as the fruits of his labor swirled down into the pipes. "I wanted to point out some of the specifics to you!"

I stayed with M for two weeks after that incident. And that, I have to admit, is no reason to feel good about myself.

Obviously, M has some pretty serious issues about control, and about respect for the women in his life.

But this incident made me admit to myself that maybe I have some issues too – about respect for myself. Why didn't I just walk away then and there, and never come back? Or at the very least, why didn't I explain – as if I needed to explain – that this was inappropriate, controlling, humiliating behavior on his part? Why did I continue to see him and sleep with him – and *want* to see him and sleep with him – until something else came up that forced me to end the relationship? Was I so short on self-esteem that I would allow myself to submit to something like that?

I never would have admitted it, till now, but I was afraid of being without a man. I can't promise that I'm over that fear now, or that I ever will be, but at least I know I have that fear. I'm without a man again – but I hope I'm stronger and smarter than I was before I cleaned that man's toilet.

Saturday, November 20

Fi Tanquiz' bit of musical engineering – the techno version of "That's the Kind of Thing They Do" – had played several times a day on WVDV Campus Radio throughout Thursday and Friday, and now it blared out of the PA system at Kees Schermerhorn Memorial Stadium as Ballou and Frank Leahy took their seats.

"Apparently at least some of our students don't much care for our beloved president either," Ballou remarked.

"They seem to think pretty highly of you, though," Leahy remarked. "Folks here are looking at you, have you noticed?"

"Oh, please. You've got a lively imagination."

"You're famous, I'm telling you. Nothing like a false accusation to make a man recognizable."

"You might not get seats this good next year," Leahy added. "We damn near beat Navy last week, down at Annapolis, and we'll be eight-and-two after we take care of these fuckers." Leahy waved to Mr. and Mrs. Plankton, who were taking their seats a couple of rows away. They both waved back, but both shot grim looks at Ballou.

For this last game of their college careers, the senior Wildens ran out onto the field one at a time, with the PA announcer introducing them, followed by "the rest of the Van Devander Wildens,

Coach Rudy Grouwinkel, and his staff, all of them ready to do the kind of thing they do."

The Wildens kicked off to the Polar Bears, and as the officials spotted the ball the PA announcer recited the usual prayer:

"Ladies and gentlemen, we remind you that Schermerhorn Memorial Stadium is a smoke-free facility. We ask you to support the team in a positive manner. Any racist or sexist comments directed at players or officials will not be tolerated, and are grounds for removal from the stadium – unless they're directed at white males."

The Wildens led at halftime, 21-0; it was hardly a contest. On his way to the men's room, Ballou got nods from three or four people whom he didn't recognize. He smiled and nodded back.

During his absence, Carrie Plankton had come over to talk to Leahy, and as Ballou neared them he could hear her voice getting louder.

"Well, why not?" she demanded. "See how he likes it!" Ballou couldn't hear Leahy's reply.

Mrs. Plankton gave Ballou another not-very-friendly look.

"Roger, that was mean, what you wrote about Faye," she said. "That was just plain mean. She was joking when she said that, and everybody knew it!"

"I didn't know it," said Leahy.

"Maybe she was smiling," said Ballou. "I wasn't there – but I don't believe for a second that she didn't mean it."

"She shouldn't have said it," Mrs. Plankton allowed. "It was stupid. But you know as well as I do that that's just the way she is..."

"Precisely," said Ballou. "That is the way she is."

"... and she was just trying to keep her sense of humor in a very tough job. Do you have any idea how hard it is to be a college president? No matter what you do, you'll be offending half the school. Any decision you make, you're putting the future of the school at stake. And the school's income – from both the students and its contributors – which believe it or not, Faye does care about."

"If she cares, she should get her ass out of the presidency," Ballou insisted. "Now. Today. You know who contributes money to Van Devander. Guys like Frank, here. The kind of people she was talking about. The kind of people she feels contempt for. And who does the work? Who teaches the classes? Some of us are evil white males, like me, whom she calls 'The Missing Link.'

"If our situation were reversed – if, say, I'd made some remark in public like, oh, I don't know, something like, 'I've always thought girls didn't belong in college,' in a joking way – what do you suppose she'd have done? Hell, she wanted to fire me for saying the Wildens should be the Wildens."

"I doubt she really would have fired you," said Mrs. Plankton.

"Hell, yes, she would have," said Leahy. "Carrie, this is not the time to discuss it." He winked at Ballou, but without smiling.

*

"I'm trying to keep calm here," said Charlotte Fanshaw on the phone to Frances Quagga, that same afternoon. "Do you have any idea – at all – of how many people you're hurting with that... that exposé of yours?" She said "exposé" as though it were the most obscene word in the lexicon.

"Charlotte, darling!" Frances replied, using much the same soothing tone she might use if one of her daughters were going off on her. "I don't understand! I would think you'd have been pleased. Under the circumstances."

"That's a whole different issue, what Martin did to me," Charlotte retorted. "His cause is still worthwhile even if he isn't. And the people who invested in that company in good faith – did you think of them, at all?"

"I guess it's true that the stockholders in Modern Diversity Systems won't like that article much," Frances conceded.

"Bingo. And guess who's one of them. But you and Don have been out to get me ever since you got to be friends with Roger Ballou — why, I don't know, unless it's because you and he all feel protective of your precious friend the Great Poet."

"Charlotte, dear, now I really don't know what you're talking about. Don and I have never even met Llandor — somebody told me he was at Runs' party the other night but I wasn't introduced — and I haven't read any of his poetry since I was in college, and it didn't impress me back then. I certainly don't remember any of it. But listen, Charlotte, why don't you call Roger himself? He writes about the stock market for a living. Maybe he can give you some advice about how to protect your investment."

"You have *got* to be joking."

"Oh, Charlotte, he's delightful! Please give him a call. And be nice to him. I'm sure he doesn't mean you any harm, and maybe he can help you. I've got to let you go now, Charlotte: I've got a showing in literally five minutes. But do please call me when you've talked to Roger and let me know how it went."

*

"Charlotte, honest, I have never been out to get you," Ballou insisted. He stood in his study in almost total darkness, still in his polo coat and fedora, having just arrived home from the football game to find the phone ringing. It was only a little after five o'clock but already nighttime. This, he thought, had become the most emotionally colorful day he'd had for some time. The exhilaration of the football game (which had ended 35-0); the delight at having been noticed by so many people; the regret that Dora hadn't been there to see it; the annoyance at Mrs. Plankton; and now Charlotte Fanshaw as good as accusing him of plotting her financial ruin: He had to admit that it added up to a pretty fun day, in all.

"Don hired me as a critic," he went on. "I thought your book sucked and I said so. But if you make a ton of money on it, God bless you. On the other hand, if you went and invested it in that company, knowing what they were up to, I have to confess I don't have much sympathy for you. They're running an arson scam. Starting fires to make money putting them out."

"That wasn't the way it was explained to me," said Charlotte. "I don't even know if what Frances wrote is true, and if it is, I had no idea that that was the way they operated. And if they do, I'm not sure they're wrong. I only bought the shares a few weeks ago!"

"If you're worried about the stock price, I'd advise you to sell out as soon as the markets open on Monday," said Ballou. "The news hasn't really broken yet. As of right now, it's still a local story. But word's going to get around in a day or two. If you sell out on Monday, I'm sure you'll still realize a very nice capital gain."

"Capital gain." Charlotte almost spat the words. "Is that the new state religion?"

"What else did you invest for?" Ballou demanded. "Never mind, I can guess the answer. But I can tell you that if you had inside information about an initial public offering, that can be a pretty serious business."

Ballou could hear Charlotte's sharp inhalation.

"Are you telling me I did something illegal?"

"How can I know? It would be almost impossible to prove, and I'm not going to try to."

Silence.

"I'm *not* trying to cause you trouble," Ballou insisted. "And I'm not trying to trick you. I'm trying to help you keep your money. If you get out of that investment now, you'll probably recover what you put in, and then some. Just go to a low-priced broker on Monday and get the best deal you can. I'm going to e-mail you some names."

Another long pause before Charlotte spoke again.

"I can't help thinking," she said, "that if you hadn't been out to get me with that review of yours, I would never have met that man, and none of this would have happened."

"Actually, if you hadn't written that book – no, that's unfair. If Llandor hadn't been attracted to you, all those years ago, you'd not have written that book, and you wouldn't have had that money to invest in Modern Diversity Systems – but your buddy Martin would still be making a ton of money by stirring up trouble."

"You call it stirring up trouble. He's working for the good of society, if you ask me. Whatever he may have done to me. And that's more than you can say."

"It may be," said Ballou, "that you and I have very different ideas about what the good of society is."

Monday, November 22

"No, I had no chance to see her," Ballou told his class on Monday morning. "I called at the county jail on Thursday to see if she was there, and they said she was still at the hospital, so I drove to the hospital and by the time I got there she'd been moved to the jail – and then she was arraigned on Friday morning and her parents bailed her out and took her back to New Rochelle right away, so that's all I know. Sher – Miss Zizmor, you knew... know her, do you know any more than I do? Or Mr. Brooke, do you?"

"I'm surprised you would try to see her," said Miss Zizmor. "What did you expect to get out of that?"

"I'm damned if I know," Ballou replied. "I expect it'd be too much to ask you to believe I was concerned about her. And I probably wouldn't believe it either if I were in your position." Ballou kept trying, every few seconds, to catch Lee Grossbaum's eye, but Lee wasn't cooperating – and he finally gave it up for fear that the other students would notice his efforts.

*

"Here are just the e-mails I've received from contributing alumni," said Leahy. He took a sheaf of papers from his briefcase and handed them across Faye Bannister's desk. "I've had a lot of others – and so have the other trustees – from parents, students, and so on. And here's a list of our biggest contributors. As you see, quite a few of them are threatening to cut off their contributions entirely. Several parents are threatening to withdraw their sons and daughters. Faye, on behalf of the board of trustees, I've got to ask you to quit."

"Oh, I suppose you had a meeting and a formal vote on it." Dr. Bannister scoffed. "Maybe over the weekend? I can only suppose, of course, since I wasn't invited to discuss the matter."

"No, I just phoned around and took an informal vote," Leahy admitted. "One of us was against asking for your resignation. But just one, I'm afraid."

Dr. Bannister drummed her fingers on her desk for a moment. "And if I refuse?"

"If you refuse we'll have to explore the possibilities of removing you. I'll tell you – I'm not going to lie to you – it wouldn't be easy for us to do it. But every day you stayed in office fighting us would hurt your future..."

"Frank, I'm not as dumb as I look. I'm just going to resign – just like that? I'd be a lot better off letting you try to fire me. Martin Wandervogel is making a documentary of this year at Van Devander, and how do you think you'd come out? How do you think the school would come out?"

Leahy sighed. "Faye, you say you care for the school. You want to destroy it?"

"I've been trying to build it back up again, for God's sake! And that's what I intend to do – even if I have to destroy it first. I'll be here a lot longer than you will."

"That's not very useful talk, Faye."

"Well, I'm sorry. But this talk about how I should just 'do the decent thing,' or whatever you want to call it, 'fall on my sword' or whatever... Look, don't think I can't make trouble for you and the rest of the trustees. I can. Plenty."

Leahy nodded, and looked thoughtful. He nodded some more, and gave a little gesture of concession.

"I know you can. I hope to create a situation here where everybody wins – or at any rate nobody feels that they've lost. I'm certainly not expecting you to just up and leave without some sort of a parachute – if that's what you decide to do. But I'm hoping it won't come to that."

Dr. Bannister tried to feign indifference, but she was nonplussed, and her expression showed it.

"You've signed a contract," Leahy went on, "and we've promised to pay you for three years. It would be very difficult for us to get out of paying you if you chose not to agree to some sort of buyout. And nobody wants that in any case. In fact quite a few of us would like to have you stay on."

Leahy paused for a moment to let this sink in.

"As president, you've pretty much destroyed your own credibility," he resumed. "There's only so much a president can do without the trustees on board. And how many friends do you have on this campus? Wandervogel is going to jail, with any luck. Even if they don't have enough to arrest him, his name's Mud around here, and I'm sure he's bright enough to know that.

"If you tried to stay on as president, against an official vote of no confidence from the Board, you'd be a laughingstock. On the other hand, you might be surprised at how many friends you'd have if you stayed with us in some other capacity. Quite a few, I'd bet. Including maybe even me. At any rate I'd love Faye Bannister living better than I'd love her dead."

Dr. Bannister's mouth hung wide open. She was too astonished to look angry or frightened; she looked more amused than anything else.

"You're telling me if I don't resign, you'll have me killed? Why am I not surprised?"

Leahy laughed aloud. "Faye, if I knew how to have you whacked I'd have done it a long time ago. What I mean is, it'd be to everyone's advantage to keep you part of the team – living, so to speak – than to have you outside and unemployed. To your advantage too. You could publish, you could speak – not a bad life.

"Faye, we'll pay your contract, all of it. The rest of this year, and two years after that if you like. You'll get some teaching and publishing chops – and meanwhile you can look for a more congenial environment. One where you'd be an even bigger wheel than you are here. If you work on it for a couple of years, you'll be a leader in... in whatever it is that you call your cause. Instead of growing old in this little backwoods college."

"And who's going to take my place? Roger Ballou?"

Tuesday, November 23

Ballou's phone rang at eight o'clock sharp on Tuesday morning. On the second ring he came fully awake, and on the off-chance it was Dora or Lee he had to get to the phone by the third ring, before the voice-mail would pick up, so he scrambled out of bed, dragging the top sheet and blankets out with him and letting them fall to the floor as he tore into his study, muttering, "Fuck, fuck, fuck," banging against the swivel chair and actually riding it forward a few feet until it bumped into his desk, and he managed to grab the phone and hit the "talk" button just as the third ring sounded.

It was Frank Leahy.

"Didn't wake you up, did I, Roger?"

"Of course not." Ballou tried not to sound thick-tongued.

"I need your professional services, pronto. I'm going to send you a draft press release right now, and I'd like you to correct the grammar and all that and shoot it back to me by this afternoon if you can possibly do it. Should be on your server in about two seconds. I'll hang on while you read it."

"Well, actually," said Ballou, "I have to admit I did just get up. I have to turn my computer on. Can I call you back in five minutes?"

"Sure. I'm at home; I'll be here till about 8:45."

FOR IMMEDIATE RELEASE
Contact: Francis X. Leahy (518) 555-0900
BANNISTER TO HEAD
NEW DEPARTMENT

Van Devander College has announced that Faye Bannister has resigned as president of the college. Dr. Bannister will remain at Van Devander for the rest of her three-year contract, as head of the new department of Women's, Ethnic, and Minority Studies.

"I've enjoyed the challenge of serving as president of this fine institution," says Dr. Bannister. "But my first love has always been teaching, and I'm looking forward to being in the arena, working with students in the classroom and nurturing them as they prepare for long and productive futures. I also feel that my personal goals can be better realized in an academic rather than an administrative setting."

"We're certain that Dr. Bannister will make many contributions to Van Devander as a member of our faculty," says Francis X. Leahy, Chairman of the Van Devander College Board of Trustees. "We have the highest possible regard for her professional skills, and this reassignment is simply a result of differences between her, the Board, and the Alumni Association as to the future direction of the college."

The Board of Trustees is now in the process of naming a search committee to begin the process of selecting a new president. Dr. Bannister will spend the rest of this semester organizing the new department, and will assume her new duties in January. Dr. J. Watson Dickey, who served as Van Devander's president from 1985-1988 and retired last year after 10 years as director of the Historical Society of the Hudson Valley, will serve as interim president until a successor is appointed.

-30-

"That's great, I guess," said Ballou to Leahy. He'd brushed his teeth and peed while the computer booted up, so he felt slightly more capable of communicating. He sat at his desk, rocking slowly in his swivel chair. "But you're giving her a whole new department? Just like that? Who's got the budget for that?"

"That department," Leahy retorted, "is going to cost us her salary plus a new set of business cards, plus *maybe* enough money so she can hire an adjunct or two. And when her contract runs out, so does the funding."

"Clever."

"I thought you'd like it," said Leahy. "Can you talk for a few minutes? Or are you running to a class?"

"No, I don't have classes on Tuesday."

"Well, Roger, first of all, you're obviously not aware of it, because you're used to it, but your chair is squeaking like a bastard. I can hear it. Get it oiled. Anyway, what I wanted to talk to you about is this: I've heard some talk about making you president of Van Devander."

"*Huh?*" Ballou sat forward sharply.

"Carrie Plankton mentioned it. At the game on Saturday. By that time I'd made it pretty clear to her and the other trustees that Faye would have to go, and Carrie was pissed as hell at you, like it was your fault, and she says to me, 'He ought to be president, see how he likes it!' And I said 'Well, why not? You want me to suggest it to him?' And she said, 'Yeah, fuck him.' Now, keep in mind that we were both being facetious, but I'm going to invite her to keep her word."

"Oh, get out," said Ballou.

"I'm serious. I'm putting you on the short list. No guarantees; it'll depend on who else the search committee comes up with, and how the rest of the board feels. But you'd be terrific. You get along with the students, you're well known, you're smart, and most of all you'd take the school in the right direction."

"Frank, that's nuts." Ballou leaned back, and noticed that Mr. Leahy was right about the chair. "I wouldn't begin to know how to run a college. And none of the other trustees know me, except for Carrie, and come on, it's crazy to pretend that she really meant it. You know damn well she didn't."

"Now wait, Roger: It gets better! When I was talking with Faye Bannister, yesterday, you know what she said to me? She said, 'Who's going to take my place? Roger Ballou?' So you see you've got several people all thinking alike on this issue!"

"Frank, she was being sarcastic."

"You were the first name that came to her mind, though."

"I don't have a degree. Shit, I don't have a Master's! I've got a lousy B.A. that's not even good for wiping my ass."

"Old Ike Eisenhower didn't have a doctorate either, when he was president of Columbia," said Mr. Leahy.

"Oh, bullshit. I'm not Eisenhower. Listen, Frank, this is silly. Okay, fine, if you want to put me on the list, go ahead, but you're sure to find a hundred candidates who'd be way better. And the rest of the trustees will think you've gone round the bend!"

"Yes, probably. But I do intend to float your name, for whatever it's worth. After all, you saved the damn school."

"Come on!"

"It's true, Roger. Maybe you didn't wield the slingshot, but you enticed Faye Bannister forward, you gave her the rope to hang herself with. As it is, it's still bad enough. She's still employed here for the full term of her contract – at Presidential pay – with her own little private fiefdom. And that was your doing, too. It was your column in the *Advertiser* that gave me the idea to make her that offer. But if it hadn't been for you, she'd still be in charge of the whole kaboodle, and we'd still be waiting for her to do something we could nail her for. You're our champion now."

"Well, shit, give me tenure then."

"You know, tenure might be a harder sell than president," said Leahy. "As you say, you don't have the doctorate. But one way or another, you can count on a job here, as long as I've got a pulse."

"If you want me to be an administrator," said Ballou, "maybe you could make me Vice President of Diversity, just to piss 'em off. Say, what's gonna happen to Wandervogel, anyway?"

Ballou could almost hear Leahy grimacing.

"Well, that's a tough one," Leahy said. "We can't prove that that e-mail he sent wasn't just a prank that didn't go over. So far. Unprofessional, yes, and in bad taste, but it might not come up to the level of a firing offense. As for his connection with that lawsuit, and with Modern Diversity Systems, so far there doesn't seem to be any criminal violation. We could fire him if we could prove that he was part of a conspiracy to harm the college, but it might be simpler to just not invite him back next year."

"Okay," said Ballou, "but by that time he'll have wrapped his movie proving that Van Devander sucks."

"All the more reason for keeping him around," Mr. Leahy retorted. "We can keep an eye on him. See you at the Brookside."

Thursday, November 25 –
Recounted At A Future Date

"And it was then – right at Thanksgiving and for a couple of weeks thereafter – that it got curiouser and curiouser," Ballou said on the phone to Linda Bierschaum. "Whatever else you may have done, I can't accuse you of having made life dull for me."

"I'm glad to hear your version of what happened, anyway," said Ms. Bierschaum. "Jack told me some of it, of course, when he and Audrey were down here at Christmas, but he didn't know much. Which I thought was strange for the chairman of a department."

"Jack keeps his head down as much as he can," Ballou said. "That's the smart play, Lord knows. Maybe he didn't want to know much, and I can't blame him. We've got more than half the school year to get through still."

"But you didn't go home at all for the holidays? Not Thanksgiving or Christmas?"

"God, no. Not that my mother didn't give me grief about it. She even called me up on Thanksgiving morning to bug me, as though she figured she could guilt me into hopping on a plane right then and there, as if that would even have been possible."

*

"I do wish you could have come home, just for today, just for Thanksgiving," Mrs. Ballou said over the phone. "I can't remember the last time you did."

"Five years ago," Ballou replied evenly.

"That's a long time to let me have Thanksgiving on my own."

"But you don't. One of your neighbors always invites you. You've told me so, often enough."

"But that's not the same as having it with family, and you know it. I know I can't cook a turkey worth a darn, but you... I still remember how you taught yourself to cook, and I'm sure that between the two of us we could make a nice Thanksgiving dinner... but you can't stand sleeping in the same house with your old Maw, I know – so okay, stay in a motel then, if a night or two in my house is so terrible to you..."

"Mom, that's not you, that's me. I'm just a little weird that way. I like motels. Less bother for both of us. But the last time I was there I stayed in a motel, remember? And I caught no end of shit from you. Do I need that? And anyway I don't know anyone else in Madison anymore, and if I did, if I wanted to go out at night, you'd be all, 'Does your old Maw bore you so much?'"

Mrs. Ballou sighed. "It does seem to me that if you really cared about me, you'd come see me every couple of years at least."

It's true, Ballou thought. I would. He almost said it, forced himself not to. He thought for a moment, then braced himself as though preparing to grasp a live wire.

"If you wanted to, I suppose you could come out here for Christmas," he said. "You could fly into Newark, take the PATH train to Penn Station, then take Amtrak up to Hudson. Or you could maybe take a bus from Newark direct to Wildenkill. And then I'd pay for your motel."

"And what would I do up there?"

"Why, I could show you off to all my friends. You'd finally get to meet all the people you've been criticizing. I'm sure they'd like you. You can be the nicest person in the world to anybody who isn't your son."

Mrs. Ballou's laugh conveyed withering scorn. "So you want me to meet your new family? I'm honored. And staying in a motel in a town where I don't know anyone? Thanks a lot."

"Mom, my house is full of smoke. You wouldn't like it."

"Fine! Be with people you want to be with, then. I hope you have a really nice Thanksgiving."

For the least fraction of a second, Ballou heard the "jing" of a metal bell, as Mrs. Ballou slammed down the receiver. She still, apparently, used the old rotary phone hard-wired to her kitchen wall. Ballou felt he'd dodged a bullet that he'd fired himself.

*

Ballou was apprehensive about showing up at the Brookside Tea Garden on Thursday afternoon, because he knew Dora would be there, and he had to expect that she'd bring Harrison Lockwood with her. Ballou hadn't seen Lockwood since Halloween, but he couldn't forget the man's existence, the threat he posed, the possibility that he'd already established himself with Dora.

Frank and Lois Leahy had got to the Brookside Tea Garden first, to claim the long table they'd reserved in the middle of the dining room. Dora had sat down next to them, but just as Ballou entered the dining room she had got up – summoned to the kitchen for a consultation apparently – and had waved to him as she crossed the floor. Ballou, noting where she'd been seated, had had his eye on the chair next to hers – thus ensuring, so he hoped, that if Harrison Lockwood showed up he would at least thus be shut out of the action. But as he moved toward that chair, Lois cried, "Roger! Come over and sit right here next to me!" and Ballou could not refuse.

"I do not remember why I love you," said Lois as Ballou sat down, "but I know I love you. No, that is not true. I am losing my marbles but I still have a few left."

"Yes, I can hear them rattling when you move your head," Ballou replied. "Both of them." Lois punched his arm. Then the Hoos showed up, and took the other end of the table; then all four of the Quaggas, who seated themselves – the elder daughter, Miffany, sat at Ballou's left – just as Dora returned from the kitchen and sat back down, directly across the table from Ballou, with an empty seat to her right. But at least no sign of Harrison Lockwood yet. Ballou would not allow himself to feel relieved, and sure enough in less than a minute Lockwood had arrived, taking the chair next to Dora as neatly as if she had been saving it for him all along.

Ballou wanted not to look, but he had to, to see if Lockwood and Dora would touch or kiss each other. They didn't, somewhat to his surprise – but, he immediately reflected, he'd have been surprised to see Dora kissing any man in public.

Runs-Away-Screaming was the last to show up. "This must be the place," the Indian growled, as he seated himself between Harrison Lockwood and Frances Quagga.

"Here's our token Redskin!" Leahy exclaimed. "Now we can eat."

The seating produced the maximum angst for Ballou. He knew the technique of "turning the table" – chatting with Miffany Quagga through one course, then finding an excuse to turn to Lois for the next course, forcing the whole table to switch – but every time he did this, Dora and Lockwood would be directly in his field of vision, and he wanted to look at Dora but could hardly bear even to let his eyes pass over the form of Harrison Lockwood. And Dora *would* smile at Ballou every time he glanced in her direction, and he would have to respond, at least with a raised eyebrow, and somehow conceal his readiness to burst from frustration.

Harrison Lockwood was his usual pontificating self. Dora mentioned to Mr. Leahy that she'd invited Lockwood along because he'd had nowhere else to go, and Lockwood took the opportunity to explain himself to whomever at the table cared to listen.

"This is my first Thanksgiving without either of my parents," he observed in his deep, calm voice. "My mother passed in February of this year, and my father two months later, just as I knew he would, because I couldn't imagine that he'd have wanted to live without her."

"Oh, no complaints," Lockwood continued. "It was time, and my mother and father had both led very full lives. But as long as they lived, our whole family would congregate every year for Thanksgiving at their home up in Rensselaer. I've got a big family, and all my brothers and sisters would come in from all over the world, wherever we all happened to be at the time. It was a... such a humbling experience: to be part of such a loving group, with so many wonderful stories and experiences that each of us brought to the table."

Dramatic pause.

"And Thanksgiving of course is the time when your mother gets to show off," Lockwood added with his big white-toothed, white-bearded grin. "My mother used to hate to have any help in the kitchen, until she got really old. She would chase us all right out of there, and for hours on Thanksgiving Day we'd hear her in there, singing to herself – and sometimes cussing – while we all watched the football on TV, or rather the menfolk would be watching the game, and my sisters and my sisters-in-law would be doing whatever they do... and I miss the cussing. It was such a part of the fabric of Thanksgiving Day."

That voice, that beard. Those teeth. Strong, masculine, white – and real: not plastic like Runs'. Ballou itched to leap across the table and savage Lockwood with his bare hands.

"But my point is, my mother was the axis on which it all turned, at Thanksgiving. Of course we all have mothers, and we all adore them, and I guess it's lucky that you only lose one of them in your lifetime. It really is remarkable, to me, how a mother can shape your life, can mold you, can give you the love and the confidence that you need to face the world... she builds a foundation, doesn't she?"

Lockwood looked directly at Ballou as he said this last, still smiling heartily, as though inviting Ballou to chime in with a verse or two of his own.

"Yes, I suppose you're right," said Ballou, dropping his gaze to his plate.

When he raised his head, Dora caught his eye and smiled again. "I'm feeling a little guilty that I haven't seen my parents in a while, but only a little," Dora said. "Serves them right for being so far away. I will see them after the New Year, though. I'm going down to Guadalajara for two weeks right after the holidays. I've never seen that part of Mexico before."

And this presented another reason for Ballou to agonize. Would she go alone? Or would this be the "meet the parents" trip for Harrison Lockwood as well? Now, he supposed, he'd have to drive into Verstanken the week after New Year's to see whether Lockwood's shop were open – and if it weren't, keep driving past it every day to ensure maximum self-torment.

It pissed Ballou off even more because he was having these thoughts in the middle of an amazing Thanksgiving dinner: possibly the best he'd ever had. Oysters on the half-shell, clam chowder, smoked salmon, an enormous turkey with three kinds of stuffing, white and sweet potatoes, any number of vegetables fresh or preserved, six kinds of bread – and dessert (Dora's desserts, presumably) yet to come. And yet Ballou had to keep reminding himself of how wonderful the food was.

"... four performances: next Thursday afternoon after school, then Friday and Saturday nights, and then a matinee on Sunday," Miffany Quagga said to Ballou. "You're gonna come see it, right?"

"I guess I'd better, if I know what's good for me," Ballou said. "After all the fuss, I couldn't very easily miss it. Are you ready?"

"God, I hope so," said Miffany. "We'll all be totally rusty on Monday. But it's tech rehearsal on Monday so we don't have to be any good. Then Tuesday is dress-dress, and Wednesday's dress, and if we're not ready by then we never will be."

Ballou had halfway turned toward Dora, to invite her to come with him to *Pinafore* – but there was Lockwood, sitting right there, and he couldn't.

"It was great how you tried to help Bonnie get her part back," Miffany said. "Even if my Dad didn't run your article. And Bonnie is doing a great job."

"Roger has a history of stepping up to the plate," said Mr. Leahy, overhearing this conversation. "He's made himself part of the family. Speaking of families. We'll see what we can do to keep him around here."

Again Dora smiled brilliantly across the table at Ballou, as though vicariously enjoying the compliment.

"I have to adopt a son every now and then," said Leahy. "Runs, there, and Don, and Hugh, and Roger. Just so I'll have left some kind of legacy when I kick off."

"And the good women have sense enough to stay here without any help from you," Dora replied.

"Oh, I always wanted daughters, too," said Leahy, "if only so that I'd have plenty of sons-in-law to intimidate."

"As long as we're on the subject of adoptions," Ballou remarked, "it looks like I'll be getting a new family member in just a couple of weeks. You know that box of puppies up at Runs' place? Pruno says the one I picked out ought to be ready to go pretty soon. He was the runt, and Pruno bottle-fed him at first, so he's likely to be weaned a little faster than normal."

"You'll have to have a dog-warming party at your house when you bring him home," Dora said, and Ballou bit his lips. Here under other circumstances would have been the perfect opportunity. He could seize upon that idea, and rather than just using the puppy to court her, he could enlist Dora's help in planning the party that she'd suggested – if only Harrison Lockwood had not sat right there.

"Maybe," said Ballou. "Seems to me we haven't had a bridge evening in a while. You'll be the first to know, if I do."

*

"Well, but that sounds like a perfect idea," said Linda Bierschaum. "So did you go ahead and have that party after all?"

"I'm getting to that," said Ballou. "Like I said, it's a hell of a complicated story. Anyway, Dora had to leave the Thanksgiving celebration early, since she had a couple of private parties elsewhere to take care of, so I drive home late that afternoon and I'm saying to myself, 'Look, whatever it takes, I have got to get her away from that son of a bitch, that Zen-master buttfucker...'"

"Roger!"

"Well, I can't help it. I loathed him the instant I set eyes on him. And he didn't improve with further acquaintance. So anyway, that was the resolution I made, then and there. Only of course I didn't have the first idea of how to go about it..."

"Act like you don't care."

"I'm not that good of an actor, and I couldn't have imagined that Dora would have missed the fact that I was half-crazy about her, but maybe I just gave her too much credit – but anyway, late that night, Thanksgiving night, out of the blue I get a phone call from this other young lady I'd been seeing on-and-off for a while..."

"A young lady? How young?"

"Young enough."

"One of your students, right?"

Ballou stayed silent.

"Roger, do you think I care? I don't care. That used to be a legitimate fringe benefit for college teachers until everybody got all politically correct. It still ought to be. Just don't hurt anybody."

*

"Sure it's okay. I hadn't turned the lights out yet. I'm just surprised to hear from you. You know, when you said you wanted to cool it, I thought we were over. Thought I'd heard the last of you."

"I just wanted to hear a friendly voice," said Lee. "I'm going to be stuck here in Greenwich with my whole boring family until Sunday night, and there's nobody here to talk to who's as fun or as bright as you."

"I might be a little tired for persiflage," Ballou replied, "but I'll do my best. I'm still kind of stunned from the Thanksgiving dinner I had. You'd have loved it. A veritable farrago of *treyf*."

"Hey, we had shrimp cocktail at our dinner, I'll have you know," Lee protested. "But what's a farrago?"

"Old word for a huge mixed-up jumble of food," said Ballou, "and obviously you haven't heard the big news, or you'd have brought it up right away."

He told Lee what Frank Leahy had told him. Lee squealed.

"Roger! President? Really?"

"No way. Mr. Leahy just pulled that out of his butt. Not that it wasn't fun to hear him say it, even if there's no chance it'll happen. But it does mean I'm going to be teaching here for another couple of years, unless I'm seriously wrong."

"Yayyy!" cried Lee. "Roger, I'm so proud of you!"

"Nothing to be proud of. I just stood back and let that old harridan do herself in. Never murder someone who's cheerfully committing suicide, you know."

*

"But under the circumstances I couldn't be sure of L... of this girl, either," Ballou said to Linda Bierschaum, "and who knows? Maybe if I'd been more seriously involved with her I wouldn't even have given Dora more than a passing thought, thereafter, but we can go on with 'ifs' until we drop from exhaustion, can't we?"

"So, you went and asked Dora to *Pinafore* after all?"

"You know, I almost saw that damn show twice. Not that I'd have minded, because it wasn't a bad show. But what happened was, the day after Thanksgiving I was fixing to send Dora an e-mail, inviting her to *Pinafore* and also telling her that maybe a dog-warming party might be a good idea after all, if she wanted to advise me on how to make it really nice. See, I figured that if Dora and I spent the next couple of weeks consulting about a party at my house, that'd be extra face-time that she's *not* spending with Mr. Snowjob. Although of course I didn't tell her that. But then just as I'm sitting down at my computer on Friday morning to write the e-mail..."

"Charlotte Fanshaw."

"I guess it had to happen. I don't know why it surprised me, in retrospect."

*

"... since you helped my daughter get her part back – or you tried to, anyway – and since it's partly your fault that I don't have a date for the opening performance now. Of course I'll be going to all four performances, one way or another, but the first one's on Thursday afternoon, right after school, and since it's a matinee you won't have to think of it as a 'date' date…"

*

"And I didn't want to go with her," Ballou explained, "but obviously she was extending an olive branch, and it would have been churlish to refuse. So that's how that happened. And in a way it was a relief, because then, instead of asking Dora to see *Pinafore* with me, and maybe have her tell me she can't because she's all booked up for the weekend, I could just tell her I was organizing a party for the weekend after that, and propose that we get together for tea or something in the meantime so I can pick her brain about it. See? Lower pressure, and I didn't make myself too available, and I spared myself the agony of wondering what she's up to on Friday and Saturday nights when she's not with me."

"Roger, you over-analyze," said Linda Bierschaum.

"Probably."

Wednesday, December 1

Frank Leahy had deliberately issued his press release the day before Thanksgiving, when students would be cutting classes to go home early, and nobody would pay much attention to Van Devander-related matters. Thus, while faculty and administration knew that Dr. Bannister had resigned, the story was news to most of the students when they returned to classes on the Monday after Thanksgiving break, and it took most of that day to get around. On the following Wednesday morning, Ballou walked into his Poetry Workshop classroom to find "BALLOU FOR PRESIDENT" written on the blackboard in ornate capitals.

"Oh, come on!" he groaned. "Who's the wise guy?" A few of the students looked surreptitiously at Tim Dance.

"It's all over campus," said Dance. "At least that's what people have been saying for the last couple days."

"People? Who's 'people'?"

"Well, I dunno," said Dance. "Just one of those things that gets around, I guess. I can't even remember where I heard it."

"Giulio," said Sherrie Zizmor, "you told me Professor Wandervogel was saying it too, in the Union cafeteria yesterday." Giulio Dellavecchia shrugged, and looked uncomfortable.

"Wandervogel said something about how Dr. Bannister had been forced out by the élite," Ms. Zizmor went on, "and that they'd brought you in as a teacher this year so that you could take her place whenever they fired her. Isn't that what he said, Giulio?"

"Is more or less what he said," Dellavecchia admitted.

"Oh, that is total Class A bullshit," said Ballou. "Forgive me for saying so, but I'd strongly recommend against believing anything that guy says about me."

Dellavecchia merely inclined his head.

Ballou handed back poems to several students, with his comments written on them. On Lee Grossbaum's he'd written, *"Samedi soir. Cz moi, diner, c'possible?"*

In his Expository Writing class, that afternoon, Firenze Q. Tanquiz invited Ballou to be a guest on his radio show the following evening, "seeing as how they're talking about you for puh... for puh... resident and all."

"I'm not aware of who 'they' are," said Ballou. "I'll be glad to come on your show, but I don't want you to be disappointed, because your premise is totally off."

"Whatever," said Tanquiz. "Show starts at eight, so get there about 7:45."

Thursday, December 2

His foot should stamp and his throat should growl,
His hair should twirl and his face should scowl,
His eyes should flash and his breast protrude,
And this should be his customary attitude
His attitude! His attitude!

"Apparently all your efforts have gone for naught," Donald Quagga whispered to his wife as they got up to stretch during intermission. "Look over there."

Frances did, and spied Roger Ballou and Charlotte Fanshaw, a few rows away from them in the Wildenkill-Verstanken Consolidated High School auditorium.

"We might want to start preparing ourselves for that nude waterfall wedding after all," Quagga added.

"Poor Roger," said Frances. "Should we pretend we don't see them?"

Quagga chuckled. "Which of them would you be trying to spare from embarrassment?" he asked.

"Roger, obviously," said Frances. "If he ends up with Charlotte, it's because he's settling — because he couldn't have Dora. That reminds me: I suppose you saw the e-mail that Roger sent everybody yesterday. About his being on the radio tonight. We'll have to be home in time to catch it. Charlotte! Roger! This is a surprise! What do you to think of it, so far? Charlotte, your Bonnie is stealing the show! If she weren't so pretty, I'd never guess she wasn't a boy!"

Indeed, the show was okay, Ballou thought. Bonnie sang well, and her brother Luke, although he had only a chorus part, enlivened his scenes with some extra antics. The waiter from the Brookside Tea Garden, Bartholomew Ashen, did the best he could as Dick Deadeye, although the part was far too low for him. Miffany Quagga had a small voice that probably wouldn't do for a professional career – it barely carried through the auditorium – but Ballou thought it a pretty voice at least.

"Once again, I apologize for having to run you home right away," said Ballou, as he walked Charlotte back to his car after the two of them had visited backstage. "But that interview should be kind of fun, and I promise I'll give you a meal another time, whenever's convenient for you." (Ballou was thinking that if he took Charlotte home immediately, he'd have time to duck into a bar for a martini and a cigarette and maybe get a sandwich to go.)

"Oh, that's all right," said Charlotte. "I know these things come up. Don't feel that you ever have to buy me a meal though – unless you really would like to."

"Well, sure, why not? But do tune in tonight. It's at 99.8, and presumably you'll get to hear me pontificate. Actually, you might be especially interested, because the guy who invited me, the host of the show, is that kid who was questioning you at your book-signing, a couple months back. Remember, the one who was asking you... well, asking you some fairly impertinent questions?"

"Seems to me that there was more than one person asking impertinent questions." Charlotte laughed a bit too loudly. "But, yes, I remember him."

"You know, I almost never got to sit shotgun in this car," Charlotte remarked as Ballou let her into his car, in the school parking lot after the show. She waited until Ballou had shut the passenger door, walked round the car, and let himself in. "My father always drove, of course," she continued. "My mother, all her life long, refused to learn to drive. And my little brother and I would sit in the back. Of course I would have been alone with my father sometimes, and then I'd have sat up front. But it's so strange, still."

"It must be just about the one-year anniversary of the last time you drove it," Ballou remarked, starting the engine. "As you famously chronicled."

"Yes, I guess so. I have so many stories about this car. You have no idea. Every little scratch or stain, I bet I could tell you how it got there. May I turn on the dome light for a minute?"

Ballou was pulling out of the parking space and didn't need the distraction, but Charlotte had turned on the dome light before he could say anything.

"You see that there are a few stains on the upholstery, as you'd expect," Charlotte said, "but do you notice that there is no big stain on the armrest on this side of the back seat?" Charlotte knelt on her seat so she could point it out to Ballou.

"Should there be?" asked Ballou, trying to drive. "I believe you. At least I don't remember seeing any stain there."

"I had an ice cream cone," Charlotte said. "I was about nine years old, and we had just bought this car new, and I had a chocolate ice cream cone, and we were driving home from the ice cream store and somehow my father swerved, or we hit a bump, or something – he was a very erratic driver – and the scoop of ice cream fell right off the cone and onto the armrest there. And I was never so proud of anything as I am about how I showed grace under pressure in that situation. Instead of gasping or crying, I managed somehow to get the ice cream into my hand, and I pressed it back onto the cone, and all the rest of the way home I was alternately licking he cone and licking the ice cream off my hand..."

"That is the worst, losing ice cream," said Ballou. "Good for you, retrieving it."

"But that's not the whole story," said Charlotte. "There was still a good bit of it on the armrest, of course. And I kept trying to scoop it up on my finger, drop by drop, as we drove along, very secretly because I was afraid my little brother would tell if he saw what was happening, and I couldn't imagine what would happen if my mother or father found out that I'd stained the car already.

"Luckily it was dark when we got home and nobody saw it. But I hadn't got it perfectly clean. So that night, after everybody had gone to bed, I forced myself to stay awake, and then when I was sure everyone else was asleep I sneaked out to the kitchen and got a rag and some Windex – that was the only thing I could think of to use – and went outside and cleaned off that armrest. Thank goodness nobody thought to lock their cars, back in those days!"

Ballou nodded slowly, to show he was impressed.

"And nobody ever knew," Charlotte concluded. "But the next morning, when we were getting into the car – I can't remember now where we were going but I'm sure I'll remember later; it's been so long since I've thought of this story – as we were getting into the car my mother asked, 'Where's that ammonia smell coming from?'"

"But you could have told her," said Ballou. "It was clean, right? The armrest?"

"It was," said Charlotte, "but it was so much more fun to leave it as a mystery. A mystery to my family and a secret to me."

Charlotte thought for a moment.

"One of the very few times in my life I've ever kept a secret," she said. "And you're the first person I've told it to."

An idea popped into Ballou's head, and he acted on it without giving it serious thought.

"Tell you what," he said, "I can give you a chance to tell that story again, if you'd like – and I can give you another crack at that kid who was giving you trouble at your reading, if you want one.

How would you like to lecture to my Expository Writing class next week? I'm sure they'd enjoy hearing from somebody other than me. And that kid is one of the students."

"That'll be such great practice!" Charlotte exclaimed. She repositioned herself, scooting just a couple of inches closer to Ballou. "I didn't tell you, did I? That I'm joining the faculty next semester? Well, no, I guess you wouldn't know yet, but Faye Bannister called me up, the other day... and I shouldn't even be in this car with you, since you helped to get her fired."

"She helped to get herself fired," Ballou said.

"That's not how I see it," Charlotte retorted. "But anyway, you know she's organizing a new department, and she's offered me an adjunct position. Which should be so much fun. To think that I'll be back teaching at my old school!"

"You never actually graduated from Van Devander, did you? Did you get a degree somewhere else along the way?"

"No." Charlotte looked both self-satisfied and defiant. "One whole semester of college, that's my story. And I'm sticking to it."

"Well, good for you," Ballou replied, not quite knowing what else to say.

"And I understand you'll be signing my paycheques," said Charlotte. "How's that for irony?"

"Oh, God!" Ballou sighed. "Is there anyone left in this town who doesn't believe that nonsense?"

"Well, it's true, isn't it?"

Ballou sighed again. "At this point," he said, "I'll just have to let you wait to find out. So how's next Wednesday for visiting my class? That gives you six days to prepare."

When they got to Charlotte's house, they found the indoor lights on, including the porch light, and saw movement within, but Ballou shut off the engine anyway, and walked Charlotte to her front door, where he offered his hand just as Charlotte was making to embrace him, so he hugged back briefly and clumsily.

*

The studio at WVDV was tiny: just enough room for a wraparound desk that contained several control panels and the DJ's chair. Fi Tanquiz had found a folding chair for Ballou, and they had to play kneesies in the cramped space.

"Remember what I said: don't be a dick," Tanquiz instructed Ballou as a song neared its end. "High energy, and no dead air." He hit a button; the music faded down and the promo came on:

"Fiiiii Tanquiz! Dynamite — joooooock!"

Tanquiz hit another button, and the sound of a door squeaking open and shut went out over the air.

"Here he is," Tanquiz cried to his listeners, "nuh... new man on campus this year and already one of the most ob... noxious instructors ever seen in the English depart... department, Professor Roger Ballou." He nodded at Ballou to indicate that an answer was required, and Ballou said "Howdy, Mr. Tanquiz," in an overenergetic voice, almost stepping on Tanquiz' last word.

"You're gonna be the new pr... president of Van Devander, that's what everybody's saying."

"Then everybody's a damn fool, Mr. Tanquiz. I have no idea how that rumor got started, but the main thing is it's not true. I lack the credentials to be president, and I'm sure I lack the support among the trustees, and I can't imagine that I'd be the best available candidate. And what's more, I don't even want the job."

"Hey, that's not what I've been hearing," Tanquiz replied. "What are you gonna do when you're president, what changes are you gonna make? You should make it an all-nude campus."

"That's not workable," Ballou protested. "For one thing we're in too cold of a climate, and for another thing we'd probably all be so busy laughing at your pathetic equipment that nobody would get any work done. Besides, if we make nudity compulsory we'll just take the fun out of it, won't we? Did you ever have fun doing something that someone was making you do?"

"Does that mean when you're president you're going to get rid of all required courses and make it all elective?" Tanquiz asked.

"Of course not. College isn't supposed to be all fun. We need structure, we need standards, we need requirements. Just as in life, without those things you go nowhere."

"So we can look forward to a conservative administration, when you're president?"

"I am *not* going to be president," said Ballou, raising his voice.

"Yeah, but come on, puh… play it with me. What would it look like, if you were president?"

"Well, my predecessor, Dr. Bannister, said that she wanted to make Van Devander 'a byword for progressive education.' I would go in the opposite direction."

Ballou's brain finally caught up with his tongue, and he realized that he'd said "my predecessor." For a fraction of a second, he thought about whether he should backtrack and correct himself, or whether that would just be drawing attention to something that might otherwise have passed unnoticed. And he remembered that dead air was to be avoided at any cost, on radio, so he plunged ahead.

"For example, the purpose of this college should not be to *nurture*, as some people have called for. Its purpose should be to educate. We should hire instructors to teach, not to facilitate. And they should be encouraged to teach what they believe to be the truth, in the way that they think it's best to teach it, and let them stand or fall on the strength of the information they impart, and the effectiveness of their methods. Students should sometimes be upset or offended by what they hear in a classroom, and they should be encouraged to exchange ideas, even unpopular ones, and examine them. Don't you agree, Mr. Tanquiz?"

"I'd rather ex… exch… ange bodily fluids," said Tanquiz.

"We hear so much on college campuses these days about diversity, diversity, diversity," Ballou went on. "But when some people talk about diversity, what they really mean is *uniformity*. They want to run every student and every faculty member through a meat-grinder so that they all come out the exact same shade of light brown, with exactly the same politically correct opinions that they repeat like fu... like parrots. We must not, we must never allow ourselves to engineer our students, to impose a uniformity of thought."

"Uh... professor, you're pounding the table."

Ballou had been stabbing his forefinger against a control panel, pretty hard, to emphasize his points, but he raised his hand quickly, as though the panel had suddenly become hot.

"Well, it's something I feel pretty strongly about," Ballou replied, and couldn't hold back a defensive chuckle, which pissed him off as soon as he'd uttered it. "This is a good school, all around, and I've been having a hell of a lot of fun here, and I hope I'll be here a while longer."

"That'd suck," said Tanquiz. "Don't you have any idea how much your students hate you already?"

"Let 'em hate me so long as they fear me," said Ballou.

"This is embarrassing," Ballou said to Tanquiz when they'd gone to a music-break and were off-mike. "You know damn well I'm not going to be president of anything. I don't know shit about academic theory, or epistemology, or management, let alone how to run a goddam college. I'm just shooting my mouth off and sounding like an idiot."

"If you d... don't sou... sound like an idiot on my show, I'm not doing my job," Tanquiz replied. "Anyway, if you really don't want to be president, then, then it's good that you're sounding like you can't, can't, cut, cut, cut it, right?"

"For all I know," said Ballou, "that'd make the trustees all the more interested."

For the rest of the program, among the song-sets, Ballou and Tanquiz chatted on-air about the football team (and the mascot), Ballou's teaching methods ("I use the Schadenfreudian Principle: I encourage my students to rip each other apart, while I lean back and enjoy the carnage"), and Tanquiz' own ideas on how to improve the school – not all of which were frivolous.

Ballou sprang for a pitcher of beer at The Old Log Inn afterwards, hoping to loosen Tanquiz' tongue enough to find out what his students thought of him, but he was disappointed. Tanquiz proved much more interested in making cruel assessments of the bodies of some of the female students in the bar – often loudly enough that Ballou was afraid they could hear.

It was past midnight when Ballou got home. On his voice-mail he found a message left at 10:00 Thursday night:

"Roger, it's Dora. I have to go to bed now so I'm going to miss the rest of the show, but I just wanted to be the first to tell you how impressed I was! You're going to make a great president; I just know it. And... about your dog-warming party next weekend: I just can't wait to meet Sir Pit Crawley, and I'm going to bring an extra special dessert for the occasion. Meanwhile this weekend is turning out to be a lot busier than I'd anticipated, so I'm going to be pretty hard to get ahold of, but you can e-mail whenever you'd like; you know how much I enjoy reading your notes! Bye!"

In fact Ballou had never suspected that Dora got any special enjoyment out of his e-mails – which was why he had been doing his best, for the past couple of months, to limit them, so as not to annoy her. Had that been a mistake?

Ballou replayed the message, then listened a third and a fourth time, straining his ears as hard as he could, trying to filter out the sound of Dora's voice, trying instead to discern the sound of a man coughing in the background, or a man's feet shuffling, or a man making noise of any kind. But he couldn't. At last he listened to the message a fifth time, then a sixth, to try to find any slight shadings of tone in Dora's voice that could indicate anything more definite than the words themselves.

Friday, December 3

It was Lee Grossbaum, though, who occupied Ballou's mind the following morning, as he entered the Poetry Workshop classroom. In about 36 hours, she and Ballou would be naked and horizontal again.

"Here are my poems for next week," Lee said, sliding some papers across the table to him. "Got them done early." Across the top of the top sheet she'd written, "Cafeteria, 12:30? *Besoin de parler.*" Ballou gave Lee a tiny nod, and tried – unsuccessfully – to suppress the rush of anxiety. *"Besoin de parler"* could not mean anything pleasant. Good news would have kept until the next evening.

The Union cafeteria was pretty crowded, and Ballou kept his eye on one of the few empty tables as he came off the chow-line, but to get to it he had to carry his tray past Martin Wandervogel's customary table, where the film teacher sat with three of his students – Giulio Dellavecchia was one of them on this day – and little Zeke, who gazed all over the big room, wide-eyed, as he worked on a hamburger that was almost as big as his head.

Ballou considered walking past Wandervogel without acknowledging him, but temptation got the better of him.

"Main Man Martin!" Ballou exclaimed. "How's tricks?"

"Actually I'm doing very well," Wandervogel said, regarding Ballou with lofty contempt. "I just did an interview this morning with your friend Frank Leahy. It'll look really good on film."

"I'm sure you'll make him look really good, anyway."

Wandervogel sighed the sigh of the patient sufferer.

"I don't make anyone look anything, Roger," he said. "I re-*veeeeeal* people, that's all. That's what my film is about. Revealing this school. Warts and all."

"Heavy on the warts, no doubt."

"And rightly so. I really should thank you, Roger. You and Leahy. You've maneuvered Faye out of her job, and I'm going to show the world the story of a fine woman who was persecuted and hounded out of office by an entrenched élite – for the high crime of trying to do some good. You've made my movie, Roger."

"Glad to be of help. And you flatter me, by calling me part of an élite. I'd had no idea, but it certainly boosts my self-esteem."

"That figures."

"I'm sure you'd love it if there were any disciplinary action against you, too," Ballou suggested.

"What's to discipline me for? Can it be proven that I ever told anyone to 'create an incident' or 'get Ballou'? That was a product of your fertile imagination, pal. But go ahead, try to get rid of me too. I wonder how it'd look, if Van Devander fired their only Native American instructor."

"What?"

"I'm a sixteenth Cherokee. On my mother's side. You didn't know that?"

"I didn't – but you would claim it, wouldn't you?"

"What's that supposed to mean?" Wandervogel demanded.

Wandervogel's little boy was listening to the conversation as though trying to figure out what was going on. He did not appear to recognize Ballou. The three students all were listening too. Giulio Dellavecchia was grinning sardonically.

"Never mind," said Ballou. "I'd like to know why you've been telling people I'm going to be president of this college. Where the hell did you get that from?"

"Are you kidding?" asked Wandervogel. "It's all over. I've heard it from I don't know how many sources. And as a matter of fact I hope you do get to be president. That'd be an outcome I couldn't have scripted better myself."

Ballou looked over again at the table he'd had his eye on. He saw Lee Grossbaum entering the cafeteria; he caught her eye and nodded over at the empty table, and she moved toward it.

"Got a conference with one of your students?" Wandervogel asked archly.

"Yes, I have," said Ballou. "Martin, what have you got against this school?"

"I haven't got anything against this school! I graduated from it. Back when it was becoming a progressive modern college. It's regressed since then, and I'm trying to bring it into modern times – just as I was when I was a student. Maybe when the public sees what kind of people hold the power here, and how they drove out a fine woman and replaced her with a caveman like you..."

"Will you get off that shit? I will not be president; that's just an idiotic rumor that you're helping to perpetuate."

"Roger, please watch your language around my son. Every time you deny it, you sound more like you're running for the job."

"Then, God damn it, you'll just have to wait till next semester, won't you? And see how you like it when they appoint somebody else."

Wandervogel shook his head in disgust. "Whatever," he said. "You'll excuse me, but I'm trying to have a nice lunch with my students and my son. And then tonight we're going to have a little homecoming celebration now that you're back living with me, aren't we, Zeke?"

"Is the crazy lady be there?" piped Zeke.

"No. We probably won't be seeing her for a while."

Ballou walked over to Lee's table, put his tray down, and sat.

"*Tu ne manges pas?*" he asked Lee.

"*Je n'ai pas faim.*"

Ballou tucked into the meat loaf, mashed potatoes, and string beans. They continued in French.

"You were magnificent on the radio last night," Lee said.

"I'm glad you think so. It's been a hell of a few days."

"It must have been. I wish I could have done something."

"You did exactly right," said Ballou, eating. "You were supportive and discreet at the same time. You couldn't have been a bigger help."

They sat silent for a minute or so, Ballou still eating. He hoped she was waiting for him to say "I missed you." But he suspected otherwise.

"I'm trying to plan the menu for tomorrow night," Ballou said. "Should I surprise you, or is there something you'd specially like me to make?" He was pretty certain what Lee had to tell him, so he figured he might as well give her that opening.

Lee took a deep breath and looked right at Ballou, as though she were forcing herself to do so.

"Roger, I'm sorry, I can't make it tomorrow night. I've been thinking. It might not be a good idea. To keep... seeing each other."

He'd seen it coming; he'd been anticipating it all morning; he was already hurting from it, so it didn't hurt much more now that she'd let it fall. The only sensation he noticed was that his mouth had gone somewhat dry, making the food feel and taste like sawdust. Ballou forced himself to swallow.

"Have I done something?"

"*Non. Non!*" Lee said. "*Tu es... formidable.* It's... it's hard to explain. I want to be a college student, you know? I want to enjoy

my 20 years. I don't want to spend this year and the next one..."
(she groped in her mind for the French term, couldn't find it, and
had to use the English) "*sneaking around.*"

Ballou couldn't come up with anything to say to that.

"Besides, be real: You're going to be president of the college!
And you want a girlfriend who's right for a president. You know.
Somebody you can be seen with. I'm not even a girlfriend for a
teacher. I'm a fling for a teacher."

Ballou was about to say, "I certainly didn't consider you a fling,"
but that was such a monstrous lie that he stopped himself.

"Lee, I will *not* be president!" he said in English. "That is purely
not happening. Tiny gorillas will fly out my ass before that happens, okay?"

"I'd hold you back," Lee said, also in English. "I wouldn't make
you happy, in the long run. Plus, I don't want to be known all over
campus as the little bimbo who's sleeping with Professor Ballou.
Or President Ballou, either way. You need someone like... like that
lady with the red hair that you took to the glee club? I can't forget
her. She's so beautiful. That's the kind of girlfriend a college president should have!"

"It won't do me any good to argue with you," Ballou said. "I'm
sorry you feel that way." He stared into Lee's eyes for a moment,
then dropped his gaze to her neck, then to her maroon sweater,
as though he were trying to fix in his mind a memory of what
lay beneath it. His throat was getting tight. "Shit," he murmured,
and his voice cracked a little, "now I'm supposed to go teach a
class?"

"I'm sorry," said Lee. "But how else should I have brought it up?
When and where else?"

"No, you done good," said Ballou, "if it's what you wanted to do,
you did it just right. You are pretty smart."

"Maybe we can hook up again in five years," said Lee.

"Yeah. Maybe." Ballou had been looking forward to the wedge of pecan pie on his tray. Now, he would not even be able to enjoy that, and it pissed him off. Lee seemed to read his mind – or maybe he really had been scowling at her.

"I should have waited till you'd had your dessert," she said.

For just a moment, Ballou started rifling through the file-cards in his mind, looking for the one headed, "How to Get Her Back." But below the heading the first line on that card read, "Above all, ask for nothing." And Ballou had just asked Lee for an explanation – which had immediately killed any chance he might have had, according to his own reasoning. And so Ballou accepted it. Perhaps not with good grace, but the discussion was over as far as he was concerned.

"You're not going to fail me now, are you?"

"What?" Ballou had tuned Lee out for those desperate few seconds of thought, so it took a moment for her question to register.

"God damn it, Lee, you know better than that," he sighed, feeling angrier than he had felt about the pie.

"Yes, I do, I'm sorry." Another pause. "Roger, I better go. Maybe we can talk more another time." Lee got up to leave, slinging her knapsack over one shoulder. She looked out the window. "It's snowing a little," she remarked.

Ballou shrugged, and watched her, staring at her backside, as she passed out of the cafeteria. He forced himself to eat the pie, scarfing it down in three bites. He held his eyes wide open as he did so, making himself not blink, until the urge to weep had passed.

*

"Okay, so that... that young chippy was out of the picture, so you started putting the press on Dora," said Linda Bierschaum.

"I don't know that I'd call it that – and the younger lady is certainly not a chippy – but I told myself I had to do something,"

Ballou replied. "At that point it was three weeks to Christmas, which gave me a very brief window of opportunity – because then there's the holidays, and right after that she's off to Mexico. I had to put myself in a position where I could make some kind of a strong move – only I had no idea what that move would be."

"Tell me," said Linda Bierschaum, "with all that going on, did you ever find out about that other girl? The one who tried to get you in trouble?"

"Oh, Lordy. That's another story. I did call her. That same day in fact."

*

It was easy enough, via google, to find the only Kampling in the New Rochelle telephone directory, so Ballou tried that number.

"Miss Kampling? It's Professor Ballou. I'm just calling to see how you're getting along. I really did feel bad about how things turned out, and..."

"Just a minute," said Miss Kampling, and then Ballou heard muffled conversation for just a few seconds before a man's voice came on the line.

"Mr. Ballou, this is Jerome Kampling. I'm Tonia's father." Jerome Kampling had a deep and tough-sounding voice; the accent was more Bronx than Westchester. "I also happen to be a retired police officer. Now, I need you to listen to me. My daughter is very upset right now, and she's very afraid of you and what you might do to her."

"Sir, just a minute, I haven't done anything to her. That incident with the cross..."

"I'm not talking about that incident. I know it looks like you didn't do that. And maybe my daughter made a bad mistake. But also from what I've heard, it looks like you've been out to get her all semester, from Day One, and we're gonna put a stop to that right now. I'll just tell you once and for all: If you ever attempt to communicate with my daughter in any way – I don't care if it's by phone, or letter, or e-mail, or text message, or anything else – you will be arrested, and the charge will be aggravated harassment. I happen to know your Chief Jorgensen, up there, and I'm going to ask him to keep his eye on you. Do we understand each other, now?"

"Sir, honestly, I had no intention of..."

"Frankly, Sir: I don't care what your intentions were. Did I make myself clear?"

"Yes, Sir."

*

"Well, Roger, you really should have known better," said Ms. Bierschaum. "I know you meant well, but still..."

"Yeah, I guess so. Only I'm pretty dumb, you know that."

"Oh, stop it, Roger. And then it was the week after that, that you got that job? And you waited this long to tell me about it?"

"Well, it was suggested to me that following week. The chairman of the Board of Trustees was pretty sure he could make it happen – as opposed to that crazy idea of making me president. Then I had a formal interview before a selection committee right before Christmas, and the board didn't officially offer it to me until just this morning. Which is why I'm talking to you right now. Because I need all the help I can get, and if I know anybody who'd know how to do a job like this, I guess it's you."

"I'll bet you told Dora right away, though."

"Yeah, but that's different. That was part of the courting process."

Tuesday, December 7

The weather had turned cold, following the weekend's dusting of snow, but by Tuesday the temperature was back up into the 40s, although the skies were grey and gloomy. Ballou couldn't believe he'd been so stupid as to volunteer to stop by Dora's bakery, since that would bring him within the orbit of Harrison Lockwood. From Verstanken's Main Street, Lockwood's shop stood to the left of the bakery, so Ballou – well aware that he was acting like a child – averted his face as he drove past. He parked to the right of the bakery, and kept his eyes as downcast as possible as he got out of the car. The front door of the bakery lay about 20 yards away, and Ballou walked slightly aslant, his face tilted so that Lockwood's storefront could not come into his field of vision.

He could not help noticing the Harley parked in front of the shop. The sight of it struck him as perhaps the most incontrovertible harbinger of doom he'd seen so far.

With some relief, he entered Dora's place of business. Of course it had occurred to him that Lockwood might be in there buying a cupcake – or getting one for free, more likely – but that, he had to chance.

Dora was not wearing a baking uniform as her staffers behind the counter did – indeed, Ballou had never seen her wearing any such thing – but a navy wool suit with matching high heels, and a bright multicolored scarf round her neck. Her wavy hair flowed loose. The effect was rather 1950s "career woman," except that Dora was so small that she looked almost like a girl playing the part.

"Come on back into my little office," she said. "I've got a list for you." She led Ballou into a little room at the back of the store, set up with desk, computer, and other standard equipment. She left the door open: From her desk she could see almost the entire work area.

"I'll e-mail you the file too," she said, taking three sheets of paper from her printer. "This is everything I could think of to tell you about how to get your house ready for a puppy, and what you should expect. And here at the bottom is the phone number of the woman who helped me train Pegeen. She's wonderful."

"My God," said Ballou. "This is scary. I'd thought of some of this stuff, of course, but this looks overwhelming. I hope I haven't set myself up for anything I can't handle."

"You'll love it," said Dora. "Just be sure above all to have your house puppy-proof before you bring him home, and don't give him the run of the house right away. I'll be there on Saturday night and I'll tell you if I notice anything you should be doing."

With Harrison Fucking Lockwood in tow, no doubt, Ballou thought, as he folded the papers and put them in his jacket pocket.

"I should tell you my big news," Ballou said. "I've been kicked off the short list for President of Van Devander."

"Ohhh," said Dora, and her eye muscles contracted in real disappointment, which pleasantly surprised Ballou.

"Frank Leahy just offered me a different job. Which he claims he's pretty sure he can get for me. The tentative official title is Director of Communications and Community Outreach. In other words, I'll be the propaganda chief for the whole school. Writing press releases, marketing materials, and all that other stuff – but Frank said he wanted me to have a pretty free hand in terms of how

I promote Van Devander to the rest of the world. In other words, I don't get to be Hitler, but I can be Goebbels."

Dora laughed her pseudo-shocked laugh.

"I guess it'll be a pretty high-profile job if I want it to be," Ballou went on. "I'll probably be the guy who catches all the complaints from the politically correct crowd, about our Indian mascot and all those other issues, and that should be fun. Like, I'm gonna get paid for finding creative ways of telling people to go umpty-ump themselves."

"Roger, you are too much!" Dora exclaimed. "Are you still going to teach?"

"Yeah, that'll be part of the job. Two classes per semester, like now. Doing PR for a college of this size won't be a full-time job, no way. And I'll probably have time to still do some freelance work – but, damn. This'll be a nice jump in my income. Not huge, but more than I'm making now, and with a lot more job security."

"Unless someone gets rid of you like they got rid of your president."

"There's that."

"And I have some big news too!" Dora exclaimed.

It was a gut-shot. Ballou thought he could actually feel himself going white in the face. *God, this is it. Harrison and I are getting married, isn't that wonderful?*

"Mine is also career-related," she added.

And we're going to combine our businesses and live happily ever fucking after, baking cookies and making furniture, and isn't that just perfectly goddamn delightful?

"I got the idea just a few weeks ago, when I was examining a new patient – or a prospective patient, I should say. You know, so many people want cosmetic surgery, but so few people know how to find the best surgeon for each procedure. And of course I know so many people in my profession, so I said to myself, 'Why not build a practice as an adviser and consultant, so that I can guide people toward the right procedures – if any – and find them the right surgeons?' That way I can stay in the business, stay current with it, without having to deal with all the *Angst* that goes with doing the procedures. I'll stay with my catering business for now too, of course – but it's something I could build on, slowly, over a year or two, and then I could decide where my priorities lie."

Ballou couldn't help himself.

"I thought you were about to tell me you were switching over to a career in woodworking."

"Oh, Roger, you're funny! Seriously, my ambition is to one day be good enough to make just one nice piece of furniture for my own house – but that's a long way off. For now, if I want something really perfect I'll have to have Harrison make it for me."

Ballou knew he'd asked for it. He almost literally kicked himself on the shin, then and there.

Wednesday, December 8

The Vegan Epicure was the little café where Charlotte Fanshaw had chosen to meet Ballou for lunch prior to Wednesday's Expository Writing class. "Not that I'm a vegan myself, exactly," she'd explained, "but I'm always telling myself it would be better if I were." Ballou figured one meal there wouldn't kill him.

"Here's what I thought might be interesting, today," Charlotte said, after she and Ballou had ordered. "You know how a few months ago, Don said that you and I could have another debate in the *Advertiser*, and we never did? So here's what I thought.

"You've had them for most of a semester, teaching them whatever you teach them – and I thought I'd give them the other side of the story. So what I'd like for us to do is, I'll talk for most of the class about how I write, and then at the end I'm going to ask you to make just a brief statement of what you think the purpose of a writer's life should be – and then I'll say what I think it should be, and we can kick that around for the last 15 minutes. Does that work for you? Because I suspect that you and I have different ideas about what a writer's purpose should be, since we disagree on just about everything else."

On those terms, an hour later, Ballou introduced Charlotte Fanshaw to the class. Ballou was disappointed, on two counts.

Mainly, Fi Tanquiz didn't say a word throughout the session — suffering from late-semester burnout, Ballou supposed. Secondly, most of Charlotte's advice was pretty standard, not that it wasn't worth repeating. One point, though, Ballou considered original and ingenious.

"A lot of writers say you should start with a premise," she said. "I would say that's close to what a writer should do, but it's not quite right. If you want my two cents, a writer should start with a defining thought. Whether you're writing about yourself, or writing fiction, or even writing a biography of a real person. You need a single thought that says, 'This is the lens through which this writer views this subject matter.' For example, if you were writing a story about your childhood, your defining sentence might be, 'I was the smartest kid in the class.' Or, 'I was always picked last for games.' Because that fact would be critical to whatever you had to say about your childhood."

On the other hand, he noticed that Charlotte seemed to be talking pretty strictly about creative writing, about writing for oneself, whether fiction or non-fiction.

"I believe the purpose of the writer's life should be to look into, and explain, the human spirit," she said. "That, if you want my opinion, is the social obligation of the writer. Although I'm pretty sure Roger wouldn't agree with me. Would you, Roger?"

Ballou straightened up in his chair.

"I'd say the writer's purpose depends on what kind of writer you are," he said. "Some of us write purely for the pleasure of it — and those people usually never get very good at it, because they lack the impetus to practice, to learn style and technique, and to deal with all the boring and anal-retentive stuff that goes with learning to write. Others write to attract attention to themselves. Which is as good a reason as any. But if you were to ask me what my purpose is, when I write, I'd say it's getting paid."

(Laughter from the class.)

"Do you think I'm being flippant?" Ballou asked. "I'm not. I write because I can't make a living any other way; I'm no good for anything else. Okay, I'm smiling when I say it, but it's the truth. I write for the money. I write what I'm paid to write. I don't care, myself, about the human spirit – but I would if I were being paid to write about it."

"Oh, now there's the big difference between us," said Charlotte to the class. "Roger would have you write to the task, and I guess that's one way to do it, but if you ask me that has as much to do with real writing as house painting has to do with art.

"There are a lot of writers like Roger, who in order to put food on the table will compromise their true, pure urge to write. They do technical writing, or catalogue copy, or public relations, and sometimes in that process they'll lose the ability to do real writing."

"Ms. Fanshaw, with all due respect, I say you're off-base," Ballou replied. "If I'm not a 'real' writer, then why are people willing to pay me to write? I'd say it takes a 'real' writer to do what I do. You might turn up your nose at it, but could you, for example, take a bunch of dry technical information about the bond market and turn it into a clear and concise article that Joe Average would want to read? Or could you write a speech for a client who only has a bare idea of what he wants to say?"

"Yes, I probably could if I cared to," Charlotte replied.

"I'm sure you could," said Ballou. "I'm saying it takes a 'real' writer to do it. It takes a 'real' writer to whip out a press release in less than an hour, if you have to – and still be sure it's accurate and readable. That's just as much part of what a 'real writer' is, as anything to do with feelings and spirituality. And you were talking about the social responsibility of the writer, too, a while ago. Let me tell you what I call my social responsibility. My responsibility is to my client. It's to give the client what he wants, on time and to length."

"And guess what else?" Ballou asked, turning to the class. "It's fun to do that. It's rewarding. When I satisfy the client, not only do I make money, but I remind myself that not too many people can do what I do, that only a 'real' writer could have done it."

"Yes, but at what cost to the kind of writing you'd rather be doing?" Charlotte demanded. "Are you going to tell me you started out – when you first realized you wanted to be a writer – wanting to do the kind of work you're doing now?"

"Oh, of course not," said Ballou. "I was going to stick to novels and essays. I wasn't going to write anything that didn't display the beauty and complexity of my soul. And again, guess what? My writing sucked! But somehow I faked my way into a job as a trade journalist. And that was how I started to become a competent writer. And you know what did it? That dry, dreary, paint-the-barn type of writing that I've been doing for a living for the past 20 years!"

Again, Ballou turned to the class.

"Writing well requires discipline," he told them. "And I can think of no better way for you to gain that discipline – and thus improve the quality of your work – than by doing commercial writing, where you are answerable not merely to your own vanity, but to a paying client. Ms. Fanshaw suggests that that kind of writing should be beneath your dignity."

A student named Dorcas Silsbee raised her hand – tentatively, as though not sure she had a right to do so.

"Isn't it prostitution?" she asked.

"Yes, it is," said Ballou. "What's your point?"

(More laughter from the class.)

"When people ask me what I do," Ballou said, "I say 'I'm a hack writer,' and invariably – invariably – they'll say something like, 'Oh, don't put yourself down; I'm sure you're a very good writer.' And I have to explain that 'hack' is not a put-down. A hack is a writer who is paid to write, and I'm proud to be one. You bet I'm a prostitute. I'm a real good one."

"Then you've made the same devil's bargain that any prostitute makes," Charlotte Fanshaw rebutted. "You get paid for what you do, but that takes you away from doing what you love. Don't you wish you were writing essays and poetry and whatever else you wanted to write when you were younger?"

"I still write essays," said Ballou. "Lord knows you've seen them in the *Advertiser*. And I crank out a poem now and then, and of course I've got the unfinished novel that's been lying around for about 10 years now."

"I rest my case!" cried Charlotte, laughing. "Thank you, Roger. And I see that it's past 2:20. Thank you so much for having me – and thank you, all of you. This has been such a wonderful experience!"

The class applauded. Ballou joined them – seething.

"Oh, one thing before I go," said Charlotte, as the class rose. "I'd like to give you all a little homework assignment over the holidays. Optional of course. I want you each to write a letter to yourself, in which you ask for advice on anything that happens to be on your mind at the moment. And then write a letter back to yourself, giving yourself whatever advice you can think of." She smiled broadly. "Roger, maybe you could give yourself a little career counseling."

*

Dear Mr. Ballou:

Couple of things. First of all, am I, as Charlotte Fanshaw suggested, not just a hack but a hacker? Am I wasting my talents here while I might be happily starving in a garret? Should I walk away from my current career, such as it is, to crank out poetry and novels instead?

Second, I'm going to have to do something decisive with regard to my dear friend Dr. Fox. Declare myself, or pinch her ass, or something. I am nearly certain that she's seriously involved with a guy who is far more attractive and eligible than I am. But there's that wisp of fantastic hope, still, that says I've got nothing to lose by trying for her – and I better try for her now, because the longer I wait, the surer it will be that she'll find someone else if not this particular guy, and I'll have lost without having ever taken a shot.

Any advice, on whether to proceed and how to proceed on either or both of these topics, would be most welcome.

I have the honor to be, Sir,

Y'r ob'd't s'v't,

R. Ballou

My very dear Mr. Ballou:

Allow me to point out, sir, that you assume facts not in evidence. The most prominent example: You seem to assume that you could – if you stepped away from your current job and wrote purely to satisfy your creative muse – produce novels, plays, poems, etc. of a quality that matches your journalism, ghost-writing, and other commercial projects. I'll not deny that your high opinion of your commercial work is justified. You're good at what you do. But are you willing, at your age, to put in the amount of study that would be required to bring your creative writing to that level?

You're not missing the boat now, sir. You missed it more than 20 years ago, in college, when you farted around instead of focusing. Back then, when you had more energy, less to lose, and maybe 60 years of life ahead of you: That, sir, is when you should have been studying literature with a view to learning from the masters. That, sir, is when you should have been honing your skills, developing a style, educating yourself so that when you reached the age you're at now, you <u>would</u> have been in a position to write great novels, plays, and poems.

Ah, but you lacked humility, didn't you? You assumed that you could excel at a difficult thing without first learning how. And when experience taught you otherwise, you tended to give up. I never saw you really work for anything, until you were out in the world and you <u>had</u> to work hard at your job – or move back in with Mom. <u>That</u> dread possibility motivated you, didn't it?

But I suspect, sir, that that was all you wanted: to scrape a living somehow. If literary greatness had been your true desire, would you not have gone out and got it? That, sir, brings me to your second assumption that's not backed up by evidence. You seem to assume that what you really want, deep down, is to be a creative writer. You assume that you've cheated yourself by not having become one, and by not abandoning your current living – which to your credit you have established by the sweat of your brow – in order to play the Delicate Starving Genius.

Sir, you like the idea of being a Great Writer – just as other men like the idea of being exceptionally wealthy. Either is attainable by any man with above-average skills. It does <u>not</u> take exceptional talent to become a great writer, any more than it takes exceptional luck to accumulate wealth. Both, however, take a lot of hard work – which very few people are willing to do. Sir, you <u>like</u> farting around, and that's <u>fine</u>. But it's no way to become a great writer, is it?

If you want badly enough to become a "real" writer – and I use that term facetiously because obviously you already are a real writer – you can do it while still holding down whatever job Frank Leahy finds for you at this college. Your work, face it, is not that arduous. You could, if you wanted to, use your spare time to work on your creative skills. By the time you're 50 – with still a few years of life left to you, and with no great risk of penury – you might be on your way to achieving the renown and respect that you claim to desire.

But, sir, I suspect that that desire is trumped by a desire to do other things. You would have to give up your bridge, your golf, your socializing, your alcohol consumption, and your pursuit of a romantic relationship. And 'tis my belief, sir, that you find those activities indispensable to your enjoyment of life. To be sure, they beat the drudgery that a serious novelist, poet, or playwright must endure.

Re your pursuit of a romantic relationship: Well, sir, you did have one – of sorts – until just a few days ago, and you have to admit that it was unsuitable and could not have been sustained. And in any case it was not a relationship with the woman you really want – or suppose you want.

This brings me to a third example of your assuming facts not in evidence.

You have no idea what is Dr. Fox's relationship with Mr. Lockwood. You assume it's more than friendship, but you have no evidence to back this up. None! If she brings him to your bridge party on Saturday, observe them, however it may pain your soul to do so. If you'll trouble yourself to look carefully and use your common sense – which, admit it or not, is not inconsiderable – you'll be able to tell what's up with them. If the situation looks hopeless for you, I advise retreat. No point making an idiot of yourself. But don't surrender without taking stock of what you're up against.

On the other hand, she might not bring him. You didn't invite him, and she might be tactful enough to leave him behind. It could be, after all, that she is not as oblivious as you insist she is. She might be aware of how highly you regard her – and of the revulsion you feel for Mr. Lockwood.

The possibility also exists that she has never considered that your feelings for her might go beyond the fraternal. They say men don't "get it," but women, sir, can be just as clueless. Even otherwise intelligent women.

Now, before we examine the question of whether or not you should resolve this issue (or rather, seek to resolve it), let us examine your objectives. Just what do you want? What do you hope to accomplish here?

Do you, for example, want to marry this lady and live with her? Where? In her immaculate house, or in your revolting one? Granted, it's very early times for you to be asking yourself "Do you want to marry her?" But is marriage a possibility you'll want to explore? Would she go for that, even if we allow that she might be attracted to you? Which we have to admit is a stretch.

<u>Or do you just want to nail her, for bragging rights???</u>

I will do you the justice to say that the latter-named possibility is unlikely. Whatever feelings or desires you may harbor toward this lady are probably honorable enough – or at least you tell yourself they are. But consider, sir, whether a marriage or a long-term non-marriage would be feasible. Why would she want either, with you? And could you be happy with her? However she might delight you now, you must know that incompatibilities will arise – some of them perhaps serious.

You will probably feel compelled to find out. That is your nature. Some experts might advise you to bide your time and let friendship develop into romance if it will, but you are not psychologically equipped to do that – and in any case that too is a highly speculative strategy.

Also, conventional wisdom states that you must never (if you're the man) attempt to instigate a romance – that you should always make it look like it's the lady's idea. Easier said than done, eh? Somebody has to make the first move, and if you wait for her to do it, you'll be taking a terrible risk – probably an unacceptable risk, for a man like you – for she may never even think about making that move.

Some might tell you, "If you wait for her to make the first move, you are very likely to wait in vain – but if you make the first move, you will <u>certainly</u> fail." I'm not smart enough to say whether this is true, but there's a real possibility that it is. You might want to just do it – just declare yourself – and get the rejection over with. Of course, that could lead to years and years of brooding: "If only I'd done it some other way."

<u>Come to think about it, my dear Ballou, "If only I'd done it some other way" might be a pretty fitting epitaph for you.</u>

In summation, we must combine an assessment of your career with an assessment of your romantic prospects. You must perceive, sir, that at this point in your life you have not made yourself worthy of Dr. Fox. If you insist on making a play for her now, the likelihood of disappointment (for you) is very high. On the other hand, if you make a speculative effort to make yourself worthy, even if you do achieve that goal, that achievement will almost certainly come too late for you to claim Dr. Fox as your reward.

I have the honor to be, sir,

Y'r ob'd't s'v't,

R. Ballou

Saturday, December 11

"Take no prisoners," Ballou instructed Mrs. Ellerkamp. "I picked this place up as best I could – it took me long enough, last night – but I hope you brought your gas mask with you anyway. And if you do a good job, maybe I can give you a steady gig."

"This is not so terrible," said Mrs. Ellerkamp, as she walked through Ballou's dining room and into the kitchen. "Ach! I spoke maybe too soon. This kitchen is a *Schweinerei*. The kitchen and the bathroom must both be perfect, if you are having a lady visitor."

"Who told you that?"

"It is common knowledge. If a woman sees a dirty bathroom, poof! Maybe you see her again, but she never forgets."

"No, I mean who told you I was having a lady visitor?"

"The angels told me," said Mrs. Ellerkamp.

"Actually it's a party, tonight," said Ballou. "But, yes, there will be a certain lady visitor. So do your best. I'm off to do some errands, now, so if I'm not back when you're done, just let yourself out. Here's your fee, and here's my cell phone number, if there's an emergency; otherwise just make a list of supplies you want me to have for you next time, or any questions. That dog-kennel in the corner of the bedroom you can leave alone: that's for the puppy I'm bringing home this afternoon. And if you get hungry, you can raid the fridge. That is, if you have any appetite after you've cleaned it. I'm warning you, there's a science fiction movie going on in there."

Ballou drove the few blocks to school and did a few hours' work in his deserted office. That afternoon, he drove along the wooded highway 212B – which was not so dark now that the leaves were down – to Runs' lot, where he swept and vacuumed the car, and put it through the wash. Done with that, he pulled the Cadillac off to the side of the garage, and waited for Sir Pit Crawley to be brought out for him.

"He just pooped and peed a few minutes ago, so he should be good for an hour or so anyway," said Pruno, emerging from behind the garage with the puppy (wrapped in a towel) in his arms, and what looked like a wistful expression on his face. "You take good care of him, or I'm gonna come get him."

"I will."

"I were you, I wouldn't leave him alone tonight. Stick with him and keep him occupied whenever he's not eatin', sleepin', or goin' to the bathroom. Otherwise he'll get anxious. And get him used to other dogs as soon's you can."

"Just what I had in mind," said Ballou. Reluctantly, Pruno passed the swaddled puppy over to Ballou, just as Runs-Away-Screaming came out of the garage.

"So, there's your courtin' tool, eh, Kemo Sabay?" said Runs, reaching over and scratching the puppy's ears. "Pruno, did Roger tell you what he wanted that dog for?"

"Hell, Big Injun, was you that told me!" Pruno retorted. "You said it wasn't gonna work, either."

Runs' face was as impassive as ever, but Ballou thought he sensed a little embarrassment. Ballou forced himself to laugh, to pretend he wasn't offended.

"Shows you how much Runs knows," said Ballou. "It's a good day to die, as Runs' noble ancestors would say."

"Maybe it's a good day to die," Runs countered, "but not by bangin' your head against a brick wall."

"What, have you heard anything else? Since Thanksgiving?"

"I don't know a damn thing more now than I ever knew about Dora," said Runs, lighting a cigarette. "But remember what I said – about Christmastime. I don't have the heart to bet on this one, but if I did, I'd bet she's closed the deal by now. Do I know she has? No. You know what she is, she's a mystery. And you know why girls like her are mysterious? Because it's more fun not to know too much about 'em. If you don't see what I mean, I can't explain it."

"Yeah, maybe you're right," Ballou conceded. The puppy had begun licking his face, which made talking difficult. "But unless you have dead-sure information that proves I got no shot..."

"You'll do what you gotta do," Runs finished.

"Cool it, Crawley," Ballou said to the puppy. "I'm gonna put you in the car for a minute before we take off, get you used to it." He opened the passenger door and put Sir Pit Crawley on the front seat, opening the little vent window in the door to give him some air before shutting him in. The puppy immediately began sniffing and nuzzling the seat.

"Wihio wouldn't give up," Ballou said, turning back to Runs. "Neither would Willie Wilden. And if you remember your Indian legends, you'll remember that every once in a blue moon, Wihio wins one. And Willie Wilden's done pretty well this year."

"True dat," Runs conceded. "And the best of the year's yet to come, like I told you before." He took another drag and gazed off into the middle distance. It wasn't even four o'clock yet, but the shadow cast by Runs' garage was already starting to stretch to the highway, and the grey sky was getting greyer.

"I love it when night comes so early," said Runs. "Somethin' about it. I never get tired of it. I wait all year for this."

Runs looked up, looked above the big sign at the front of his lot, at the banner of Willie Wilden flying to the left of the American flag. The wind picked up, and the flag rippled a bit, lending some motion to the picture of the defiant, indomitable little Indian.

"If Willie Wilden's doing okay," Runs added after another few seconds, "it's partly 'cause you helped him. You done old Willie pretty good in just a few months, gotta admit."

"Oh, that," said Ballou. "We beat 'em back. We won a small battle. There's worse to come — not *the* worst, just worse. Willie Wilden, there, he won't last forever. We saved him for this year, but those bastards will kill him eventually. As sure as they'll stop you smoking that Marlboro, or stop me from 'looking inappropriately' at my students."

"That little guy stands for a lot more than just that school, after all, don't he?" Runs reflected.

"What he stands for, that's what we fight for," said Ballou.

"To the last fuckin' Injun, Kemo Sabay."

Runs gazed out across the highway. "God, what a pretty day."

"It is," said Ballou. "It's a good day to die."

Midnight

Sir Pit Crawley had an exhausting few hours on Saturday, his first day as Roger Ballou's dog: being admired, fussed over, and tormented – first by Ballou and by whatever neighbors they'd met while out walking, and then, in the evening, by the bridge-playing crowd. When the card game began, Ballou had locked the puppy in the wire kennel in the bedroom, hoping for the best.

Runs-Away-Screaming had been the first to leave, toward midnight. "Good luck, Kemo Sabay – with whatever," he said as he and Ballou shook hands.

"Yep, bedways is rightways," said Frank Leahy, getting to his feet. "Ready, dear?"

"We should help Roger clean up," said Lois.

"Yes, Roger, are you sure we can't help you?" Frances Quagga asked. "You're just one person, after all!"

"No, thanks," Ballou replied. "There ain't enough room in my kitchen for the whole boiling of us." Ballou took a deep breath, and physically braced himself. "But, Dora, could you do me a favor and stick around for just a minute? I wanted to ask you a couple questions about that little beast of mine. If you don't mind. You can keep me company while I put the food away."

"Of course," said Dora. "Not for long, because I need my beauty sleep. I have to get up again at four, you know. But I'll help you wash up. No, Roger, I insist! I'm very small, so I won't crowd your kitchen, and you need an extra pair of hands. The two of us should be able to do it before you can say Jack Robinson!" She picked up an armful of plates from the dining room table and carried them into the kitchen.

Ballou could feel his innards turning over. But, after all, this was what he'd been angling for.

"Thanks ever so, old thing," said Hugh Hoo, shaking hands with Ballou at the front door. Effie Hoo kissed Ballou on the cheek, then looked at him sidelong, giving an ironic little head-toss in the direction of the kitchen and rolling her eyes just a bit. "Lord help ye," she muttered. As the Quaggas left, Frances gave Ballou a wink and a secret little pinch on the arm.

Ballou heard water running in the kitchen. He almost literally could not move, for terror. He imagined a gigantic hand pressing into his back – slowly and with difficulty, but irresistibly, forcing him through the living room, through the dining room, toward the kitchen. No doubt if he could have seen himself he would have seen that he was walking normally, but at the moment he supposed that his gait was that of Frankenstein's Monster, shambling forward step by step. He could not swallow. He felt, rather than heard, a rapid throbbing, thumping, throughout his body: ba-*bump*, ba-*bump*, ba-*bump*, ba-*bump*...

"I'll wash and you dry," Ballou said, his voice nearly croaking with fright – he could not keep a slight tremble out of it – as he joined Dora at the kitchen sink. "I don't want you getting dishpan hands on my account."

As he sponged off a plate, he heard the flapping of wings, and a single Black Demon appeared, hovering at his shoulder.

Ballou passed Dora a plate to dry, and she inspected it skeptically.

"Oh, Roger, really! Men and dishes! Here, you let me wash, and you dry. No arguments."

A second Black Demon appeared.

"Men will wash dishes properly when women learn to parallel park," Ballou replied, as he and Dora traded places. He would go down fighting.

"No Harrison tonight?" he asked, drying plates.

Dora laughed. "He really isn't your favorite person, is he?" she exclaimed.

"And why did you say anything about that guy?" inquired a third Black Demon, whispering in Ballou's ear as he materialized.

"Tell her what's on your mind, dipshit," said a fourth Demon. "Here you are, it's midnight, you're side-by-side. Go for it. Declare yourself."

"No! No!" cried a fifth Demon, frantically waving his pterodactylous wings. "No way! *Never tell a girl you're into her until you have her in your arms!* You're guaranteed to fail otherwise. *Guaranteed!*"

Ballou knew this. He'd tried more than once, in high school and college, to simply confess his feelings for a girl as they'd walked together or sat across a table from each other. And he remembered what the results had been.

And here he was, right next to Dora at the kitchen sink, and why not just reach over, take her in his arms, and kiss her?

"Yeah, Rog, that'd work," said Demon Number Three. "No ceremony, just grab. That'd be a nice graceful move, only not so much. Specially when you both have wet soapy hands."

Now there was a thought. Playfully flick some soapsuds at her. Get into a little foam-fight, there at the kitchen sink, and end up laughing in each other's arms. But what if she took exception to that sort of thing? You never could tell how she'd react to flecks of dishwater in her hair or on her blouse. Ballou held back.

But he had to do something. Here, now, somehow, Ballou told himself. Whether or not she'd closed the deal with Harrison Fucking Lockwood, he could not know. But it was now two weeks to Christmas – another busy time for her – and right after New Year's Dora would be in Mexico for two weeks, with or without Harrison Fucking Lockwood. More than a month it would be, before Ballou could possibly see another opportunity.

"He really should wait," said Demon Number Five, the apparent leader of the conservative faction. "Give it a month. Even if the Harrison thing is going on, give it time to burn itself out. He should *not* make a grab right now. The time is *so* not right!"

"Right or not, he's pretty much got to try it now," said Demon Number One.

"I'm saying he shouldn't," said Number Five. "But I guess he will drive full-tilt into the grave he's dug for himself."

"And that's that," said Dora, handing Ballou the last dish. "See how fast it went?"

Yes, indeed Ballou had noticed. He had to keep her there, if only for a minute or two more. Before Dora could make to leave, he said, "Come check the little guy. See if he looks okay to you. I mean, tell me if he's kenneled properly and all."

"Ooooo, into the boudoir," crooned Number Three.

"Be vewy, vewy quiet," Ballou whispered to Dora as they tiptoed into his dimly lit bedroom. "We're hunting wabbits! A-heh-heh-heh!"

"Poor little guy," Dora whispered. Sir Pit Crawley was curled up on a pillow in the kennel, sound asleep. "He must be worn out after such a long day. But it looks like he has everything he needs. You won't get a full night's sleep for a few months, I'm afraid. But it'll be worth it."

"I hope so," Ballou whispered back.

Dora and Ballou stood side-by-side next to the kennel, and Ballou was pretty sure that in just a matter of seconds Dora would say that she had to leave.

"*Go for it, Roger! Now!*" commanded Demon Number One in a voice almost shrill in its urgency.

"No, don't, Roger!" cried Number Five. "Not if you value your dignity!"

"This is your one chance, Hamlet!" screamed Number One. "*Now or never,* you wuss! *Do it! Oo-ga-cha-ga! Oo-ga! Oo-ga! Oo-ga-cha-ga! Oo-ga! Oo-ga!*"

All but one of the other Black Demons picked it up.

Oo-ga-cha-ga!
Oo-ga! Oo-ga!
Oo-ga-cha-ga!
Oo-ga! Oo-ga!

Ballou couldn't help it. Frozen with fear as he was, he laughed aloud.

"What's so funny?" Dora asked.

"I wish I had the guts to tell you," Ballou replied. "But you'd never believe it."

Dora raised her eyebrows.

"Oh, the hell with it!" cried Number Five. "*Oo-ga-cha-ga! Oo-ga! Oo-ga! Oo-ga-cha-ga! Oo-ga! Oo-ga!*"

And the chanting of the Black Demons reached a crescendo as Roger Ballou – unable to breathe, his heart pounding – wet his lips and placed his arm round Dora's shoulders, gazing into her eyes as he drew her closer and brought his mouth to hers.

9593400R0035

Made in the USA
Charleston, SC
25 September 2011